Into

the

Blackness

Into the Blackness

Into the Blackness

Edited by Progressive Edits

Cover Design and Layout by
Ellie Kay Bockert Augsburger
Creative Digital Studios
CreativeDigitalStudios.com

Cover Images by
© pio3 / Dollar Photo Club

Published by It's Publishing
PO Box 14402
Parkville, MO 64152
www.normajeannekarlsson.com

ISBN: 978-0-9911873-7-9
ISBN e-book: 978-0-9911873-6-2

Table of Contents

Dedication...

To my husband. The man who helped me learn how to thrive.

Acknowledgements

Dedicating this novel to my husband seems like a tiny recognition of everything he does for me. I live the life I do because I have the best partner, teammate, cheerleader, supporter, caregiver, ass kicker, distracter, debater, brainstormer...my muse. Writing stories of strong women that find happiness with strong men originate from this strong woman finding her strong man. I love you with every breath I take.

My children remain my greatest reward in life. Someday I'll show them the characters that have been borne from the love they teach me with every single day the sun shines on their adorable faces. Love is too small to describe the feeling I have for my boys. They encapsulate my soul with happiness.

There are days that are harder than others. On those days, I reach out to my lifeline. My best friend. Chris, you make tough days easier, good days better and everything in between joyful. A life without you wouldn't be a life at all for me. It would be a sad, dreary space. Whether you're an ocean away or at my side you give me solace. Loving you is the simplest thing I do every day.

Amanda...you're a shining star in my life. I'm not known for my abilities with the ladies, but you're an exception to the rule. You teach me something new every time we talk. Whether it's how girls feel at fourteen or that I have serious issues writing with commas, I'm always learning from you. It's not often I think my life is anything other than wonderful, but I can admit something was missing before you came into it. Thank you for being an amazing friend to me. Thank you for helping me grow. Thank you for having my back at every turn. I love you to bits, lady. Always will.

Professional and personal lines no longer exist with you, Ellie. Hours of talking about our lives, loves and work are effortless and fulfilling. I've never looked forward to Fridays as much as I do now. One of the best parts of writing for me is imagining how we'll dress it up in the end. If not for you talent, I wouldn't have the success I do. If not for your generous spirit, I wouldn't have an amazing friend that's always there for me. Loves and hugs to you.

Ruth you've given me such support and kindness that I don't have words to express how you mean to me. A life on an island all alone withered away when I met you. Thank you for offering me your friendship when I needed it more than I was willing to believe. This next year will be a joy, knowing I'll get to share it with you.

Pam and Michele, you ladies have been the most amazing supports in the blogging world. I'm honored that you've taken the time to sing my praises. I hope you continue to enjoy the series and fight against the blackness right along with me.

My readers, reviewers and fans are AWESOME. I've received some of the sweetest words and reactions from all of you. Your trumpets are loud and verbose, causing me endless joy. Thank you for taking the time to come on this journey with me. I couldn't do it without all of you!

Into the Blackness

Chapter 1

Kat

The Domestic Crime Agency, better known as the DCA, has a certain set of criterion they utilize when recruiting new agents. Potentials must be unattached, unaffiliated, unassuming chameleons, of questionable moral fabric and above all willing and able to use deadly force without hesitation in any situation. Oh yeah...and you're supposed to have a dick too. I met and surpassed the initial requirements easily. I'm in no control of meeting the final unstated requirement of being male. My recruiter told me upon our first interaction that I would be an ideal candidate for intelligence monitoring, in other words riding a desk. I didn't then, nor do I now, have any inclination to ride a desk. Desks are where people like me go to die.

That's funny because most people would think being an active operative in a clandestine government agency under the umbrella of the FBI would be where people like me go do die. They'd be wrong. This is where I came to flourish, meet my full potential. The DCA is where I was brought to life, not back to life, *to life*. I wasn't alive once and then looking to be reborn. I was searching for my birth, the place where I fit in the world. June 1, 2003 Katherine Russell was born at eighteen years old weighing 138 pounds and measuring five feet eight inches in length. Nothing before that date exists for me other than my training and life skills that created the woman I am today. I carry the memories of my parents and the lessons they taught me, but other than that, people, places and relationships from before that date ceased to exist. Not that there was much hanging around.

These thoughts often run through my head on mornings like this. I think they enter of their own accord to ground me and remind me that this is who I am. I take one final look in the mirror, the reflection I see today I'll be glad to rid myself of tomorrow. Severely dyed midnight black stick-straight hair hanging three quarters of the way down my back. I look like Demi Moore in *Strip Tease*. My dark brown colored contacts change the entire look of my face. With the caramel tan, inky hair and chocolate button eyes, I appear Mediterranean when that couldn't be further from the truth.

There was a little "enhancement" for this undercover operation (op). I had injectable fillers put in my lips and cheeks causing me to look younger and fuller in the face. My striking high cheekbones now have a soft curve beneath them, making me look closer to twenty than my closely approaching thirty. The lips were specific for my mark, the target of my op. He enjoys women with fat lips, so I now have fat lips. Thankfully, these augmentations are temporary, only requiring me to have the procedure once more while I've been undercover as they wear off in a matter of months. Months, which I've spent living with my mark as the stunningly beautiful Camilla Bruno from upstate New York, sadly discovered by the wealthy arms dealer Marco Bianchi, while working as a stripper in one of his establishments. Poor Camilla grew up in foster care and was in desperate need of a powerful man to sweep her off her feet and plant her securely on her back beneath him. My back fucking hurts.

After five months of living and breathing Camilla doused in expensive perfumes always surrounded in a cloud of Marco's cigar smoke, I'm ready for a cleansing deep lungful of fresh air. I saturate myself in Marco's favorite scent and shove down the gag at the back of my throat. I pull my hair over my naked, more than a handful, boobs à la *The Blue Lagoon* and take one last glance at my heavily make-up covered face—a porn star's face. Disgusting. Marco will love it.

I stride from the marble encased bathroom into the bright light beach-facing hotel bedroom. White linen everywhere with hints of local Belize mahogany, this place is truly a paradise. I'll come back for a vacation someday...like that will ever happen.

Marco sits up on an elbow in the king-sized bed, intensely perusing my appearance. He likes what he sees so much that he hisses sharply through his fake teeth. Marco is an extremely attractive older man. He dyes his hair a chestnut color to avoid appearing his age of fifty-eight and it works since his body looks at least fifteen years its junior. At only six feet tall I've been cautioned to be sure my heels allow him an inch over my height at all times. No skin off my back.

His hazel-blue eyes dance over my form as I approach. He's fallen in love with me, Camilla. It's more for my body, the sex and the arm candy, but he's taken the time to learn the back-story that's been carefully crafted by the DCA. Marco knows everything about Camilla and wants to own her mind, body and soul. I can sense a proposal coming any day now. I'm glad this will be over before I have to endure that.

"Camilla," he purrs in his gruff voice.

As I reach the edge of the bed, I offer him a seductive smile and peer down at him with lust-filled eyes.

"I made you coffee," I whisper back in my most submissive voice.

Marco likes a morning fuck, but he needs his coffee first.

"Later," he growls pulling me onto the bed, rolling me beneath him.

I giggle.

"I'll have my breakfast first and then my coffee," he announces before sweeping my hair off my boobs.

He roughly palms one while his mouth closes around the other's nipple. I hiss sharply as he bites harder than I like. He always bites harder than I like. Marco smiles around my nipple misperceiving my reaction. Pushing

3

sixty and still can't get sex right, it's a good thing I'm putting him out of his misery.

He pinches and rolls my nipple, again too hard, so I moan and arch my back like a good girl would. Descending the plane of my stomach, he rips the delicate pink lace Agent Provocateur thong painfully from my body. I'm waxed within an inch of my life just like Marco likes. The only hair remaining on my body at this point is on my head and my eyebrows. Everything else is waxed regularly. I have no problem with a Brazilian and a leg wax, but my arms and the faintest peach fuzz on my knuckles is a bit outside my realm of normal.

Marco buries his face in my pussy, sucking too hard and fingering me too aggressively as I fake a few orgasms and will myself to get wet for the production. Finally, he decides he's given me enough and sits up on his rickety knees.

"Roll over," he commands harshly.

I quickly flip to my stomach and raise my hips to the appropriate height.

"Once you have my name I'm takin' this ass," he informs me tracing his finger along my crack.

I nod into the mattress again grateful that will never happen.

Marco spits and rubs his hand through my folds before plowing in like he's storming an enemy fortress, violent and unyielding. I use all my strength to keep my body planted where it is as he powers into me, bruising my hips with his fingers. After a few minutes, I fake another orgasm and feel that spur him toward his.

A few stunted strokes later Marco pulls out and shoots his load on my ass and lower back. He then does his classic move of rubbing it into my skin like lotion until he's convinced I'm good and marked. Collapsing on the bed next to me, he shoves his come-covered fingers in my mouth. I suck them clean and moan, just like he likes.

4

"Good girl," he breathes out, pinching my bottom lip before releasing my mouth. "Ready for my coffee now."

Finally.

I climb off the bed and move into the suite where the pot of coffee is staying warm in the coffee maker. I pour him a large mug and then add my chemical concoction that will end this op once and for all. There are two guards at a post outside the room and a few more working the perimeter in various places. I'll have to make this good.

I saunter into the room and hand him the mug before retrieving my black silk robe from the plush white chair in the corner. Marco takes two giant gulps as I start forcing the tears to come. It'll take a few minutes to get them good and flowing for an Oscar-worthy ugly cry.

I sit on the end of the bed with my back to Marco as the first tear runs down my enhanced cheek.

"Camilla," Marco gasps through labored breaths. I love fast-acting compounds.

He moans loudly, thrashing around the bed as his mug hits the floor with a thud. I take this moment to stand from my perch and retrieve my torn thong from the floor. I deposit it in the small trashcan in the bathroom while continuing to work up tears at a more constant rate.

"Please," he pleads through a whisper when I enter the bedroom again.

"No," I respond coolly watching the realization and panic hit his eyes before the last few moments of life slip from his body.

I wait for a full minute before checking him for a pulse. Of course, there isn't one, but you can never be too careful. I'm not a fan of the moment where you think the bad guy is dead and then he pops up behind you in one last effort to win the fight.

Sucking in a giant breath, I scream a blood-curdling wail and dissolve into hysterics. The guards race into the room guns at the ready until they spot the scene. I continue to sob and convulse as they try dutifully to revive Marco, calling for all the men to return to our suite.

Seven more men barrel into the bedroom, barking orders at each other and attempting CPR, as I play the role of girlfriend in shock. My body is shaking so violently that the arches of my feet are beginning to cramp, which causes more wailing to burst from my throat.

The compound has done its job in creating heart attack type symptoms. If and when they do an autopsy, they'll find the drugs and I'll be so far gone it won't matter. It's only this moment of my acting, and his apparent heart attack that matter.

"Camilla," a guard named Torch soothes in my ear.

He has this nickname because he likes to set people on fire as a form of torture when needed. He's an animal I wish was on my hit list.

"We've gotta move. Marco's gone and we got a shipment that has to fuckin' move outta this country before cops and shit come sniffin' around. Get your shit together. We're leavin'." There's no longer softness to his voice, now harsh and commanding.

"I can't leave him," I blubber. "You go. I can get back on my own. I can't just leave him here alone."

"You're on your own here. If they arrest you for bein' associated with him we won't fuckin' come for you. You get that?"

I nod and look as lost as I can muster. Torch grunts and moves away from me quickly. As he leaves the room, he casts one more look on his boss's dead body before barking orders to the other men. They leave the suite as swiftly as they entered.

When they land, they'll be taken in by federal agents from many different branches of the government thanks to the five months of intel I collected. Killing Marco was just a bonus.

Once I'm certain I'm alone I move to the bathroom and wash my face, ridding myself of the horrid make-up that's camouflaged my skin for months. I pile my hair into a bun on the top of my head before pulling on a plain white sun hat that shields my entire face. Thong sandals, a pale yellow halter maxi sundress and boy shorts on...I already feel a bit more like myself.

I move out to the patio that leads to the beach and grab my bag before walking along the white sand, taking that long needed deep cleansing lungful of fresh air.

Chapter 2

Kat

I pull up in front of DCA headquarters and feel a bubble of excitement creep up within me. This is my home. I don't own anything in this world other than some clothes, a fairly good amount of weapons and some practical luggage. That makes headquarters the closest thing to a home that I have. Just across the Potomac from CIA headquarters stands our unassuming four story business-looking building. All vehicles are parked beneath the building in a parking garage manned with state of the art security and guards. Every car is weighed and scanned as it enters the garage. No one is coming in here with a bomb or chemical weapons.

Once I park my car and sling my messenger bag across my chest, I head for the elevator. ID badge, retina and hand scan combine to allow me access to the elevator. Once inside, a TSA-style body scanner scrutinizes my person until satisfied I'm only armed with allowed weapons, a holstered Springfield 1911 and my secondary Glock around my ankle.

The best thing about working for a small clandestine government agency is the dress code is lax. No sad FBI pants suits here. I'm wearing boot-cut dark wash jeans, a soft blue V-neck T-shirt and a grey canvas jacket. I'm more comfortable than I've been in half a year.

I took the standard four weeks off that are allowed to agents after being in the field for extended periods after an initial debrief is conducted off-site. I spent my time off up in the Rockies near a summer resort town. I did nothing other than read, cook and celebrate the last of my fillers leaving my face and my hair painstakingly returning to its natural honey blonde. I had the girl restoring my hair take a few inches off, but it's still falling at the middle of my back. Today I have it in a loose braid swept over my shoulder.

My high cheekbones are back, though my lips are still a bit puffy. I'm hoping it will go away soon but have been informed they may stay a slightly swollen for a long time to come. Not wearing colored contacts has my eyes forming a loving relationship with me once again, instead of being dry and irritated all the time. My hazel blue-green-grey eyes seem a bit brighter now than they were before. I'm sure that's not the case, but it feels that way all the same.

Then there's make-up. I went without a stitch the entire time I was in the mountains. My pores needed to breathe and reacquaint with natural sunlight. My skin as a whole has lightened from the shade caused by the constant tanning, but I still have a deeper olive color than I normally would. I look good now. Today I'm sporting light natural make-up and lip-gloss that took me all of five minutes to complete. Ah, it feels good to be home.

The elevator opens ushering me into a long well lit corridor benefiting from a glass roof with warm light grey walls and similarly colored tiled floors. I make my way to the reception desk, which is housed in an open three-story center point of the building. All of the corridors shoot out from this area like hands on a clock.

I make my way past the guards scanning my badge as I go, walking directly to the glass elevators to head up to intelligence monitoring on the third floor. There are a lot of people in the corridors and the elevator, but none I'm familiar with. We work in small teams in different areas of focus. My team's specialty is arms dealings and human trafficking, as they often go hand in hand. There are teams for drugs, organized crime, terrorism, espionage. You name it we have it. Some agents move around within the company, but there are others that have been on the same team their entire career.

Exiting the elevator, I make my way down a suspended walkway leading to a small corridor with four team rooms housed behind two doors on the right and two on the left, with intelligence monitoring behind the last door at the end of the hallway. I scan my way in to be hit with the serenity of quiet agents sitting dutifully behind desks in rows facing a massive multi-media center of large and small screens on the back wall. I move to the far right, my eyes landing on her before I'm within arm's reach. Her thin lips curve into a welcoming saccharine smile as she stands from her desk. My pace quickens.

"You look phenomenal," Jess murmurs into my neck as her short stature only allows her to reach that far.

I pull her tightly to my chest, relieved at the weight of my best friend in my arms.

"Fuck, I missed you," I huff into her chocolate curls.

"Obviously, you're squishin' the shit outta me and I had Thai last night. I'd loosen up if I were you," she snarks.

I let out the first real laugh I've uttered in months and relish the vibration in my chest as I let Jess go.

"Shane's excited you're back. He's been poppin' in here all morning hopin' you'll be here so he can get the next op on the move."

Jess rolls her pale green eyes. Shane is the head of our team and is constantly planning, executing and running ops. He's the youngest team leader in the history of the DCA and is dead set on being the youngest department head before he takes the helm of the agency all before he's forty. It's exhausting thinking about it much less having a conversation with him about it. Unfortunately, Jess lives it every day because Shane is her fiancé. They went through the same training class together and have been inseparable since Jess schooled his ass in covert monitoring during training. She's like Houdini with computers.

I met Jess my first day out of training and we bonded instantly. Her funny bluntness won my heart and endeared her to me after only a few sentences. Shane was still a field agent at the time and he and I clicked as quickly as Jess and I did. Shane taught me so much about this job, more than any mentor I had at the DCA training farm. He never belittled me for being a woman in a field of men. Shane saw me as an equal and treated me as such. They've been my best friends for the past seven years and I can't imagine doing this job without them having my back.

"I better go find him. I'm ten minutes early as it is. I'll probably get in trouble," I scoff.

"No shit," she huffs flopping into her chair behind her fortress of computers.

"I'll come back once I know where I'm headed next. Dinner tonight?"

"Yes, I need some wine and girl time."

"Can't imagine a better way to spend my evening."

I offer Jess a broad smile and move away from her desk back into the corridor. I'm supposed to meet Shane in room one so I head to the last door on my right and go in.

Shane's sitting at the end of an eight-person dark wood conference table in a perfectly tailored navy designer suit, setting himself outside the team in appearance and position. If you can imagine a real life Ken Doll that's what Shane is—tall, lean, blond perfectly styled hair and dazzling blue eyes. Those stunning eyes lock on mine and an award-winning smile kisses his broad lips. He stands from the table smoothly, approaching me with a promise of a rough hug to follow.

He fulfills his unspoken promise yanking me off the ground in a bear hug. Now I know how Jess felt a few minutes ago when I squished the life out of her. I smile at the equality of our relationships and squeeze him as hard as I can.

"You look great, Kat," he murmurs into my hair. "Way better than that porn star hooker look you had workin' a month ago. Felt the need to bleach my eyes after the debrief and seein' you in those pictures." He shudders before setting me down.

"At least you didn't have to fuck like one too," I snark pushing him back a bit. "And just so we're clear, I'm done with those ops. I've had enough to last me a long ass lifetime."

"Last one. I swear." He crosses his heart dramatically before pulling me under his arm and leading me to the conference table.

The door to the room opens behind us and we turn around in tandem to greet our visitor. The man facing us has an inquisitive look on his chiseled face, but drops it as soon as we make eye contact. His eyes are so dark brown they're practically black. His hair is buzzed short, a russet brown color. He's tall, probably six feet three inches tall and built like a brick shit house. He's wearing almost the same outfit as me other than a more masculine form. He's gorgeous and I have no idea who he is.

Shane drops his arm from my shoulder, quickly returning to professional mode.

"Nick, allow me to introduce Katherine Russell."

Nick strides toward me, his large hand outstretched.

"Kat, this is Nick Cooper," Shane continues the introductions.

I nod and grip Nick's hand once he places his palm in mine.

"Nick's joining our team. He's recently left the organized crime team lookin' for greener pastures," Shane informs me as Nick releases my hand and offers Shane a stern glare.

"Not lookin' for greener pastures, Shane. Tryin' not to end up dead," Nick says pointedly in a deep menacing voice. Now there's a bit of tension in the room. So much for a nice welcome home.

"It's nice to meet you, Nick. I hope you enjoy it over here," I offer politely trying to diffuse the pressure building in here.

"It's nice to meet you too, Katherine. I look forward to workin' with you. I've heard great things," he responds kindly.

13

"Kat, please."

"Kat," he says through a slight smile.

"Why don't we have a seat and I can read you both in on our op?" Shane suggests motioning toward the table.

I take the seat to Shane's right, while Nick sits across from me at Shane's left. We both turn our attention to the end of the table where a screen is projecting Shane's presentation as the lights dim.

"These are the Bookers," Shane starts, advancing the slide to the most normal white picket fence couple I've ever seen. They look like they belong as a stock photo in a picture frame.

Blonde haired, blue eyed, polo and khaki wearing generic people. Not my usual game.

"Trish and Tony Booker live in the sleepy, affluent Connecticut town of Maybelle."

The slide advances to various shots of Tony looking like he's running for political office.

"Tony is a self-employed computer engineer. He enjoys running, golf, poker on Thursdays with his neighborhood pals and church on Sundays."

The slide advances to Trish looking like June Cleaver.

"Trish is a housewife that spends her days volunteering at the local library for a literacy group, knitting, baking, bridge on Thursdays and church on Sundays, where she's a bible school teacher for children."

The slide advances to two children that look like clones of their parents. Creepy.

"These are their two children. Bradford is ten and Annabelle is eight."

The slide advances to Bradford playing a lot of different sports.

"The boy is an athlete year round. Baseball, football, basketball and soccer all figure into his yearly schedule."

The slide advances to Annabelle dancing and singing in photos.

"The girl spends most of her time in the arts. Dancing, singing, acting and some gymnastics."

The slide advances to the family in various family portraits and candid shots around the picturesque town they live in. I study the photos looking for the angle, the mark, something that shows me what's wrong with them. I don't see it on film. They're perfect, which to my trained brain says they must be totally screwed up.

The slide advances to a room full of filthy young girls draped in FBI blankets. Their cheeks are stained from tears and their faces are in various stages of exhaustion and panic. I immediately feel the need to hit something...hard.

"The Bookers are running a human trafficking ring from what our intel has gathered. We don't have much to go on, so we need eyes and ears. They've been at this goin' on fifteen years without the slightest slip-up or rat. They're untouchable."

The slide show stops and Shane slides dossiers in front of Nick and me.

"You two are going in as Nick and Kat Johnson. All of the relevant information and details are in front of you. I suggest you two spend some time together working through your back-story before you head out tomorrow. We're also in the unique position of having acquired a kid for the two of you. Well kind of. He'll be the nephew of Nick's deceased older brother. Jake's eighteen and just completed his first three months of training. He looks nowhere near that so we're sending him in with you as a fifteen-year-old sophomore in high school. Jake's flying in from the training farm now. Should be here in an hour or so. Any questions for me?"

"Timeline?" I ask without looking up from my dossier.

"Unknown. They're good at what they do. My best guess is a year, maybe more." Shane sounds wounded as he says it. I look up to see I'm right. I nod in understanding. I just got back and now I'm already gone again.

"Better than my last assignment," Nick scoffs under his breath.

"Bad one?" I ask quietly.

"You could say that," he huffs not looking at me.

"Nick ran a small op team in organized crime for ten years. He just got out in December," Shane explains.

"Jesus Christ. I didn't know any ops ran that long," I say shocked. The longest operation I'm aware of in the agency was five years and that was by far the most time an agent had been under.

"They don't," Shane says blankly.

Well clearly, they do, but gauging his response, I'll leave it for now.

"I've got another meeting to get to. You have the room for the day so feel free to use it. I'll send Jake this way once I've met with him. I'll see you later, Kat," my friend finishes softly.

"Nick, I'll see you at five," Shane states professionally before scooping up his black leather document case, squeezing my shoulder and exiting the room.

Leaving me alone with my soon to be fake husband.

Chapter 3

Kat

"I've never worked with a partner before," I admit sheepishly.

"Me neither," Nick grunts without looking up at me. "You wanna go through some of this now?"

"Sure." I shrug off my jacket and get comfortable. Nick does the same, revealing a ripped body beneath his tight white T-shirt. As far as fake husbands go, in the looks department, I've hit the jackpot.

"So we met at college," Nick reads finally looking up at me with his dark eyes.

"In psychology class," I confirm.

"We went to the University of Kansas and both come from small towns in the state." There's a slight chuff to his voice as he reads.

"Is that funny?"

"I have some close friends in Kansas City, so I spend a bit of time in the area. I'm from Chicago originally. You familiar with the Midwest at all?"

"I'm from Sioux City."

"Well at least they've given us some comfort in our back story."

"That they have. I've never used my real name before," I say a bit surprised.

"With long term ops it helps sometimes. Living by another name for years at a time can wear down your morale."

I nod. It makes sense.

"I own a securities business and you stay at home now that we have Jake to take care of. Before that you were a pre-school teacher."

"I'm an only child and your older brother and his wife died in a car crash a year ago. Both our parents are deceased. We have aunts, uncles and cousins that live in our hometowns that we visit rarely," I continue reading.

I realize that I'm at the end of the page and there's not much else listed. Our new home is beautiful and our cars are BMWs, a sporty version for Nick and an SUV for me. *Stepford* here I come.

"We'll fill in the rest with real details about each other," Nick says in a softer tone than he's used up to this point. I look up at his kind face peering across the table at me.

"I guess we need to catch up on years of dating and getting to know each other in a few hours."

"We'll learn a lot about each other since we'll be living together. I'm not too concerned with that. I think you need to lay out some ground rules about this though."

I furrow my brow and wait for a further explanation.

"We'll obviously have to be physical and intimate when we're in public. I'd like to know how you feel about that. What you're comfortable with."

After the operation I just finished I'm somewhat blown away. Shane loves me, but it was made clear to me that I did whatever was necessary to win Marco over. I'm not a whore. I keep telling myself that. I don't know that I believe it, but I keep saying it. All agents make sacrifices to work for the DCA. Mine has, three times now, been to sacrifice my body to get close to my mark. Marco was the last time.

"What are you comfortable with?" I ask, letting him know I don't need to be coddled by the big strong man.

"I'm comfortable with whatever you're comfortable with," he responds coolly.

"Nick, let's get this out on the table. I just got back from an op where I was basically dressed up and treated

18

like a porn star for five months. I'm pretty comfortable with anything. In this op I fear you're the one that'll have more hang ups than me."

"Did you enjoy your last op?" he asks in a harsher tone.

"Fuck no," I scoff.

"Then you aren't comfortable with *anything.* You do your job and clearly, you do it well. I'm not a mark so I don't wanna put you in a situation that's uncomfortable for you or puts you in a position where you feel like you're sacrificing. You set the boundaries," he instructs. I can tell he was a team leader because he's leading me. I'm not used to being led on an op. I've always worked alone and I'm starting to realize I like working alone.

"Thank you for your concern. I'm fine with whatever we agree upon mutually. I don't feel the need to set the boundaries. We can discuss them and set them as a team," I respond professionally.

"From the photos of the Bookers they're affectionate so we should be on par with them or even surpass them. Holding hands a lot, in each other's arms, you sit in my lap rather than an open chair when appropriate, kissing lovingly. I doubt there'll be a need for a steamy make-out session, but there could come the time. How does all of that sound for you?"

"Horrible," I deadpan.

His gaze widens and I lose my straight face tumbling into laughter. After a moment, he falls into chuckles right along with me. His deep baritone vibrates through the room like a symphony exposing the acoustics of the greatest opera houses in the world. Nick's voice is sultry, but his laugh is intoxicating.

"I'm fine with all of that, Nick," I say gaining my composure. "Do you think we should share a room? A bed?"

"Yes. Once we get the Bookers in our home, we need it to look like we're a normal couple sharing a home, room, bed and life. I'm anticipating people poking around our house to check us out. I'm good on the floor if you're more comfortable."

"Nick, if you don't stop pussy footin' around me we're gonna be a constantly fighting couple," I warn.

"Noted." He pauses for a moment. "Do you like to spoon?"

I look up from my dossier to see a mischievous grin playing on his succulent mouth.

"If you need me to hold you at night all you have to do is ask," I tease.

We both snicker again. I think we'll be fine once Nick loosens up a bit.

"What's your feeling on pet names?" he asks with a serious face.

"I've been called every one you can think of. What do you think a couple like us would call each other?"

"Something awful like Kitty for you and Darling for me," he says with pure disgust in his voice.

"I think a little puke just came up my throat."

"We could try the generics of babe, honey, baby," he suggests with a shrug.

"I'd rather not. That feels almost lazy."

"I know. Okay, if you were just gonna give me a pet name what would it be?"

"Right now?"

"Yeah," he says encouragingly. No pressure!

"Button."

"Button? What the fuck is that?"

I laugh quietly before answering, as he's clearly offended.

"Your eyes look like chocolate buttons. You know...the candy in the UK?"

"I'm not familiar."

"Hey you asked me to pick something off the top of my head. You do it if you think it's so damn easy."

"Sunshine," he replies immediately.

"How's that?"

"You're a bright beacon of light from head to toe and your hair looks like something out of a fairy tale, golden and shiny."

Well shit. His was definitely better.

"Okay, you're better at this than I am," I admit slightly defeated.

His smug smile makes his win less impressive. He's probably used that same line on hundreds of women.

"Can I make a suggestion?" he asks quietly looking at his hands.

"Of course."

"Nicky," he whispers almost pained as he says it.

"You don't seem to like the name," I observe.

"It's personal for me. Maybe someday I'll tell you about it. It's a good choice though and I don't have an issue with you calling me that."

"I'm not steppin' on your real life wife's toes with that or something am I?"

He furrows his brow looking up at me.

"I don't have a wife. None of us are married that go on extended undercover ops. You know that," he admonishes.

"I know. You just seem...I don't know. Never mind."

I let it go because he obviously doesn't want to talk about this with me. I'm a stranger. I have no desire for him to start poking around in my life.

There's a swift knock at the door before it swings open. A kid walks in startling me a bit until I remember Jake.

"Hi. I'm Jake Rivers," he introduces himself sweetly. He looks like he just started puberty. He's long and gangly with shaggy blond hair curling over his ears and big brown eyes wide with excitement. No way is this kid eighteen.

Nick and I stand up simultaneously to greet our third.

"Kat Russell," I say sticking my hand out to him.

"Nice to meet you, ma'am," he responds respectfully. Yeah he just came from the training farm where everyone is sir and ma'am.

Nick comes around the table in confident manly strides.

"Nick Cooper."

"Sir."

"Why don't we sit down and run through some things?" Nick suggests.

I retake my seat while Jake slips off his backpack and takes the seat next to mine.

"You're pretty young to be in the agency," I point out the obvious.

"Yes ma'am. The FBI has strict rules on age and college education. The DCA doesn't and recruited me straight outta high school."

"I was recruited right outta high school too. And please stop callin' me ma'am. You're makin' me feel old."

"Sorry, ma...Kat."

I smile and he offers me a sweet almost timid grin in return.

"I'm guessin' you have a skill-set that didn't require a college education," Nick suggests.

"Yes sir. I'm a sniper."

"Welcome to the family, Jake," Nick says through a broad smile, pleased at the kid's prowess.

"Thanks," he beams back.

"Let's bond," I instruct and we go about doing just that.

Chapter 4

Nick

Jake may be new to the agency and young as fuck, but the kid's bright. He'll be easy to work with. My only concern is high school girls wanting a piece of him. Maybe he can do it cougar-style and get an eighteen-year-old if the need comes. It will.

Kat...wow, she's a lot. The job has mindfucked her a bit. It does that. I'm no beacon of normalcy. I'm not sure what kind of team Shane's running, but pimping out field agents should be against his goddamned policy. I felt every muscle in my body twitch when she laid out the briefest description of her last op where she was basically a whore for hire. That shit stops.

We have three departments that oversee teams at the DCA. I come from the same department and have been moved to this team because the department head, Hal Gelding, wants me to take over this team. When this op is wrapped, Shane's goal is to move to a different team or take Hal's position as he's looking for a promotion to run the agency. Shane may be taking his ops in unconventional directions, but he's running the most successful ops of any team. If he can rein his shit in, he'll make a great department head.

I know Shane pretty well. We went through three years of training together before I went back to Chicago to work undercover in my own family. My uncle was the head of The Mancini Crime Family and I worked undercover as the enforcer for that family for a decade. It was torturous (pun...intended) to live my life in the family that had murdered my parents in one way or another before I was an adult. My father got what most mob men get, dead. I never needed the specifics, but I figure it was a drug deal gone wrong. Nothing to really shed tears over.

My mother got cancer while I was away at "college", meaning DCA training. She only lasted six months after the diagnosis. I was a miracle baby born to parents in their forties so my grandparents were long gone before my mom died, leaving me to be taken in—inserted by the DCA—by the great Vito Mancini. My uncle is a piece of fucking shit.

I spent most of the decade I was in the Family carrying out DCA sanctioned hits, torturing and murdering at my uncle's behest, collecting intel about every crime organization we had dealings with and in the end gathering recorded information on Vito Mancini himself once we'd sucked the Family dry of information. I wish I could say after a decade it was easy to get that, but it wasn't. He was religious about sweeping for bugs and checking everyone for wires and listening devices. Even though I'd been killing for him for years, he never trusted me enough not to search and scan me.

He finally fucked up though. After years of me trying to get enough shit to pin on him, he fucked up big time. Vito orchestrated the abduction and torture of Shannon Kelly. Shannon is a family attorney in Kansas City. For the last twenty-two years, it was believed she and her father, the State's Attorney at the time, had died when their car was caught in a gang crossfire. I met an eight-year-old Shannon a few months before the shooting. I played with her for hours and fell madly in love with that little girl. I may have only been ten at the time, but she stole my heart and soul that day. My Shanny.

When the press conference announcing her and her father's deaths came on the TV, I threw up all over the carpet in front of me. I was destroyed by that information. It was in that moment I knew I never wanted to be anything my uncle was. I wanted to be good, to do good. I wanted to be worthy of the afternoon I spent with a girl that shined so brightly it hurt my eyes. Auburn hair, bright green eyes, a smile that could melt glaciers and a heart so big the world could fit in it two times over...that was the eight-year-old I played baseball with for an afternoon. She rocked my world.

Twenty-two years later I get a call from my uncle that a job isn't going as planned and he needs me to go wrap it up. Not an uncommon request from him. I show up at a farmhouse outside Chicago and look at the monitors connected to the cameras where the team was holding their captive to see auburn hair, bright green eyes, a naked body with its back ripped to shit from torture and Tony Gallo moments away from raping her. My heart finally returned to a beat I'd lost as a ten-year-old boy and my veins ran ice cold.

I stormed into the basement room where they had her and slit Tony's throat before he could do much to fight me. I spent the next few days tirelessly trying to find a way to rescue Shanny and keep her alive and safe. I failed in that effort because her new adopted family showed up to rescue her just as the rat that had infiltrated her family—planted there by mine—showed up. "Taylor", as he was known, shot Shanny four times in the back as she flung herself around my body to save me, as I was his intended target. I felt every shot wrack her thin frame before I watched the life drain from her stunning emerald eyes. I died for the second time in my life that day.

I wrapped my hands around her head when she curled around me and ended up stopping the bullet to the back of her head with my hands. The DCA has some amazing surgeons who have fixed my hands and removed my scars. That was the least of my worries.

After a week in a coma, Shanny came back. My heart beat again. The only issue, Shanny is no longer the girl I met twenty-two years ago. She's been hurt and tortured in ways nightmares are made of. The woman has a strength and determination that has carried her through her life that's unparalleled.

Once she was rescued I set about putting away my uncle which was made easy by information Shanny's father had hidden proving on paper what my uncle is, as well as a dirty politician that my uncle was in cahoots with. That politician is currently recovering from surgery after I put a bullet in him yesterday. He came for Shanny for the third and last time. He ordered the hit that was made to look like a gang turf war twenty-two years ago. He ordered the abduction and torture of Shanny in December to cover up his dealings with Vito twenty-two years prior. Yesterday, Governor Grady showed up with three Mancini Family lowlifes to try to force her to testify at his trial by stealing her infant son. Before Shanny, who's a weapons expert the agency would love to get their hands on, could blow his brains out, I put two rounds in his chest.

That's the last time harm will come to Shannon Kelly on my watch.

As much as I love that woman, she's taken. She has a man who loves her the way she deserves, in a way I'm not sure I'm capable of. So instead of fighting for the love of a woman who's had my heart for more than two decades I've let her go. Shanny's my friend. My closest friend in the world and I love her fiercely. But I had to let her go. Eight months have passed since I found her in that basement and the ache from losing her still stings, but the joy in sharing her friendship lessens the blow.

Yesterday, Shanny learned she's pregnant with twins. Her life is full to the brim with love and I can't be hurt by that. I take pleasure from it. I'll fill my life with good to prove to myself that I deserve even a fraction of what that woman offers me as a friend if it's the last thing I do on Earth.

"So should I call you Uncle Nick?" Jake brings me back to the table away from my thoughts.

"Yeah," I grunt still stuck in my head a bit. I'm a fairly rough person to begin with so being a family man for the next year or so is going to be a challenge.

"Please don't call me Aunt Kat. It sounds like the name of some old lady's dead cat that she's had stuffed after it died and still shares her meals with," Kat explains seriously. She's fucking funny. I chuckle right along with Jake.

"What would you like me to call you then?" Jake says through a snicker.

"Is there an aunt I'd like to fuck acronym we could use?"

That sets the whole table alight.

"Not that I'm aware of. I'm not sure that would be a very wholesome option either," Jake points out sweetly.

"What about Aunt Kay? That sounds better," she suggests.

"I'm good with that if you are."

"Nick?" I like that she diverts for my approval. I like it more than I should.

"I'm comfortable bein' married to Aunt Kay," I respond professionally.

"This has been fun boys, but I've got a hot date tonight that I can't put off gettin' ready for any longer," Kat informs us pulling her jacket on as she stands up.

"I believe we're staying at the same hotel. Would you like me to go back with you?" Jake asks politely. The kid is sweet, professional and smart. There's nothing about him that suggests he's a cold-blooded killer. I like him.

"I'm good on my own but thanks. I've gotta run to a lingerie shop and I doubt you wanna accompany me for that errand."

That's a lucky motherfucker she's seeing tonight. Kat's gorgeous, no doubt about it. Her hazel eyes are in a constant state of a sexy slant. Her golden hair would look good spread across any number of surfaces, but it would look best covering a pillow. Her body is soft yet toned, something she works at. Her tits are more than a handful and when the air conditioning kicked on a few hours ago, it made apparent her nipples are made to be sucked on for days. Kat has a narrow waist and shapely hips that my hands would wrap around with ease taking her from behind. And I've promised myself to keep this nothing but professional with her. This agency has made her use her body too much for its own gain. I won't be another person to put her in that position.

"Have a nice evening," I say politely.

"You too, Nick. I'll see you in the morning. Jake, if we're at the same hotel you can hitch a ride with me in the morning."

"Thanks," he says through a broad smile. He thinks she's gorgeous too.

She offers us each a stunning smile and then leaves the room with a slight sway to her hips that I'm sure she's unaware she has.

"Jesus Christ that woman's somethin' else," Jake says with wide eyes.

"She's good at what she does," I state blankly.

"She's better than *good* at what she does," Jake admonishes.

"You're right, she's a very talented agent and she'll be stellar on this op."

"You gay?"

"What?" I snap.

"I got no problem if you are. But I figure I should know goin' in on the op."

"I'm not gay," I growl. I don't give a shit if people are...to each their own.

"Are you blind?"

"What the fuck are you talkin' about?"

"Katherine Russell is stunning, smart, funny, deadly and gettin' ready to share a bed with you for the foreseeable future. You got nothing to say about that other than she's good at her job? Either you're gay or blind," Jake says pointedly.

"I'm not gay or blind. I'm a professional. She's an agent just like anyone else in the company. It's called respect. Learn it before I'm forced to teach you," I threaten.

"Acknowledging a woman's beauty is nothing but respectful when done appropriately. I may be young, but I've learned in life that women enjoy bein' complimented and admired when it comes from a place of genuine appreciation. Kat is a woman meant to be admired,

28

often. If you're gonna play her husband with any believability you'll need to learn that skill quickly. Other men'll be sniffing around her at every corner in Maybelle, Connecticut. She's grade-A in any world, but playing the role in this op she'll draw a shit load of attention.

"And this will be the first and the last time you threaten to teach me anything in life. I've learned my lessons the hard way and any-fuckin'-thing you believe you can teach me I'll school your ass in. I may not be a full agent yet, but I'm not some stupid kid you need to educate. We clear?" he finishes curtly.

The look in his eyes has changed from young sweet kid to the heartless killer I now have no doubt he can be. Okay, the day is full of surprises.

"Noted."

He offers me a chin lift before slinging his backpack over his shoulders and leaving the room. I wait for a moment and then climb to my feet. I make my way out of the corridor, across the suspended walkway beyond the elevators to another suspended walkway that leads to our offices. I glide into mine and close the door with a soft click.

I flop into my chair at my glass desk and get to work researching every classified document that I can get my hands on about Kat Russell and Jake Rivers. I'm hit with a severe lack of information that tells me my team members come from the same fucked up background that I do. The "Johnson" family is made up of three people without a past looking for a future.

Chapter 5

Kat

"Silk PJs and wine may be the best present I've ever received," Jess says through a sleepy long stretch on the couch.

"I'm a pretty good gift giver," I state confidently.

"You gonna give Nick Cooper some of your gifts?" Jess says through a tipsy smirk.

"I don't think Nick Cooper has any interest in my gifts. He practically shut down at the idea of havin' to share a bed with me."

"Really?"

"Yup," I pop my *p* remembering the pale shade his face turned when I told him about my last op.

"You think he's gay?" Jess asks with a furrowed brow.

"I don't know. He could be." I shrug. I don't care if he is. Actually, it would make this next year even easier if he is. He never checked me out or acted suggestively toward me. Jake was sweet and genuine in his compliments. Someone has taught that boy how to swoon the ladies. Look out Maybelle High School, Jake Johnson is coming to town.

"No sex for a year. That sucks, Kat." Jess pouts on my behalf.

"I've gone longer."

"Did it close back up?"

"No," I say through a chuckle.

"I'm glad you're not takin' *those* ops anymore. It's not good for you," Jess says seriously with a little sadness on her face.

"I knew the job when I started. There have only been a handful like that, but I'm glad to be done."

"Be safe this time, Kat. These people look like *Stepford*, but they're really a fuckin' horror movie."

"I'm not alone this time, Jess. I can take care of myself and with Nick and Jake with me, I'll be even better. No worries." I rub a comforting hand across hers.

"Shane said a year, maybe more," she huffs.

"We work until the job's done. If the Bookers have lasted this long it'll take time."

"You're gonna miss the wedding," she whispers.

"I'll be there in spirit in one of those hideous pink dresses you're forcing your bridesmaids to wear."

"They're really bad. I can't be upstaged on my big day," she says definitively.

"That logic is baffling."

"You love me," Jess states with a mischievous smirk.

"You know I do."

"Okay, let's say goodbye now so I can cry all night and make Shane feel really bad for hours on end."

She stands up and pulls me to my feet squeezing me tightly around my middle. I constrict around her even harder knowing I'd wear one of those ugly fucking dresses if I could be by her side. A sob breaks through her chest and I steel the emotion bubbling within me. Only one of us can crack at a time and this time it's her turn.

Jess tips her head up to peer at me through wet lashes, a small smile playing on her lips.

"See you soon, Jess," I whisper.

She nods unable to speak for fear of tumbling into a state of uncontrollable blubbering. I let her go and leave her home without looking back because I have the same fear as Jess.

As I slide into my sheets, I release the tension of saying goodbye to my friends for the millionth time, knowing my life works this way. I hate saying goodbye,

but I love my job. I'm brilliant at my job. Agent Kat
Russell is who I'm meant to be.

Welcome to Maybelle the ornate sign reads as we pass
by in my white BMW SUV. The town is something out of
a postcard. The streets are lined with towering full green
trees. Lawns are manicured to perfection in front of
colonial and Georgian houses. As Jake and I drive down
Main Street (because these people are imaginative), we
enter the downtown space with Nick following behind.
The store fronts are homey and inviting with a good deal
of foot traffic on the sidewalks. There are cafés and
restaurants all locally owned, not a Starbucks in sight.

As we move through the small quaint downtown and
beyond a lush park, the roads begin to turn and sweep
with the landscape giving way to sprawling estates. I
follow the GPS only a few minutes further before it
informs me I've reached my destination. I pull in the
driveway of a massive colonial palace.

"Holy shit," Jake mutters.

"I second that."

We smile at each other and put on our Maybelle
faces. Jake is wearing a turquoise polo shirt and khaki
shorts with leather sandals. He looks cute and fifteen.
I'm wearing a white halter cut dress with a pale violet
flower print that sports a banded waist and a pleated A-
line skirt. I look the part with comfortable wedge
sandals.

Nick is at my door before I'm able to swing my legs
out offering me his hand and a broad smile.

"We're already bein' watched," he says through his
smile leaning in for a brush of his lips against my cheek.
I squeeze his hand to let him know I heard him and
plaster a bigger smile on my face.

Nick leads me around the hood of the car with his
hand on my lower back, guiding me toward the massive
gleaming black front door. He moves around me to
unlock it and gestures for Jake to go ahead. I make my

way to follow when Nick sweeps me off my feet bride-style and carries me over the threshold careful to keep my skirt hiding my business from the neighbors. I giggle genuinely because this is one of the sweetest things a man has ever done for me, real or fake.

Nick kicks the door shut and rights my feet on the glossy parquet floors. A grand staircase is just in front of us with a formal living room to the right and a library with solid thick wood shelves lined with books two stories high to my left.

"Fuck me," I whisper taking in the grandeur of the space.

The entryway we're in is open all the way up three stories with a stunning modern chandelier glistening in the sun streaking through the windows above the front door. Nick pulls my hand and leads me beyond the staircase toward the back of the house. We enter the most magnificent kitchen with light marble countertops white cabinets in some areas and dark ebony wood in others. The mix is complementary and modern, but works perfectly with the home. With the size of this kitchen, we could entertain hundreds of people easily.

Off to the left is an eating area with an eight person espresso-colored wood table and white upholstered chairs. The French doors and windows on the back wall show a glorious view of our deck, in-ground pool and basketball/tennis court with a few acres beyond rolling with trees placed perfectly throughout. Beyond the breakfast area is a relaxed family room with two large couches and two large chairs facing a fireplace with a TV hung above it. The furniture is plush and inviting, a light cream color for the chairs a warm chocolate for the couches. I'll definitely be napping in here.

On the other side of the kitchen is a formal dining room with seating for at least twenty-four. What the hell do you do with that many seats? It's stunning and pretentious, with no comfort in sight. I hope to never have to be in this room for more than a few minutes. Yuck!

There are a few more doors on this floor. One leads to the finished basement that houses the home theater, gym, game room, wine cellar and storage. Another door opens to a humongous laundry room and another to the three car garage. There's a home office between the dining room and the formal living room. This is too much house for the three of us. I get that it's defining we have money, but it's definitely too much.

Nick leads us up the staircase where we come to the master bedroom. It's gigantic. It must cover half of the first floor in size. There's a freaking sitting area in here! A large bed occupies the main wall with an ornate wooden mahogany headboard and white and navy patterned linens. There's a bathroom off to the left that could house most New York apartments. Separate sink and vanity areas on either side of the space ensure limited interaction with my spouse. There's a large jetted tub that could fit at least four people comfortably and a walk-in shower sporting more nozzles than I would know what to do with—two sets.

At the end of the bathroom there are two doors leading to his-and-hers dressing rooms. I feel like I'm on *Cribs*. My dressing room is completely full of every clothing item known to man ordered in color and garment type. There's one wall housing only bags and shoes. In the middle of the room is a large light marble topped island with drawers full of lingerie and sweaters and a whole bunch of other shit my brain is too overwhelmed to deal with right now.

Moving back out of our room we head across the hall where there's another home office and a nursery already fully prepared for a newborn's arrival. Gorgeous pale greens and creams adorn the room.

"That's a lot," Jake whispers in my ear as we make our way to the third floor. Jake's room is on the opposite side of the house from ours. It's a typical teenage room for a boy who loves basketball, which Jake does. He'll play on the team at the high school if all goes well. A black queen-size bed, a desk and chair, two dressers and a TV, it's very normal and still very high-end. Jake makes his way around the room with an emotion on his face I can't quite place. He looks pained by whatever he's thinking.

"You good, Jake?" I ask trying not to belittle him since he's really an adult, not my nephew.

He shakes his head free of wherever he just was and clears his throat before giving me a quiet, "Yeah."

The doorbell rings sending us all into op mode instantly. The three of us hurry down the stairs before I move to answer the door. I swing it open wide with a toothy smile plastered on my face.

"Hi!" the woman says excitedly. "We're your neighbors from across the street. I'm Trish Booker and this is my husband Tony. These two are Bradford and Annabelle."

And so it begins.

"It's lovely to meet you. I'm Kat Johnson," I introduce politely and offer my hand. She grips it limply making my stomach turn at the weak behavior, but I smile through it. Nick slides his arms around my waist from behind as I release her wet noodle.

"Nicky," I admonish his forwardness sweetly. I feel his body tense behind me for a millisecond before he's back on his game. He brushes his lips on my bare shoulder before moving to my side wrapping an arm around my upper arms.

"Nick Johnson," he offers his hand to Tony. Tony responds with a warm smile and a firm shake before wrapping an arm around Trish similarly to how Nick's holding me.

"This is our nephew Jake," Nick introduces.

Jake gifts them a kind smile and a low wave.

"Well, we won't keep you. We just wanted to introduce ourselves. Kat, if you'd like, I could introduce you around some, pull you into the Maybelle fold," Trish offers with a giant smile. Her eyes run down to my left hand, which is sporting a giant radiant cut rock with smaller diamonds running down the band. My wedding band is made of large round diamonds that encircle its entirety. Trish's smile lets me know she approves of my ostentatious ring.

"Thank you Trish, I'd like that."

"I host a weekly poker game on Thursdays. If you play, you're more than welcome to join us," Tony says to Nick.

"As long as you promise not to steal all his money," I joke causing everyone to fake snicker.

"Thanks for the invitation. Maybe next week when we're good and settled in," Nick accepts politely.

"You guys like basketball?" Jake asks the kids.

"Yeah," Bradford says with a huge grin. Annabelle frowns and rolls her eyes.

"We've got a court out back if you wanna shoot the ball sometime. It gets old beating Uncle Nick all the time," Jake teases causing both kids to smile.

"Hey," Nick feigns offense.

"I used to play with the kids that lived here before you. Mother, would it be all right?"

My stomach turns when he calls her mother. Who does that in the twenty-first century?

"Of course, dear." Her response is warm and slightly fake. I'm certain Nick and Jake pick up on it along with me.

"Welcome to the neighborhood. Let us know if you need anything, we'd be happy to help," Tony says turning his family and walking down our stone skirted driveway.

The three of us stand in the doorway watching them go before offering a final family wave as they reach their own driveway.

Nick ushers us in the house and shuts the door before locking it.

"You're fuckin' amazing, Kat," Jake beams at me.

"Sorry?" I furrow my brow. I think we all did awesome just then.

"He's right. You were perfection," Nick compliments squeezing my wrist before moving toward the kitchen.

Jake and I follow with gigantic smiles smeared across our faces. We can do this.

Chapter 6

Nick

"This bed is heavenly," Kat moans as she slides into the sheets wearing a white silk and lace nightie that hits her ankles.

"It's pretty good," I respond telling my dick to slow the fuck down.

"Sorry about the nightie. My closet doesn't have a single T-shirt in it and I didn't bring any with me."

"It's fine."

"I considered sleeping my sportswear, but they only have me in tiny shorts and sports bras. Not really comfort clothes in my book. I thought about goin' into your dressing room and stealing some undershirts, but I didn't know if you'd be down with that. So, you're stuck with nighties I thought only existed in soft porn. I'm convinced a man styled me for this op," she huffs.

The image of her in only a sports bra and barely-there shorts gets my dick at full mast. Her in one of my T-shirts...now I'm painfully hard. I keep my laptop firmly in place telling her, "Help yourself to whatever you need in my closet."

"Thanks. It's probably not a good idea, now that I think about it. I have to be in op mode here, not bunny slippers."

"True."

It's definitely not a good idea and for more reasons than just the op.

"I'm no good at pillow talk. At least that's what my last mark told me," Kat apologizes pulling the duvet up to her chin before rolling to face my side.

"I'm no good at most kinds of talking," I admit.

39

"Well, I don't believe that. You've talked to me just fine. Thanks for carrying me over the threshold. I know it was for the eyes of the neighborhood, but that's one of the sweetest things a man has ever done for me even if it was fake."

That's just fucking sad. I have no clue how to respond.

"I'll try to be the best fake husband I can be."

"And I'll be the best fake wife. Does that nursery freak you the fuck out?"

"On principle?"

"No, it's not like I hate babies or anything. I love kids actually. But if it's in the house and all of *Stepford* knows about it they'll expect it to be filled at some point. How's that gonna work?"

"Infertility."

"Okay."

I shut my laptop and lay down, uncomfortable sleeping in a full pajama set. I wiggle around getting settled on my side facing away from Kat.

"Night," Kat whispers in her soft sweet voice.

"Night," I mumble.

A few minutes later, I hear her breathing even out. I wait a good five minutes and then climb out of the bed and pad to the office across from our room. I flop into the leather chair at the large L-shaped mahogany desk and plug my laptop in. I write a quick email to Shanny letting her know I'm on an op and that I'll call her when I'm able.

I read through some briefs on our secure DCA network about the Bookers and the human trafficking ring for the next three hours until I'm finally exhausted enough to fall asleep. When I walk into our dark room, the moonlight is casting a cool glow on Kat's skin. She looks ethereal...if that's a thing.

I step lightly to my side of the bed and pull off my pajamas, leaving my boxer briefs. No way I'll be able to sleep in that shit. I'll be up before anyone else is so Kat won't be uncomfortable finding me mostly naked next to her. I only get a few hours of sleep a night normally. I've never needed more than that. I guess I haven't needed it because I sure as shit haven't gotten it.

I slide into the bed carefully, hoping not to disturb Kat. When I move to lie down, she flies across the bed away from me, curling into a protective ball at the edge of the bed. She doesn't seem to be awake even though her actions suggests otherwise.

"Kat," I whisper.

There's no response so I let it go and swing my forearm across my eyes, quickly falling asleep.

I wake up to a loud scream and launch myself from the bed. Kat's already ahead of me with her gun at the ready taking the stairs two at a time her nightie flowing romantically behind her as she holds the hem to run easier.

We burst into Jake's room to find him on the floor in a ball. Kat drops to her knees beside him wrapping her arms around his body. I quickly scan the room for a threat, knowing there isn't one.

"I've got you. You're okay," Kat murmurs into his hair.

Jake's arms fly around her waist as she cradles the top half of him in her lap. His entire body is convulsing. I move into his attached bathroom and fill a glass of water.

"Jake, drink this water. Get yourself back together," I instruct more harshly than I'd like.

That earns me a scowl from Kat as she runs soothing fingers through his shaggy hair.

"Sorry," Jake finally murmurs against Kat's torso after a good five minutes of being comforted and stroked by Kat. I've just been standing here avoiding Kat's icy glares with a glass of water in my hand.

"Nothing to be sorry about. You think you can get up?" Kat asks in the softest voice I've heard her use.

"Yeah," he croaks.

I reach my hand out to help Kat off the ground and she smacks it away from her. Okay, I've clearly pissed her off with my lack of kindness earlier. She climbs to her feet and leads Jake to his bed sitting down on the edge and pulling him to sit next to her under her arm. She holds her hand out for the water without looking at me and I oblige swiftly.

"Here you go," she encourages Jake to take a drink.

Jake takes the glass in his still tremoring hand, carefully easing it to his lips. After a few small sips, he hands it back to Kat who places it on the bedside table. She wraps both arms around Jake and holds him for a long time in silence. I have no clue what to do right now. I barely know the kid, but I get this is heavy...whatever it is.

"You want me to stay with you tonight?" she murmurs into his hair.

"You don't have to do that," he mumbles.

"I don't have to do anything, Jake. If you'd like me to stay with you, I'd be happy to do that. It's whatever you're comfortable with."

"Just for a little while," he whispers so faintly I barely pick it up.

She nods and stands up to let him scoot between the sheets. Jake moves quickly into place. Kat climbs in next to him and pulls him snugly into her body, his head cradled into her chest. Her long fingers run lovingly through his hair, smoothing it away from his forehead. His body begins to calm and his breathing evens out, but he's still wide awake. Once I'm satisfied they're okay on their own I turn on my heel and leave the room pulling the door almost closed as I exit.

I slide into my own sheets shaking off the vision of the young man in a ball on the floor fighting demons that will never get him again. I hate that for him, fucking hate it. I should have gone gently at him. Kat's right to be mad at me for being gruff. Tender is something I don't do with ease. I'm tender with Shanny and that's it. She brings out a softness in me that I had as I child and no

42

longer possess. I'll have to learn it again to spend an indefinite amount of time with two people who deserve soft. I can do that for them.

Coffee. I crack my eyes open to the heavenly smell of coffee. I turn to the clock to see it's just before 9:00 am. Fuck, I slept late. Not really because I didn't fall asleep until after 6:00 am following Jake's nightmare. So I've had a one hour nap followed by a three hour nap. I should be good to go.

I lumber out of bed and pull my pajamas on quickly before grabbing my navy robe. Kat pointed out last night that it's cashmere which from the look on her face means it's over the top for a robe. I think getting used to the affluent money-growing-on-trees lifestyle may be the hardest thing for the three of us. Eventually we'll get the hang of it, just not yet.

I have quite the nest egg from my time in organized crime so if I wanted a life like this I could have it. I could probably have more than this now that I think about it. I grew up in something so opposite of this I can't imagine wanting a life that looks like this. I feel better in the streets at this point, but I'm trying to let go of that. This op should help that transition along.

I enter the enormous kitchen to find Kat sitting on the counter sipping from her mug, a newspaper in her lap. She has on a silk and lace robe that matches her nightie and her golden hair piled on top of her head. It's a glorious sight first thing in the morning.

"Good morning," I say pleasantly before beginning a search for a mug.

"Fifth cabinet on the left," she murmurs into the edge of her mug.

"Thanks."

No response and still no eye contact. Not good.

"Jake still sleeping?" I ask while pouring my coffee.

"Yes."

"Did you get much sleep?"

"No."

"Are you still pissed off at me?" I ask stepping in front of her attempting to force more than one word responses.

"Yes."

"Kat." I pause and clear my throat hoping the right words will come to me. "I'm sorry that I was harsh with Jake. I'll apologize to him once it's appropriate."

"'Kay."

"Will this continue much longer? The one word responses?"

"Yes."

"Fuck me."

There are many reasons in life that I've remained single. This is very near the top. I don't understand women...at all. I said I was sorry and I meant it, yet she still isn't happy. What the fuck am I supposed to do beyond an apology?

I move away from Kat and plant myself at the ridiculously long breakfast bar choosing the closest of eight brown leather stools. This house is too much for three people. It has eight damn bedrooms! I tried counting bathrooms but gave up after eleven feeling like I'd already missed some. The three of us could live in this house every day and not see each other. I have the feeling Kat's going to try that out.

Jake strides in the kitchen a few minutes later, looking worse for wear in sweats and a hoodie.

"Morning," he says quietly.

"Good morning, Jake," Kat beams brightly at him causing a low inaudible grunt to rumble in my chest.

"Morning," I respond in the kindest voice I can find with only half a cup of coffee in my system.

"I need to visit the high school today. Look around, get my class schedule, stuff like that."

Jake saddles up next to Kat and kisses her on the cheek before taking the stool next to mine.

"I'll drive you," Kat says jumping off the counter and gliding to the sink.

"I can take him so you can get some sleep," I offer.

Maybe she won't hate me so much if she gets some decent shuteye.

"You must be worn out, Kat. I'll go with Nick," Jake says sheepishly.

"I'm fine. I'll turn in early tonight. No biggie," she says waving him off before pinning me with a glare. It's starting to get funny at this point. You'd think I kicked his puppy the way she's acting.

"I'll take him, Kat," I command as her hackles go up.

"I said I'm fine," she grits out through her teeth.

It's better than one word responses.

"And I said I'll take him. I'm glad everyone is doing a good job of listening," I snark.

"Jake can you give us a minute?" she asks turning around from the sink to face us.

"Sure," he replies with giant eyeballs pointing at me. I know, man.

Jake bolts up the stairs and Kat waits until she's sure he's gone before she lays into me.

"You don't run me. You may be my pretend husband when we're in public, but when it's just us you don't run shit," she seethes stopping on the other side of the bar in front of me.

Her hazel eyes are narrowed and her chest is heaving with quick breaths, but otherwise she's completely in control. Let's see what I can do about that.

"That's where you're wrong, Sunshine. I run this shit. I run anything and everything that I do so that now includes you. You wanna be pissed about that? Fine by me, but you'll do what I say for two reasons. One, this is my op. If you wanna question Shane or Hal be my guest, but they'll tell you the same thing. Second, I'm a man through and through. I don't take shit from anyone. I can be respectful and kind when necessary, but at the end of the day, what I say goes. You're my wife for all

45

intents and purposes so you need to get used to this. From now on we're the Johnsons twenty-four seven. We have no clue what we're up against here so the op is on at all times. Get that or get your ass on a flight back to Virginia and ride a desk until Shane can find you something else," I finish blankly and stand up to find myself some breakfast.

"Are you a caveman?" she asks astonished, watching me walk past her with the same big eyes she's had since I started my diatribe.

"I've been called worse."

Cereal it is. I make myself a bowl while Kat processes my words.

"I'm aware this is your op because Shane told me before we left. I was *not* informed you were some sort of crazy alpha male that I was required to submit to. I'd love nothing more than to tell you to go fuck yourself and climb on a plane, but I know Jake won't come with me and I'm sure as shit not leaving him with you. So I'll stay and be your little woman. I've lived with monsters before. I can do it again."

I move quickly, pinning her to the counter from behind with my arms braced on the counter smashing her hands beneath mine. I keep my body flush with hers before dipping my head to her ear.

"I'm a monster you've never fuckin' experienced. You'd be wise to steer clear of pissin' me off just for the fun of it. I'll take your mouth when it's warranted, but only to a point. I've been nothing but kind to you since the moment you met me and I'll continue to be kind to you. I fucked up with Jake last night and again, I'm sorry for that. It was a moment in a new house with virtual strangers, cut a motherfucker some slack. I'll fix it with Jake today when I take him to school."

I let her go and take a small step back. Slowly she turns around with a murderous glare on her face.

"Thank you for your kindness," she sneers. "And for your warning, I'll heed that information. If there aren't any other orders I'll go back to sleep now after sitting up all night with our *nephew* who was so fucked up over his nightmare that he clutched me tightly enough that I now have bruises on my back. Learn some softness, *Nicky*. It'll take you miles beyond your cave."

She pushes to move past me, but I grab her arm. Kat quickly executes a release move twisting away swiftly then punching me in the chest. I accept the blow noting she's got some power before I encapsulate her in my arms spinning her away from me.

"I don't wanna fight," I whisper in her ear.

Her back is flush against my chest, her shoulders heaving with the urge to continue assaulting me.

"Show me your bruises," I demand in a gentle tone.

I release my grip on her preparing for an attack but none comes. Kat dramatically unties her robe letting it fall to the floor before slipping off her spaghetti straps. The nightie tumbles to her waist before she stops it with her palm. On her back are small circular bruises from fingers digging into her skin. There are eight, four on each rib cage. I gently rub my thumbs down her back across the bruises. Goosebumps rise on her tan skin beneath my touch. That's interesting.

"Do they hurt?"

"No," she whispers the anger gone from her voice.

I wrap my arms around her waist pulling her snugly into my chest. She has one arm covering her tits and the other maintaining her nightie in its place.

"I'm sorry," I whisper into her ear before pulling her straps back up her body and turning my head so as not to see anything when she slides her arms through the wholes. Bending at the waist, I tag her robe off the ground, holding it open for her. Once it's around her body, I reach around, gently tying her sash.

"Thank you," she whispers.

"Can we be done fighting?"

"Yes."

"Are we back to one word responses?"

47

"No, Nicky, we're not. I'm tired and I don't wanna fight with you. I understand how you want things now so I'll be accommodating. I don't need you to be soft with me, but I need you to be soft with Jake. If you'll do that for me, you and I can coexist peacefully," she says softly with her back still to me.

I spin her around and tip her chin up with my finger. Her face is stunning, but her eyes are tired.

"I'll be soft with you and Jake both. I spent a decade bein' a monster and that's not an easy skin to shed. We have to be able to do this thing between us all the way. If you're gonna hate me most of the time it won't play. Do you want me to call Shane? I can pull you outta this today, but it needs to be now."

"I'm good. I'll get some sleep and feel better. I appreciate your apology and I accept it. It's been a rough few days for me and I'm a bit off. I won't be this difficult most of the time. Let's put it behind us and move forward."

She leans up on her tiptoes and pulls my face down to her with her hand behind my head before pressing a soft kiss to my cheek.

"Have a good day, Nicky," she murmurs into my skin.

"Get some sleep, Sunshine."

She nods pulling away and offers me a sweet smile before leaving the kitchen and my head in a clusterfuck.

Chapter 7

Kat

Fucking prick! Nick Cooper is a fucking prick and I'm tempted to put my gun down his throat. *I run shit.* Well fuck you buddy!

I hurl myself into our mammoth bed and punch my pillow twenty times before I collapse. Yes, I was hard on Nick for how he treated Jake last night. The tone he used with him was so devoid of any sincerity it riled me up. If Nick had just let me cool down, take Jake to school and get a nap, we never would have had an argument just now.

I'm glad we did though. The jerk almost had me fooled. I thought he was sweet and quiet. Turns out, he's some raving controlling lunatic. He can't be worse than Marco and I don't have to have sex with him so that's a bonus. I'm a chameleon. I can do this. I can be the good little wife that lets her man run shit. This is just another op.

I get up on my knees and attack the pillows a bit more before I hear a throat clear.

"You're a good actress, Sunshine," Nick purrs from behind me.

Shit. I punch the pillow.

Double shit! Two punches.

"There's a reason I have this job," I huff diving face first into the mattress.

"Wanna punch me?" His voice is now at the edge of the bed.

"Yes," I shout into the duvet.

He chuckles his warm belly laugh.

"All right. Come on."

49

I turn my head as he's peeling out of his robe and then his shirt. Good God this man's body looks better in daylight. I caught a glimpse last night during the craziness with Jake, but this is a treat. His chest is perfectly sculpted completely bare of any chest hair with smooth olive skin. His arms are thick and chiseled all the way down to his wrists. I can't see it, but his back is surely defined at the same level as the rock hard unflexed eight-pack I'm currently ogling. Hello man V of the gods.

"Like something you see?" he teases.

He's trying to lighten the mood back to joking between us.

"Just the target I'm painting on your chest."

"Are you shooting me or punching me?"

"Today?"

He nods.

"Punching. I think Shane'll fire me if I shoot you day one."

He chuckles again. I stand up off the bed and remove my robe before squaring my shoulders and unleashing a torrent of body blows. I wish I had my garish ring on right now. That thing would cause some damage. Nick stands and takes it until I land a hit under his ribs causing him to stumble back.

"Feel better?"

"Mildly," I say with a shrug.

Actually I feel a shit ton better. Good idea Nick.

"Let's do this next time instead of the acting and then walkin' off to attack innocent pillows," he suggests seriously.

"Fine. I'll enjoy kickin' your ass," I sneer flopping onto the edge of the bed.

"I need you to be real with me, Kat. You can do fake in front of everyone else but with me you're real. You're pissed we deal. You're sad we deal. You're something else we deal. That's how this works. I know I seem like a fuckin' prick right now, but I promise I run a good op. I

50

have to be able to trust you completely for this to work and that means you're real with me."

"You win. I submit and all that other shit you demanded downstairs. I don't know if you could tell when you met me, but I usually run my own shit. You runnin' it will take some gettin' used to."

I fling myself to my back dramatically, throwing my arms over my head. I'm too tired for this shit. He could tell me to do a strip tease to the "Macarena" right now and I'd do it if I could go to sleep afterward.

"I can see your nipples," he says in a husky voice I'm not sure I've ever heard from a man.

"You're my husband. Get used to it."

"Noted."

I wait for a moment and finally turn my gaze from the ceiling to him. He's staring at me with lust filled dark and dangerous eyes. Oh my.

"Like something you see?"

"Kat," he warns.

"Gonna do somethin' about it?"

Two can play at this game.

"Careful." His tone menacing.

"Careful of what exactly? You're the one starin' at my tits."

"Kat," he growls.

"Yes," I purr.

"Don't," he seethes, never leaving my eyes with his gaze.

"'Kay."

I flop my head back down on the mattress and listen to him thud away into the bathroom. Ha! Now he's as pissed off as I was. I slide into the sheets and pull the duvet up to my face before quickly finding sleep.

"Kat," a male voice whispers in my ear.

"Huh?" I grunt.

"Kat, wake up. You've slept the day away. I'm a growing boy that needs to be fed," Jake teases.

I open one eye just a slit to see Jake lying in bed with me peering sweetly into my face with his big brown eyes.

"Hey," I groan stretching my arms above my head. "How'd it go at Maybelle High?"

"Fine. Found my locker and my classrooms. I'm not sure signing up to go back to high school was my brightest choice though. I forgot how awful that shit is," he huffs rolling to his back.

"It's good to get your feet wet on an op at your age. You've got three more years of training before you're an agent. This'll be good...in a shitty way."

"I'm sorry about last night, Kat. I haven't had a nightmare that bad in a long time," he whispers.

"There's nothing to apologize for. Life has a jacked up way of dealin' with shit. Nightmares are part and parcel of life and this job. I struggled my first few years with 'em. I always felt better when I had someone with me afterward...even a mark."

"You still have 'em? The nightmares?"

"Not really. I don't know how to explain it. One day they were just gone. Maybe I'd done so much fucked up shit by that point my brain couldn't pick what to torture me with so it gave up." I shrug.

Jake moves his gaze from the ceiling back to my face.

"It's the bedroom."

"The bedroom?"

"Never had one of my own. Whenever I've slept in one..." he trails off not needing to finish.

I saw the fear and I'm pretty good at math. Someone in his life did some fucked up shit to him.

"Can I help you with that?" I ask softly running my fingers through his shaggy light hair.

"I need to do it on my own. But thanks, Kat. I just really...thanks," he breathes out closing his eyes.

"You're welcome. You need anything I'm always here."

I stroke his hair a few more times before patting his cheek and sitting up. I look over at the clock that reads 3:32 pm. Shit I slept all damn day!

Sliding off the bed, I right my extremely annoying nightie.

"You and Nick gonna be all right?" he asks standing up from the bed.

He looks so cute in a white polo and plaid shorts.

"You and Nick all right?" I return.

"We're fine. I get that you were pissed at how he talked to me, but that shit doesn't faze me. I wasn't mad at Nick. I wasn't offended by Nick. He's a good guy. He apologized and offered to help me out just like you. You can call off your dogs if you're only pissed because he was a kinda rough during a weird situation."

When he puts it like that, I feel like a complete drama queen. I have too much pride to admit that though.

"He also informed me that he *runs* shit and that I'm expected to just take what he dishes out. That's my bigger irritation at this point," I huff.

"Can you imagine Nick not runnin' shit? Have you met him? Do you know anything about his last op?"

"I don't know much. I know it was ten years long, which is well outside company norms. I know he informed me he's a monster like I've never encountered. I've been with the company long enough to know how guys like Nick work, all bossy and demanding. Just never had it laid out for me like he did this morning."

"He was an enforcer in a crime family. I know that much. There's not a lot of detail in his files beyond that, but from what I gathered, he's lived a long time runnin' shit in a way you and I haven't. That doesn't just go away because he has to play family man now."

Well, that gives me a bit of insight into the man pretending to be my husband. A decade of murder, torture and God knows what else would be hard to break out of.

"Did Shane tell you Nick was runnin' this op?"

"Yeah," he says like I should know that too.

I lied when I told Nick I knew. Well, that entire interaction was me lying and faking just to get away from him before I did something that would surely get me fired.

"Damn it. Shane did *not* tell me. He's got an ass whipping coming his way once we're back in Virginia."

"I suspect he didn't tell you because you wouldn't have taken that news very well. He needed you here. Shitty move, but it makes sense."

"You're too sweet and too logical for me to talk to anymore."

He beams a bright shiny smile at me and I beam one right back.

"Nick did say we're now workin' the op twenty-four seven. I think that's a good idea. I feel like there are eyes on us wherever we turn. When we walked around the high school there were definitely interested eyes on us."

"It's easier to work an op that way. It gets exhausting going back and forth, at least for me. I can't be super *Stepford* all the time though. My brain'll rot. But I can do the housewife roll with ease. So with that in mind I need to get dressed and begin preparing dinner."

"You a good cook?" he asks excitedly.

"I do all right," I lie. I'm a damn good cook when given the opportunity.

"Liar," he snorts. This kid reads people too well. I'll have to keep that in mind.

I scrunch my nose at him gaining me a tickle of laughter that warms my soul. I like Jake...a lot.

"I'll be down in a bit," I say turning toward the bathroom.

After a miraculous shower that took me a good ten minutes to figure out how to operate, I feel like a new woman. I would love to sink into a pair of jeans and a hoodie, but I have nothing close to that in my closet. I did find a pair of blush colored Marc Jacobs twill pants and a coordinated striped crew neck capped sleeved shirt. There's a manual in the dressing room that helps me out (instructs with precise detail) with my wardrobe. I'm not an idiot when it comes to fashion, but I'm not from the multimillion-dollar-mansion thousand-dollar-pants world either. I'm happy for the assistance.

I leave the make-up light and nude with a pink lip and my hair in an off kilter chignon at the base of my head. No fluffy bunny slippers so I settle on low heeled strappy sandals. Small drop pearl earrings and a pearl bracelet with diamond accents are in place with my Franck Muller diamond faced watch. I'm a vision of *Stepford*.

I step into our bedroom and quickly make our bed before heading to the kitchen to feed my family.

When I enter the massive space I find it empty, save for a murmur coming from the family room. I take a few steps in that direction to find Jake and Nick stretched out on the couches watching ESPN.

"Good afternoon boys," I call out to them.

Jake, like a good teenager, simply waves his hand over his head without looking at me. Nick swiftly scissors up off the couch to come and greet his wife properly. He makes his way through the room slowly, allowing me to drink in his appearance. Perfectly tailored dark wash jeans hug his thighs just enough to let you know the legs beneath are defined and powerful, paired with a snug charcoal polo. His wrist is adorned with an all black Franck Muller skeleton watch. His wedding band is wide and shiny, glinting in the sun streaming through our wall of glass in the breakfast area.

"Sunshine, you look good after some rest," he murmurs into my cheek before placing a kiss there.

"I feel better. Thanks," I say softly.

Nick slides one powerful arm around my waist before pulling me firmly into his body.

"We good?" he questions, a thoughtful look on his face.

"We're good, Nicky," I coo leaning up on my tiptoes to kiss his cheek.

He bends forward slightly so that I can reach my intended destination. When I drop back down, he squeezes me once before letting me go.

"Any requests for dinner?" I ask moving toward the kitchen.

"Somethin' more than the sandwiches we threw together for lunch."

I pull on an apron and set about making lemon and rosemary pork with a chickpea salad. All of the ingredients stocked in our kitchen and pantry are organic and fresh. This I could get used to. As I prep vegetables and begin cooking Jake and Nick sporadically join me to check on the progress, both of them sweet and tender with me at all times.

"Jake will you set the table please?" I ask on his most recent visit to my side.

"Sure."

"Wine?" Nick asks standing near the door to the basement, which houses a good sized wine cellar.

"White please," I respond with a smile.

Nick offers me a tip of the chin before descending the stairs. I prepare our plates and move them to the table as Nick rejoins the area, wine in hand. I doubt Nick drinks wine so I move back into the kitchen and pour him a glass of Stella.

He smiles broadly at my return to the table. I set his beer down and take my seat, relishing how good it feels to enjoy a normal sit down family meal. The sounds that the guys make as they dig in causes a tingle inside my chest and I feel even better about our normal end to an uncomfortable day.

Chapter 8

Kat

"Play nice with the other kids, dear," I call to Jake as he climbs from my SUV on his first day at school.

He snorts through a broad grin before swinging his legs out and fading into a mass of teenagers. He's a braver man than I.

I take a leisurely drive back to our house enjoying the gorgeous scenery of our new town. The rolling hills mixed with the Metacomet Ridge provide a picturesque dawdle for this newly appointed housewife. The green canopy that surrounds Maybelle will surely be breathtaking once autumn is upon us. Ambers and hues of gold mixed with the changing season will be a nice experience to have with my new family.

I swing my BMW into the driveway curving around to our three car garage before parking. I float into the kitchen in my black high wasted trousers and sky high wedges. A crisp tailored white button down to finish off the look with my pearls and designer watch...too much shit first thing in the morning.

I have no clue what to do with myself now. This is going to be a slow op. Slower than any op I've been on. I've been on some slow ones where I had to work hard to get close to my mark, but I was always working. In this scenario, we have to be seen and then be brought in by our marks. Seeking them out will blow us faster than just tattooing that shit on our foreheads and running naked through downtown.

What the hell does a housewife do all day? If we had small children I'd be busy, but we have a self-sufficient teenager. I'm not associated with any committees or boards and if I want to be that'll take time to work into.

We have a gardener and a pool guy and no need for a housekeeper. What am I supposed to do all day?

"How'd drop off go?" Nick asks striding in the room looking like a Hugo Boss ad, navy suit, white shirt unbuttoned at the neck, and shiny red-hued brown leather shoes. Sexy as hell.

"He's a brave man wading into that. You couldn't pay me in orgasms to convince me to go back to high school," I joke.

Nick barks out a laugh before offering me a coy smile.

"I'm glad to know what your motivations in life are."

"*Pfft*, I'll give you a list if you want."

We move together to the breakfast table with fresh mugs of coffee, Nick sitting at the head of the table me at his left. These have become our spots it would seem over the last week.

"Where are you off to today looking all dapper?" I ask over the rim of my mug.

"Work," he says like I should know this.

"Oh, I didn't know you had anything lined up already."

"I set up some meetings at the end of last week. Just getting my face seen in town more than anything."

"I have no idea what to do with myself. What do women like me do all day?" I ask with a little hurt in my voice at the idea I'll actually be alone all day.

"Shop? Go out with other women? Fuck, I don't know," he says with a grimace feeling my pain.

"What should I shop for? This house is stocked to the gills with everything we could ever need. I'll feel like a hoarder if I start buying more stuff."

"Sunshine, I don't think it's lost on you that I have no clue what you should shop for. I'll hand you my credit card with a smile whenever you figure it out," he says sweetly.

"I don't have my own credit cards?" I ask in shock.

"It was a joke." He breaks into a low chuckle.

"Well I wasn't sure how far your controlling caveman routine went in life."

"I'm not controlling or abusive so please don't paint me with that brush," he grunts getting irritated with me.

"You *are* controlling, but no, you're not abusive. I'm sorry if I've offended you."

"What kinda man do you want in life, Kat?"

"I'm married now so a pool boy would suit my needs just fine," I say through a wry smile.

That gifts me a pointed glare.

"I don't date so I can't really answer that. The last boyfriend I had was in high school. The agency recruited me the day I graduated and sent me to training a few days later. You know this job doesn't allow for personal relationships. Any I've had were with marks, so they don't count. What about you? You spent a decade on an op. Have any relationships during that time?"

"Not anything serious. The op didn't allow for anything beyond casual. You're dodging my question," he says with a raised brow.

"I want the dream like every other woman, Nick. I'm a lot to handle so I need someone that can do that without difficulty. I want someone that takes care of me not because I need it but because he wants to. I want time and attention without feeling guilty about wanting it. I want the man that women want and men want to be. A good friend, a soft place to land at the end of the day, a kind soul, a partner and a man that would like to be a father because in this hypothetical world I'm creating at the moment I get to have kids." I offer a slight shrug when I finish.

"Would he be a pussy?"

"What?" I ask horrified and annoyed at being abruptly pulled from the perfect vision I had just produced in my head.

"Your man...would he be a pussy?"

"No," I scoff at the idea. I could never be with a pussy.

"Would he be at your back in a crisis or standing in front of you, shielding you as best he could?"

"My front."

"Would be weak and let people walk all over him?"

"No."

"Would he speak his mind and be honest at every turn?"

"Yes."

"Would he make decisions, difficult or not, with his family's best interest in mind?"

"Yes."

"Would he allow his family to act in any way that would endanger them?"

"No."

"Would he love and cherish them even in the moments where tough decisions were made and crises were dealt with?"

"Yes."

"Would you call this man controlling?"

"No."

"I'm not controlling, Sunshine. I'm a man doin' all the things I just said and more. Get that."

"Nick—"

He cuts me off with a finger.

"Controlling men tell their women what to wear, what to eat, where to be, how to live, how to breathe, and how to serve their men. I'm not that. I will never be that. I *detest* men like that. I am a man though, Kat. I'm the head of this family and comfortable with what that role requires. You've spent your adult life without the ability to count on someone offering you that support. I'm here to do that so allow yourself that comfort if just for a while. You deserve that man you created. You deserve to be a mother if that's what you want. Don't buy into the company line that you only get to choose one spot. You're a field agent now, but that can change to grow with your life. You're permitted a life beyond the DCA," he finishes softly.

"You're a complete and total mindfuck," I huff flopping back in my chair.

"Sorry?"

"Every time I think I've got you pegged you flip the script. I have no clue what to make of you. You can be a monumental ass that's infuriating and exhausting to live with. You can also be the kindest gentlest person to share a space with. What the fuck is up with that?"

He offers me a sly smile and a wink, no response though.

"What do you want in a woman?" I turn the tables on him.

"I want a woman that can take care of herself with ease and allows me to take care of the rest. A woman that needs for nothing and wants for the things that only I can give her. A woman that's happy in sweats and no make-up because that's how she looks the best in my eyes. I want soft and gentle to even out my rough and harsh. I want as many kids as she'll allow herself to give me. Proud, confident, high self-esteem, a friend, an equal and above all...mine."

"I hope you find her someday. She's sounds like a good woman," I say softly.

"I already found her but it wasn't meant to be," he responds staring into his empty mug.

"I'm sorry to hear that." I reach my hand out and wrap my fingers around his trying to convey I'm truly sorry because his face looks wounded at the mention.

"I never had a shot because someone like me doesn't deserve someone like her. I'm tryin' to shed the skin of the monster I was, but that shit'll always follow me. She deserves a world untouched by that because she's had her own brand of awful enough in life. She also found a man that's capable of loving her in a way I'm not certain I possess. She's better off without me and that fuckin' sucks. She's still my best friend in this world and I would do anything for her...she'd do the same for me,"

61

he whispers looking up into my face with sad eyes that I know aren't his natural color.

I noticed the other night that he wears colored contacts, but I haven't mentioned it and I don't plan to. If there's a reason he has to hide his eyes, he can tell me when and if he's ready. But the deep dark brown color looks horribly gloomy right now and all I want to do is make that go away for him.

"Even DCA agents are deserving of what they want in life. This smart guy I know just told me all about it," I tease a little, hoping to lighten the mood.

The sadness vanishes from his face to be replaced by a small smirk.

"I've gotta head out. I'll be home this afternoon. Have a good day tryin' to figure out what to do with yourself."

He stands from his chair and presses his lips to my hair before rinsing his mug and leaving the house. Home alone with money to spend and nothing to buy. This op will surely turn me into a hoarder.

I didn't buy anything, but I did spend the day meeting shopkeepers and a few people that were kind enough to introduce themselves to me. It was a good day even if a bit lonely. I spent a week with Nick and Jake with me at all stages of my day. That was definitely a nice departure from my norm on an op and better than spending the day walking around Maybelle.

I look out the passenger side window to see Jake approaching with three boys that look like carbon copies of him save for variations in hair color following at his heels. I roll the window down to see what I'm in for.

"Hey, Aunt Kay," Jake calls with a broad smile and a huge wave. He's so damn cute.

"Did you have a good day?" I yell out the window forgetting that's probably not what the other moms are doing. Oh well.

Jake arrives at the window and leans his folded arms on the edge.

"Is it okay if some guys come back to the house to shoot hoops for a while? They said they'd get rides home later." He looks nervous, like he'll get in trouble for asking a normal question. I swear I'm going to find out what happened to him someday and then I'm going to tell Nick and let him go all caveman alpha male and avenge Jake right along with me.

"Of course, honey," I coo.

"All good," he calls over his shoulder pulling the door open.

The back door opens and the first boy gets in wearing the apparent teenage boy uniform of polo shirt, khaki shorts and flip flops, topped with shaggy hair.

"Thanks, Missus Johnson. I'm Cole," he says climbing all the way through before sitting behind me. Cole has blond hair and soft blue eyes. I'm going to have to use these small traits to keep the boys straight.

"No problem. It's nice to meet you, Cole."

"Hey, I'm Sawyer," the next kid says. Sawyer has black as night hair and big brown eyes.

"It's nice to meet you, Sawyer."

The last boy with dirty blond hair and honey eyes climbs in and shuts the door.

"Thanks for the lift, Missus Johnson. I'm Dane."

"It's nice to meet you, Dane. You boys can call me Kat."

Every time they say Mrs. Johnson, I feel old and out of the loop, even knowing they're just being polite and well mannered. They all nod in agreement before I turn my eyes to Jake and offer him a loving smile before pulling out of my parking space.

"How was the first day?"

"Sucked balls," Dane huffs.

"Dude!" Jake warns.

"Oh God, I'm so sorry, Missus...uh...I mean Kat. Sorry," he stutters his cheeks flaming red as I eye him in the rearview mirror.

"It's fine. My day kinda sucked balls too," I say through a smile and a chuckle. Maybe I have more in common with teenagers than I thought.

The three in the back chuckle at me while Jake shakes his head, a smirk on his lips.

"Why was your day bad?"

"Will Burke," Cole huffs.

"Who's Will Burke?"

"It's nothing, Aunt Kay," Jake cuts in quickly.

Oh, now I want to know for sure.

"Jake," I prompt.

"He's a dick," Sawyer says and turns bright red from his language slip.

"Who was he a dick to?" I ask, ignoring Sawyer's embarrassment. I'm not a mother. I'm sure I should scold these boys and their language, but I don't give a shit. Have you heard my mouth?

"Jake," they respond in unison.

I pull up to a stop sign at this announcement and turn my gaze to Jake with a deep scowl on my face. Yeah I may not be a mother, but I'll be damned if anyone mistreats Jake...ever.

"Aunt Kay, it's not a big deal," Jake says softly.

"Jake, you better start talkin' and I mean now," I growl.

I drive through the stop sign and wait in a silent car. Either he talks or I'll find out on my own and he knows that's what I'll do.

"He's a senior and his ex-girlfriend mentioned she thought I was hot or some shit. He didn't like it and got in my face," Jake mumbles.

"Got in your face how?"

Again, silence.

"Jake!" I bark.

He closes his eyes and drops his head. My blood is boiling.

"One of you tell me what happened...now," I command.

"Will slammed him into a locker and then choked him with his forearm in his throat while he said nasty shit like he always does. He let Jake go before any teachers or staff saw anything," Cole explains.

I grab Jake's chin and rip it toward me at the next stop sign looking at his throat where there's a small bruise. I'm going home and getting my gun!

"I'm okay," he whispers squeezing my wrist trying to soothe me. "Just let it go."

"He touches you again and I'm gonna rip his fuckin' balls off and feed 'em to him. You think about lyin' to me about it or not tellin' me, you and I will have problems," I say pointedly holding his chocolate eyes long enough for my words to soak in.

He nods and I let go of his chin, continuing the drive home in tense silence.

When we pull into the garage, the boys pile out quickly, moving into the house, no doubt in search of sustenance.

"I've got chicken nachos in the warming drawer and caramel pecan popcorn. You boys grab some seats at the table," I instruct.

I wasn't expecting a house full of teenagers so I hope this is enough food to satisfy them. They look like they could eat me out of house and home. They all bolt for the table and dig in the moment the plates hit the table. It's like they've never seen food.

"Did you not eat lunch?" I ask appalled at how ravenous they seem.

"Fight happened at lunch," Cole says through a full mouth of...too much food.

So not only did Will Burke bruise Jake he also ruined his lunch. My blood is back to boiling, but I play it off and move into the kitchen.

"I've got a pot roast in the oven. You're all welcome to stay for dinner if your parents don't mind." I know they won't go home hungry that way.

Dane snorts around a mouth of popcorn.

"Our parents don't give a shit."

"Maybe you should call or text to be sure," I suggest not wanting to step on unknown parents' toes day one of school.

"Our parents aren't like you, Kat. We eat alone most nights while our parents go out or aren't even in town. They don't care if we aren't home," Sawyer explains blankly and my stomach drops.

I had a vision of wealthy attentive parents fawning over their children. Why wouldn't you when you make enough money to not have the stressors of the typical middle class family? I'm out of my depth here and yet again getting pissed the fuck off.

"Then you boys will come here after school every day and eat a good dinner and then you can do your homework or hang out or whatever it is you boys like to do," I command a little harsher than intended.

"Your aunt's the shit, Jake," Dane says through a smirk.

"I know," Jake says tenderly, holding my gaze with an adoring look.

They go about eating while I fix a salad and wash some dishes, listening to the conversation between the boys.

"Regan's hot, Jake," Dane spouts when the conversation turns to the ladies.

"She comes with too much baggage," Jake dismisses.

"It's not her fault. Her parents and Will's parents put them together from the time they were babies. She never had a choice. The only reason she got to break up with him was because her parents were out of town when shit went down between them. By the time they got back, Will was already bangin' half the cheerleading team.

Regan's parents were pissed at *her* for not doin' more to get Will back," Sawyer huffs.

"That's fucked up," Jake scoffs shoving a handful of popcorn in his mouth. "Still not sure I wanna weigh into that scene."

"She's a nice girl. Not like most of the chicks at Maybelle. Just talk to her. You'll see," Cole encourages.

These boys are pretty sweet for a bunch of fifteen-year-olds.

"How'd your parents die?" Dane asks Jake in a kind manner.

"In a car accident just over a year ago. The car in front of them lost control of their car on the highway and my parents over corrected tryin' to miss the car. They flipped into on-coming traffic. Died on impact," Jake explains quietly sounding as sad as he should.

"Fuck, man. I'm sorry. Were you close?" Sawyer asks genuinely.

"Yeah," Jake doesn't elaborate.

"Must've been nice," Cole says.

"What's that?" Jake asks confused, a slight beam of irritation coming from his eyes.

"Bein' tight with your parents. Ours could give a shit most days," Cole huffs.

"I'm sure you're good with that. Nice not to have 'em up in your shit all the time."

"I used to think that. We'd take advantage and fuck around all night, skip class, party," Sawyer whispers the last part trying to hide that piece of information from me.

"What changed?" Jake prompts.

"Just got old. Cole and I got in trouble last year for too many absences. With our parents and with the school. My dad told me I had one fuckin' job to do and that was to go to school and follow his legacy to Yale. If I didn't do that he'd cut me off financially. Cole got a similar threat. Fucked up thing is they do nothing to ensure we're gettin' good grades. They just expect that we'll do it. We've been told, so we better follow through," Dane finishes and chugs his Gatorade.

"What if you need help in a class or on a project or somethin'?"

"They'd hire us a tutor and make sure no one knew about it," Sawyer scoffs like the idea is completely preposterous.

"Maybe yours would, but mine are never around enough to even ask for help at this point. I've been told what they expect and that's the end of it," Dane explains in a irritated voice.

"Not around? Where are they?" Jake asks in an irritated voice that mirrors my mood.

"Out of town and shit," Cole dismisses the issue.

Time for the grownup to wade into the conversation.

"Are your parents out of town a lot?" I ask wondering how alone these kids are.

"Cole's and mine are," Dane admits with an annoyed tone in his voice.

"My mom's...uh...busy a lot. My dad works really long hours, but ends up home most nights. I think," Sawyer explains.

I'm guessing his mother is a drunk or has a boyfriend occupying her time based on Sawyer's description. I'm hoping for the latter.

"Do you all stay at your houses alone at night?"

"We have staff that lives in," Cole says with a snort. I second his snort.

"You're all welcome to stay here with us whenever you'd like. We have plenty of space to accommodate you. Now if you'll excuse me I need to run upstairs for a few minutes. I'll be back," I say turning on my heel and swiftly making my way to the stairs.

"You're aunt rocks, man. You think she'll really let us come and eat dinner here every night?" Cole asks disbelieving.

"Yeah. She's good like that," Jake offers nonchalantly.

"Stay here too?" Dane asks in shock at the idea.

68

"If she said it she meant it. No bullshit with Aunt Kay," Jake states with conviction.

"She's fuckin' hot," Sawyer pipes in.

"Dude, that's his aunt," Dane admonishes.

"They aren't related by blood and he's not blind."

"She's hot and she's my aunt so let's not talk about it," Jake growls.

"Aunt Kay's my new favorite," Cole states.

There are agreeing grunts before Jake suggests, "Let's go shoot."

I make my way up the rest of the stairs as I hear them exiting the back door.

Chapter 9

Nick

I arrive home to a mostly quiet house smelling like slow cooked meat. This I could get used to. I spy Jake out back with three guys playing two-on-two. They're having a good time based on the smiles plastered on their faces. I've got to get out of this suit jacket. I climb the stairs and pick up my pace when I hear the sounds of grunts coming from our room.

I fly through the door to find Kat beating the shit out of pillows again, with no shirt on but still wearing heels, pants, her bra and most of her jewelry, her wedding ring on the bedside table.

"I figured out what I'm gonna buy," she states through a ragged breath not looking at me.

"Yeah?"

"A fuckin' heavy bag," she growls before unleashing vicious punches into the pillows. I stand in the doorway watching in amazement as she pummels the poor things.

Once she's worn herself out, she collapses face first into the mattress and screams at the top of her lungs in anger. I shut the door and shrug out of my jacket before approaching her.

"Kat what's goin' on?" I ask from the end of the bed.

She pops up on her knees, shuffles over to me and starts waving her hands around crazily as she speaks.

"Did you know that there are parents that are millionaires that just abandon their children and force them to fend for themselves?" she screeches.

"Yes." I thought this was common knowledge.

"Did you know they have to eat alone and sleep in houses with live-in staff?"

"It doesn't surprise me."

"Well, it shocked the shit outta me. And that was the easy part of my day, Nicky. Some motherfucker slammed Jake into a locker and held him against it by his throat, bruising him," she seethes.

"What?" I growl low and menacing. Now I feel like accosting a pillow or two.

"You heard me. And Jake wasn't gonna tell me. His new friends let it slip and then I had to drag it outta Jake. He doesn't want me to do anything about it either. So instead, I'm up here beating the shit outta pillows which does nothing to release the fury boiling inside of me!"

"Why aren't you wearin' a shirt?"

"Really? That's what you ask right now?" She rolls her eyes but continues. "I couldn't get a good swing workin' and I was gettin' sweaty. I was tryin' to preserve my outfit. Why the fuck aren't you as pissed as me? Big talk this morning, you're lettin' me down a bit."

"I don't attack pillows when I'm pissed. I attack people. Get cleaned up. I'll deal with this...like I told you this morning. I'll take care of you both. Trust me," I say trying desperately not to look at her tits, which are on display through her white lace bra.

"I may have also adopted three teenage boys," she informs me like she's talking about the weather.

"Is that right?"

"They're left on their own all the time according to them. We have a gigantic house and I like to cook. I don't think it should be an issue. I'm trying to find something to do and four teenagers is something to do."

"It's a lot to do. We are runnin' an op here, Sunshine," I point out.

"Well, I'm not a stripper suckin' dick to get to my mark this time. I'm a housewife tryin' to be brought into

72

a tight knit fold. More kids, more ins. It's not like we're hiding tactical gear in the spare rooms."

"I'm not arguing with you. I'm just talkin'," I point out because I can feel her hackles rising. I'm also reminding myself to calm the fuck down because her talking about sucking dick to get to a mark makes me see red.

"I'm talkin' to you too."

"All right, so we've unofficially adopted three teenage boys?"

"Yes."

"You're happy with this?"

"Yes."

"Then I'm fine with it."

Her face goes soft and she throws her arms around my neck, squeezing me tight before smashing her lips roughly into my cheek with a wet smacking kiss. I've just taken a very calculated risk. Involving civilians in ops isn't unusual. Taking on minors could prove disastrous. But the look beaming at me from Kat's hazel eyes breaks any resolve I have to remain a professional right now. I'm just being her husband. An even greater risk.

"I have the best husband," she squeals scurrying off the bed and racing to the bathroom. Totally worth it.

I roll up the sleeves on my shirt, make my way downstairs and out the backdoor in the space of a few seconds.

"Jake!" I shout getting all the boys' attention.

He drops his head to his chest and palms the basketball. The other three look at me with fear on their faces. I ignore them and stalk onto the court to Jake.

I pull his chin up and find the bruise on his throat and take three deep breaths before speaking.

"What happened?" I growl.

"It's not a big deal. I'm fine," Jake huffs ripping his chin from my hand.

He's a grown man and I'm treating him like a child, but for all intents and purposes, he's my child for the foreseeable future so this is what he gets. We stare each other down for a few beats before a kid with black hair chimes in.

"Will Burke happened, Mister Johnson," he says quietly.

"What's your name?"

"Sawyer Lancaster," he again says in a quiet voice. I'm scaring him.

"You two?"

"I'm Cole Bennington, Mister Johnson," the kid with light blond hair says.

"Dane Ashcroft, sir," the darker blond kid finishes.

They all look just like Jake except different hair and eye color. This'll be fun to keep track of.

"I'm Nick. My wife's informed me she adopted you boys this afternoon," I say in a kinder voice.

None of them respond, just turn a little pink with embarrassment.

"They're alone a lot," Jake murmurs.

"You guys respect my home, my rules and above all my wife and you're welcome to be here as often as you like."

"Thanks," Dane says through a giant smile. "Aunt Kay's the shit by the way."

"That she is," I agree. "Now that we're all acquainted I wanna know what the hell happened today."

"Will's ex told her posse that Jake was hot and he got all up in Jake's shit about it," Cole explains.

"How old is he?"

"Eighteen," Sawyer huffs.

"How big is he?"

"He's the same height as Jake," Cole explains. "But he's more filled out."

Jake's about six feet tall, but still kind of skinny. The other three are just starting to sprout up, all a few inches shorter than Jake.

"He puts his hands on you again you beat his fuckin' ass," I order.

"I'll get kicked outta school. They've got a strict no fighting policy," Jake quickly informs me.

"You let me worry about that. He puts his hands on you again you fuck him up."

"Yes, sir." He says it in a way that can be interpreted by the boys as respectful, but I recognize it as him obeying an order. They're both true in some way.

"Can you fuck him up?" Dane asks shocked at my instruction.

"Yes," Jake responds never leaving my gaze.

"I can't wait for this shit," Cole hoots with excitement.

"He touches you first, Jake," I remind him.

"I understand."

"Go in and get cleaned up for dinner. You four gonna be playin' ball most days while the weather's good make sure you bring a change of clothes. I don't wanna eat in a locker room."

"You guys can borrow from me tonight," Jake says to his friends as they all head for the house.

I follow the stinky boys inside to find them all staring into the kitchen in shock and awe. Kat is standing with her back to us at the stove doing something with food I suppose. Her hair is piled on top of her head in some kind of twisted thing that surely has a name that I don't know. She's got on a short sleeved navy sweater that's falling off her shoulder halfway down her arm. The sweater stops abruptly at her waist where black skin tight spandex pants begin and leave nothing to the imagination all the way down to her ankles where her black high fuck me heels finish the show. She'll be the death of me.

"Get movin' guys," I grunt.

"Twenty minutes boys," Kat calls over her shoulder.

They all stumble away while Jake offers me a knowing smile. Teenagers.

"Wine?" I ask moving toward the basement door.

"I already got it."

Fuck that means I have twenty minutes with nothing to do other than stare at her like a teenager. I head to the fridge and grab a beer before settling myself at the breakfast bar.

"Told Jake to fuck that kid up he puts his hands on him again," I inform her.

"Good. I'm second in line once Jake wipes the floor with him," she says seriously.

"Guess that means I get the leftovers."

"Won't be anything left when I'm done."

"Noted."

We each go silent for a while as I listen to the boys banging around, showering and changing clothes. Kat finishes whatever she's been working on at the stove and pulls out the roast. It smells like heaven in this house and the view is pretty fucking nice too.

"You look nice, Sunshine," I finally break the silence.

"Nicky, these leggings still had the tags on 'em. They cost two hundred and seventy-five dollars! I've been instructed by the *manual* to only wear them in the house or for brief errands. Is that insanity or is it just me?" Kat looks at me completely blown away by this.

"It's a waste," I grumble.

"Yeah when I can buy some leggings at Target for thirty bucks."

"It's a waste you can't wear 'em to show off your legs and perfect ass," I state pointedly.

"I've mostly been outfitted in dresses and skirts. I think my ass and legs will get plenty of public display for the neighbors and whatnot. Am I tryin' to draw attention with my ass and legs?" she asks incredulously.

"Don't think you've got much control on that front, Sunshine," I say through a snort.

"Whatever," she says rolling her eyes. I don't think she gets that I'm complimenting her right now. "This isn't about me bein' some dim witted sex pot for the locals to ogle. It's a fairly conservative space that I'm tryin' to fit into."

"We're not very good at communicating. I'm complimenting you. You look great and it's a shame the DCA has us in this conservative space because I could look at your ass and legs in those things all day long and never get sick of the view. But even in your conservative dresses, skirts and pants the view's just as good."

"Mindfuck," she murmurs turning away from me.

"What's a mindfuck?" Sawyer asks striding in the room with his black hair still wet, wearing a hoodie and gym shorts. He walks right up next to Kat and leans against her bare shoulder watching her work.

"Men," Kat huffs.

The kid puts his arm around her waist in comfort like he's had to do that a lot in his life. She leans her head against his and pauses what she's doing.

"Group hug," Cole bellows and runs into the room followed closely by Dane and Jake. The three take the remaining open parts of her body and squeeze the hell out of her until she giggles.

"All right you four, get off my wife and set the table," I demand in a light tone that still lets them know I mean business.

They quickly obey and go about it while joking around. Ah, to be young again. Kat bends over at the waist and retrieves a pan of homemade rolls causing Cole and Dane to gawk thereby running into each other, both of them falling to the floor in a thud. Jake and Sawyer bust a gut laughing while I shake my head.

"What in the world? Are you two okay?" Kat asks, panicked at their state when she turns around. They're both dying laughing along with their friends at this point.

"They're fine, Kat," I assure her moving into the kitchen, stalking toward her.

I wrap my arms around her waist before cupping her ass in both hands. Fuck, it's better than I imagined it

77

would be, soft and firm at the same time. The perfect size for my large hands.

"Your expensive pants caused a fender bender," I purr into her neck before placing a soft kiss on her bare shoulder. "House full of teenage boys, probably a good thing you've got a closet full of conservative clothes."

I pull back to look at her face which is now flushed with embarrassment, at what I'm not sure. I pat her ass twice before moving away. The teenagers are all staring at us with weird looks on their faces.

"What?" I ask the room.

"How long have you guys been together?" Cole asks with his brow furrowed.

"Since college," Kat answers in a lie from behind me, moving to my side.

I swing my arm around her shoulders and gently brush her smooth bare skin with my thumb.

"How old are you?" Sawyer pipes in.

"I'm twenty-eight. Rude question by the way," Kat admonishes playfully.

"So you've been together like ten years?" Dane does some quick math.

"Yup," Kat pops her *p* offering me a stellar smile.

"I don't believe it," Cole says shaking his head. Kat goes rigid at my side and Jake's eyeballs bug out of his head. I prepare myself for damage control.

"Why's that?" I ask nonchalantly squeezing Kat's shoulder in reassurance.

"I've never seen my parents like that. And I've been around longer than ten years. There's no grab ass in my house. The only ass my dad grabs is his latest mistress's and even that's short lived. Right guys?" Cole asks for some backup from his friends.

They both nod in agreement waiting for us to tell the truth.

"Any of your moms look like my wife?"

"No," they respond in unison.

"Any of the mistresses?"

"No."

So fucking wrong they know an answer to that question.

"Any of 'em as sweet?"

"No."

"Any of 'em cookin' you dinner and handin' out group hugs to horny teenage boys?"

"No," they grumble and blush a bit.

"If you're lucky enough to have a woman like this you'll be all over her every day until the day you die, gentleman. You admire a treasure when you find it, at any moment you're able. Get me?"

"Yes," the three chime together.

Jake offers me a proud smile as Kat turns her body across the front of mine. She leans up on her toes, barely because of the fuck me heels, and presses her fat lips to mine. It's a soft sweet closed mouth kiss meant as a thank you. I'd like to take it as an invitation, but I give her soft and sweet before pulling away from her face stroking her jaw with my thumb.

"Mindfuck," she whispers before untangling from my arms and moving back to the dinner.

"Can I move in tomorrow?" Dane asks as I stride toward the table where the guys are all settling in.

"Sure," I say jokingly thinking he's giving me shit about Kat.

"Seriously? Because my parents are in Europe until January."

"What?!" Kat yells from the kitchen making the table jump, except for Jake. "Sorry, I'm not yelling at you, sweetheart."

"We always go to Europe over the summer, but this year they didn't come back with me before school started. My mother wanted to visit some health spa so she can try to look like you and my dad's screwin' a girl that wishes she looked like you," Dane explains in an annoyed tone.

"We'll pick your stuff up tomorrow after school. Would you like me to speak to your parents or whoever's takin' care of you?" Kat asks carrying the roast to the table.

Even if I wanted to argue that it's not a good idea to move this kid in, I know I'd lose. Kat's on a mission with these boys. I can see the determination in her face. It would definitely be a losing battle for me.

She hands me the carving utensils without looking at me, her eyes trained on Dane's light brown ones.

"It's just house staff at my place. I'll tell 'em. They won't care. Whenever my parents call I'll let 'em know."

"When's the last time you spoke to your parents, Dane?" I ask becoming concerned at how alone these kids seem to be.

"At the airport last month," he says blankly.

"Jesus fucking Christ! I swear to God, Nicky," she pleads with me to fix this for her. I set down the knife and fork to wrap her in my arms, pulling her back to my front.

"Where are your parents?" she asks Cole who must also have shit for brains adults in his life.

"Italy," he answers sheepishly.

"How long?" she growls.

"Our parents left together. I think they'll be back after New Year," he says with a shrug looking to Dane for some help.

"Sawyer?" she asks fighting back the emotion caught in her throat. I place a kiss on her naked shoulder and grip her tighter.

"My situation's a little more complicated," he murmurs staring at his hands.

Kat pulls out of my arms and slides into the seat next to Sawyer. She tips his head up with her finger under his chin. I set about carving our dinner because I'm starving while my wife tries to save the planet one neglected child at a time.

"What do you need?" Kat whispers holding his chin firmly in place.

"A mom like you," he says honestly.

Fucking hell, these kids are killing me.

"You've got it. You understand me? You need me for anything I'm there," she states emphatically.

"I looked into getting emancipated this summer. But it got to be pretty complicated so I quit."

Kat looks up at me signaling it's time for her man to step in.

"Sawyer, how about you and I talk after dinner and see if I can help you figure some stuff out?" I ask as pleasantly as I can, wishing we had that heavy bag right now.

Parents that forget their children should be shot in the street and left for dead. I'd be happy to have that job if it becomes available.

"Thanks, Nick," Sawyer breathes out, relieved for the assistance.

I finish carving the roast and serving it to the boys while Kat fills their plates with vegetables, potatoes and fresh rolls. When she finally sits down, we tuck it away with deep satisfaction. Kat is talented in the kitchen, but her heart is her true aptitude in life. She's blowing my mind all over the place right now. And she calls me the mindfuck?

Chapter 10

Nick

"Guys you gotta get movin'," I order gruffly up the stairs where the teenagers live. Six weeks now, I've had a full house of teenage boys and it's been pretty good for the most part.

Kat immediately schooled them in keeping their rooms clean and picking up around the house, but other than that, they've been good kids. Cole and Dane moved in without incident. Both their mothers talked to Kat at her behest and acted like it was the most normal thing in the world. They told her since she was here and they were *so* busy abroad it was a convenient solution. We're complete strangers to them and they agreed to let us be responsible for their children after a twenty minute conversation! Fucking worthless people. Kat went at the heavy bag for thirty minutes after that talk.

Sawyer has been another ball of wax. His mother, if you can call her that, is doped up on any and every prescription she can get her hands on. She's overdosed twice in the last year. Both times, found by Sawyer. His father lives in a dream world where he works tirelessly and then fucks any twenty-two year old he can get his hands on. They're both around enough that Sawyer doesn't feel comfortable moving in, but he's here every night. According to Kat, more than half his shit is in his room here too.

The op is crawling at this point. I've gone to poker at the Bookers every week for the last five and the only fucking thing that's happened is I've made some decent money. I'm welcomed like everyone else, but shit is mostly superficial. So I keep plugging away.

Kat has had three lunches and two brunches (is there a difference?) with Trish and some of the other *Stepford Wives*. All five interactions were much the same as mine at poker night, polite and uneventful. We knew this would be slow going in, but I think we're getting a dose of reality now. A year may not even cut it at this point.

Kat and I are getting along for the most part. We've improved our communication. She only calls me a mindfuck a few times a week now instead of multiple times a day. I've done an award winning job of keeping my hands to myself. We're affectionate in the house when we have an audience—all the time—and in public, but at the end of the day we stay on our sides of the bed and crash. By affectionate I mean brief lip brushes, hand holding, a hand on her thigh or an arm around her shoulders. There's been no more grab ass because I'm a tough motherfucker, but I can only tempt myself so much before I crack.

At some point Kat got a hold of the DCA and was able to have some different sleeping clothes shipped in. Now she's mostly wearing button down cotton tops with shorts. It doesn't make a difference...she's still fucking hot. So my resolve is struggling, but I'm working hard to remain a professional and not to be a monster. Kat, Jake and the boys make it easy. They're good for me.

I hear the elephants descending the stairs at a rapid pace because they're running late for school this morning. They blow past me into the kitchen and start snatching breakfast burritos Kat made them for breakfast off the bar. She's standing in the kitchen with her hands on her hips trying to look pissed. It's successful.

"Boys," she admonishes.

"Sorry, Aunt Kay," Sawyer says sheepishly. "We'll do better."

"I'll set your alarms for five in the morning and break off the snooze buttons if you don't get your shit together, you four," she growls.

They all nod in understanding and move to the garage. She rolls her eyes at me before following them to begin her never ending chauffeur duties. I watch her perfect ass swish away in a blood red skirt that hugs everything just right and offers me the tease of a high slit in the back as she goes. It's always a nice view around here.

Today is a big day for me. I have a meeting with a few of the guys from the poker group that want new security at their law firm downtown. In a town as small as Maybelle, I find it interesting that there are quite a few law firms, but we are in Ivy League hell so I'm not surprised.

I gather my briefcase and head into the garage to meet with potential holes in the human trafficking ring. Game face on.

I pull into our sweeping driveway relaxed and satisfied. I got the job and now have the ability to bug their office. Two weeks from now, I'll have feeds inside every room in that place. Finally, some damn progress. Now I have to hope they have something to do with this shit.

The SUV is gone and it's not time to pick the boys up. That's a rarity. If Kat's going out she always texts or calls. Once I'm in the kitchen, I check my phone to see twenty-five missed calls. FUCK! I had it silenced for the meeting and completely forgot to check it. I run to the office to see if she left me a note while simultaneously dialing her.

Straight to voicemail.

No note on the desk.

I dial again.

Straight to voicemail.

I try Jake.

No answer.

I try Sawyer.

"Dude, where the fuck are you?!" Sawyer chides in a whisper.

"At home. What's goin' on?"

"Shit's fucked up. Get here now!"

He hangs up.

I jump in my car and speed through the calm town, making it to the high school in less than five minutes, more than twice as fast as it would be legally. I bolt from my car and high tail it into the building to be met by Cole, Sawyer and Dane. They're all scowling at me in disgust.

"What?" I growl.

"They've been goin' at Aunt Kay for over half an hour. Where the fuck were you?" Cole seethes.

"Workin'. Where are they?"

I don't know who *they* are, but if they're going after Kat, I want to be there now. They march off and I follow until we reach the school office. As soon as I breach the door, I can hear a man yelling. Oh, fuck no. I blow past the receptionist who's ninety years old and attempting to stop me by calling me sir. Fat chance.

I follow the bellowing to come to a conference room where I can see a man standing inches from Kat's face pointing at Jake, screaming. I take a breath and then throw the door open. This motherfucker doesn't miss a beat.

"He's a fuckin' trouble maker," he yells as I enter the room.

"I don't know who the fuck you are, but if you don't get away from my wife in two seconds I'll rip your fuckin' throat out," I growl in a menacing tone I recognize from my monster years. It's cold, ruthless and terrifying on its own, but matched with the look on my face it's a promise of unbridled pain and anguish.

"And you are?" he asks in a cocky snide voice.

"Get the fuck away from my wife. Now!" I roar.

Jake jumps while Kat remains still. Her back is to me so I have no idea what her face looks like. Jake is also facing away from me and right now, I want their eyes.

The motherfucker takes a step back and I approach Kat with caution. I step between her and Captain Douche to see her face is a mask promising the same things mine was earlier. She's livid. She's looking through me to get to him. I glance away from her to see Jake's face is bruised at the jaw and beginning to swell beneath his eye. I see.

"Do you need a hospital?" I ask in a painfully mustered soft voice.

"No, sir," Jake replies instantly holding my eyes to let me know he's fine.

I turn my gaze back to Kat's fiery hazel slits and grab the side of her neck. Her eyes finally cut to me like she hasn't been aware of my presence until I touched her.

"You good?" I ask again in a tortured softness.

"No," she growls.

"He touch you?"

"Not really."

"Kat," I demand in a low timbre.

"He poked my chest."

That's all it takes. I spin away from Kat and launch at the piss-ant behind me, catching his throat and pinning him to the wall.

"Did you poke my wife you pathetic piece of shit?" I seethe into his face constricting tightly as he flails to get free.

"Yes," he rasps.

"Are you Hoyt Burke?" I fume.

"Y-es," he sputters.

"Did your son get his ass handed to him by my nephew?"

He nods because he can no longer speak.

I release his throat and he drops to the floor.

87

"You're fired as of now. Get your sorry ass outta Maybelle along with your piece of shit son. If you're not gone by nightfall, I'll have the State's Attorney file felony charges against Will for assault of a child, since Jake's only fifteen. Then I'll have him file assault charges against you for touching my wife. I suggest you leave the state if you know what's good for you."

"You just assaulted me you psychopath," he chokes out.

"I was defending my wife and nephew who you had held captive in a room where I found you assaulting my wife. Explain that to a judge and see what they have to say about it."

"I've been the assistant principal at this school for a decade. My family has lived here for five generations. I'll take my chances," he scoffs climbing to his feet, his pussy fingers still clutched around his neck.

"Suit yourself," I say blankly. I turn to Kat who has a small smirk on her lips matching a similar one on Jake's.

"Kat, call the police and tell 'em you and Jake have been assaulted on school property by a school official. Jake, run out to the boys and have 'em round up witnesses to the first assault and this one. I'll sit here and keep Assistant Principal Burke company."

Kat dutifully pulls out her phone as Jake rises from his seat. Three, two, one.

"Wait," the pussy says dejectedly. "We'll go."

I spin around and pin him with a gaze that holds all the promises I've just made and then some.

"I'll be drivin' by your house at nine tonight. If there's any sign that you're still in that house, I'm comin' in and what I just did to you will look like child's play."

He nods briefly.

"Let's go," I instruct my family holding out a hand to Kat.

She places her sweaty palm in mine, shaking from head to toe with unused adrenaline. Heavy bag is in for some torture tonight.

I move my family down the hall and back past the ancient receptionist as the boys run up to us from the waiting area. From our faces they know now is not the time to talk. With my arm tightly around Kat, I pull Jake into my other side as we step outside.

We swiftly arrive at Kat's illegally parked car half on a median. I let Jake go, but he stays right at my side. I cage Kat's body to the driver's door and cup her cheeks in my hands, staring as deeply into her blue-green-grey eyes as I can so she can't lie to me.

"You good?" I ask softly.

"Fuck no," she whispers.

"Can you drive?"

"Yes."

"I'm takin' Jake with me and followin' you."

"'Kay."

I press a long kiss to her forehead before I let her go and stalk to my car a few medians down. She can handle anything...I know this. Still, walking away from her right now is making me sick to my stomach, but I don't have a choice. We have to get both cars home. I'll take care of her once we're there and away from prying eyes. Then I'll plot the untimely deaths of the Burke men because the monster within me has the taste for blood on his tongue and craves immediate satisfaction.

Chapter 11

Nick

Jake and I climb quickly into my car, waiting for Kat and the boys to drive off. I turn to him and grab his chin so I can get a good look at him. Not bad. Will maybe got two hits.

"You fuck him up?" I ask letting his chin go.

"Yes," he responds without hesitation.

"He hit you first?"

"Sucker punched me in the jaw."

"Pussy."

"Yeah."

"Where's he at?"

"Hospital."

"Bad?"

"He'll live. Maybe have a limp."

"Good."

"Kat flipped the fuck out in there," he whispers with pride.

"I bet," I snort as we pull away behind Kat's SUV.

"She was wasting time waiting for you."

This stops my breath for a second. Kat was waiting for me. I wasn't there and she didn't know when I would be...she was willing to wait for me. Because I run shit. Fuck me.

"I silenced my phone for the meeting and forgot. I came as soon as I figured out what was goin' on. Think I broke about twenty laws gettin' to you guys."

"Thanks for comin'. Never had anybody stick up for me like that. Today I had the boys, Kat and you. I kinda dig bein' fifteen again."

"I'll always fuckin' stick up for you whether you're fifteen or fifty. Get me?"

"Yeah," he whispers with a glint of satisfaction. He gets me.

"This shit about homecoming?" I ask as we legally wind and weave through picturesque Maybelle, which I'm finding houses the scum of the Earth behind its towering hills currently covered in shades of gold, copper and emerald. Nothing is ever what it appears.

"Yeah," he scoffs. "I've stayed the fuck away from Regan and her girls. Today at lunch, she saunters up to our table and asks me to go to the dance with her. Will was two tables away and lost his shit. I couldn't turn her down in front of the whole school, Nick. That woulda caused a whole new level of drama. Before I could say anything he came at me from the side and caught my jaw while I was tryin' to get Regan outta the way. I launched at his ass, took him down fuckin' his knee up and pounded his face until he wasn't movin' anymore."

"Hands hurt?" I ask with a smirk on my face. Kid did good. There's a piece of me that wishes I was there to watch it. Looking at Jake you wouldn't think he could hurt a fly...he wouldn't. Jake would never be aggressive unless necessary. He's not like me. I *like* that he's not like me.

"It's a good hurt. Split a couple open, but other than that I'm solid." He shrugs it off. I glance over to his hands resting in his lap and they're pretty torn up. That'll piss Kat off even more.

Finally, we pull in the garage next to Kat. The boys pile out looking exhausted, stressed and a little crazed. Kat stays in the SUV, not moving, her hands tight on the wheel. I climb out and gesture to Jake to go clean his hands up as I make my way to her door. I pull it open and brace my forearms at the top of the opening leaning into her.

"I kill people for a living. I track 'em, work 'em, squeeze information from every pore and then I kill 'em...most of the time. There's a need to kill at the end of most ops because the marks I've had have been demons preying on the innocent. There's no loss in the world when they're gone. I don't wanna kill 'em...it's my duty. I *want* to kill Will Burke. I *want* to poison his Gatorade and watch him struggle for his last breath, begging for his daddy to help him. What the fuck do I do, Nicky?" she asks turning her hazel eyes to me, pain and fury setting them alight.

"You get outta this SUV and go inside to take care of those four kids. They need you right now more than you need blood. Let me handle this. I promise you I'll make those motherfuckers pay. Then once the boys are calmed down you head to the basement and kick the shit outta the heavy bag and eat a pint of ice cream like you do when I piss you off." I keep my tone light but intensely pointed so that she knows I've got this. I've got her.

"I'm beyond ice cream," she sneers. "My parents had me late in life. Really fuckin' late and I only had them into my teenage years. It was a good life, but I was always unusual because of it. My perspective on life was different from the kids that had parents in their thirties. I lost them six months apart my senior year of high school. My father was a Korean and Vietnam War vet...he loved that he served his country. He wanted that for me. When the DCA came calling, I knew it was what he would want me to do. That he'd be proud of me. I kill people and my father would be proud of me. He would not be proud of me wanting to murder a child because he hurt someone I love."

"If your father was there today what would he have done?"

"If my father came in a room and thought someone had hurt me when I was Jake's age, he woulda done what you did. Without question."

"Then he was a good man. He was a loving father and a strong caretaker. And you're just like him. You wanna take care of Jake, but you've learned a different way of dealin' with shit. That doesn't make you anything less than the hero your father was. You're just more lethal. He'd be proud. Trust that, Sunshine," I finish softly and peel her fingers from the steering wheel that's at risk of being crushed under her grip.

"Mindfuck," she mumbles as I pull her from the SUV.

I put my arm around her shoulders and place a firm kiss on her hair as we make our way into the house.

"I've gotta call this in," I whisper into her ear as we hit the kitchen where the boys are huddled around Jake who's trying to clean his hands.

"'Kay," she says pulling away from me and heading to her boys. She immediately takes over cleaning Jake up while the others close in on her, trying to get a bit of comfort from her presence.

I run up the stairs two at a time before locking myself in the sound proof office across from our bedroom.

"Code in," a male voice directs.

"Alpha Bravo seven four six three," I respond.

"The line is secure Agent Cooper," the voice notifies me.

"Shane Hollander please."

"One moment."

The DCA could work on their hold music. Kenny G doesn't really fit the scene.

"Cooper, you're not due for a brief for two weeks. Tell me you've got somethin'," Shane insists excitedly.

"Nothing. We had an issue at the high school today," I explain annoyed at him and his constant pressure to end an op that he fucking knows is going to take months to even begin to dig into.

"Local authorities involved?" he asks professionally, thank fuck.

"Not yet, but I may need to involve 'em. William Burke, a kid at the high school, has been fuckin' with Jake since day one. Got physical the first day but has laid off to just verbal shit since then. Today he attacked

94

Jake in the lunch room in front of the whole school. Jake fucked him up good, put him in the hospital. I gave the order if this kid touched Jake again that Jake had clearance to retaliate with force. He did."

"Fuck! High school is such a pain in the ass. That shit doesn't change. Jake good?"

"Yeah, nothing a Band-Aid and a hug won't fix."

"Didn't know you gave out hugs, Cooper. I'll put that in your file for future reference," he snarks.

I snort but don't respond because he's getting on my nerves.

"Burke's father is the assistant principal. He was in Kat's face when I got on scene. Shit got physical and I told him that his current career was done and he had until tonight to vacate Maybelle."

"I'll deal with this from here. Shouldn't be an issue to remove the family. Send the details to me through the network and I'll get it done before end of business. Jake doesn't need any more shit to deal with, that's for fuckin' sure. I worried about sendin' him in with his history. Kid's unreal with a rifle, but with people things can get bad."

"He was followin' orders, Shane. He didn't go off half cocked. Jake's fine here with me...doin' really good in fact. I've got the op under control. But if local authorities get involved I need you to squash it to keep us where we've settled in Maybelle. Had a meeting with some of the poker group today at their law firm and got the contract for full security upgrades. Should have eyes and ears in two weeks. It's the biggest move we've been able to make so far."

"You think it'll flush anything out?"

"No clue. But it's somethin'."

I see movement on my surveillance monitors at the front of the house as two Maybelle Police cruisers pull into our driveway.

"Shit! Shane, I've got local PD pullin' up in the driveway. Start makin' moves," I bark.

95

"On it. Call you once it's settled."

He hangs up without a word. Shane's a piece of work, but this type of shit is his bread and butter.

I grunt my way out of the office and thud down the stairs, pulling the big black door open as a cop has his hand at the ready to knock.

"Mister Johnson?" the officer whose name badge identifies him as Burke asks. I'm guessing he's related to the pussy and his son. Fuck me.

"I'm Nick Johnson. How may I help you, Officer Burke?" I ask clinically.

"We'd like to ask you and your nephew a few questions about an incident at Maybelle High this afternoon. Can we come in?" he asks blankly, but his blue eyes are fiery, itching for a fight.

"Please," I offer, opening the door wide and extending an arm for them to pass.

The four men stride past me with confidence, none of them making eye contact as they do. Pussies.

"This way officers," I direct and lead them to the kitchen where I can hear my big weird family talking.

"Kat, we have visitors," I announce as I hit the room finding all four boys at the breakfast bar and Kat pulling something out of the oven. The boys are going to eat us out of house and home.

"Hello officers," Kat beams vibrantly, walking a tray of homemade Hot Pocket looking pastries over to the counter in front of the boys.

"Ma'am," Officer Burke greets for the group.

"Would you boys care for a snack?"

She's good at her job. No...she's fucking amazing at her job. Kat can play any role at anytime and no one knows what's actually going on behind her eyes. She appears calm and cool right now, when I know she's boiling to the hilt.

"Yes," one of the officers spouts as Burke declines.

Kat offers Burke a warm smile before loading up a snack pocket into a napkin and walking it over to the officer that requested one.

"How can we help you officers?" Kat asks as I pull her under my arm, hers going around my waist.

"We've been informed there were a couple incidents involving your husband and your nephew at Maybelle High this afternoon. We'd like to ask them some questions," Burke explains.

The boys are dutifully attentive while they eat their snacks. I offer Jake a brief look to let him know we've got this and he returns an imperceptive nod.

"Please come in and have a seat. We'd be happy to answer your questions," Kat says with an arm held out toward the breakfast table.

"We only need to speak with Mister Johnson and Jake, Missus Johnson," Burke responds coolly.

"I'm sorry. I thought you were here to get statements about Jake and I being assaulted on school grounds this afternoon. Is there something else you're here to discuss?"

The three officers standing around Burke turn questioning eyes his way before schooling their features back at us.

"William Burke has been hospitalized and Hoyt Burke is currently being attended to in the emergency room from injuries he claims Mister Johnson inflicted upon him," Burke says his eyes flaring at me as he does.

"Well, I'm sorry that Will is in the hospital after *he* attacked Jake. But as all the witnesses in the lunch room will tell you, Jake was defending himself. This was the *second* time Will attacked Jake without provocation on school grounds. Hoyt Burke then kept Jake and me against our will in a conference room before repeatedly shoving me in the chest for half an hour. My husband entered the room and found Mister Burke assaulting me. Nick defended me as I'm a woman and Hoyt Burke is much larger than me. If you'd like to ask questions about those assaults, we'd be happy to answer them. If

97

you're here to ask questions about anything else, I believe we should contact our attorney and join you at the police station," Kat finishes emphatically.

Suck on that motherfucker!

Burke is stunned stupid and has no response so the officer that's just finished eating Kat's incredible cooking takes the lead.

"Why don't we just take statements from you for now and we'll progress with our investigation," he says kindly offering Kat a small smile.

"I think that's best. It is a felony in Connecticut for an adult to assault a child under the age of sixteen isn't it?" Kat asks knowingly.

"Yes, ma'am, it is," the hungry officer replies.

"Well, Jake is fifteen and I'm aware Will Burke is eighteen. I believe we should press charges at this stage."

"Yes, ma'am. We'll gather more statements, interview witnesses and if you'd like to press charges we'll move forward with arrest warrants."

"I'd also like Officer Burke removed from this case. He's obviously related to our perpetrators and I feel this is a conflict of interest," Kat lowers the boom.

"Yes ma'am. Junior, why don't you head back to the station? We'll finish up here," the officer directs. He moves around Burke so I can see his name on his chest. Harrison.

"Sure," Burke, I'm guessing Hoyt Junior based on what Harrison just called him, responds glaring at me.

"I'll show you out," I say devoid of any emotion, indicating he goes ahead of me with a nod. When he moves I kiss Kat's hair and then follow behind.

"You touch my father or my brother again and I'll make you sorry," he growls leaning into my face at the threshold of the front door. I chuckle.

"You go ahead and try that."

"I don't make idle threats," he seethes.

I move into him so that my chest is touching his before the monster that lives within me unleashes his threat, "Neither do I. You tell your pussy father that. Get the fuck outta my house."

The fury in his eyes changes to fear at my tone and force. Then he gets the fuck out of my house. Pussy. I slam the door and head back to my family.

Chapter 12

Kat

"I went at it too hard," I groan, rolling to my stomach on my side of the bed. My body hurts from head to toe from the violence I unleashed on the heavy bag tonight. If only I had sweats to wear, I'd lounge around all day tomorrow and let the ache take me over. Jake and the boys have sweats, maybe I'll steal some of theirs.

"You feel better though, don't you?" Nick asks rolling to his side to face me.

I snort. I feel exhausted enough that I don't feel anything else, so that's something.

"Shane leaked the video of the fight in the lunch room and some possibly Photoshopped images of Hoyt pushing you in the conference room. Of course, my action is magically missing from the footage. I think this'll all go away by tomorrow," Nick explains, ending with a yawn.

"Jess is a magician with a computer. I'm sure she did all that in an hour flat," I say with pride at my best friend's super powers.

"Jake said you were waitin' for me," he says softly.

"You run shit. I was pretty certain protocol in that situation was to await your arrival. I also didn't think me unmanning the assistant principal would've done a lot to maintain our cover," I finish with a shrug. Well, an attempt at a shrug with my aching muscles.

"I appreciate your thoughtfulness," he drones in a sarcastic tone.

"What? Did you want me to unman him?" I ask disbelieving.

"No. You did good. Thanks."

That was a brush off if I've ever received one. Have I mentioned this man is a mindfuck?

"Nicky, I'm worn the fuck out. If you've got somethin' to say, say it. We can fight for a while, but I need some sleep," I order.

"Nothin' to say. Get some sleep, Sunshine."

"Mindfuck," I murmur into my pillow and fall asleep five seconds later.

I wake up to shrieking screams and fly out of bed. I know it's Jake. Nick beats me up the stairs this time.

"Get back boys," Nick directs as we barrel into the room to find all three of them huddled around Jake's shaking frame on the floor.

I collapse next to him and gather as much of his body as I can into my lap.

"What's wrong with him?" Cole asks with terror in his voice. These boys have shitty home lives, but nothing compared to where Jake's come from.

"It's just a nightmare, guys. Why don't you three head back to bed? We've got him from here," Nick instructs kindly, offering the softness he didn't a month and a half ago.

I nod, smiling encouragingly at them and they all move back to their rooms slowly, watching Jake as they go. I keep rocking and shushing Jake, rubbing my hand across his shaggy hair.

"Come on, bud," Nick says reaching down and heaving Jake off the floor, cradling him to his chest.

Jake remains tense as Nick carries him, but eases a bit under his touch. Nick pads down the stairs back to our room still carrying Jake. I follow behind quickly as the boys peek their heads out of their rooms.

"Can we come too?" Sawyer asks sheepishly.

"Come on," I whisper, realizing they won't sleep if they don't know everyone is okay.

They all run into their rooms and come back out with blankets and pillows. When we make it to our room, Nick is laying Jake down in the bed. Nick eyes the boys standing behind me for a second and then nods his head for them to come in. They quickly make pallets on the floor before snuggling in.

I slide into the sheets and Jake wraps his arms excruciatingly tightly around my middle. I take the pain. This I can do for him. I'll take the tiniest amount of his hurt if it gives him even the slightest relief. I still don't know Jake's story and I really don't need to. He comes from fucked up and it still lingers. I don't need a road map to figure that shit out. Jake can tell me when he's ready. I'm not a pusher.

I feel Nick's body come flush with my back before reaching across me, placing a hand on Jake's shoulder.

"Easy, Jake," he soothes and Jake responds, letting up on his pressure.

None of us move from this position for the rest of the night. Nick is vigilant in keeping Jake calm and relaxed with a hand on his shoulder and gentle reminders that he's okay, while I cradle and hold Jake to my chest. It's not a restful night's sleep, but it's a safe one for Jake.

I wake to the sound of the doorbell. I lean up on my elbow and the clock reads 9:27 a.m. We slept in...I don't give a shit. I wiggle free from Jake and Nick before grabbing my robe and hurrying down the stairs.

Through the peephole, I see Trish Booker standing patiently looking like perfection in a pair of light colored chinos and a thin maroon sweater covered with a deep gold jacket. Her platinum hair is swept away from her face, which is bright and sparkly. She looks like autumn personified. Game face on Kat.

I pull the door open and her smile drops at my appearance.

"I'm so sorry. I figured you be up and at the day already, Kat," she says judgmentally but plays it off as concerned. It would work on ninety-nine percent of the population. I'm happy to be the other one percent in moments like this.

"It was a rough day and night around here. We're slow moving this morning," I say grimly, working the tone as much as I can.

"I heard what happened at the school yesterday. Then that footage on the news last night...Just horrible." Shaking her head, it reads as sympathetic, but I see disgust behind her eyes and it's not directed at the Burkes.

"Yes, it really was a frightful day for my family. We've decided to take the day off and recover. We'll be back at it tomorrow. I really appreciate your concern, Trish."

"Well of course I'm concerned. You're my friend and you were assaulted. I'm horrified for you. Is there anything you need?"

Fake as fuck. This bitch makes my stomach turn.

"Thank you, but I think we're all set. Some junk food and a day of movies should suit us just fine," I reply nicely.

"If you do need anything please don't hesitate to call."

"That's very kind."

"Well, I'll let you get back to..." she trails off and looks beyond my shoulder with something resembling embarrassment on her face.

"Good morning, Trish," Nick says brightly, sliding up behind me.

His arms are bare so I'm assuming he's only wearing pajama bottoms and giving our mark quite the show. Eat your heart out honey. Nick's damn good at his job.

"Good morning, Nick," she replies with a rosy flush to her cheeks.

Nick presses a long kiss into my neck not responding to her or looking her direction.

"Morning, Sunshine," he murmurs into my neck.

"Morning, Nicky," I reply in a husky voice, closing my eyes to add to the affect for Trish.

She clears her throat and I pop my eyes open as Nick stands up straight, keeping me in his clutches.

"I can see you two are busy, so I'll let you go. I'm really sorry about yesterday. I've known the Burkes my whole life and am truly shocked at their abhorrent behavior. They're certainly off my Christmas card list," she says as though that's a real blow against the Burkes.

"Thanks for comin' by, Trish," Nick responds for us. "Kat'll call you this week once we've recovered from all this."

"Please do," she replies in her *Stepford* façade.

"I will. Have a lovely day, Trish," I beam cheerfully at her.

"You too," she says with a wave as she turns and makes her way back down our driveway.

Nick burrows his head in my neck and aggressively works his stubble across the sensitive skin causing me to yelp and giggle. Trish stops and turns back to see the commotion. I offer her a magnificent smile and a wave as Nick drags me backward, continuing his assault before closing the door.

"You two are kinda gross first thing in the morning," Dane grumbles as he thuds down the stairs, the other boys nodding in agreement behind him.

"So are you," Nick snarks, receiving chuckles in return.

"Jake's still out," Sawyer informs us.

"We'll let him sleep a while. He didn't get much after the nightmare," I explain sweetly, sweeping an arm around his waist and leading the group to the kitchen.

"Does he get those a lot?" Cole asks sliding onto his— all the boys have their spots—stool at the breakfast bar.

"Not a lot. Yesterday was hard for him. I'm sure that's all it was," I say knowing there's probably more truth to that statement than lie.

I set about making omelets while Nick gets the coffee going.

"Aunt Kay?" Dane asks pulling me from my chopping of peppers.

105

"Yes, sweetheart?"

"Will you let us stay here even when are parents are back?" he asks quietly.

"Of course you can stay here. Why would you even ask?" I'm surprised at his question, frankly.

"I just figured you'd be sick of the charity case by then. And since we wouldn't *technically* be alone anymore you'd be done," he finishes with a shrug, the other two nodding in agreement.

I slam my knife down and round the island, stopping at the counter in front of the boys, who now look nervous due to my apparent displeasure with their thoughts.

"That's a fucked up thing to say to me, Dane Ashcroft. What's worse is that you actually believe what you just said. Let me tell you boys somethin'. You may come from people that have used you, thrown you away like trash and expected you to grow up way too soon, but that's not okay. And it sure as shit isn't how I would *ever* treat you. You are not a charity case! I care about you all and I want to keep you happy and safe because of that. Not some fucked up selfish reason you three seem to have created. You're in our home because the thought of you anywhere else at the end of the day makes me sick to my stomach with worry and concern. Do you understand me?" I finish harshly.

I'm pissed. I'm pissed the fuck off and shaking because of it. I'm not mad at the boys, it's their parents that are the current sore spot for me. These are good kids. They're sweet, polite, thoughtful, smart boys that most parents would die to have as their children instead of rude, mouthy teenagers that occupy most homes. If their shit-for-brains parents don't get that, it's their loss and my gain.

"Yes," they reply in unison.

"Good."

I return to my chopping, albeit a bit more aggressively than I was previously going at it. I'm twenty-eight and have fallen in love with four teenage boys like they're my own flesh and blood. It's bizarre and I can't explain how it happened or why, but it did. DCA protocols be damned. If I could figure out a way to adopt all of them, Jake included, I would. I'd take them out of *Stepford* and give them everything I could to ensure they get a few good years of love in them before the real world ruins shit.

"You'll be a good mom, Aunt Kay," Sawyer says tenderly, bringing me out of my murderous veggie assault.

"She already is," Jake calls from the entryway of the kitchen.

I offer him a demure smile as he approaches me with purpose. Jake wraps his arms around my waist and buries his face in my neck as my arms go around his shoulders.

"I love you, Kat," he whispers into my skin and I feel tears prick my eyes. I refuse to cry, even happy tears.

"I love you too, Jake," I whisper back and he squeezes me harder, holding me for a long while before letting me go.

Jake pads over to Nick, who's been silent since Dane leveled his blow, just watching us from his perch against the counter. Jake stops a breath from Nick and they simply stare at each other for a moment before Nick sweeps a hand behind Jake's head and crushes it to his shoulder. Inaudible words are exchanged along with some manly back pats before Jake pulls away and joins his boys at the breakfast bar.

The four of them settle into their normal banter and I get back to breakfast. I never look at Nick during this time. I know he gets that was a huge moment for all of us. Not just with Jake, but the boys too. I don't need eye contact to share that with him. There's a part of me that doesn't want to share it with him because this op is becoming more reality and less of an op as each day passes. That's dangerous where emotions are concerned. I'm not losing my focus on the op; just falling in love with four teenage boys I'll have to leave. Fuck if that doesn't hurt like a bitch right now and it's only been six weeks. If we're at this a year or more it'll be the death of me. Just thinking about it brings tears to my eyes that I can't hold back any longer.

I keep my head down and my back to the room facing the stove as I prepare omelets. The tears stream down my cheeks, but I keep the sobs buried in my chest. This is bad. I'm not one of those women that can shed tears, look gorgeous doing it and refreshed afterward. No, I'm the woman who has blotchy skin, a runny nose, red-rimmed eyes and look sickly when I'm done.

I load five plates for the men in my life, lining them up on the counter next to the stove. Then I turn tail and run up the stairs to our room to get my face presentable before they can tell what a blubbering mess I've become. A shower is necessary to begin accomplishing this task.

I turn on every jet, including the rain shower and let the hot water soothe my aching muscles in tandem with my aching heart. I don't regret taking the boys in or creating a bond with Jake. I feel something good for the first time in years that doesn't involve killing a mark. No, there are no regrets in loving four teenagers. I'll spend the time I have with them offering those boys everything my parents gave me. Love, support, concern and above all I'll give them all the happiness in the world that I can wring out of the op.

Once I have my shit together and my emotions back in check I climb out of the shower and inspect my face in the mirror. A little blotchy and red-rimmed, but overall it's not too bad. I'll take my time getting ready and doing my hair. By then I should look as *Stepford* as Trish.

"You need to come out here and talk to me or I'm comin' in," Nick demands roughly at the bathroom door.

"I'm fine, just needed a shower," I lie in a sweet tone.

There's no response. That was easier than I anticipated. I move into the dressing room and peruse my outfits hoping to find something comfortable to go with my horridly expensive leggings, which have become my go-to when in the house. Digging through the drawers, I find a plush plum three-quarter sleeved turtleneck sweater. This will do the trick. I slip into a tiny black thong and lacy matching bra before heading back into the bathroom while securing my navy silk robe.

Nick is leaning against his vanity with his massive arms across his chest and a scowl on his face. I walk past him and begin lotioning my face, avoiding his icy glare in my mirror.

"It's not gonna work," Nick informs me in a low tone.

"What's that?" I ask innocently.

"You can't hide from me or the boys. They're easier to hide from than I am, but you sure as shit can't hide from me so knock it off," he demands.

"I'm in our home, in our bathroom. Not a great hiding spot, Nicky," I huff.

"No shit. Next time you should leave the house if you wanna run away from us."

"I came to take a shower."

"You ran outta the kitchen like your fuckin' hair was on fire."

"I needed a shower."

"Kat."

"Nick."

We stare at each other in the mirror for a long moment before I break eye contact and take my wet hair out of my towel. I set about combing and running product through it, all the while feeling Nick's deep brown eyes boring into the back of my skull.

"I'm not dressed. Maybe you could give me some privacy," I suggest without meeting his irritated gaze.

"No," he growls.

"That's not very considerate," I say with warning in my tone.

"You runnin' outta the kitchen wasn't either," he retorts pointedly.

"What the fuck do you want from me?" I grind out harshly, turning to face him.

"You to quit fuckin' hidin' from me," he barks loudly.

This argument began between Kat and Nick Johnson. Kat Russell is pissed and coming out to fight now.

"Why do you give a shit? I'm here doin' what I'm supposed to. Lettin' you run shit and takin' care of the boys. I've worked my way in with Trish enough that she showed up first thing this morning. I fail to see where I'm doin' anything wrong."

"You're my wife," he says like that's an answer.

"No, I'm not. I'm your team member and you should remember that in moments like this. You run the op, you run your wife and nephew, you run yourself and the boys most of the time. You don't run me."

That breaks the standoff because Nick stalks to inches from me, glowering as he leans into my face.

"You. Are. My. Wife," he growls low and menacing. "Every minute of every fuckin' day you're my wife. That doesn't stop because you have a moment. That doesn't stop because you get scared. That doesn't stop because you say it does. That doesn't stop because you wanna break from it to pull that goddamned mask back over your face and run into the blackness that's been your home for the last decade. You're my wife."

"Get outta my face with your shit, Nick. I'm not you're fuckin' wife and I never will be. Go growl at some other girl, I've had enough of your alpha male routine," I seethe.

He pins me with a fierce stare before smashing his lips to mine. I move to push him off me, but he traps my hands beneath his, pressing them into his naked rock hard chest. He works his mouth across mine and I feel my resolve fading, passion building. His tongue slides out, tracing my lips, requesting entry. Goddamn him! I was really doing a good job of being pissed and not letting him get his way.

I part my lips and a small moan crackles from my chest as Nick buries his hands in my damp hair,

110

slanting his head to get better access at my mouth. We tangle our tongues together, drinking from each other. His mouth is warm and minty with a male muskiness that's just him topping it off. I run my hands up his bare chest, over his sculpted shoulders and around his neck.

I start to work my nails over his scalp and arch my back, pressing my hard peeked nipples against him. A deep satisfied groan bubbles up his throat and I breathe it in before sucking his plump bottom lip into my mouth then tugging it between my teeth.

Nick takes over after that, nipping and licking at my mouth. Holding my head where he wants it to get the access he requires as his tongue plunders my mouth with fervor.

Then he's gone. My eyes pop open to see Nick shaking his head and running his hand roughly over his hair. The look on his face is defeated, frustrated and worst of all...disgusted.

"Fuck!" he roars tipping his head up to the ceiling.

I close my eyes and take a calming breath. Game face on Kat.

Chapter 13

Nick

I've lost my goddamned mind! I just attacked Kat like a horny teenager. I'm spending too much time with the boys.

I'm still staring at the ceiling after roaring like an animal. When I lower my chin and make eye contact with usually fiery hazel eyes, I find them blank. This moves me from frustrated at myself to pissed off at her, again.

"Feel better?" she asks calmly.

"No," I growl.

She shrugs and turns away from me, switching on her blow dryer. Kat goes about drying her hair and ignoring my presence like she was when I first came in here. This woman drives me insane. She's so soft and sweet with the boys and with me most of the time. I know it's genuine when she does it too, her mask is nowhere in sight.

Then there are moments like this where she runs. She's hiding from all of us and I don't get it. We're here for her like she's here for us, but she won't take it. It infuriates me.

Then she runs that mouth and it's so fucking sexy when she does, I lose my shit. I lose my shit and ram my tongue down her throat to shut her up. Not just to shut her up, but that was my initial goal until she purred and pressed her soft tits against me. Then shit got real and it felt perfect. She felt perfect. The weight of her in my arms, the taste of her in my mouth and the sounds echoing from her that I caused snapped me back into reality.

I'm not certain what that reality is anymore. Kat's gotten under my skin. The glow that beams from her has penetrated my hard shell and filed down those rough edges I've spent a lifetime sharpening. That's what I should tell her. I should tell Kat that I'm feeling for the first time in my adult life and it freaks me the fuck out. I know it freaks her out too. That's why she bailed on the boys and me.

Listening to Dane question her loyalty to him and the boys set off a storm in my chest. I didn't utter a word during their interaction. I simply leaned against the counter and watched Kat put herself on the line emotionally, no Agent Russell in sight. I'm not stupid enough to believe we haven't been creating emotional connections since we got here, but they're becoming more intense and that's problematic as the team leader. The first no-no in the DCA, no emotional ties while undercover. Then Jake came in a dropped his love bomb and anything the DCA has ever dictated flew out the window. Kat may have spoken the words that I didn't have the balls to say, but at the core of my being I feel the same way. I love those boys; they're a piece of me. When Kat bolted, it pained them and that pissed me off.

Now I'm in an emotional shit storm and I can't see my way clear. So I do what any dumb ass man would. I shut down my emotions and become a robotic dick.

I stomp over to her vanity and rip her hair dryer out of its socket. She turns her blank gaze to mine in the mirror and waits.

"The op is twenty-four seven. If you can't comply with that I'll have you reassigned. We can use the altercation yesterday as an excuse for you to leave. If you decide to stay this shit won't happen again. You cannot break character at any juncture. Perfection is expected at every turn. If anyone bugs the house you'll blow us. I apologize for kissing you. That was inappropriate and unprofessional. It won't happen again. I'll let you finish gettin' ready. I expect your decision when you're done," I say in my Agent Nick Cooper voice.

114

"Thank you for your apology, Agent Cooper. I would like to remain on the op and will comply with the directives you've just set out. I apologize for having a weak moment. It won't happen again, sir. As for the kiss, it's not an issue. We can forget it ever happened and move forward with the op professionally," she responds in her Agent Katherine Russell voice.

This is worse than when she was blank. She's now devoid of anything, running deeper into the blackness than I thought she could. I don't know what to do to fix this, so I do nothing. I nod and leave the bathroom. I fucked up.

Kat's alarm begins to beep and she has it silenced before the sound can even tickle my ears. She floats effortlessly into the bathroom without a glance in my direction. I pull my phone off the bedside table and wait for her to finish her shower before going to take mine. The only thing of interest on my phone is Angry Birds, so I play that like a five-year-old in a timeout until I hear Kat banging around in the bathroom.

I enter the space staring that the woman that's completely shut me out. It's been a week and she's said maybe two words to me when we're alone. I think one has been *yes* and the other was some version of *uh huh*, not exactly and in depth conversation.

The woman is perfection in a slinky deep purple long-sleeved dress that hangs mid-calf. It clings to her curves like it was painted on without seeming inappropriate for the day. She's wearing her hair down today. I've learned how she's going to style her hair based on which electric contraption she's wielding. Today it's a curling iron. The curling iron is my favorite.

I hop in the shower wishing it were encased in glass instead of stone so Kat could see the effect she has on me. That's a perverted thought I've become used to since I tasted her luscious mouth. I'm aware I'm the dipshit that ended things with Kat. It doesn't mean my dick's on board with my brain.

After willing my hard on away, I take time soaking my tense muscles. I've been in our home gym twice a day since I shut Kat down. I need a release and beating the shit out of the heavy bag only does so much. I've been running, lifting and any other exhausting activity I can find in order to burn off steam. Jake's joined me twice and I've gotten a good workout on the mats. That boy may be smaller than me, but he's got skills. He even bested me once. The pride I felt when he did was matched in the confidence beaming back at me when he helped me off my back. Love that kid.

Another relief came when the Burkes left town like the bitches they are. Kicking the shit out of Hoyt Burke would have been a nice release but a death sentence for the op, so I take the win at face value. Junior is still here on the force, but he's steered clear of all of us. I get the feeling he's plotting some dimwitted plan against us, and it makes me about as nervous as a mouse fart would. He's a pussy.

Once I'm good and clean I head into my dressing room. Today's a big one so I opt for slacks and a button down. Not my usual Saturday wear. Back in the bathroom, I find it empty save for the lingering light, airy scent of Kat. She smells like citrus and a crisp breeze off the ocean. It's become my crack. I can't get enough of it and it may end up killing me.

Back in the bedroom the bed is made and my shit it picked up and put where it should be. She still takes care of me, or she hates that I'm a slob and curses me while she picks up my shit. I prefer the former.

As I descend the stairs, I can hear the jubilation that follows the boys wherever they roam. Kat's bellowing laughter is what catches my ear though. Her fucking masks keep this sound from me. I pause on the stairs and cherish the sound before continuing on my path. When I enter the room I find Kat at the stove. The smells enveloping my nose tell me she's whipping up some French toast.

"Morning," I say in my I-haven't-had-enough-coffee voice.

"Morning," the boys respond in unison.

Jake nods his chin toward Kat, silently asking if things are better. I return with a slight shake of the head before pouring myself a mug of coffee. Jake hasn't asked me what's going on. Not even when we're kicking the crap out of each other in the basement. He knows. He's completely aware that something is off. He's not a pusher though, much like Kat. He'll wait until something needs to be said and then we'll have to listen.

"What's the plan for today?" I ask the boys while plopping down at the head of the kitchen table.

"Aunt Kay's threatening haircuts," Dane responds with huge honey-hued eyes begging me to make that request go away.

"I didn't say a haircut, Dane. I said a trim," Kat playfully interjects. I miss that.

"Uh, scissors plus hair equals haircut," Dane argues.

"I just want your hair outta your eyes for the pictures," Kat urges, sliding a plate of French toast, bacon and eggs in front of me.

I take my opportunity. This is a fucked up thing to do, but it's the only way I get what I want from Kat.

I slide my arm around her waist and pull her into my lap. She willingly falls against me with a glowing smile on her face. I know it's fake. I fucking hate that it's fake. So I pretend it's real. I had the shot at real, but I let Agent Nick Cooper fuck it up. I pretend right along with her.

"Compromise?" I ask with my brow raised.

She rolls her eyes dramatically before turning in my lap to face the boys. Her ass feels so good against my dick I miss the first half of the discussion.

"...can take you to practice driving later this week. How's that, Nicky?" Kat finishes rotating in my lap again to look at me. Her hazel eyes shift from warm and soft to blank when they lock with mine. She shuts down so easily I'm impressed. I'm gutted that I did this, but it's extraordinary to witness.

"Sounds like a good compromise," I lie. I have no idea what I'm agreeing to.

"Badass! Can we drive the em six?" Cole questions excitedly.

The M6? Why are we discussing the boys driving my sports car? I shift my gaze to Kat and I see the pleased look on her face. She did this shit on purpose. Sliding around in my lap was a calculated move to distract me so I wouldn't hear her offering up driving lessons in return for haircuts. I told you she's good at her job.

Kat hops off my lap announcing, "It'll have to be your car, Nicky. I've got a lot goin' on this week."

"Is that so?"

"Uh huh," she dismisses me and starts cleaning the kitchen.

I glance over at Jake who has a smirk playing at the corners of his mouth. Kat just gave him a master class in misdirection techniques and I was the mark. Great.

"How much hair are we talkin', Aunt Kay?" Sawyer yells into the kitchen, lovingly petting his black locks.

"As much as I want!"

"Shit," he mutters under his breath.

Kat pokes her head around the corner and innocently asks, "What was that?"

"I didn't say anything," Sawyer lies.

"Liar," she says with a knowing look. "Careful, I'll shave you bald in your sleep if you're not nice."

She could too. These boys sleep like the dead.

After we finish our breakfast with Kat unsurprisingly missing from the table, she appears at my side.

"I'm off to collect corsages. I'll be back in an hour or so and then I'll take you boys to get haircuts," she says brightly.

"You said a trim," Dane grumbles.

"Did I say that? I don't remember."

"Aunt Kay," Cole whines.

"Oh stop. I'm just playing with you. Be good while I'm gone."

With that she presses a soft kiss to my forehead and I again take the advantage, pulling her face lower before brushing my lips across hers.

"Bye, Sunshine," I murmur against her lips.

Her fat lips turn up in a grin before she gifts me another kiss.

"Bye, Nicky," she says in a breathy voice.

The sound tricks me and I look up into her eyes to find them as blank as they've been since the last time I caused them to be hot and ravenous. What I wouldn't give to see that again.

I release her with two pats on her ass and she floats out of the house swinging those damn hips with every step.

"Aunt Kay's more like a mom to me than my own mom has been, but she's still fuckin' hot as hell," Dane announces before draining his orange juice, wiping his mouth with the back of his hand.

Cole and Sawyer nod in agreement while Jake glares at his boys.

"What?" Dane questions ingenuously.

Jake rolls his eyes and shakes his head without comment. The boys love Kat. I don't question it one bit, but Jake really does see Kat as his mom. He doesn't want anyone talking about her like she's a piece of meat. I don't either, frankly. Dane's not being crude when he says shit like that though. He's just admiring the woman and I can't fault him. He just needs some lessons in tact. I'm not the one to teach him those lessons. I think Jake's the man for that job.

"When you wanna pay a woman a compliment, don't say anything you wouldn't confidently say to her face. And if you think women wanna hear shit like you just said, you're wrong. Tell Aunt Kay she's beautiful, gorgeous, hot as hell or whatever else you think, but say that shit from your heart. Not your dick. Do it again and I'll beat your ass."

"Yes, Sensei," Dane retorts. "You're the master of the ladies. I have much to learn."

Sawyer and Cole burst into laughter and Dane follows suit. Jake holds out as long as he can and then he joins his boys. That's all it takes to break the tension in the room and I release a few chuckles along with them. These boys are good for my soul. If it weren't for them right now I'd be in a dark place. I'm in the dim jail cell Kat's imprisoned me in, but these boys offer me the sunshine missing from my days. I'm thankful for teenagers. Stranger things have happened.

Chapter 14

Nick

"No ties?" I ask as the boys come into the family room just before their dates are set to arrive. The four of them look almost identical in suits and button down shirts.

"No," Dane scoffs as if that's the stupidest question he's ever heard.

"Nervous?" I question them while climbing to my feet, switching off the TV.

"No," they all grumble, telling me they are.

"It'll be a fun night, boys. Be the gentlemen I know you are and you'll have the time of your lives," Kat encourages as she strides into the room. Her make-up is darker for the evening and her hair looks freshly primped, flowing curls cascading around her face. Her dress looks even better with high heels that surely cost an arm and a leg. A large diamond pendant hangs just above her cleavage drawing my eyes to her perfect tits. It's always a great view in Maybelle.

"You look gorgeous, Sunshine," I compliment, moving to wrap her in my arms.

Her arms enfold around my neck as I burrow my face into hers. I kiss her succulent skin and she dutifully giggles. I hate that sound as much as I love it.

"You look pretty delicious yourself, Nicky," she says in a fake husky voice, blank hazel eyes meeting mine.

"I was right about the haircuts, wasn't I?" Kat asks the boys moving away from my grasp. I take a calming breath before facing the group.

"You know you were. Quit askin'," Cole teases.

The doorbell sounds, alerting us to the ladies' arrival and I lead the parade to the front door. When I pull it open I remember this feeling, the excited nervousness that accompanies formal dances. The girls all look the part in short pretty dresses, none showing or covering too much.

I don't pay much attention to the girls or their parents, preferring to keep my distance. I don't know how many pictures are normally taken on nights like this, but I have the feeling we're working on a world record.

The boys loosen up through the process, their usual jokes and banter making their dates giggle. Kat beams like a beacon within the group. Her smile should surely be causing her cheeks to cramp, but it never leaves her face. She's happy and full of pride as the boys load into the limo with retina damage from flashes going off for an hour. Jake's the last to fold into the car and I offer him a wink as he disappears with a two finger wave in return. He'll keep everyone safe tonight. I have no worries. After the kids leave, Kat invites the other parents in the house for coffee, and I dutifully sit and converse with strangers about New England's chances this season.

As always, I watch Kat out of the corner of my eye. She moves around the kitchen without effort, filling glasses and mugs, offering food and pleasant smiles as she goes. These people have no idea the dazzling performance they're witnessing, which makes it even more impressive. Kat catches my gaze and blows me a big kiss before tipping her head back and laughing at something one of the women says. Why was it that I pushed Kat away?

I wanted her to feel powerful and in control. I didn't want her to feel attacked by a horny man yet again on an op. If I'd had the balls to tell her that maybe I wouldn't be watching her from afar right now, getting glimpses of what I'm missing. She's sweet with the men here, a few of them lingering too long around her. But her kindness with them seems to have a limit that they all acknowledge. She's a taken woman. My woman. If only that could be true.

She ran from me that day in the bathroom. While this self-imposed sentence is irritating, Kat constantly hiding behind her masks is infuriating. How am I supposed to open up to her, when she always shuts down on me? Kat uses her talents as craftily as I use weapons. I can't take this where I want just to be another mark to her. That's all I am at this point and it's torture. If we started a physical relationship, I'd lose my mind. I don't work like this.

I need her...all of her. Kat's never shown me she's capable of that. Before I met her, I wasn't sure I was capable of that. I am now, with her. I won't take anything less. I can live in this prison because it allows me the façade I've grown used to in the DCA. Anything beyond this has to be on my terms. All or nothing.

The evening with the other parents winds down after a few hours of coffee, wine and conversation. Kat and I usher the crowd to our door, promising to do this again soon. I hope not. When the door closes, leaving Kat and me alone, I feel it. The emptiness of our op settles like a heavy fog between us.

"I'm gonna head down to the gym," I mutter as I climb the stairs.

She doesn't respond. So I push.

"You can continue to be pissed at me, but I'd appreciate it if you'd respond when I speak to you," I demand.

"I'm sorry, Nicky. Enjoy your workout. I'll be in the family room reading," she says in the appropriate tone and inflection, her eyes hauntingly devoid of the emotion her voice just offered.

I think the lack of speech was better. I nod in response and she floats away to read. I wonder if she reads books about men that sweep women off their feet in romantic overtures and is waiting for me to be that man. She'll wait a lifetime if that's the case. I'll snoop around in her Kindle tomorrow just to see what I'm up against.

Dripping with sweat, I climb the stairs from the basement, well and truly exhausted. I went at it harder tonight than I have any other. My arms are like jelly and my mind can barely produce a coherent thought.

When I reach the kitchen, I find the space clean and empty. I silently glide into the family room to find Kat curled up in a ball in her favorite cream reading chair asleep. I make a snap decision to carry her to bed, knowing I could end up assaulted and unmanned. It's worth the risk. I promised the first time we fought I'd be kind to her and I'm a man of my word.

I lift her with ease and pause for any indication she's playing opossum. Her breathing continues to tickle my neck at the same rate and her soft body remains limp in my arms. I take measured steps so as not to disturb her. Climbing the stairs after my workout was one thing. Carrying another person is testing my reserves. I do it though. I'm happy to have her relaxed in my arms. If she'd give me this all the time, this could be our reality. I guess it's not meant to be.

"Thank you, Nicky," she murmurs as I slide her between our sheets.

"You're welcome, Sunshine," I mumble into her hair, placing a kiss there.

I pull back hoping to find warm inviting eyes, only to be hit with the serenity of her sleeping face. I hold onto the sweetness of her voice and imagine this is the life I deserve. If only for a little while, I bask in the glow of the fairy tale before I have to move back into the blackness of my reality. Alone.

The boys rode on the high of homecoming night right into a week later when Halloween came around. There was a big party at a guy's house that all the boys and girls went to together. I was sure we'd end up getting drunk phone calls and having to set some real punishments and boundaries, but we didn't get any calls or any drunk boys. They had a blast dressing up as some boy band that was a huge hit with all the ladies.

The surveillance is in place in the law firm and streaming to the DCA. So far nothing but a lot of boring ass shit is going on; I feel bad for our intel monitors having to watch it. I have to hope that it'll shake something our way soon.

Tonight's poker night and the boys are at some school play. Kat and I are currently eating a silent meal that she also prepared in silence. It's been two and a half weeks since homecoming. Nothing's changed and nothing's gotten worse. We're just going through the motions like we would on any other op. It's depressing.

"I've got a late meeting tomorrow. I'll meet you at the school for the game," I inform Kat.

Jake made the basketball team easily and is gaining even more popularity because he's in the starting lineup. Cole made the team too, but isn't starting...yet. Sawyer and Dane are so proud of their friends. It's refreshing to see teenagers supporting each other instead of fighting to see who can stab the next in the back the fastest.

"All right," Kat responds in the appropriate inflection and timing with nothing in her eyes.

"I'm gonna head out. I'll try not to be too late," I say standing from the table.

"Enjoy your evening," she says in the same tone that haunts me at this point. I'm sorry I ever asked for it.

I drop my head in defeat and go to the front door, with a few grand in my navy pea coat I move out into the cold night air.

Tony greets me at his door and ushers me down to the basement playing room where all the guys are setting up around the table. There's a new guy that I don't recognize, but think nothing of it.

"Nick, this is Phil Ganesly. He's been out of the country on business since your family moved in," Tony introduces the man.

He's refined in a tailored three-piece suit with a Cuban hanging from his teeth. His hair is salt and pepper, heavier on the pepper. I'm guessing he's close to fifty, but can pull off forty in a push. There's something

125

about his eyes that lets me know he may live in the affluent world now, but he doesn't come from here. It's like looking in a mirror fifteen years into my future.

"Phil, this is our new neighbor, Nick Johnson," Tony finishes.

I slide my palm into his and respect the firm grip he offers. He holds my eyes for a moment before smiling around his cigar.

"Hear you're beatin' the pants off these boys every week," he says in a deep gravelly voice.

"Don't believe everything you hear," I say through a chuckle retrieving my hand.

"Never do. I will tell you I've heard you've got yourself a looker for a wife," he says with a brow raised.

"That you *can* believe."

He lets out a loud bark of laughter before clapping me on the back.

"Make sure you hang onto that. Women in this town have a tendency to upgrade," he informs me with a knowing look.

I notice a few mumbles from behind me and realize that some of these men must have been downgraded at some point. Maybelle is a cut-throat world in every facet.

"Thanks for the advice," I respond through a smile before moving to the table.

The evening progresses normally with me kicking everyone's ass, including Phil's.

"You sure he's not a professional player?" Phil asks after he loses yet another hand to me.

"I grew up playin' a lot. You get good after a few decades," I reply nonchalantly.

That's a true statement. Growing up in a crime family, poker was a part of my life as long as I can remember. I'm good, really fucking good. I take it easy on these guys most of the time. They all have horrible tells and no strategy. I think they like losing their money.

126

"How long you been in security?" Phil asks as Tony deals another hand.

"Since college, about eleven years."

I peek down at my hand. Pocket kings. I'm not even going to have to pay attention this game.

"How'd you get into that?" Tony asks. This is the most these guys have asked about my past making me somewhat wary and very excited.

"It was my father's business. When he retired I took over and expanded it beyond the Midwest."

"Expanded your bank account too," Phil scoffs before throwing back two fingers of whiskey. His sixth by my count.

"That was the intended goal," I say through a sly smile.

"Get your woman before you got your money?" he asks slightly slurred.

"Met Kat in college."

"That's good, she'll be less likely to upgrade."

I don't respond because I'm not liking the direction of the conversation. I push all my chips to the middle of the table and win the hand because they all fold. Pussies.

I need to get a bug in this house, but the only room I've ever been in is this one and I doubt they're doing business down here. Slow and steady wins the race. It's killing me.

"Why don't you come by my office next week? I could use some added security," Phil suggests nonchalantly.

"Sure. I've got some availability on Tuesday if that works for you. Here's my card. Give me a call."

Supposedly, Phil's in marketing and advertising. I'm not sure why he needs more than basic security, but I'm willing to check out everyone that spends time with the Bookers.

"Will do," Phil says, placing my card in his inner jacket pocket.

We play a few more hands before calling it a night. I'm up six grand, so I say the evening is glowing success with Phil being an added bonus. Progress.

Chapter 15

Nick

I walk across the street and am surprised to find an Audi SUV in my driveway. Who the fuck is at my house at midnight? I pick up my pace and enter my front door to be knocked in the face with the full belly laughter of Kat along with that of a man. Not one of the boys, a man.

I remove my coat and head in the direction of the jubilation, which is coming from the kitchen area. I enter the room and find it empty, but hear more chuckles coming from the family room. The sight that my eyes find makes my stomach drop.

Kat is sitting on the couch with her back to me, her hair piled on top of her head in a messy bun still dressed in her skin tight pants with a black sweater that even though I can't see, I know has a low-hanging cleavage-revealing neck-line.

On the same couch is a man facing her dressed in jeans and a button down, rolled at the sleeves and unbuttoned exposing a bit of his chest. He has lust in his light blue eyes and his brown hair is messed in a way that says he runs his fingers through it a lot. I'm not entertaining any other way it got that fucked up.

Kat's blocking his view of me and I'm currently breathing slowly, schooling my features. I've had too much whiskey to get it completely together.

"I'm back," I announce loudly.

Kat leans her head all the way back so I get a view of her face upside down, it also allows the man a better view of her tits where his eyes are currently fixed.

"Did you win?" she asks, again the right tone with the wrong look.

"I did all right," I lie.

Kat sits back up and continues talking to her guest. I move to the fridge and grab a beer.

"Who's your guest?" I ask making my way to them, done with this shit.

"This is Jason Ross, the boys' coach," Kat explains.

"Are we havin' late night practice?" I ask moving into the family room standing behind Kat, glowering at *Jason Ross*.

"He offered to bring the boys home after the play. I guess we lost track of time," she replies nonchalantly.

"I should get outta your hair," he finally speaks, climbing to his feet.

The guy is in great shape and has a few inches on me. I'd kick the shit out of him before he'd know I was coming.

"Thanks for the nightcap," Jason says offering Kat a panty-dropping smile.

"Thanks for keepin' me company and makin' me laugh my head off," she responds while rising to her feet.

"Any time," he responds with a promise of more masking his features.

This motherfucker has balls. I'm so shocked I'm just standing here like a fucking idiot.

He smiles at her again before hugging her. Hugging her! He's fucking hugging my wife two feet from me. Then, while she's in his arms, he opens his eyes and smiles knowingly at me. Before I launch at him he lets her go.

"See you at five tomorrow," he purrs and then moves away from us.

Kat goes to follow him catching my eyes for the first time and stops in her tracks. Jason continues on his own as I keep her pinned with my gaze until I hear the front door open and shut. The blank mask is gone from Kat's face now. She looks terrified.

She moves her mouth to talk and I stop her with a small shake of my head. If she starts with her shit right now I can't be held responsible for my actions. I would never put my hands on a woman, but I will wreck this house in a rage I'm certain she's never experienced.

Kat tries to move around me and I take a step, blocking her path. Her chest is heaving in deep labored breaths. She's scared of me. I know what my face and posture look like right now. This is not Agent Nick Cooper. This is the monster that murdered and tortured people for a decade and he's feeling homicidal.

"Nick," she whispers, pleading with me to stop.

I move into her space and she steps back. I follow. We continue this dance until she backs herself into the wall and panics when she collides with it.

"You're scaring me," she says in a shaky voice.

"Good," I growl and her face pales. "I feel fuckin' scary right now."

"I—"

I cut her off. "Don't you fuckin' think about it. You're not talkin' your way outta this so just stand here and keep you goddamned mouth shut."

Her mouth snaps shut, her eyes remain huge.

I breathe. I breathe and breathe, trying to get my shit together. I can do this.

"You've given me nothin' for a month. I walk in just now and you're givin' him everything. What exactly did you wanna accomplish with that?"

"I wasn't." She stops speaking when I spin and hurl my bottle of beer across the room shattering it against the wall.

"You wanna lie to me? I swear to fuckin' God," I mutter running my hand over my head. "Tell me the truth!" I roar.

"I don't know. He was bein' nice to me," she whispers, tears pricking her eyes.

"Am I not nice enough to you? I take your shit at every fuckin' corner. What the fuck do you want from me?!"

"Nothing," she lies.

"I warned you about lyin'. I'm at my motherfuckin' limit tonight, Kat." My hands begin to shake at my sides and I know I'm going to have to walk away from her soon.

"Please don't hurt me," she pleads with a tone that I haven't heard from her before.

"You just gutted me. You're not the one in danger."

"I wasn't trying to hurt you."

"Yes, you were and you know what? I'm fuckin' done. I don't need this shit. I've got an op to run and I don't need your emotional shit hangin' over my head. You wanna fuck Jason Ross or half the town, be my guest. You're not my wife. My wife would never let another man touch her, much less eye fuck her for hours in my home."

She flinches like I just hit her, but I see a fight building in her eyes.

"You hurt me," she states indignantly. "A month ago you fuckin' gutted me in the bathroom. How does it feel, Nick?"

"What?" I ask in disbelief.

"You ranted about me bein' your wife and then gave me a glimpse of what that would actually be like and acted as though it was the most disgusting thing you'd ever experienced, kissing me. I've had men make me feel like trash before, but I've never had a man discard me with the ease you did that day."

"Kat," I whisper.

"So when an attractive man showed me some attention I fuckin' liked it. He made me feel good when I've spent weeks feeling repulsive. I'm human beyond anything else. I have feelings and you crushed them. Jason made me feel better," she sneers.

"What do you want from me?" I snarl, feeling infuriated at a level I didn't know I could reach. I'm pissed at her for not talking to me. I'm livid at Jason Ross for existing. But more than anything, I'm enraged at myself for not seeing this.

Panic sweeps across her face and her voice shakes as she answers me with, "Nothing."

"What do you want from me?!" I bellow and move further into her face, her breath brushing across my throat.

"You," she says as a sob breaks from her chest and a tear runs from one glimmering hazel eye.

I watch that tear roll down her perfect face until it drops off her jaw. When I meet her eyes, I see it. The vulnerability I've been begging her for since day one, she's giving it to me. There's no mask, no running into the blackness. She's here and present with me in this moment.

"You have me," I say softly and her breath hitches. "As long as you give me you, you'll have me."

Another sob breaks from her chest as she nods.

"Kissing you was one of the best things I've ever experienced. I stopped it because I felt like I was attacking you. I wasn't disgusted by you. I was disgusted with myself for molesting you. I didn't want that for you...not after the other ops you've been on. I'm fuckin' sorry I hurt you that day. I was pissed at myself and then you went blank on me. If I ever hurt you again, you tell me. Straight up. No runnin'."

She nods again, unable to speak through the tears that are running down her cheeks. I run my thumbs over her face, wiping away the wetness as she closes her eyes at my gentle touch.

"I'm sorry I hurt you tonight," she says softly.

"Don't do that again, Sunshine. If we do this, it's my way and I don't fuckin' share. You're mine. I don't think I need to explain this to you, but I need to know you get how I work. I know that's intense, but that's me. Can you do that?" I'm soft with her even though the words are extreme.

"Yes," she says her voice quivering as she opens her eyes to meet mine.

She can do it. I see the tenacity in her eyes that says she can be everything I need in life. Fuck me but it looks better than anything I've ever seen.

I tip my head an inch and press my mouth to hers, tasting her tears mixed with wine and the sweetness that's just Kat. She melts into me so much so that only my body being pressed against hers is keeping her upright. I reach my hands under her arms and drag her up the wall until her face is level with mine, never breaking our kiss. Once I have her positioned where I want, she encapsulates me with her arms and legs. I slant my head and as I do, Kat opens her mouth without hesitation.

I slowly pass my tongue between her soft lips meeting the tip of hers as she moves to enter my mouth. Our tongues tangle and massage each other's as I grab a hold of her ass and knead the supple cheeks. A moan filters into my mouth from hers causing a growl to rattle in my chest. I'm not fucking her up against a wall. I want her in our bed, laid out beneath me to worship every inch. So I move in that direction.

As I begin to walk with Kat still wrapped around me she releases my mouth, dragging her teeth along my jaw before moving to my ear. She teases the shell with her tongue and teeth as I pick up the pace. When I hit the stairs her warm breath tickles my neck before she suckles and nips the sensitive skin. My dick is straining against my zipper, begging to be released.

I enter our room and quickly shut and lock the door before depositing Kat on the bed, crawling on top of her. I grab the hem of her sweater and pull it off before reaching behind my head yanking mine off. I snake my hand behind her back and unclasp her bra dragging it from her arms. I draw in a hissed breath at the beauty in front of me. She's fucking unbelievable. Perky tits with pink peaked nipples, a slight flush decorating her chest and cheeks. She's a vision of perfection.

I hook my fingers in the waist of her pants pulling them down her legs, leaving her in a scrap of a black lace thong. Up on my knees I quickly get free of my slacks before covering her body with mine, her soft delicate skin warming beneath me, as I capture her mouth and palm her tit.

Her back leaves the mattress as I roll her nipple between my forefinger and thumb with gentle pressure. I leave her mouth trailing my tongue down the slope of her neck to the valley between her tits. I lick my way across the soft flesh before devouring her nipple. I suckle and nip while she moans and thrashes, her nails digging into my scalp.

I switch my mouth and hand and I swear to God she's about to come. Her body is trembling and her hips are rocking against my thigh trying to relieve the pressure that's building.

"Nicky," she whispers.

My dick twitches and I increase my pressure and action with my fingers and my mouth. Her chest is heaving with short labored pants as her head falls back and her breathing stops while her orgasm rips through her.

Her nails bite into my head while I slow my motion and let her come back down to earth.

"Fuck me," she gasps.

"Gettin' there, Sunshine," I purr.

A deep guttural moan flows from her lips as I drag my teeth down the plane of her stomach to the edge of her thong. With delicate fingers, I slide the fabric over her hips letting the lace tickle her legs all the way to her ankles. Then I kiss my way back up her long stems until I reach her bare pussy before placing a chaste kiss at the top.

I push her knees all the way back planting them on either side of her chest. She keeps them there as I run

135

my hands down the backs of her thighs until I round her ass and tip her up for me to feast.

One long slow sweep of my tongue from back to front and Kat cries out, her body shuddering. I continue to lick slowly building the pressure in her once again before settling on her clit. I harden my tongue to flick firmly before plunging a single finger in her tight pussy. She clenches around me and rocks her hips to get more.

I match my tongue's pace with my finger before adding a second and with that she drenches me in come, thrashing her head from side to side whispering my name, "Nicky." I don't let her come down this time. I rip my boxer briefs off, palm my dick and slowly ease it into her.

Kat's eyes pop open and she leans up on her elbows to watch my cock disappear inside her. I'm stretching her so I go slowly, enjoying the show of her taking me. Once I'm seated to the hilt I cover her with my body and enjoy the feeling of her warm wet pussy squeezing my dick trying to accommodate my size.

"Your fuckin' big," she groans with pleasure.

I offer her a seductive smile before taking her lips. She hungrily licks her come off my mouth and chin before ramming her tongue into my mouth and moving her hips to let me know she's ready.

Slowly, I slide out before pounding back in, causing her to convulse in ecstasy. I continue to power into her wanting more, needing to get deeper. Kat wraps her legs around my waist and her arms around my shoulders, clinging to me with desire.

I release her mouth and bury my face in her neck increasing my thrusts, growling like an animal as her pussy closes around my cock and her nails score my back. "Ahhhh," breaks from her lips almost silently before she starts to go limp from the exhaustion of her orgasms wracking her body.

I savor the moment. She's here in our bed, giving me everything. There's no mask, no mark. This is us entirely. I rest my forehead against hers and lock my gaze with fiery hazel eyes that set my soul alight. I'll never lose this again. Fuck the op. Fuck the DCA. I have a treasure in my arms, she's mine. Mine.

As this realization hits me I drop my head back to her neck and surge forward with intensity. Her pussy clamps down on me as she whimpers with passion. Kat's heavenly scent mixed with citrus and sandy beaches envelopes me as I thrust purposefully. She's mine. With her juices drenching my balls one last time, I slam into her, filling her with months' worth of come, smothering my own screams of release into her neck.

Slowly, I rock in and out until we both catch our breath and then I collapse, smashing her beneath me. I know I'm crushing her because her breathing is labored, but she doesn't say a word, just pets my head and back.

When I start to feel like I'm probably suffocating her, I go to push up on my elbows. Kat constricts her arms around me before softly requesting, "Not yet."

I stay still. If she wants me on top of her and inside her I'll stay here until morning.

I start kissing her neck, shoulder, collarbone, jaw and then I take her fat sweet lips. Kat kisses me with passion and want in a way a woman has never kissed me. Her arms and legs are still wrapped around me as her tongue licks and massages mine.

My dick comes back to life after twenty minutes of making out like it's our first kiss. Sliding in and out of her pussy slick with my come I make love to a woman for the first time in my life, wanting to never touch another one as long as I live.

Chapter 16

Kat

I wake up naked, sore, satisfied and unbelievably happy. Nick and I are a tangle of legs and arms as my alarm sounds. I roll away from the warmth of his gorgeous smooth olive skin and turn off the clamorous beeping. Knowing I need to get up and get the boys moving, I flop back in the bed. That was the best sex of my life, bar none.

I can feel him on every inch of my skin, like he branded me with passion. I've never had a man pay such attention to detail, worshipping me. I feel like I'm high right now and last night was an out of body experience.

I was actually scared of Nick when he got home last night. Terrified. The look on his face combined with his looming presence was enough to make me think I was going to have to fight him. That I would have to use everything the DCA has taught me and then some against Nick. That's why I was frightened. I care so much about him, the idea that in that moment he would be just like any other enemy was crushing.

Then I saw it. He was hurt. Hurt that I gave Jason a piece of myself I've been holding back from Nick since last month. It honestly wasn't my goal. Jason was sweet, hot and obviously interested. When Nick turned me down and went into agent mode it wrecked me. It felt like being a hooker at the end of an evening. Nice try but you'd never be good enough for me, that's how it felt.

Jason acting like I was the sexiest thing he'd ever seen gave me a much needed boost. I figured he'd be gone before Nick got home and I could ride the high for a few weeks. A few glasses of wine, good conversation and

139

I finally forgot about Nick and the hurt. Not a good thing because Jason was still there when Nick got home and that about started World War Three.

Maybe it was the push we needed though. We were stuck in a pattern that was sucking the life out of me. Putting on my mask everyday was weighing me down in mind and spirit. I'm good enough at playing happy that no one noticed—other than Nick who I didn't care if he saw it—I was beginning to crumble.

Then there's the op. I'm getting closer and closer with Trish. Well as close as you can be in *Stepford*. Everything's still superficial, but we're spending more time together. We're both on the winter dance committee at Maybelle High, so we lunch a few times a week together with the rest of the snooty bitches on the committee. I'm getting there. I have to believe that.

But I've been frustrated with the pace and combine that with Nick's shit last month I haven't been in a good place. So waking up this morning twisted with his glorious body, aching in the best way possible and feeling happiness beaming from my pores is like waking up from a month long nightmare. Fuck, it feels good.

I push up on an elbow to climb out of bed when Nick's giant hand tags my arm and drags me back to him, spooning me tightly from behind.

"Morning, Sunshine," he murmurs into my neck, his stubble tickling my skin.

"Good morning, Nicky," I purr interlacing our fingers around my waist.

His dick is rock hard and rubbing against my thigh. So much for getting a head start this morning.

I rock my hips back into him and a groan thunders from his chest. His hands move up to my breasts while I reach back and stroke him slowly. Nick made me come last night by working my nipples. I have never experienced that. He's a master of sexual prowess. After months of being used by Marco, I forgot the pleasure possible from sex.

As he starts to work my nipples, I slowly feed his dick (giant dick) inside me. I'm swollen and sore and I don't give a shit. I move my hips against him for a few moments before Nick takes over, releasing one nipple and grabbing my hip to anchor me to him as he thrusts powerfully.

He's slow and methodical with his movement, paying attention to my pleasure more than his. He's been worshipping me since last night. I was afraid maybe that was the newness and months of sexual tension, but now I realize it's just Nick.

My heart hammers as he increases his speed and begins to pay close attention to my clit. The perfect pressure. The perfect speed. This is nothing like I've experienced. Nick knows my body like he's owned it his entire life and is teaching me a master class.

As he's licking and sucking on my neck, I can feel the orgasm building at my toes, a warm tingle of pleasure burning up my body. I arch my neck and he captures my mouth in a searing kiss swallowing my moans of ecstasy when my orgasm quakes through my body. A few more deep thrusts and he crushes his head into my shoulder grunting out his release.

"Good morning," he murmurs against my skin, his lips curved in a smile.

I hear the boys moving around upstairs, getting my brain out of the sex fog. I reluctantly pull away from him, immediately missing his touch. His come is hot and leaking from me…a shower is necessary after three rounds.

"We're gonna fill that nursery sooner than later if we're not careful. My birth control shot just wore off," I say scooting out of the bed.

"Huh?" he asks following me into the bathroom.

"Did you not get the birds and the bees talk?" I snark, starting up both sets of nozzles.

This double shower is finally making itself useful.

"Kat." Nick's tone carries a warning, causing me to turn and inspect his face. He does not look happy. Fuck.

"I'm not supposed to be on birth control, Nicky. I got the shot when I wrapped up my last op. I didn't know I was headed here and jumping into family planning. It was in my medical report. You know the op backwards and forwards...you didn't know?" My voice shakes at the end.

Goddammit, I misread him. I thought he knew and was willing to take the risk. Because why wouldn't an active DCA operative want to get a team member pregnant after knowing her for a few months and fucking her for the first time? I'm an idiot, a classically stupid woman. SHIT!

"I'll call into headquarters and have a morning after pill sent here today," I say blankly before turning away from him and climbing into the shower. Game face on Agent Russell.

I let the hot water wash away my ignorance and quickly begin scrubbing my hair. I need to get out of this shower before he gets in here. I'm running after I promised I wouldn't, but old habits die hard.

I rinse my hair and slather on conditioner before quickly buffing my body clean, removing any remnants of Nick from my skin. As I tip my head back to wash away the suds and conditioner, Nick climbs in. My eyes are closed, but I hear the door and feel his presence.

"Do you remember the conversation we had when we first got here about what we want from our ideal partners?" Nick asks quietly.

I bring my head forward and lock my eyes with his deep dark browns, wondering what color his real eyes are.

"What color are your eyes, Nicky?" I whisper.

He closes his eyes and drops his chin to his chest dejectedly before turning his back to me. Yeah, maybe this isn't going to work after all. How can I be with someone I know nothing about? I know the bits and pieces he's given me, but in truth I know very little. The idiot I've become is getting on my damn nerves.

I shut off my nozzles as Nick spins around to face me. He lifts his head and staring back at me are the most beautiful sapphire blue eyes I've ever seen. My breath catches in my throat behind the lump growing there.

I move to him, cupping his cheeks in my hands to get a closer look.

"Beautiful," I breathe out.

"These eyes belong to a monster, Kat. A monster that died last December. I'm not hiding from you, but these eyes can't be in the world anymore," he explains softly.

I don't understand, yet I do. His decade long op must have ended in his supposed death. Eyes like these would make him very easy to identify. I hate that for him. I hate that he seems to hate his eyes as much as his need to hide them.

"Thank you for showing me," I say, leaning up onto my tiptoes to press a soft kiss on his cheek.

"Answer my question now, Sunshine," he instructs gathering me around the waist.

"I remember the conversation."

"Do you still want that?"

"Of course I do."

"All of it? Kat, I remember every word you said and I'm that man. I'm your man through and through. I found another woman, had to give her up almost as soon as I found her and thought that was it for me. You give me more than she did and I never thought that would be possible. I've had you as my wife for almost three months and the idea of you being anything else is stomach turning. I get how fast this is, but I know what I want in life and it's you. Fuck it's the boys too as insane as that is. I want kids of my own. I want a family to share my life with. This is my last op, Kat. I'll be takin' Shane's job when we wrap this. I can settle down and live a normal life...with you. Can you do that with me?" he asks nervously. I've never seen this man nervous in all my days with him.

He's asking me to give up ops and ride a desk. I'll die behind a desk. I don't know how to live any other way. I love the masks and the change. How can I just leave that behind to be with Nick? Is that really the question?

No, it's not. I had sex with him knowing there was a possibility that I would get pregnant and I never even thought to stop it. Living in Maybelle has given me a taste of real, mask-free life. I'm still wearing a mask when I'm engaging in the op, but at night when I'm home with the boys and Nick, I'm me. I haven't been me in so long I forgot how good it feels, freeing and comforting. Fuck me I like being a *Stepford Wife*. I like being Nick's wife. No...I love being Nick's wife. Because even after everything we've been through this last month I've fallen in love with the man in front of me with no mask on. He's given me all of himself from day one and I've soaked up every ounce.

"Is this a lame proposal?" I tease.

"You're already my wife, so that seems kinda pointless," he says seriously.

"So we jumped from strangers to married and you just wanna keep that as the status quo? I don't get romantic dates and wooing? The heartfelt proposal after years of learning every detail about each other? The wedding of the century with a dress so poofy I can barely walk down the aisle? The honeymoon in the Seychelles? The year of being newlyweds and fighting to figure out how to make our marriage work, while buying our first home and planning a family? We just jump to the end?"

"Wooing?" he asks with a smirk.

"Wooing," I say sternly.

"I don't need to *woo* you, Sunshine. You're already mine," he points out with a brow raised.

"Okay, what about the rest?" I ask in a huff since he's avoiding me.

"Do you want the rest? Do you wanna lose me for a few years while we go back to square one? Wait two years until I've earned the honor of asking you to be my wife? The stress and exhaustion of plannin' a wedding that neither of us have family to involve in? The two days it takes to travel to the Seychelles when we can be buried in each other in any room in the world because all we need is each other? We've already learned the lessons of newlyweds so I consider that part squashed. So?" he asks with a cocky smirk on his lips.

He runs shit. Fucker.

"Maybe I do," I state defiantly, offering him a glare.

"Okay. I'll ask you out on a date in a year or so when we're done here. Since you're still an active field agent, hopefully we'll get a week before I have to send you on a new op. Then when you get back we'll see if your schedule allows for a few more dates. Maybe by the time you're aging out of the program at thirty-seven we'll have a chance," he replies blankly.

I pinch his side as hard as I can and he flinches away, shock spreading across his face.

"Ow! What the hell?" he grumbles rubbing the spot I've just bruised.

"You. You're a mindfuck! Fine, I'll be your wife because all the other options don't work in reality. Thanks for bein' so sweet about it all," I huff and pull away from him.

He could use some work on his people skills. At least I can fake it.

Chapter 17

Kat

I stomp into the dressing room to get clothes on quickly because I'm seriously behind schedule now. A simple emerald green cable knit sweater dress and knee high Jimmy Choo black boots are a simple decision. I pull everything on over my bra, thong and stockings before racing to my vanity to do a rush job on my hair and make-up.

"You know I'm not sweet, but I'm sorry if that was too harsh for you," Nick states, prowling toward me from his dressing room.

I watch him stride confidently in the mirror. His black slacks unbuttoned and his barely blue pinstriped shirt open and floating out from his perfectly sculpted torso. Fuck, he's hot.

He stops a few feet back and talks to me through the mirror while buttoning his shirt, his fake brown eyes holding mine.

"If you wanna slow down and go back to what we were, that's up to you. I won't push you if this is too much, even if it's what I want. But please don't get a morning after pill. Enough lives have been lost at both our hands...I can't bear the idea of us doing that to something that could turn into a life. It's too much for me. We may be able to get you the pill or maybe another shot, but it's iffy. The op is set up for infertility and if we move in that direction you can't have any birth control in your system. I can't take the risk of condoms bein' in the house with the boys here or if anyone ever gets in the house to check us out...it's a bad idea."

"Mindfuck," I mumble as I finish my mascara before turning to face him.

"So you wanna go back to our sexless marriage?" I ask with my brow raised.

"No," he states emphatically.

"And you don't care if you just got me pregnant?"

"No," he responds immediately his eyes and nostrils flaring.

"And if I'm not pregnant, you realize that I will be sooner rather than later if we don't use some form of birth control?"

"Yes. Though my best friend used some weird form of birth control where you time your sex with all kinds of stuff like your body temperature, ovulation and other shit. I could ask her about it," he says with a shrug.

"The woman you lost?" I ask softly.

"I didn't lose Shanny. She's still my best friend and always will be. But not bein' with her got me you and I'm good with that trade."

"See, you can be sweet," I say walking to him and wrapping my arms around his neck, enjoying my heels bringing me closer to his height. "Did her weird birth control work?"

"She's pregnant with twins and has a five-month old," he says through a chuckle.

"Jesus Christ! Are you sure you didn't misunderstand what she was doin'? Maybe she was tryin' some super fertility regimen."

"It's a long story. I think she got knocked up with the twins before starting the birth control thing."

"Well, you can ask her if you want, but I'm skeptical. Even still, there's a good chance I'll end up knocked up like your friend. You sure you're good with that?"

"Yes," he mumbles before pressing his lips to mine in a chaste reassuring kiss. He pulls back an inch and asks, "Are you?"

"It would change everything for me. There's no way I could go out into the field and leave a baby behind. But I'm not cut out for a desk so I don't know what I'd do without the field. That said I *want* to be a mother so

148

badly that I'd give up everything to have it. So yes, I'm good with whatever happens, but I'll probably have multiple freak outs."

"You're a good housewife. I like you bein' *my* housewife. You could retire after this op. I know this is a lot so don't make any decisions now, but give it some thought," he encourages gently.

"'Kay," I respond as I hear pounding on our bedroom door.

I hurry away from Nick and unlock our door to find four teenage boys looking at me like I've grown two heads.

"I told you she isn't sick," Sawyer admonishes the group.

"Well, we haven't seen her and we need to leave. She's never up here when we get downstairs and she *always* makes us breakfast," Dane points out.

"I'm sorry boys," I say embarrassed that I've left them on their own. Cole and Jake have a game tonight too. I'm a horrible mother and these boys aren't even mine (yes they are).

"It's okay, Aunt Kay," Jake soothes, reading my mood. "We made some instant oatmeal, even put blueberries in it."

"Good for you four," Nick says coming up behind me smelling like heaven, musky and spicy.

"They're fifteen, Sunshine. They can feed themselves breakfast," he chides, pushing me from behind with his warm hand in the small of my back.

"You guys make up?" Dane asks as we all descend the stairs.

"What?" I ask horrified at the idea that they heard us fighting.

"There's a beer bottle shattered in the family room and a stain on the wall where it hit," he says with a dark tone in his voice. I'm guessing that's not the first time he's found a house in that state. I am a total fuck up!

"I lost my temper last night guys. I shouldn't have thrown the bottle and I sure as shit shouldn't have left the mess," Nick states emphatically, embarrassed by his irresponsible behavior.

Jake sweeps an arm around my shoulders when we hit the foyer and pulls me away from the group into the formal living room. He bores his soft brown eyes into mine for a few breaths, waiting for the guys to be far enough away that they can't here the impending interrogation.

"Did he hurt you?" he grinds out.

"No, Jake, he didn't hurt me," I say softly running a hand up to his cheek.

"Promise me?" he whispers.

"I swear."

He wraps me in a tight hug when we hear a throat clear from my husband.

"We good?" he asks in a concerned tone.

"Just makin' sure I don't need to kill you," Jake says grimly, uncurling from my embrace.

"I would never hurt her, Jake. Never," Nick states ardently.

They stare each other down for a few moments before Jake offers Nick a manly chin lift.

As we make our way to the garage where the boys are already in my SUV, Nick grabs my bicep to stop my progression letting Jake go ahead.

Jake stops and turns toward us. His face is ridged and I see the often missing man take over his features. Nick's hand drops from my arm as he notices the change along with me.

"Some kids at school have been talkin' about a rise in domestics available around here. I haven't gotten much detail because what the fuck should a fifteen-year-old care about that for. The pace of this op is wearing me out and you two fighting and whatever else is goin' on isn't helpin' shit. Get it together for the op's sake," he finishes sternly.

"We're good, Jake," Nick assures him.

"'Bout fuckin' time," Jake huffs, striding away from us before climbing into my SUV. I move to follow, when Nick stops me again with his hands on my shoulders.

He turns me to face him before wrapping his big hand around the side of my neck, holding me in place.

"I would *never* hurt you, Kat. I'm sorry for last night and I'll make it up to you. That said, you need to cancel your date with Jason Ross before I put him six feet under and have another temper tantrum."

There's no joke or smirk, he's dour.

"I don't have a date with Jason. It's a team dinner. No need to get homicidal," I soothe trying to pull away so I can get the boys to school.

He keeps his hand on my neck, not letting go.

"Nicky, the boys are gonna be late," I complain, pulling his hand off me.

He ignores my plea and yanks me against him with one strong arm behind my back.

"He doesn't touch you again. He doesn't eye fuck you. He doesn't breathe your air," Nick dictates in a low growl with some fury flaring in his eyes.

"I'll do my best. I don't think I can control eye fucking though, Nicky," I say, again trying to pull away. He just clutches me harder.

"Kat," he warns.

"Do you want me to stab him if he eye fucks me? I don't know what you want me to do to stop that behavior from happening. He's not the only man that does it. It happens. It doesn't mean I'm gonna go home with 'em and make it a reality. Now let me go so I can get the boys to school," I demand, pushing him in the chest with both hands as my horn sounds.

Instead of letting me go or acting like he hears the horn, he devours my lips in a bruising assault, one hand forcefully grabbing my ass the other at the nape of my neck. I no longer hear my horn and melt into him as his tongue massages and caresses mine. Nick pulls my

151

bottom lip between his teeth nibbling and suckling before letting me go.

"I'll see you at the game," he murmurs into my forehead after placing a chaste kiss there. "Don't ever talk about another guy fuckin' you, eye or otherwise. *That* makes me homicidal."

I snicker but nod in agreement. He pats my ass twice, indicating I've been released. I turn and hurry toward the SUV, the boys staring at me like I've grown two heads on top of the two they're already struggling with.

"Sorry," I mutter, speeding out of the garage and driveway.

"Must've been good make up sex," Dane declares with a shit-eating grin smeared on his face.

I glare at him in the rearview mirror until we all fall into fits of laughter. He's right though. Best make up sex ever.

Chapter 18

Nick

Kat flies out of the driveway at top speed to get the boys to school, as I make my way back into the kitchen to get some coffee before I clean up my temper tantrum mess. My dick got in the way of my ability to think about the aftermath of our fight. I never should have left it for the boys to find this morning. The looks on their faces are some I never want to witness again.

So yeah, it's been an interesting nine hours. Let me start by saying Kat is un-fucking-believable in bed. She rocked my world and then some. Then she dropped her birth control bomb this morning and my brain glitched out.

In truth, I know she's not supposed to be on birth control. It was stipulated in the dossier for the op, but I never really thought about it. Never thought it would be an issue. It's an issue now that I've pumped her full of my swimmers. And I can honestly say, I don't give a shit.

That's not true, because if she's pregnant I'm going to want her off the op. I'm aware that won't fly with Kat and will end in an ugly fight that I don't want to have. I also have the overwhelming urge to pull her and all the boys out of Maybelle and live off the grid for the rest of time. I've turned into a caveman worse than I already am.

I meant what I said to Kat this morning. I want her. I want to keep her as my wife without doing all the other shit that leads up to it. As far as I can tell, it's overrated. I can't really date my wife. I've been dating her for the last three months. I take her out to dinner, we've been to the movies, we had a picnic in the park in September when the weather was still warm, and we've had family excursions to the fall festival and a couple hikes in the . mountains. I don't need to start over with her. I'm right where I want to be. This last month has shown me what I'm missing without her. And now that she's willingly giving me all of her, I'm not letting go.

I'd like to put my own ring on her finger and exchange vows for real though. I have no desire to see her in a "poofy" dress. I'd settle for her and the boys on a beach barefoot any day. This relationship with the boys is complicated. We're going to have to leave them. That's going to kill Kat and I won't fair much better. We've become a strange family that works seamlessly. If we could get the three of them emancipated we could take them with us. We'd have to tell them the truth about us and that could be tricky, but it would be worth it in the end. Kat and I need to discuss this and come up with a plan.

I rinse my mug out and start cleaning up the shattered glass when the doorbell rings. Checking my beyond expensive watch I find it's just after nine. A little early for visitors. I peer through the peephole and crack my neck from side to side at the face grinning on the other side. I pull the door open with a blank expression, preparing for any and everything.

"Nick, I wasn't expecting you to be here," Jason says with a sly grin. "Kat around?"

"My wife is not home," I state with a glower, causing his grin to widen.

This motherfucker has a death wish.

"I'll swing around later."

"No, you won't," I command taking a few steps toward him.

"Kat's a big girl, Nick. I think she can decide who she makes friends with on her own."

"She can and does. I, however, don't let men around my wife that have the desire to fuck her. So *you* will stay away from *my* wife."

"I'm the boys' coach. She's their transportation most of the time so I'll be around... a lot. We'll see if she wants

154

to continue our *friendship* after a few afternoons with me," he says smugly.

"You've got some fuckin' balls. I'll put this another way. You come around my wife again, touch my wife again, look at my wife in any way in other than blankly...I'll destroy you. Anything and everything that you love in this world will meet untimely and unfortunate accidents. You'll suffer in ways horror movies attempt to scare people with. Your life will disintegrate around you until I dump your body in the wilderness where you'll be praying for death," I growl.

His face has paled and he's taken two steps back from me.

"You're fuckin' crazy," he says with wide eyes.

"When it comes to my family I am. Get the fuck off my property and don't come back. And if you even think about fuckin' with Jake or Cole to mess with me, the promises I just made will get twice as bad. Now nod your bitch head so I know you get what I'm tellin' you," I command.

He tries to buck up, but fails, offering me a chin lift and practically runs to his SUV. I watch his punk ass speed out of my driveway. Pussy.

Shutting the door, I go about cleaning and getting ready for the day. I can't wait to see what rumors that interaction causes.

I walk into the gym just before tip-off. The boys are in a huddle with Jason, so they don't see me enter. I scan the bleachers to find Kat standing with Sawyer and Dane, bouncing with excitement. Quickly, I squeeze and climb my way to half my family.

"Hey!" I yell over the roar of the crowd as the cheerleaders finish off their routine to the amazement of the boys who are glued to the two girls they went to homecoming with. I think condoms need to be purchased soon for the boys. Maybe I can snag some of theirs...that's not weird or anything. Plus they'd notice when a few were missing. So much for that plan.

"Hey!" Kat yells back, beaming a huge smile at me.

She's wearing slim chinos and a short sleeved cream colored sweater with a low sweeping neck-line. I've already caught a few of the men in here staring at her and a lot of the teenage boys. My wife is hot so I can't blame them even if it makes my blood boil.

So I behave like a caveman and tag the back of her head crushing my mouth to hers in an inappropriate kiss for a high school basketball game. I don't give a fuck. What's even better is she wraps her arms around my neck and leans into me. She likes it. I pull away from her when the lights go down for the team introductions. Kat looks up at me with hazy sex-filled eyes before shaking it off and coming back to reality.

I kiss her forehead swiftly before shrugging out of my suit jacket and rolling up my sleeves to the elbows all while the crowd boos at the opposing team as they're introduced. I'm still getting a few looks after my alpha male claiming of Kat, but no one is looking at her anymore so my plan worked.

I sweep my arm around her shoulders and she reaches up interlacing her fingers with mine. We're still standing waiting for the team to be introduced when I feel eyes on my back. I turn to find Phil standing a few rows behind us. I offer him a chin lift and he returns it with a cocky grin indicating his head toward Kat. That's either props for having a hot wife or props for marking my territory, I don't know which. It doesn't really matter so I smile back before turning my attention to the court.

The starters are all seniors other than Jake so I'm surprised when he's introduced last. I'm even more surprised at the raucous applause that follows his name being announced. The bleachers vibrate with force and my ears wince in pain from the squeals of the girls around us. Kat, Sawyer and Dane lose their shit right along with the crowd. Jake turns his gaze to the bleachers, finding us quickly. The smile that lights his face makes my stomach flip. That kid loves us. I don't know where or what he comes from other than it's deep and dark. Fuck me if that's nowhere to be seen in his eyes in this moment.

I smile down at him with pride like a father to a son. I know Jake's a grown ass man, but I feel responsible for him. And I'm so fucking proud of him right now I can hardly contain it so I put my fingers in my mouth and release a deafening whistle just for him. Kat squeezes my fingers as the boys line up. I look down into her gorgeous hazel eyes where tears are holding themselves at bay but only just. I kiss her nose and she closes her eyes, pushing down the emotion before pulling me to sit next to her.

"That was some show your boy put on," Phil congratulates clapping me on the back.

We're waiting in the gym for Jake and Cole after an earth shattering performance by Jake. I've never seen him with a rifle, but what I just witnessed...Jake has more talent than he gives himself credit for.

"Twenty-four points, twelve assists and ten rebounds...he was fuckin' amazing," Phil continues.

"That he was," I agree, catching Kat's eyes from across the gym where she's talking to some other moms.

She beams me a smile before excusing herself from the group, making her way back to me. Her movements are effortless, yet they seem to require so much. A flip of her hair, the sway of her hips, the swing of her arms, it's all overwhelming to take in.

Kat slides an arm around my waist before sticking her free hand out to Phil.

"I don't believe we've met. I'm Kat Johnson," she says brightly.

"Pleasure's all mine," he says, roughly pressing his lips to her knuckles before letting her go.

I steel myself against the desire to rip his lips off his face and sew them to his ass when Kat gives me an encouraging squeeze. I return the pressure with my arm around her shoulders.

"Your husband kicked my butt last night," Phil informs Kat.

"I'm sorry to hear that. I've asked him to ease up on you boys," she says sweetly.

"I doubt that," he scoffs. "I'm sure keepin' a woman like you in shoes and bags can always use some padding in the bank roll."

I take a deep breath before I unleash, only to be cut off by my amazing wife.

"Actually, we donate his winnings to charity. Always have. My shoes and bags come from the sweat off his brow and he enjoys workin' for what we've got. He also likes the reward of me beneath him at the end of every day. I'll be sure to have another talk with him about bein' so successful at the poker game though. It was nice meeting you, but you'll have to excuse us. We've got four boys to get home," she finishes coolly.

Phil is stunned stupid and simply nods as Kat steers me away.

"I fuckin' hate these people," she grinds out through a smile directed at a group of parents.

I grab her left hand to pull her to me and find it's a little light in the jewelry department. In fact, it's a different ring all together.

"A couple of the diamonds came loose on the other one," she explains. "The local jeweler said he'd have my rings back tomorrow. Gave me this as a 'place holder'."

"Do you like your ring?" I ask wondering if I could convince her to not pick up her old one and let me get her a new one.

"Yes and no," she says with a shrug.

"How's that?"

"Not really the place to discuss it, Nicky," she admonishes, curling into my side a bit more. Almost immediately she's gone, running toward Jake in a full sprint as he exits the locker room. Jake's face splits in two with a wide grin as she heaves herself into his arms, almost knocking him down. They hold each other tightly, drawing some looks from the other parents that are merely trading smiles and back pats with their children. Pussies.

Cole comes out of the locker room and I see his face drop when he finds Kat's already occupied. Fuck that. I move to him in a few strides and wrap him in a bear hug clapping his back firmly.

"Good game, bud," I congratulate, releasing him and squeezing the side of his neck.

"Thanks, Nick," he says with a relieved smile.

Kat passes me Jake and wraps Cole up in her arms with no less intensity than she offered Jake. I grab Jake similarly to how I'd grabbed Cole, squeezing the shit out of him.

"Proud of you," I murmur in his ear before letting him go, again with a neck squeeze.

Jake gifts me a giant toothy cocky grin and I chuckle. Sawyer and Dane come barreling over to us, fist bumping the guys and immediately start rehashing the game highlights giving Cole's performance off the bench plenty of attention too.

I notice Regan and her posse hovering near the exit of the building as we make our way out.

"Can we go for ice cream?" Sawyer asks, eyeing the girls with his big brown eyes beneath his shaggy black hair that I heard Kat threaten to cut in his sleep if he doesn't keep it out of his eyes. Apparently, the homecoming haircuts have grown out faster than she likes.

"You boys wanna go on your own?" I ask knowing no fifteen-year-olds want to hang out with their parents— even if we're not parents—on a Friday night.

"You don't wanna go with us?" Sawyer asks with a hurt tone in his voice and I want to kick myself in the balls. Of course they want us with them. They've missed out on the normalcy of a family outing after a game.

"No place I'd rather be. Just thought you'd want some alone time with your ladies," I reply, nodding toward their admirers.

"They'll be there too. Everyone will be," Cole responds coolly, like he couldn't care less if the girls are there or not. I furrow my brow before Dane explains his reaction.

"You're just pissed because Avery went down on Beckett last weekend. Fuckin' forget about her," he admonishes his friend.

"Was she goin' down on you too?" Kat asks sheepishly.

Cole turns bright red and stares at his shoes.

"Sunshine, kinda my department, not yours," I inform her with a pat on her ass as I let her go and wrap my arm around Cole's shoulders.

"Hey, I know about suckin' dick," she argues somewhat loudly for the venue, causing the boys to chuckle nervously.

"Kat," I chide with my own chuckle as she realizes what she just did and bursts into her own laughter.

I pull Cole aside after settling Kat in the passenger seat while the boys maneuver into the SUV. It has seven seats, but the third row is a little crammed for growing teenage boys to squeeze into.

"So what happened with Avery?" I ask leaning against the tailgate.

"Just what Dane said," he says quietly, not meeting my eyes.

"And what about what Kat asked?" He blushes again and stares at his feet. "Eyes up here, Cole. You're man enough to do it, you better be man enough to admit it and talk about it like an adult because that's adult shit."

His soft blue eyes snap to mine and I see a bit of maturity sparkling behind them.

"I'm not in trouble?" he asks softly.

"For what?"

"For you know..." he trails off unable to say the words.

160

"Should you be?"

"I don't know. Everyone does it. It's like kissing people do it so much."

"So she's goin' down you because you want it or because that's just what you think you should be doin'?"

He shrugs.

"Cole," I urge him.

"It just kinda happened. I was curious and then she was just doin' it," he huffs.

"Is that all that happened?" I ask, hoping like hell that's all that happened.

"Yeah."

"Cole, I'm not your father, but I'm responsible for you and I give a shit about you. I was fifteen too so I know what it's like. I fucked up plenty at your age and I wish someone woulda talked to me before I made those fuck ups. You're too young to be goin' that far with a girl you just started seein' a few weeks ago. It's tempting to just get sex over with, but that's the wrong way to go about it. Find a girl you wanna share that with and make it special. I don't expect you to be a monk. I'm not sayin' wait for marriage or college even. I'm sayin' you get one shot at firsts in life and you wanna be able to look back at that shit with pride not shame. You don't look proud right now, bud."

"You've been more of a father to me than mine ever has been. I'm sorry I've disappointed you," he says dejectedly.

"I'm not disappointed in you. I'm proud of you for havin' the courage to stand here and listen to me. I'll only ever be disappointed in you if you break our rules. You remember what those are?"

"No lying, no disrespecting, no drugs or alcohol and if there is drugs or alcohol and we get in a car are asses are grass. Oh yeah, and Aunt Kay says if we don't keep our rooms clean she'll empty the garbage in our beds and make us sleep in 'em."

I chuckle because I didn't know the last rule. Cole chuckles slightly too, breathing a sigh of relief I'm not mad at him. I clap him on the back before moving off the tailgate.

"Nick?" he calls as I walk away. I turn and see a reluctant look on his face, so I return to stand in front of him, peering into his soft blues.

"You can say anything to me, Cole," I reassure him as I notice he's clamming up.

He takes a deep breath and then clears his throat.

"My parents don't tell me that they love me. I don't think I can remember them ever sayin' it when I think about it. But I tell Aunt Kay all the time and she tells me even more. And I just...I just want you to know that I love you too," he whispers the last part.

"Love you too, bud," I say pulling his head to my shoulder roughly with my hand in his messy blond hair.

Tentatively, his arms wrap loosely around my ribs until I pull him tighter against my chest and he squeezes in return. I look across the parking lot to see Trish Booker staring at me with an odd expression on her face. I hold her gaze for a few beats before slapping Cole on the back a couple times.

"Let's get some ice cream and go home and watch a movie," I say softly as he wipes his face discreetly. I know he was crying and I don't give a shit. There are kids in the world who have it way worse than what he's had, but he still hurts. His pain is no less important.

"Let's watch something where a lot of shit gets blown up," he suggests with a grin.

"Good plan," I reply as I see Kat climbing out of the passenger's seat.

"Everything okay?" she asks sweetly, looking at Cole.

"Just gettin' the birds and bees talk, Aunt Kay," he jokes, moving into the backseat.

Kat quirks a brow at me.

"Let's go get our ice cream so I can go home and practice birds and bees shit on you," I say, causing a chuckle to bubble out of her throat.

I put her back in the SUV before climbing behind the wheel and heading to the ice cream shop, which is packed and erupts in applause as Jake enters. Kat sits in my lap and we share an ice cream cone while the boys sit with us bantering and fucking around like they always do. None of them pay any attention to the girls in the corner. Avery fucked with their boy so the rest of the pack is guilty by association. I like that and Kat loves it based on the satisfied grin on her lips as she watches our boys with pride. Our boys...fuck, I love that.

Chapter 19

Nick

The Booker family walks into the ice cream shop as we're finishing up. Bradford runs up to our table almost tipping it over as he crashes into it.

"Jake, you were awesome tonight!" he squeals.

"Thanks," Jake responds with a kind smile.

"You did great off the bench too," Bradford says to Cole. "Coach Ross should start you instead of Grant."

"Thanks, kid," Cole says with a big grin.

"It really was a fantastic showing, Jake," Trish agrees excitedly.

"It certainly was," Tony pipes in, the three of them hovering above us. I notice Tony's gaze settling on Kat's cleavage for a moment before moving away. Trish catches it too and winces a little before throwing on a dazzling *Stepford* smile.

"Thank you," Jake says politely.

"Where's Annabelle tonight?" Kat asks in her fake voice that I hate hearing, but marvel at every time.

"She's at home with Sarah," Bradford replies. "She's our new nanny."

Ah, a new nanny. Why don't the women here take care of their own children? I grew up in the mob and in the streets. The women I grew up around took care of their children or if they worked a grandparent or aunt or a cousin, somebody in the family helped out. None of these women work and none of them take care of their children. Maybe I'm old fashioned, but it makes me fucking sick.

"That's nice, sweetheart," Kat coos at Bradford.

"Can I come over and play tomorrow?" Bradford asks Kat.

"That's up to your parents."

"I don't think so, son. You have a lot of activities that will fill the day before your father and I are out for the evening," Trish responds without the coo that Kat offered the boy.

"Ah, man," he complains, receiving a stern look from his mother and immediately stops.

"Hey, Bradford, you think your coach would let us come hang out for a while at your next practice?" Jake chimes in.

"Yeah!" Bradford replies excitedly.

"That's a very kind offer," Trish says, irritation hidden on her face. If I didn't know any better I'd think she doesn't want my boys around her son.

We've offered multiple times to have him come over and shoot hoops with the boys or watch practice, always to be met with a polite decline. Seeing it in person instead of relayed through Kat, I recognize the disgust. I saw that enough as a kid. I was never good enough to play with the "regular" kids from school and their parents weren't so subtle in making that known.

"When's your next practice, bud?" I pipe in.

"Tomorrow at two."

"I'll make sure the boys are there. I should get my family home. Glad you could make it out to support the team," I say to Tony standing Kat up out of my lap.

"I'll see you Monday," Kat says to Trish.

"Yes. Perhaps we could have lunch after the meeting if you're available," Trish says in her scary *Stepford* voice.

"I'll check my schedule and get back to you. With the boys off next week for Thanksgiving I'll be busy."

"You can surely leave them on their own for a lunch date," Trish scoffs.

"Of course I can. I just prefer to be with them when they're home," Kat says with annoyance in her voice

166

though covered well enough, I know I'm the only one that picked it up other than Jake.

"You could use some help in the home anyway. It can't be easy to run a household full of strays." Her fake as fuck persona just slipped.

"Trish," Tony warns in a growl. "I'm sorry, Nick. She doesn't always think before she speaks."

Wow, that was belittling. Kat would cut my nuts off if I ever apologized for her behavior and then demeaned her in public...not that Trish doesn't deserve that or worse for what she just said.

"Kat, I—" Kat cuts Trish off, turning to face the boys.

"You're *not* strays. Do you understand me?" Kat rumbles at them.

The boys nod, but I can see shame on each of their faces, Jake's included. That breaks my resolve to keep my mouth shut.

"It'd be wise to keep her on a shorter leash if she can't behave in public, Tony. Let's move, boys," I command.

Kat sweeps her arms around Jake and Cole, stomping away without another word.

"I apologize again," Tony says, holding his hand out to me. I grasp it firmly, showing my displeasure. Bradford looks horrified at his mother but not surprised. Trish is studying her feet intently.

I give Tony a chin lift and then wring Dane and Sawyer around their necks, moving us out of *Stepford's* fucked up reality and into the safety of our family fold.

"You all right?" I ask as we approach the SUV.

"She's a fuckin' bitch. Always has been. Jacked up thing is, she's tight with our parents," Dane says in an annoyed tone that speaks volumes.

"You're not strays. You have a home with us as long as you want it. Don't listen to her or anyone else that says otherwise. In fact, if someone else pops off at the mouth like that you tell me," I instruct letting them go so they can get in the backseat.

I can see Kat sitting in the car fuming. I'm surprised the car's not full of smoke.

"Aunt Kay's fuckin' pissed," Sawyer points out before climbing in.

"So am I," I say in a grunt.

Sawyer chuckles and shakes his black hair before saying, "Tell me something I don't know."

I offer him a grin before closing the door behind him.

"I almost punched that bitch in the mouth," Kat seethes as we slide into bed.

Things were fine with the boys by the time we got home. We watched *The Expendables 2* and ate candy and popcorn down in the home theater before heading to bed. It's like once we're all in this house we can each relax easier than we can out in the world of Maybelle. Kat kept her happy mask on for the boys and in moments like that I'm glad she can. They don't need to feel guilty for her emotional reaction, which is what would happen.

"I'd like to see that," I say pulling her to my side.

She rolls over half on top of me so she can look into my face.

"You think I fucked the op up? I couldn't keep quiet. I should've just smiled and walked away, but if I did that would've told the boys I agreed with her."

"You didn't fuck up. Tony was pissed and made it a point to try to smooth shit over with me. I've worked my way in good with him. If you've fucked the relationship with her, I'd be surprised. She'll probably be here in the morning with apology muffins. Use it to your benefit when she grovels," I say running my hand through her silky golden locks.

"Tony was pretty brutal with her. Well not brutal, but that was rough to watch even though I was fuckin' pissed. I guess he runs shit too," she says teasing me.

"I don't run shit like that. I'd never disrespect you like he did. I'll always have your back and we'd never be in a situation like they were tonight because you're a good person. My wife would never say something that horrible to a bunch of kids."

"No shit I wouldn't," she scoffs. "And I'd cut your balls off if you did what he did."

See, I know her and how she works. I snicker at the thought.

"Good to know, Sunshine," I purr flipping her to her back beneath me. "Let's do something more productive with my balls."

"You want me to show you what I know about suckin' dick?" she asks playfully, threading her hand into my boxer briefs, stroking my hard cock slowly.

"Hell yes," I groan.

Kat flips me to my back and removes my underwear before cupping my balls in her hand, settling between my legs. I prop one arm behind my head to watch the show. I'm prepared for the usual licking and teasing woman usually do and thusly shocked as shit when Kat licks her palm strokes me a few times and then pulls the majority of my dick into her throat.

"Fuck!" I shout, my eyes bugging out of my head.

Kat moves up and down my cock with her cheeks hollowed, forcing down more of me. She gags a couple times, but powers through, seemingly enjoying the challenge. With one hand massaging my balls and the other steadying me at the base, Kat finally fits the entirety of my dick down her throat and then pulls off with a giant gasp from holding her breath to get there.

I'm silent because I have no words. Kat offers me a seductive grin and goes back to work, fucking my dick with her mouth, bouncing it off the back of her throat with tenacity. I feel my orgasm building at the base of my spine and my toes curl.

"Kat," I warn, but she keeps at it. Playing with my sack and sucking me deep. Moments later I shoot my load and she swallows every drop. My entire body jerks as she licks and kisses my deflating dick until she's satisfied with her job.

"Nightie off," I command in a gruff voice.

Kat removes it immediately and sits next to me awaiting further instruction, which turns me the fuck on even more. I sit up and scissor off the bed. I crook a finger at her as she walks to me on her knees.

"Turn around. Chest in the bed. Knees tucked up under you," I grunt in caveman style speech.

Kat bites her plump bottom lip and does as instructed. I run my fingers through her folds, which are drenched before slowly sinking one finger inside her. Kat hisses with pleasure as I work her, curving my finger against her front wall. I add a second finger and pick up the pace. She presses her hips back begging for more. So I give her more. I work her clit with my thumb and drag my teeth down the curve of her ass cheek. That's her undoing. Her body tremors and bucks, screams of ecstasy muffled by the mattress.

I don't let her come down before sliding in. I want to slam into her, but Kat's tight and I refuse to hurt her. Her entire body is quaking in ecstasy as I anchor myself, gripping her hips. My dick is bottoming out inside her at this angle so with each thrust her body jolts with pleasure.

I pick up my pace and pound harder when her moans indicate she's about to come again. With powerful long strokes, I pull her toward me by her soft hips as I surge forward. Fuck she feels good. I knew the moment I saw her body would it mold to mine perfectly. I didn't know it could be this good though. The silkiness of her skin, the curve of her hips resting in my palms like only my hands were meant to hold them, her scent intoxicates my lungs and her cries of passion make me dizzy with emotion. The realization that this is real and I'm finally feeling something good and pure for the first time in my life, makes my heart hammer and my dick surge.

Her hands fly out, fisting the sheets as, "Nicky," moans from her throat. It's my undoing. And while I had planned to pull out until we figure the whole birth control thing out, I don't. I fill her to the brim loving it in a primal way.

My chest is heaving as I bend and trail kisses down her spine. She tastes like sweat and something sweet that's just Kat. It's the best thing I've ever tasted...other than her pussy, which is becoming a new obsession.

"I swear to God I felt your dick in my stomach," she mutters.

I laugh quietly as I pull out. Kat groans in protest which makes me glow internally. I have absolutely turned into a primitive being that should cause me shame, but fills me with something else resembling pride.

"Let's clean up, Sunshine," I say, patting her perfect ass.

"No. Can't walk," she grunts.

This causes a full laugh to rattle my chest as I move to the bathroom. I hop in the shower and do a quick rinse-off before returning to find Kat missing, the bedroom door open wide. I hurriedly drop my towel and tug on my pajama pants before sprinting from the room, a feeling of dread crawling up my spine. I burst into the office and scan all of the monitors for anything unusual.

Kat comes on screen pushing open the back door with her gun drawn. FUCK! I grab my weapon out of the gun safe and fly down the stairs. Kat's nowhere to be seen, so I move outside securing the door behind me and move around the perimeter.

"Don't move," I hear Kat command and quicken my pace in the direction of her voice.

When she comes into view, I see her holding aim at the back of a figure a few feet from her.

"On your knees," she orders.

The figure swiftly complies and Kat hastens her steps. I follow. I haven't announced my presence, but I know I don't need to. She knows I'm here. The figure is small, I'm guessing a female. If this is Trish Booker, shit is going to get complicated.

Kat moves around to face our trespasser while I keep my gun trained on the back of her head. Definitely a woman now that I'm close to her. When Kat gets in front of her she immediately drops her weapon, confusing me.

"Nick, lower your weapon," Kat says softly. I pause a moment until she catches my eyes and I see that we've misread the threat. I move from behind the woman and stumble to find a girl looking at us terrified and shaking from head to toe, barely dressed.

"It's okay. We're not gonna hurt you," Kat soothes, taking a tentative step toward her as the girl jerks away in fear.

"My name is Kat Johnson and this is my husband Nick. Do you need help?" she asks taking another step. The girl's eyes are wide and panicked. She's going to run at any moment.

The girl holds Kat's eyes for a long while not saying a word, only panting in fear. I keep completely motionless other than my eyes scanning for another threat. It's cold outside and I'm shirtless, Kat's wearing my button down from earlier and the girl is in some kind of nightie, inappropriate for her age from what the moonlight is showing.

Eventually the girl nods her head with the tiniest movement.

"Can you get up on your own?" Kat asks remaining a foot from her.

The girl shakes her head no and begins to tremble, releasing a little tension from her face.

"I'm gonna have Nick pick you up." The girl flinches and cowers. "He won't hurt you. You're safe here with us. I promise nothing bad will happen to you. I'm not gonna be able to carry you on my own. I need Nick to do it for me. Is that okay?"

Warily, she meets my gaze and I force my features to soften to a point of looking like a pussy. Eventually, she gives another minute nod. I wait a moment and approach her with caution, holding her big eyes the entire time.

"I'm gonna put an arm around your back and another behind your knees. You just sit tight and I'll have you into the house in a few seconds," I explain in a whispered voice.

I crouch down beside her before saying, "Here we go." I consider going slowly, but I figure she may panic, so I try to go quickly though not too quickly. Her body goes stiff and a yelp breaks from her throat as I come in contact with her. I ignore it and scoop her to my chest. She can't weigh eighty pounds. Her bones are grinding into my bare chest as I swiftly maneuver around the house and through the back door Kat opens for me.

I intentionally don't look down once I have her in a lit room because the girl might as well be naked. I move into the family room where Kat is sitting on the couch holding out a plush throw blanket like she's waiting for me to hand her a baby. I set the girl down and Kat wraps her up tight, pulling the girl into her lap. Once I can tell she's completely covered out of my periphery I move my gaze to her face. Fuck she looks young. She can't be more than fourteen, if that. Even though she's dirty, I can tell her face is pale like a porcelain doll and her big green eyes are looking up at Kat swimming with emotion. Her deep auburn hair is a mess around her head and face. She looks like a younger version of Shanny. I feel my stomach turn, bile rising up the back of my throat. Fuck!

I sit on the edge of the coffee table and hang my head in my hands. This vision is hitting too close to nightmares of my best friend's past. I breathe deeply trying to get a handle on myself.

"Can you tell me your name?" Kat questions in a whisper.

"Dee," her tiny voice croaks.

"Dee? Is that short for something?" Kat asks and I bring my head up to see her brow furrowed as she cradles the small girl to her chest.

"It's my letter," Dee says with a trembling voice.

Now we both have furrowed brows. Her letter?

"Can you tell me where you came from?" Kat asks with an encouraging smile.

173

"I don't know. I just ran when I broke the lock."

"Was someone holding you against your will?"

"Yes."

"Who?"

"I don't know their real names. I never saw their faces in the shadows of my dungeon," she shudders as she finishes.

"That's okay. Don't worry. You're safe now," Kat soothes, finally making eye contact with me. I know, Sunshine...this is fucked and a good lead for us, is what my gaze returns.

"Dee," I start quietly causing her to jump and curl into a ball, burrowing further into Kat. "You can't stay here in this town. It's not safe for you so I'm gonna call some authorities that will come here and collect you. Take you to a safe place."

"No please," she pleads clawing at Kat. "I'll be good. I promise I'll be really good. Don't send me back to them!"

"No one is sending you back to them. Nick and I work for a special agency that helps people like you. You're safe now. I promise," Kat states firmly, letting Dee know there is no risk as best she can.

"You won't let them get me?" Dee asks disbelieving.

"I swear to you," Kat insists demonstratively.

Dee studies Kat for a long time in silence, her green eyes searching for a monster lurking within Kat.

"Okay," she agrees when she doesn't find the evil she's lived with.

I know this seems rushed, but we have to get her out of the house before the boys find her here or someone comes looking for her. I silently excuse myself to call this into headquarters and get the ball rolling. First things first though, I grab a pair of Jake's sweat pants and a hoodie out of the laundry room for Dee. It's the most comfortable clothing in the house even though she'll swim in them, she'll be comfortable. After leaving the pile of clothes on the coffee table I hurry from the room.

I've got a matter of hours before this girl becomes a real issue for us and the op.

Chapter 20

Nick

"Jake," I whisper, shaking his sleeping body a bit.

His eyes pop open and he takes a wide swing at me.

"Jake, calm down. It's me," I soothe, moving away from his hovering fists.

"Shit, sorry," he apologizes rubbing his eyes with the heels of his hands.

"We've got a situation."

The teenager falls from his features and the agent comes into view. I hate seeing it. He deserves the teenage years he's getting here.

"Got a young girl downstairs that just broke out of her 'dungeon'," I say with air quotes.

"Fuck," he groans, climbing out of bed, dragging a hoodie over his head.

"A team's flyin' in to an abandoned air strip about forty-five minutes away from here. I need you to run interference with the boys and anyone that might show up here this morning. We need to move out now before we're racing daylight."

He offers me a chin lift as we quietly descend the stairs. The boys won't wake up. They sleep like the dead. I'm thankful for that right now and need to remind myself of this moment when I'm bellowing at them to get it together every other time I can't wake them up. Daily.

We enter the kitchen as Kat's leading Dee in from the family room. She's absolutely swimming in Jake's clothes, making her look even younger. Her mahogany hair's been smoothed back and piled on her head like Kat's. I'm guessing Kat did that for her. Dee's face has been cleaned making her shine brightly in spite of darkness lurking behind her breathtaking features.

Dee's eyes are locked on Jake and his on her. She seems less nervous and more curious with another "kid" in the room.

"Hoodie looks better on you," Jake says with a kind grin.

She looks down at the navy waffle textured material covering her body and raises a questioning brow.

"It's yours?" she asks in a whisper.

"Yours now," Jake responds.

"Really?"

"Sure, sweetheart."

Her face flames at the endearment. Good God this girl is stunning and her resemblance to Shanny is eerie. I can't shake the feeling I've moved back in time with my best friend. It's haunting and comforting at the same time.

"Thanks," she says softly, staring at her socked feet.

"We better move out," I suggest.

Kat steers Dee toward the garage and Jake's eyes follow the girl's every movement. I'd be worried, but his gaze carries concern like none I've seen from him.

"I'm Cara," she says quietly, coming to a halt and directing her information at Jake.

"It was nice to meet you, Cara. I'm Jake," he responds, striding toward her with his hand out to shake hers.

She delicately places her palm in Jake's and he just holds it. He doesn't shake it or make a move to let go. The moment is so intimate that I feel like Kat and I are intruding. Kat must feel the same because she locks eyes with me almost asking if we should give them some privacy. I know the feeling Jake's experiencing right now. I had it as a ten-year-old boy when I met Shanny and again a few months ago when I met Kat. Something in the air changes when you meet someone that matches your soul. It's a beautiful thing to witness.

"Have a safe flight, sweetheart," Jake orders like a man to his woman, soft yet commanding. Fucking hell it makes me proud.

"Okay," Cara responds with the same blush from earlier dotting her cheeks.

Jake moves his free hand to push a loose strand of hair behind her ear and she shocks the shit out of me by not flinching or cowering, but leaning into his touch. My eyes catch Kat's and I see motherly pride brimming in her hazel eyes along with relief for Cara. There's hope in this moment.

"Bye," Jake whispers as Kat approaches to move Cara away.

"Bye, Jake," Cara whispers back and offers him a small smile that warms my guts.

Kat pulls Cara into the garage as I move to Jake.

"I'm gonna end whoever hurt her," Jake seethes.

I clap him on the back.

"I'm lookin' forward to it, bud," I say through a chuckle. Maybe Jake's more like me than I give him credit for.

I notice Jake rubbing his palm over his heart, the same hand that held Cara's.

"Feels good doesn't it?" I ask heading toward the garage.

"Huh?" he responds in a bit of a daze.

"Your hand feels like it's on fire, right?"

"I guess so," he answers in a shrug and drops his arm to his side.

"Feel that every time I touch Kat. No better feeling in the world."

"Doesn't that make me a sick fuck? She just got outta God knows what and I'm creepin' on her," he huffs and runs his hand through his messy blond mop.

"You made that girl feel good for the first time in years. Don't beat yourself up over that. I'm so fuckin' proud of you right now I'm considering adopting you." I beam a broad smile at him.

His face pales and I feel my grin fade. That was over the line.

"Shit, Jake—" he cuts me off with a slight shake of his head.

"That's...I...Thanks, Nick. That means more to me than you know," he says softly. "You better head out. I've got things here."

"I meant what I said, Jake. I know you're a grown ass man, but I feel like you're my kid too. I'm proud of you every day and not just on the op. Know that," I say confidently.

"Dude, you gotta quit or I'm gonna start cryin' and shit'll get too intense. But just know I feel the same. I've never had this." He gestures around at the house. "If I ever got to have a dad I'd pick you, no doubt. But seriously, you gotta get outta here."

I swallow the lump in my throat and offer him a chin lift before leaving the house feeling immensely better than I have in weeks. I've got my woman, a kind of kid and a great lead on the op. It's amazing what twenty-four hours can provide.

I climb in the SUV where Kat and Cara are mostly asleep in each other's arms. I study the girl's face for a moment. Every feature is striking from the slight curve to her nose to the dip of her upper lip. This girl could grace the cover of magazines...just like Shanny. I keep coming back to that thought. If this is a sign for me to watch over this girl like she's my family, I'm getting the message.

Her green eyes pop open as I finish admiring her. She furrows her brow, wondering what the fuck I'm doing staring at her.

"You look like my best friend," I say softly.

"I look like a boy?" she asks horrified.

"No, my best friend's a woman," I say through a smile, turning my gaze out the windshield and backing out of the garage.

"Oh," she responds quietly.

180

"His best friend is gorgeous, Cara. It's a huge compliment," Kat mutters sleepily.

"Is she as pretty as you?" Cara asks with her big green eyes almost pleading for a yes.

"Yes," I say confidently. "I hit the jackpot with my wife and my best friend. Two prettiest women on Earth and I have both of 'em."

Kat and Cara grin at each other before Cara giggles and my heart stops at the sound. It's like hearing an angel sing, airy and hypnotic.

"How old are you, Cara?" Kat asks gently.

"I think I'm seventeen. I could be older or younger. I'm not really sure," she answers in a shrug like it doesn't matter.

"How long have you been in the dungeon?" Kat continues.

"They took me when I was seven."

"Do you know your last name?"

"I don't remember one," she admits sheepishly.

"Do remember where you're from originally? What state or city?"

"Chicago," she mumbles.

Kat meets my eyes in the rearview. Why is all of this hitting so close to home? I nod minutely to let her know this is getting to me too.

"We'll try to get you home as soon as we can," I reassure her.

"I don't have a home," she says blankly.

"Someone is surely lookin' for you, honey," Kat coos.

"No," Cara responds annoyed. "I don't have anyone. I never did. I probably never will." With that she closes her emerald eyes and shuts us out.

We ride quietly discussing what happened with Cara while she sleeps against Kat's side. Eventually, Kat also succumbs to exhaustion. So I spend the last of our journey with my eyes on the road as much as on the girls in the backseat.

As we pull onto an old dirt road I see the jet waiting in the distance. No one has trailed us. Jake hasn't called to alert us of any issues on the home front. We're going to get Cara to safety and I'm beyond relieved I haven't had to kill anyone to make it happen. The day is coming though and I'm getting more and more excited for the blood. The monster within me is beginning to wake and he craves bodies to torture and maim. Soon.

I park and gently wake Kat, which wakes Cara. I see the panic wash over her features and Kat holds her tightly, shushing and reassuring her. Jess and Shane descend the stairs of the jet and approach the vehicle. I climb out and meet Shane while Jess moves directly into the backseat. I keep a wary eye on the ladies while talking to Shane.

"What're we lookin' at?" he asks glancing in the backseat.

"Fucked up and then some. Her name's Cara. Doesn't remember her last name. Taken from Chicago when she was seven and thinks she's somewhere around seventeen. Doesn't know where she came from before she got to our house. Kat got a bad feeling and checked the security monitors, found her in the back yard. We scared the shit out of her before we realized she was a kid. Held her at gunpoint for a few moments. Cara said she broke a lock on a dungeon she's been in, doesn't know the names or the faces of the people that had her."

"Doesn't matter how long I do this job. I'll never get used to this shit," he huffs with pain on his Ken Doll features. "This is a good lead for the op. We'll get her in with psych as soon as she's able. I don't wanna push her though, so we'll go slowly."

That's a shock coming from Mr. Hungry. Could he finally be pulling his head out of his ass?

"On a side note. You hurt Kat and I'll have you eliminated," he says with no waver or joke.

"What's that?" I ask, taken aback by the forwardness.

"Kat called Jess and asked her to get Kat a birth control shot before we left Virginia. I'm guessin' that means you two are no longer playin' house and are actually doin' this thing for real. I cleared the use of birth control. I figure if you're doin' this it can work for the op. To be honest, if I could pick a man for Kat it'd be you. I wanted you on this op because I trust you above any other agent to keep her safe. I've fucked up with Kat for a few years and allowed shit to happen I'm not proud of. I wanted you to have her back. But if you hurt her, I swear I'll put a bounty on your head with every hit man I know and every agent in the company," he finishes emphatically.

"You doin' drugs?" I ask stunned at his monologue.

"I'm sorry?" he asks confused.

"You're takin' it easy on Cara, backing up Kat and apologizing for pimping her out for years. What's the change?"

"Tell me how you really feel," he scoffs. "Look, I've made mistakes with Kat and I'm tryin' to fix that shit. I'm a little too hungry sometimes and it clouds my judgment, but don't question whether or not I love Kat. She's the closest thing to me in this world other than Jess. As for the rest, my fiancée has been putting her foot down with my shit and I'm makin' some changes so she doesn't quit fuckin' me because that was her latest threat."

"I'm likin' the new and improved Shane Hollander," I say through a chuckle, appreciating Jess and her skills. "I'll tell you this. I won't hurt Kat and I appreciate the threat you've given me. I'm glad you're lookin' out for her, but I've got her from here. You're right to trust me. I won't let anything happen to her at anyone's hands, mine included."

"We'll see how much you like the new Shane when I make my next suggestion."

"What?" I growl, immediately losing my good feeling.

"Is thing with Kat a fling or permanent?"

"Permanent," I answer without hesitation.

"Good. Don't give her the shot. Get her pregnant. The sooner the better, frankly. It'll work the op. You can reach out to the Bookers for domestic help. There's no way you can spin that you're lookin' for a young girl to lock in a dungeon. You've gotta work the domestic edge. A nanny is the way to go."

I stand in stone-faced silence. I don't know what to say to him. I'm fucking livid that he's yet again asking Kat to sacrifice her body for an op. This is beyond anything that a team leader can ask. I can't believe he's even suggesting it. The worst part is, I'm considering it. What the fuck is wrong with me? I'm about to rip into him when he speaks again.

"She needs an out, Nick. Kat loves the job and she's better than any other agent I've ever known, you included. But she's more than this and she deserves a life. She's my best friend. I owe her a life and this is the best way I can give it to her. You can give it to her. I'm askin' you to give that woman something outside of the blackness this job requires. She's been alone since her parents died and this job has become her only focus in life. I know this means a change for you, but you're takin' my job. You two can settle in Virginia and have a family. Kat can be safe and happy. That woman deserves that and so much more. I can't give it to her, but you can."

"I don't know whether to knock you the fuck out or hug you," I grunt. "It's a good move for the op. I agree with you as much as that annoys me. But I'm not forcing her to get pregnant for an op. She's given enough of her body for this agency and I refuse to let her give anything else. I'll talk to her about it and see where she is. We'll take the shot with us and I'll let you know what we decide," I say with a shake of my head. "And if I find out you try to push her into this I'll take you out myself...my way."

He smiles a dazzling grin at me.

"Now I trust you with her life and her heart. Don't fuck up."

Shane turns on his heel and approaches the SUV. He pulls the backdoor open for Jess and Cara to slide out. Kat follows and wraps Shane in a tight hug. She loves him and he loves her in some warped way. I move over to the group to say goodbye.

"Bye, Cara," I say softly, gazing into her haunting eyes one last time.

"Bye, Nick," she whispers. "Tell Jake thanks for the hoodie."

"I will, sweetheart." She blushes when I say it, but not the same way she did at Jake.

"Will I see you again?" she asks Kat shakily.

"Yes," Kat answers emphatically and engulfs her in a tight embrace, but Cara remains rigid.

Kat hands Cara over to Jess, but Cara refuses the contact and just stands next to Jess. Jess doesn't push the issue and they move off together. I see a few people on the plane waiting for Cara. It looks like a medic and maybe someone from psych. God knows she needs both. Shane and Kat talk a bit before the medic runs out to us with a box in hand.

"Agent Russell," he greets and hands her the package.

"Thanks," Kat says nicely and the guy runs back to the plane.

"Nick, have you got anyone left in Chicago you can reach out to?" Shane asks cautiously.

"I'm a dead man, Shane. What the fuck do you think?" I growl.

Kat watches us with big eyes. I haven't given her many details and now this asshole has just opened a can of worms. Dick.

"How dead?" he asks honestly.

"Have you fuckin' taken a look at me lately?"

My natural hair color is back from the blond it was dyed for six months after I "died", but the contacts alone change my appearance greatly. I also had a bump removed from my nose. Those two changes allow me to move through life without looking over my shoulder too much. That and the fact that the people that would want to kill me if they knew I was alive are either in prison or idiots that couldn't pull off the hit necessary to take me out.

Even so, I'm a dead man in Chicago. Well...mostly dead.

"You're right. Sorry. I just thought if you could dig back into Chicago we could figure Cara out quicker. If she's been gone a decade this is gonna be difficult," he says backing off.

"I've got a guy I can reach out to, but it'll be expensive," I huff at the prospect.

"Budget is a non-issue. But don't risk your safety. We can work this ourselves."

"Mindfuck," I mutter and Kat giggles.

"I'll talk to you soon, Shane," Kat says through a giant smile before nuzzling into his chest.

I stamp down the feeling in my gut, knowing he's been her friend for years. I still don't want her touching him like that. Now I know why Shanny's man always looks at me like he wants to eat me for breakfast. Not that I'll stop hugging my best friend for his benefit, but I get it now.

"Keep her safe," Shane orders as Kat disappears into the SUV. "Jake too."

"I will. I'll let you know what my guy in Chicago says. I'd tell you to be gentle with Cara, but Jess seems to have your ass under control," I say through a cocky grin.

"Wait till Kat has you by the balls. You won't think it's so funny then," he chides through a kind smile glancing at his friend. I snort, but fear he's right.

"Safe flight." I offer him a low wave and join my wife. Time to kick this op into high gear.

As I drive away, Kat interlaces our fingers and I pull our hands into my lap. She's pissed and relieved just like me. It's nice to have someone to share the op with. I'm done being alone. I have a family now...and I may be adding to it sooner than later.

Chapter 21

Kat

Nick and I amble into the house, exhausted and bone weary. Jake comes charging into the kitchen from the family room looking as worn out as us.

"She okay?" he asks me urgently.

Jake is smitten and I love it and hate it. I love it because he was soft and strong for her at the same time. He was a man caring for a woman that he had an instant connection with. It was beautiful to witness. I hate it because if he tries to go after her, it'll be a rough time for the two of them. Jake comes from ugly and Cara's been in a living nightmare for a decade. I can only hope maybe they'll heal each other.

"She will be," I say through a sad smile. He nods in understanding.

"Let's make pancakes," I encourage, hoping it will get all of us out of our haze.

"How about Jake and I make pancakes and you grab a shower?" Nick murmurs into my hair.

"'Kay."

"You know how to make pancakes?" Nick asks Jake, letting me go.

"No," Jake says through a laugh as they go off to make some surely disgusting pancakes.

I climb into the shower and scald my skin trying to wash the night from my mind and my body. When I locked eyes with Cara for the first time in the back yard, I felt like I'd been shot. It jolted me in a way I wasn't prepared for. I expect the unexpected at every turn, but I never thought I'd find a kid in our backyard basically naked running for her life. Some sick fuck in Maybelle had her as a sex slave for a decade. When I find him...I can't even formulate a proper punishment but it will be gruesome.

The only good thing about finding Cara was getting the chance to see Shane and Jess. Not that I got to talk to them much, but just seeing their faces gave me a piece of joy that I miss when I'm away from them. Shane and Nick seemed to have a heated discussion while Jess and I were in the SUV with Cara. I didn't pay much attention because we were trying to get Cara comfortable with Jess, but Nick definitely looked pissed a few times while Shane was talking. Shane also looked tense. I hope they worked out whatever they needed to because it'll make the op a pain in the ass if they're butting heads.

The strangest part of this whole thing is Cara. She looks like the pictures I've seen of Nick's best friend Shannon Kelly. Even in blurry cell phone pictures the woman is drop dead fucking gorgeous and Cara is right on par with her. Nick looked like he'd been stabbed in the gut when he got a good look at Cara. I hurt for him in that moment. I hurt for him now as I remember the anguish washing out his always strong features.

I have the feeling we're up against more than we know with this and I hope it doesn't destroy the people I've fallen in love with. I'll protect what's mine to the death and I fear that tenacity could end up costing me everything. But more than fear, I feel strength in knowing I have a family to love and a family that loves me. My parents are gone and I've hidden myself away from anything resembling a family since the day I entered the DCA. I told myself it was because I was a good agent and I needed to be completely unattached to be the best I could be. All bullshit when I think about it. When you lose everything you love, you tend to not want to love anything again. I love Shane and Jess, but what I feel for the boys and Nick goes beyond. It fills the cracks that my parents left. It's healed my heart and opened my soul to the possibility of moving forward.

I roll out of the shower feeling better, but still wiped. I'll be napping today. I pull on my go-to pricey leggings and the biggest fluffiest heather grey sweater I have. I'm actually comfortable in my clothes and with my toes warming in a pair of sweater boots I feel normal. I don't give a crap if my outfit goes against the manual or if the entire town sees me and decides I'm no better than shit on the bottom of their shoes. I feel good and that's all that matters right now.

I don't put on any make-up and just pile my half-dried hair in a messy lump on top of my head. Fuck, I feel good looking like a mess.

I leave our room to be met with the smell of burning food. Yeah, they can't cook. I chuckle all the way down the stairs and burst into full-blown laughter when I enter the kitchen and all five of my boys are in the kitchen, trying desperately to salvage breakfast.

"We suck," Sawyer admits in a shrug.

"At cooking...yes."

"Good thing we've got you," Cole says in relief like he was afraid he was going to starve.

"You've got me," I say, pressing a kiss to his flour-covered cheek.

It looks like a bomb of ingredients has gone off in here. I think I spy some batter on the ceiling too. What the hell have they been doing?

"Hey, mine turned out okay," Dane protests.

"You mixed up the sugar and the salt. It tastes like shit," Jake says pointedly.

"At least it's not burnt," he says shoveling a bite in his mouth and then immediately spits it out. "Yeah, that tastes like ass."

"Tasted a lot of ass?" Sawyer snarks.

"Only when I kiss you," Dane fires back.

We all fall into laughter as I wrap my arms around Nick's waist. He's trying at the stove, but I can tell he's just burning more food.

"Why don't you let me take over?"

189

"I'm a failure as a husband," he huffs as he turns around.

He looks down at me and his breath hitches at my appearance.

"I know I look like crap, but I'm too tired to care," I explain.

"I've never seen you look better," he says in a husky sex-filled voice.

Oh.

"Oh."

Nick slams his mouth on mine as he picks me up under my arms. I dutifully wrap my arms around his neck and my legs around his waist as he palms my ass aggressively. He slants his head and plunges his tongue into my mouth. A moan purrs from my throat and coaxes a groan from him. Whistles and cheers break out behind us and I start to laugh again. Nick follows me with a chuckle deep within his chest as I slide down his body. He pats my ass twice before I move to the island to fix our pancake mess. Okay, there's no fixing, I just have to start over.

My pancakes are a success, much to the glee of my boys. Our doorbell rings as the boys are finishing cleaning up the giant mess that they created in the kitchen. Nick stalks to the door his mask firmly in place. I can only imagine who's here. If it's Trish and her apology muffins, I may choke her to death with them. I'm not in the mood today.

"Kat," Nick bellows and I hurry toward him. Jake and the boys fall in step behind me.

Cock sucking Officer Burke is at our door with sweet Officer Harrison. Game face on Kat.

"Good morning, officers," I greet them brightly.

Nick sweeps me to his side.

"Missus Johnson," Officer Harrison responds with a kind smile.

"How can we help you?" I ask knowing why they're here.

190

"There was a report of a suspicious person in the neighborhood last night. We're just making the rounds to see if anyone saw anything unusual."

"I didn't," I lie. "Boys did you see anything unusual last night?"

"No," they answer in unison.

"Like I told you," Nick grunts. "We didn't see anything."

Burke glowers at Nick and Nick rumbles with tension.

"Well, we'll be in contact if any of us remember anything. If there's nothing else, we have a food explosion to clean up," I say sweetly.

"Ma'am." Officer Harrison offers a departing nod. "Great game last night boys."

"Thanks," Jake and Cole reply in harmony.

They turn off our porch and climb in their cruiser with Nick and I watching them retreat. Once they're out of our driveway Nick shuts the door and releases a giant breath. The boys left when the cops did and are either cleaning or making another mess based on the noise filtering in from the kitchen.

"Go take a nap, Nicky," I suggest running a hand up to his cheek.

"Come with me," he murmurs into my palm.

"The boys need me."

"They'll survive a few hours on their own," he assures me while tugging me up the stairs. "Boys we're gonna take a nap. Don't burn the place down."

"'Kay," a few of them yell back.

Nick shuts and locks the door before backing me to the bed and collapses on top of me when my knees hit the edge. His large hands run beneath my sweater and palm my breasts as his mouth teases my jaw.

"This isn't napping," I chide weakly.

"I'll be quick," he mumbles into my neck.

"A true romantic," I tease and then moan as he pinches my nipples and rolls them.

I stop talking because Nick captures my mouth in a rough kiss at the same time he threads a hand into my pants and a finger deep inside me. His tongue matches his thrusts and I'm writhing in moments. Okay, quick it is. Nick adds a second finger curling them up to hit my spot while he circles my clit with his thumb. Oh, that's it. I buck my hips and encourage him onward as I suck his tongue causing a growl to roar from his throat.

"Shit," I sigh as my orgasm lights from my core.

Before I have a sense of what's going on I'm naked and so is Nick, thrusting in me.

"Fuck," he groans as I lift my pelvis to meet him stroke for stroke.

Nick buries his head in my neck and pounds me in such a quick pace that I have to give up meeting his thrusts. I wrap my legs around him and he threads his arm below my lower back pulling me flush with him as he drives into me. He's panting in my neck, his breath warming my skin as his fingers dig into my hip. He's grinding into my clit and bringing a second orgasm my way quickly. My eyes roll back in my head as I arch off the mattress, clenching around his dick.

Nick reaches a fevered pace, plowing into me. I hold onto his sculpted back loving every ridge and ripple. There's a sheen of sweat covering his skin causing his musky manly scent to fill our room, intoxicating my senses. I do my best to roll him to his back and when he realizes what I'm doing he happily complies. I grind into him before riding him roughly.

He encourages my pace with his hands on my hips as he sits forward to capture my nipple between his lips. His stubble scuffs my skin adding to the warm sensation of his mouth devouring me. I dig my nails into his scalp as I feel yet another orgasm building. Nick's hips power up from below me almost throwing me off him as he collapses to his back pulling me down on top of him.

I hold myself in place over him and let him lead. I offer him my mouth and he takes it aggressively while he gifts me with a swift smack to my ass causing my pussy to clench and my orgasm to topple over. I scream my release into his mouth as he finally lets go and fills me with long powerful strokes, groaning in relief.

When his hips still, I collapse, nuzzling into his chest. Nick pulls the duvet over us and a few moments later I pass out with him still inside me, encapsulated in his massive arms. Best nap ever.

Chapter 22

Nick

I woke up from the best nap ever with a naked Kat draped over me like a flesh blanket. I rolled her beneath me and made love to her slow and sweet before I dragged her to the shower and took her again hot and heavy against the cool tiled walls. I'm like a teenager with her. I can't get enough and she doesn't seem to be complaining.

When we got out of the shower, she collapsed naked in bed while I left to take the boys to Bradford's practice. I received knowing looks from all the boys but no comments about my day of endless sex. Fuck, I feel good.

That cunt Trish Booker wasn't at practice, thank fuck. I didn't have the stomach for her shit today. Bradford was ecstatic to see the boys and his coach appreciated the help at practice. I watched and worked some until it was time to head home. Bradford's very nervous looking nanny picked him up, avoiding eye contact with everyone as she did. She scurried around and collected him before he could say bye to the boys. Weird.

Now I'm home in the office getting ready to make an important phone call. Kat's downstairs with the boys in her sexy ass tight pants and giant sweater with no make-up and her hair a mess on her head. It's the sexiest I've ever seen that woman look. Maybe that's why I'm counting down the minutes until I can get my dick in her again. I'm becoming concerned about chafing at this point. I'll power through, no matter.

"Shannon Kelly," she answers professionally.

"Hey, Shanny," I breathe into the phone, relieved at her voice in my ear.

"Nicky," she sighs.

"How are you?"

"Fat, tired, hands full with Johnny who has learned to sit up on his own, preparing like mad for Thanksgiving and fuckin' thrilled you called."

"You're not fat, you're pregnant with twins," I admonish.

"I look like I ate an entire turkey. It's hilarious," she says through a warm raspy laugh.

"I bet you're glowing."

"Nope," she pops her *p*. "I look like hammered shit on crap crackers."

"You're insane," I say through a chuckle.

"How are you?"

"Workin'," I offer little detail. I can't and I hate it.

"All right, Jason Bourne," she teases but doesn't push for details. She respects what I do and the boundaries I have in place. If she wasn't a mother and soon to be wife I'd try to get her in the DCA. Her skills are remarkable and if Shane knew what she's capable of he'd trip over his own feet trying to get to her. She's where she belongs in life though. I'm glad she has my back.

"I actually need a favor."

"Anything," she responds immediately.

"I need Kieran's number," I ask quietly.

"Hang on," she instructs and I hear the phone move around before she comes back. "Just texted it to this number you called on. You want me to email it too?"

This is why I love this woman. No questions, no hesitation, just trust.

"Nah, this is good. Have I told you how much I love you?"

"Not lately," she goads.

"I love you, Shanny. More than you'll ever know."

196

"Well that's a fuckin' lie. I know how much you love me because I love you just as much."

"I never can win with you can I?"

"My team never loses," she offers a very true line that's kind of a motto in her life. "I miss you, Nicky. This is the longest we've gone without seein' each other since I got home," she finishes softly.

"I miss you too, Shanny. I told you this is my last op, promise. I'll be around more. Time to live a more normal life."

"I agree. This shit drives me nuts. Not knowin' where you are. Not bein' able to get a hold of you. Worryin' I'll never know if somethin' happens to you," she trails off with sadness in her voice that crushes me.

"You're my contact if somethin' happens, Shanny. You'll know," I try to reassure her.

"'Kay." She's not reassured.

"Hey, don't worry about me. I'm not as badass as you, but I'm pretty good. This op isn't like others. I'm fine. You just worry about Johnny and the twins. I'll be in Kansas City before you know it and...I have someone for you to meet."

"Holy fuckin' shit! You met someone? Who is she? How'd you meet her? Oh never mind you won't answer me. Nicky...you met someone?" she asks tenderly, genuinely happy for me.

"Yeah."

"Well thanks for all the details," she huffs, but I know she doesn't mean it. "Nicky, I'm so thrilled for you. You know that right?"

"I know."

"When do I get to meet her?"

"Once I'm done with this op. We'll be on a plane the next day, Shanny. This won't seem real until you know her. You'll love her."

"Of course I will," she says emphatically. "Well hurry up and knock off some bad guys and get your woman to Kansas City. I'd like to be able to walk when I meet her."

"I'm workin' on it." I laugh at her exuberance.

"Work faster!" she demands. "Is she hot?"

"Yes."

"Your dick raw yet?"

This is the other thing I love about Shanny. She's more guy than girl. I've never met anyone like her. She has a commanding presence that's peaceful at the same time. I thought she was the woman for me, but now that I have Kat I realize that I can't handle Shanny. I need the sweet and soft that Kat gives me that Shannon Kelly just isn't. Shanny runs shit, until her man puts his foot down. She's my best friend and that's the perfect place for her in my life.

"It's gettin' there," I answer in a chuckle.

"That's the best. When it hurts so good," she purrs.

"Quit talkin' about it or I'll have to go hit it again. I've got work to do," I scold her.

"I've turned into a fiend bein' pregnant. Kel ran away from me two days ago because I'd worn his ass out," she says in a full belly laugh and I imagine her doubling over, her green eyes alight and her auburn hair cascading around her face. Beautiful. Dylan Kellerman has his hands full. I have even more respect for him now. He's a stronger man than I am tangling with the force that Shanny is. I've got my hands full with Kat. The best hand I can imagine playing.

"I almost feel bad for him," I joke.

"Liar."

"I'm sure he's caveman happy."

"I swear me bein' pregnant has lowered his IQ exponentially. It was bad after Johnny was born, but now...it's ridiculous."

"It's biological. Can't be helped."

"Wait 'til you talk to Kieran. He's just as bad."

"I'll keep that in mind. I should get off here and call him," I say a pretty bummed to end our conversation.

"All right. Keep yourself and your woman safe. I hope you have a good Thanksgiving if I don't talk to you," she says with capped emotion in her voice.

"I'll call," I assure her.

"'Kay," she sighs. "Bye, Nicky. Love you."

"Love you too. Bye, Shanny."

I take a moment and let the good feelings I have from that conversation roll over me before I have to call and make a deal with the devil. Well, he's not the devil. He's actually a good man that happens to be the head of an organized crime family. Still, this might be rough.

"Yeah," Kieran Delaney's whiskey and tar voice reverberates through the phone.

"Kieran, it's Nick," I say professionally.

"Man, you're gonna have to be more fuckin' specific than that," he scoffs.

"Nick Cooper."

There's a long pause and I hear him moving away from the laughter of kids in the background.

"Is Shannon okay?" he asks in a growl.

"She's fine. I just got off with her. She gave me your number," I assure him before he flips the fuck out.

"You must be in a fucked up situation if you're callin' me. What's up?"

Kieran is one of the smartest men I've ever met in any kind of life, criminal or otherwise. He can read a situation and people faster than anyone. He's also a deadly fighter and a generally scary motherfucker. I respect him and always have. I've known him for most of my life, while I was undercover and before when I was a kid in a crime family. Kieran just took over a local crime syndicate in Chicago and cleaned it up a bit. He removed the guns and drugs in favor of protection and illegal fighting. He may be a criminal, but he's not morally repugnant like most people in the life are.

"I'm runnin' an op that may lead back your way. I need some background, but I've got pretty much nothin' to give you to go on."

"What's in it for me?"

"Whatever fee you want. Plus an opportunity to squash some fucked up shit in your neck of the woods."

"Twenty-five to start and if I need more I'll let you know."

"Fine. I picked up a girl last night. She's from Chicago. Been missing for ten years or so. She's not sure. She was seven years old when she was taken. Her first name is Cara."

"That's all you got?" he asks shocked at my lack of intel.

"She's been locked in a dungeon according to her. She was in shock and totally fucked up when we found her. Not really a good time to press for more."

"No shit. What's she look like?"

"Like Shannon at seventeen," I say in a growl.

Kieran draws in a hissed breath.

Shanny was attacked and almost raped at seventeen. It's a hard memory for Kieran because he wiped out the trash that attacked her. I'm sure that part brings him joy...I know it would me. But the memory of what she looked like after the attack has to have stuck with him.

"Fuck. I bet that fucked with your head," he grumbles letting me know it's fucking with his.

"Yeah and then some," I grunt.

"I'll figure it out. Give me some time. Quinn's a little crazy with the pregnancy so I'm kinda handcuffed right now." He's happy about it based on the tone of his voice. Kieran Delaney badass master criminal has a fiancée, her two kids—which are just as much his as hers—and another on the way. I never would have believed it until I saw it with my own eyes in September.

I made a quick journey to Kansas City for Shanny's birthday. Shane and Kat about flipped out, but I couldn't miss it. It was a fast in and out that I sold as a business trip to the prying eyes of Maybelle. It played just fine. Kieran got engaged that weekend. Talk about a shock. If a man like him can find happiness and a family I've got hope that I can have it too.

"How's she doin'?" I ask politely. Kieran is as much of a caveman as I am so I don't want to come off as disrespectful, even more after Shanny's warning.

"She's good. Tired and pissed at me for knockin' her up most of the time. Nothin' new really," he says through a chuckle. "Nothin' hotter than a pissed pregnant woman."

"I'll have to take your word for that," I respond in my own chuckle.

"Okay. I'll get on this for you. Send me your contact details."

"I appreciate it, Kieran."

"No problem. I'll be in touch."

We hang up and I feel better than I thought I might after talking to Kieran. I'm ready to be done with work for the day and enjoy the evening with my family. After talking to Shanny and Kieran about pregnancy and babies I realize it's time to talk to Kat about Shane's idea. I feel slightly insane because the idea of getting Kat pregnant excites me. It should freak me out or make me nervous, but it doesn't. I want this life with her. I want everything with her. I can only hope she wants it too.

Chapter 23

Nick

"Can a vagina swell shut?" Kat asks as we slide into bed.

"I don't know," I answer in a snicker.

"I think mine's closed up like Fort Knox."

"Sorry," I say sincerely.

I've broken my favorite new toy from playing with it too much like an over eager five-year-old on Christmas.

"I'm sure it'll go back to normal. Or maybe it won't and I'll have to go get vaginoplasty."

"What the fuck is that?"

"I don't know, but it's a thing and I might need it because your giant dick broke my lady bits." She tries to deadpan but breaks into gut busting laughter.

I scoop her body beneath mine and smile down at her glowing face. Happiness looks so much better on her than any of her masks.

"Can I kiss it and make it better?" I ask with an eyebrow wiggle.

"No."

"No?"

"No. If you put your face down there your dick will follow and I won't be able to walk tomorrow and that's not classy. I think that's a good way to get crotch rot and nobody wants that business."

"Did you just say crotch rot?" My body begins to shake with amusement at the disgusting image.

"Don't tell me you have some weird fetish for creamy discharge."

"Stop!" I scream with laughter and force back a gag. She's cracking me up and grossing me out. We both laugh until my face hurts and our breathing is labored.

"We need to talk about something," I say bringing the mood down.

"Oh God!" She looks at me with wide eyes. "You do have a thing for crotch rot."

"You're disgusting. No, I don't have a thing for crotch rot. We need to talk about us and the op."

"Oh," she says relieved. "Should we sit up and talk or do I need to be pinned down?"

"Let's sit up," I suggest. I don't want her to feel pressured by me looming over her.

We both sit crossed legged and face each other. I take a deep breath and admire the perfection before me. Tussled honey-hued locks, bright sexy hazel eyes, high cheekbones, perfect fat lips, a long slender neck, a body that's soft and firm in all the right places, tits made for my hands, hips and ass too and beyond anything a heart of gold. She's everything I need. I want her like I want my next breath. I feel like a pussy and like I've become the best kind of man I can be at the same time.

"I just want you to hear me out," I lead.

"Okay," she says with a wary nod.

"I don't want you to take the birth control shot you had Jess bring you."

I leave that in the air for a moment as her brow furrows.

"You're gonna have to explain that sentence," she says with a tinge of annoyance in her voice.

"This is complicated and I don't wanna fuck it up, but I probably will. Stick with me here."

She remains quiet so I launch in.

"This was Shane's suggestion, but I've thought it through all day and I've realized it's what I want. His suggestion was that we get you pregnant for the op. That we use you bein' pregnant to solicit domestic help, use that as our in. It's a good plan, but I can't ask you to do something that drastic just for an op. Shane then told me he wants you to have an out. He wants you to have a life beyond the DCA and havin' a baby is the only thing that'll make you leave. He loves you, Kat. He's fucked up with you and he knows it. Your friend wants you to have a life you deserve.

"But beyond that...this is what I want. I want you. I want a life with you. I want a family with you. I *want* to marry you. I love you, Kat."

Her face hasn't changed the entire time I've talked and now I'm fucking nervous. I thought she'd be pissed or happy, but she's blank. It's like she's looking through me. I want to urge her to say something, but I wait. I wait for that enormous amount of information to sink in.

It's been five minutes and we're still sitting in silence. I've gone from nervous to concerned. I need to say something, do something. I have no clue.

"Kat," I whisper.

"Don't," she breathes out.

I freeze and shut my mouth. I'll wait.

After twenty minutes Kat climbs out of the bed and walks into the office, shutting and locking the door. This is not going well. Shit!

Kat

"Hollander," Shane mumbles sleepily into the phone.

"You selfish motherfucker!" I shriek. "Do you have any fuckin' clue what I've done for *you* for the last five years that you've led the team?!"

"Kat? What's wrong?" he asks equally confused and concerned.

"What's wrong? What's wrong?! *You* are what's wrong!"

"Kat, calm down. What happened?"

"You told Nick to get me pregnant for the fucking op! You selfish son of a bitch! I've given you and this agency every piece of me. Everything!" I screech. "I've sacrificed my body, my mind, my soul, my dignity, everything that's good in me."

"Kat, please just listen," he implores me.

"Fuck you, Shane. I cannot *believe* you. You're supposed to be my friend. You're supposed to love me! The one thing I had left in this life you just stole from me. You make me sick!"

"Kat, please." His voice shakes with emotion and regret.

"No, Shane. You don't get to ask anything from me ever again. I'll finish this op because I'm too invested personally with Jake and the boys to cut loose. I don't give a shit if that breaks protocol. I don't ever wanna speak to you again. Did Jess know?"

"Kat," he pleads.

"Did. Jess. Know?!" I scream at the top of my lungs.

"No," he whispers. I feel a slight relief at that but only just.

"I'll complete my briefs with her for the duration of the op. I'll do my op debrief with Hal. Consider this my resignation. I'll send you an official letter tomorrow. I hope your fucking job was worth this. You just tore my heart out and dragged it through the dirt. I'm horrified at you. Goodbye."

I hang up and hurl the burner phone into the wall, shattering it to pieces before releasing a feral scream and collapsing in a heap on the floor. Having this soundproof room is a saving grace in this moment as my cacophonous sobs echo through the space.

The one thing I've wanted in life they just made dirty. Have a baby for the op? What kind of demented fucking shit is that? I feel sick to my stomach with rage and pain.

Nick. Fucking Nick. He starts that shit off telling me what Shane wants and then tells me after spending the day thinking it over it's what he wants too. What woman in the world wants that? I'm not the most romantic person, but that was agonizing. If he had just come to me and told me he loved me and wanted a life with me I would have melted. I don't need much. I haven't asked him for shit. I just want real and happy. I don't want to be a vessel for an op. I don't want to be a convenient option.

I heard what Nick said. Those words were nice. They felt good until I remembered what precipitated them. It's like Shane dared Nick to take the next step. I know I'm hurt and emotional right now and maybe I'll see things clearer once the sorrow seeps away, but I'm fucking struggling right now. How could he do that to me if he loves me? If Jess told me to convince Nick to knock me up for the op, I would have told her to go fuck herself. I never would've asked Nick to sacrifice something so personal for an op. Never. Even if it's what I wanted.

If I wanted that with Nick I would have just told him, without anyone telling me to. I would have led with that before anyone had the chance to try to convince me. I'm sure Nick wants me. I saw the love in his face as he spoke. He believes the things he said, but he fucked it up. I'm too heartbroken to see anything else right now.

I pull my gun out of the safe and attach the silencer. If I have to shoot him...I will and I don't want to alarm the boys. I steady myself on my feet and brush away the last of my tears before opening the office. Nick is leaning against the wall across from me as I exit. His eyes widen when he sees the gun.

"Kat," he whispers in astonishment.

"Don't. If you come near me, I'll put a bullet in you," I seethe. "I can't believe you just did that to me."

I move past him into the bedroom, then the bathroom and stop in the dressing room. I pull on the same clothes I wore today as Nick hovers at the door deciding what to do.

"Please talk to me," he pleads softly.

"You and Shane broke my fucking heart," I say as tears spill over my lids, hot angry pain-filled tears.

"Kat, it came from a good place. I obviously didn't do a good job of explaining it if you're this upset." He nods at the gun in my hand.

"Did Shane say he wanted you to get me pregnant for this op?" I demand.

"Yes, but—" I cut him off.

"See that's where you fucked up, Nick. There's no but in that conversation. I have nothing left. I've given the agency everything. Every single piece of me has gone to the DCA. And you know what? I gave it willingly. I love what I do. But it has a fucking limit. My reproductive life is where my goddamn limit is. I would *never* use a baby for an op. If you knew anything about me you'd know I would fucking die before I'd do that.

"And then you. Jesus Christ, I don't even know what to say to you. You start off tellin' me that shit about Shane and then tell me it's what you've thought about all day and realize you want it too. How the fuck is that supposed to make me feel? It's like you were standing on the edge of a cliff afraid to jump and Shane had to push you."

"That's not how it was," he growls.

"Don't fucking growl at me!" I shout.

"I'm tryin' to keep my shit together. Give me a little latitude."

I remain silent with a brow raised.

"Yes, it was Shane's suggestion and no, I wasn't thinkin' about plannin' a family seriously before he said it this morning. We already had sex and knew there was a risk of you gettin' pregnant. We fuckin' talked about this shit. I told you then I didn't care if you ended up pregnant. I still don't."

"You're movin' between two things that have nothing to do with each other. If we get pregnant because we're together and it just happens that's one thing. Doin' it intentionally for the op is another. The fact that you don't see the difference is a fucking issue above and beyond the rest of this mess."

"I don't want this for the op," he argues ardently.

"No? That's not what it sounded like. It sounded like you found a way in on the op and decided it fit in with your plans so why not."

208

"You're twisting this shit in a way that it doesn't need to be," he grumbles.

"How the fuck would you see it from my point of view? Think about it for a minute. I find out that a person I thought was my best friend just asked my...whatever you are...'boyfriend' to get me pregnant for the op. That on its own is gut-wrenching. Then I find out I can use the baby to get out of the DCA because my friend doesn't give a shit about me enough to just talk to me and let me know I deserve more on my own terms. Then my boyfriend has a convenient epiphany that he wants that whole life with me, baby and all. How would you feel? Would you feel loved and adored? Or would you feel dirty and used?"

"I don't know," he answers honestly.

"Well, I feel dirty and fuckin' used. If you'd come to me tonight and said, 'Kat I love you. I want a life with you. Let's have a baby.' I probably would've agreed. But knowing this whole thing originated with Shane and the op, I can't see past it."

"I meant what I said tonight. I understand why you're hurt. I didn't do this the right way, but it doesn't change how I feel about you. I love you, Kat. I'm sorry I fucked this up. I'm really fuckin' sorry," he finishes in a wounded voice.

"I need a break. This is too much for me to process right now. I'm remaining on the op, but I gave Shane my resignation. I'm done after this. I'm gonna sleep in the guest room tonight. Tell the boys I'm sick when they ask. I'll get my mask back on tomorrow, but not tonight. I can't."

I move past him, climb the stairs and lock myself in the guest room. I push my gun under my pillow and curl into a ball. I want to cry and sob, but I feel numb right now. I feel empty and lost. The DCA has been my home and now it's my enemy. Game face on Kat. One last time.

Chapter 29

Kat

I pull my aching body from the guest bed, hiding my weapon in the back of my pants beneath my fluffy sweater. I hurt everywhere, but it's my heart that's taken the brunt of the assault. So much for a good night's sleep being the cure. My mother always used to tell me that and she was usually right, but she got this one wrong. I know better than to get emotionally involved. One, it's against DCA protocol to become emotionally attached during an op. Two, I lost the two people I loved the most in life and had no control in those losses. I decided when I joined the DCA I would never experience grief like that in my life again. I naïvely believed I could do this, have Nick and the boys, and everything would be okay. I'm an idiot. No, it's worse than that. I know better.

I plod down the stairs exhausted and embarrassed, realizing it's early afternoon. I can do this. It's just another op. I'm the best agent the DCA has ever had. I can play any character at any moment. Damn it, I can run circles around Nick Cooper. He'll see.

I climb in the shower and scour away the anguish covering my body. This is it. The moment where I'll be tested like I've never been before. Shane warned me about this when he inserted himself in my life. He told me one day I'd be on an op and I wouldn't be trained for what I was going to face, that no training can prepare an agent for every scenario. I never thought it would be a moment like this. I thought it would be me fighting a ninja in a pitch-black room (What? It could happen). Instead, my test will be my broken heart and myself. I can do this. I will do this.

211

I can't do this. The moment I enter the kitchen and the boys light up at the sight of me, I know. I can't fucking do this. I feel the color leave my cheeks and my stomach rolls just like when a roller coaster is hovering at the edge of the big drop, only mine doesn't stop at the bottom. Game face on Kat. Come on.

"Aunt Kay, you look rough," Dane announces my grotesque appearance to the group. Nick is finishing making sandwiches for lunch while the boys look on from the breakfast bar.

"I'm still not feelin' great," I lie.

Jake furrows his brow but doesn't comment. Instead, he climbs to his feet and presses his hand to my forehead.

"No fever. What's wrong?" he questions sweetly, peering into my eyes with concern and searching for a lie.

"I hurt all over and I'm exhausted."

Jake's satisfied with my answer because he doesn't find a lie. That's because I wasn't lying. If I'm going to pull through this op I'll have to hone my lying to surpass Jake's detection. He'll be my greatest adversary. No, Jake's not my opponent, he's someone I love. I can't have him in my life for long, this has an expiration date, but for now, he's here and I love him.

I meet Nick's fake chocolate eyes and offer him nothing. He's hurt and I could give a shit because I'm completely demolished. Nick sees that in my face and remains the distance from me my gaze is demanding.

"Sunshine, why don't you get back in bed? I've got the boys covered. Some rest should help." His suggestion is more than his words appear to be on the surface.

"I'm gonna need more than a nap," I grumble. Shit, that's not what I would say. The boys look at me slightly confused at my attitude. "Sorry guys. I guess I could use a nap. I'll come down once I feel better."

With that, I trudge toward the stairs, leading me to the bed I've shared with Nick for months. This always felt like a safe place to fall. After what transpired in here last night, it feels like I'm willingly climbing back into a nightmare. I hate Nick and Shane for this. Absolutely. Fucking. Hate them.

"Don't touch me!" I wake up yelling.

"It's just me, Kat," Jake's soothing voice hovers at the edge of the bed. When I open my eyes his hands are in the universal don't shoot pose and I feel like shit all over again.

"Sorry, Jake. I must've been having a nightmare," I lie.

"Thought you didn't get those anymore?" he questions the lie.

"Sometimes when I'm sick, I do."

He believes this information. Again, it's not a lie. I do get nightmares when I'm sick from time to time.

"You feelin' any better?" he asks softly, sitting on the bed facing me.

"Not really."

"Should we get you an appointment with the doctor?"

"I'll be fine. It's just a cold or flu. Nothin' too big," I finish off rubbing my neck to add to the effect I'm using with my voice.

"I'm sorry you're sick. You want me to stay with you for a while? We could watch movies and I could rub your back." He adds his dazzling smile to his kind words and I almost lose it. I can't do this.

"As good as that sounds, I think I should just sleep some more. Is that okay?"

"Whatever you need is okay, Kat. I just wanted to offer what you've given me when I needed you."

I use everything I have to steel myself against the emotions raging within me and offer Jake a small weary smile. He brushes a strand of hair from my face and stands up. I watch as he walks away and wait for him to shut the door with a soft click. Only then, do I shove my face in my pillow and sob like a baby.

I never knew. I had no idea I could love like this. My entire adult life I made sure I never ventured in this direction. It was unknown and scary as hell. I was right to fear it. I think I'm dying this hurts so badly. I love those boys like they're my own and I'm not going to get to keep them. Nick made that clear last night with his shit. This is an op and we're all just moving cogs within a large wheel. I need some distance from the five of them to get myself back in the game. Once my head's right, I can do this. When my heart is less broken and functioning like it did only a few months ago, I can do this with ease.

"You look better, Sunshine," Nick purrs into my neck and I force myself to act. I melt into his embrace and imagine this doesn't rip my heart out.

"I just needed to rest," I murmur against the skin of cheek before pressing a soft kiss there. In typical Nick fashion he tries to push for more, but I can't. I move away from his embrace and flop down on the couch holding Cole and Sawyer, effectively removing any chance of sharing a space with Nick.

The boys are oblivious and snuggle into me. I was "sick" for a full forty-eight hours and they want their chance with me. I cuddle into a blanket with Sawyer and turn my gaze to ESPN pretending to be enamored by *SportsCenter*. It works on the boys and not on Nick. I don't care.

"Aunt Kay, I'm glad you're better. I can't eat anymore sandwiches," Dane grumbles.

"I'm sorry I left you all to your own devices. How will you ever survive without me?" I shouldn't have asked that question. All of the brows in the family room are furrowed at my question. I don't even want the answer to that question. "You are gonna be in college in a few years." My quick recovery ends the questioning looks immediately. I can do this.

"College kids survive on mac and cheese and ramen noodles. We'll be fine," Cole explains.

"Please don't tell me shit like that. I'll have to cook and bring you food every day. I don't think you'll enjoy that daily visit."

"Like you'd be able to stay away from us for more than a day. You were sick and still dragged your ass out of your room a few times a day to check on us. You probably got us all sick doin' that," Dane pretends to scold me.

"I'll take care of you," I whisper, feeling those damned emotions bubbling up.

"You always do," Jake interjects happily.

"We tried to do laundry," Sawyer informs me looking a little guilty.

"How'd that go?"

"We shrunk some of your sweaters and everything's really wrinkled."

"That's great," I snark.

He chuckles along with the other boys, pulling me closer to him.

"Love you," he murmurs into my hair.

"Love you too," I whisper in return.

I don't know if I've ever meant those words as much as I do right now. When I was lying in that damn bed for two days, their love pulled my head above the waves of despair trying desperately to pull me under. I may not be meant to be with Nick, but I won't leave these boys. They've been left by their asshole parents and I won't leave them until I have to wrap the op. I won't have any control beyond that point, but until that time comes, I'll be here for them in every way I can. I can do this.

Fresh flowers sit on the island in a towering arrangement of whites, purples and greens. I bury my face and inhale the intoxicating scent.

"Nick has been doing this at least once a week since we moved to Maybelle," I explain to Trish.

"That's lovely," she lies. I control my eye roll and set her coffee down at the breakfast bar in front of her. "I wanted to wait until the holiday passed before I came to apologize for my behavior at the ice cream parlor. I can't begin to explain how awful I feel about my cruel words. I don't know what possessed me to speak that way, but I can assure you that's not how I feel about the boys."

"I accept your apology, Trish. I understand how stress can affect a woman in your position."

"It can be difficult at times. I think what you're doing for those boys is admirable. Their parents should be ashamed of themselves. Having strangers take responsibility for their children? Just dreadful."

Notice she doesn't blame them for abandoning the boys, just that they didn't provide better accommodation. Now that I'm in full op mode I'm able to smile a broad fake smile with ease at her disgusting face. It's taken a week and a half and a truly gut-wrenching Thanksgiving to get me here, but I made it.

"The winter formal is shaping up nicely," she changes the subject to the superficial.

"I agree. I'm glad we decided against a themed dance. It's so clichéd," I repeat the words I've heard spoken by all the *Stepford Wives*.

"Absolutely, winter is theme enough. I appreciate you taking the time to see me this morning. I've got another meeting over at the library in a half hour so I have to run, but I'd love to set up a lunch date later in the week," she says through her fake façade that sounds inviting and warm, yet I find it cold and disconcerting.

"I'll check my schedule and let you know when I'm available," I respond air kissing her cheeks and pushing down the puke at the back of my throat.

"Wonderful! Have a lovely day, Kat."

I follow her to the front door and wave goodbye as she climbs in her white Range Rover. Once she's down the driveway, I slam the front door and begin sweeping for bugs she could have left. An hour later I'm satisfied she didn't.

Unfortunately, Trish wasn't the part of my day I've been dreading. This is.

"Code in," the male voice instructs.

"Delta Charlie three zero nine four."

"The line is secure, Agent Russell."

"Jessica Evans please."

"Evans," Jess's sweet voice fills my ear and I steel myself for a battle with my best friend.

"Agent Russell," I reply tentatively.

"Katherine Russell, how nice of you to call your best friend," she drones sarcastically.

"I just completed a meeting with Trish Booker. The meeting was not productive beyond pleasantries and continuing to build a relationship with the mark," I state professionally.

"Don't you fuckin' dare do that to me, Kat. I'm your best friend and some fucked up shit happened two weeks ago. The first thing you do is start a brief without so much as a mention of it? Huh uh. I'm not doin' this with you. Talk to me," she finishes in a command.

Jess has called me every day since I ended my relationship with Shane. I haven't answered a single call or listened to any of her messages. Shane's her fiancé and I won't put her in the middle of us. It's not fair to her and I love this woman like a sister. I have to approach her like a colleague to get through this right now. I can't break again and if I talk to her about what happened, I'll break.

"I've only had contact with Trish Booker one other time since my last brief. It was an altercation involving Jake Rivers and the civilian boys currently residing with us. Agent Cooper felt that the tension wasn't detrimental to the op as Tony Booker was concerned and tried to remove any issues on his wife's behalf. I agree that the incident didn't hinder the op in any way and we can

217

move forward as planned. Agent Cooper can expand during his brief."

"Kat, please. You're scarin' the shit outta me. If you don't wanna talk on this line, call me back on a burner. I'll call you if that's easier, but don't do this. I've got your notes. I'll update the file. Talk to me. Are you okay?" my best friend pleads with me. I can't. Not yet.

"I have nothing further to add. I'll call in on..." I reach over to check the calendar for the date of my next brief. "December tenth. Thank you for your time."

With that, I hang up on Jess and drop my head in my hands. I feel like complete and utter shit doing that to her. She doesn't deserve the freeze out, but I have to be strong right now. Jess is my soft spot and if I get a glimpse of that softness I'll disintegrate. My only option to complete this op is to hold it together until holding it together doesn't take so much work. Right now...it's the most difficult work I've ever done.

Chapter 25

Nick

I stride into the house to be met with a kitchen full of teenagers. Not that unusual these days.

"Hey, Nick," Sawyer says gloomily.

"What's up?" I ask the solemn group.

"Aunt Kay has a headache again," Dane informs me with a grunt finishing off his statement.

"Any plans for dinner?" I avoid the topic of my wife, just as I've been doing for almost three weeks. None of the boys have asked outright what's going on, but I've gotten a lot of looks and grunts.

"We burned it," Sawyer responds, nodding at a plate covered in something charred beyond recognition.

"Let's go out for pizza. Give Kat a break from us for the evening."

"She needs a lot of breaks lately," Cole points out as he shrugs on his coat.

"That's how it goes sometimes, bud." I clap him on the back a couple times trying to reassure him.

"I know," he scoffs, moving out of my reach.

The SUV is silent as I maneuver through the snow-covered streets of Maybelle. Downtown is dripping in twinkle lights, wreathes adorning every door. This place is like a poison dart frog, beautifully captivating and filled with venom.

After we're seated at a booth, the mood lightens slightly. The boys are dealing with the aftermath of breaking up with Regan and her posse. Things were strained between the two groups after the incident with Avery and Cole. He ended it with her instantly. Once Jake connected with Cara he immediately ended things with Regan. Dane and Sawyer followed suit a few days later with their girls. I never knew what it meant for someone to blow up a phone. I'm now intimately acquainted with the term and its visual representation.

Jake's phone buzzes for the fifteenth time when he rips it off the table, turns it off and shoves it in his coat pocket.

"How hard is 'I'm done' to understand?" he grumbles.

"Apparently, pretty fuckin' difficult," Sawyer mumbles around his straw.

"Women can be difficult to understand," I chime in with pathetic words of wisdom.

"You've got the best lookin' wife in this town and probably on the eastern seaboard. Not only that, but Aunt Kay's awesome. She isn't nuts like most chicks," Dane scoffs.

"Kat's an amazing woman, no question. But figuring out how a woman works takes patience and teenagers aren't great at that. I know. I was one."

"Like two decades ago," Dane teases me.

I give him a hard stare causing the group to burst out laughing. I love that sound. It warms me when I feel empty and cold. I feel like that most of the time now. I wasn't lying when I said women are difficult to understand. I wish I didn't understand why Kat's done with me. Unfortunately, I do. I fucked this thing up so badly I'm not certain there's a way back. The last time I messed up with her, I pushed and prodded her. This time I'm leaving her alone. Kat's hanging on by a thread and I refuse to be the thing that snaps the string.

Watching her struggle to get through the heartbreak I've caused is torture I'm unfamiliar with. And I'm familiar with every type of torture ever created and some I've made up on my own. I never knew emotional torture had such power.

So as I keep my distance from my wife that hates my guts, I bond with my boys.

"Were you with a bunch of chicks before Aunt Kay?" Dane's question pulls me back to the table.

"Not sure that's appropriate dinner conversation."

"I didn't ask for details."

"I was with women before Kat," I answer quietly.

"A lot?"

"I'm not Gene Simmons."

"That's good. I don't think you'd look good in make-up."

"Me neither," I retort, offering him a wry smile.

"I think we should try it out. Maybe seein' you in a full face of make-up will get Aunt Kay outta her funk," Cole adds.

"I think she'll be fine without me traumatizing her with that experience."

"You sure about that?" Sawyer questions disbelieving.

"Things have been difficult for Kat lately. I think she took on too much with the dance committee and all your activities. Winter break will be a nice reprieve for her," I explain thoughtfully.

"Is it us? Are we too much?" Sawyer whispers.

"Fuck no!" I growl a bit too loudly for the venue. I look around and thankfully, no one seemed to notice. "Sorry, no, it has nothing to do with you. You see how much happiness you boys bring her. Trust that."

"Kat's a stronger person than you're all used to. She'll be fine. Just give her a little time to recover," Jake interjects his opinion.

Jake's been watching Kat like a hawk throughout this whole thing, but she's done a good enough job of avoiding and wearing her mask that she's got him mostly fooled. He knows she's pissed at me, but that was inevitable. The fact that the boys are asking tells me the cracks in her façade are starting to show through. This could be disastrous for the op. I'm going to have to do something soon if she doesn't get it together.

I'm still being the best fake husband I can be. It's not much but it's something. I love her and nothing's changed that. If anything, her putting up with me and the op even though she's heartbroken and lost makes me love her more. I'll wait a lifetime if I have to, I'll get her back. I can't push this time though. I have to wait it out and serve my sentence like a good prisoner. I can do that for the love of my life. That's what Kat is. I'm certain of it.

"Ready to go?" I ask the group as we finish four large pizzas.

"Hello, Nick," Trish Booker says sweetly at the edge of our booth. "Boys."

"Hi, Trish," I greet her warmly.

"Boys' night out?" she asks too eagerly for my liking.

"We didn't get a chance to celebrate the team's win last night. Thought pizza was a good choice tonight," I lie.

"Well done last night, boys. I'm impressed with how well you've improved. Cole, starting is quite the accomplishment."

"Thank you, Missus Booker," Cole replies politely, even though it's forced.

"Give Kat my best. Enjoy your evening," she finishes brightly before sauntering away.

"I can't stand her," Dane grumbles under his breath.

"She only came over here to find out why Aunt Kay isn't here so she can try to get her claws in you," Cole informs me.

"She can try all she wants. I'm a one-woman man. Speaking of, let's get home to my wife."

They all nod their heads enthusiastically and we swiftly leave. I'm not sure why Trish just approached us, but I fear it's the reason Cole thought. She sat behind us at the game last. Kat put Dane and Sawyer between us and Trish settled on the bleachers behind me. I felt her looming presence often during the game. I just thought she was being nosy. Now I fear she wants on my dick. I refuse to do that. I won't betray Kat and I won't whore myself for this op. Before I met Kat, I would've done anything for the DCA. After my latest fuck up, I've got more boundaries in place.

We pull in the garage and pile into the house, the boys laughing at some video on Facebook.

"Aunt Kay," Dane calls out lovingly when he catches sight of her in the kitchen. The burnt embers of the boys' attempt at dinner is cleaned up. Kat's already in her pajamas, covered in a silk robe.

"Hi boys," she coos as they envelope her in a group hug.

"Headache gone?" Jake asks pulling her into another hug when the others release her.

"No. I just wanted to clean up before I go to bed," she lies.

I take her in my arms when Jake steps away to get her pain relievers.

"I hope you feel better soon," I whisper against her cheek.

"I don't think I will," she responds in a weak voice.

I nod feeling defeated. I did this to her. I stole the glow that beams from this woman and I don't know how to give it back to her. The only thing that brings the smallest glimmer of light to her is the boys. So I leave her with them and go upstairs to get myself ready for bed. Kat curls into a protective ball on her side of the bed every night. Just like she did the first night we moved in. I'm her enemy now. My hands are tied and I'm the person that did the binding. If I prayed this would be the moment where I'd ask for some fucking help because I'm so far into the blackness and I can't see my beacon of light to lead me out. She's been doused by my insensitivity. I've trapped us when I swore I'd keep us safe. I've failed.

Chapter 26

Kat

No, no, no! This can't be fucking happening. I rip open another package, the sixth. I pee on the stick and wait. This is some kind of sick joke from the universe.

Positive.

Damn it. I pee on the other stick from the package and wait. Terror and insanity blurring my vision as I read the same thing again.

Positive.

I feel a maniacal cackle rise from my chest that sounds so foreign as it escapes my lips I fear it's from someone else. I'm in the house alone so I know that's not the case. It's just the crazy officially setting in.

The last three weeks have been brutal. Completely and utterly brutal. I've barely spoken a word to Nick except when necessary for appearances. I've been completely secluded from everyone and everything. I've had a lot of "headaches" so I can excuse myself in the evenings and go to bed before the boys start to notice I'm off.

The first time I had to kiss Nick after everything, I almost cracked. It took every ounce of ability I have to keep my mask in place. I've gotten better over the weeks, but the agony is still heart-wrenching. I'm treating Nick like any other mark. He gets what he needs from me for the op to be successful and that's it.

I think the boys suspect something's off, but none of them have asked yet. Not even Jake. The boys have had their hands full after ending their relationships with Regan and her posse. I'm thankful right now because I have no answers. I have nothing.

"Well, not nothing," I think, looking at the twelve positive pregnancy tests decorating the cream stone floor. This is beyond bittersweet. Shane and Nick have fucked this moment up for me too. I want to be happy and squealing with joy while I run to call Nick and tell him. Instead, I'm locked in the bathroom crying, terrified.

I can't call Jess and talk this through with her because I still refuse to put her in our shit. I have no one. I'm alone and pregnant with a baby. What the fuck am I supposed to do now?

The only reason I bought a test is because I needed to in order to take my birth control shot. I never expected it to be positive. I was just going through the motions. Now everything has changed. This is no longer an op. This is my life and the life I'm carrying. How the hell am I going to do this?

I let the sobs wrack my body until I need to get myself cleaned up to go get the boys from school. I jump in the shower willing the water to soothe away my aches and pains. It doesn't. It gets my face to look okay, but large sunglasses are needed to hide the mess. I'm a damn mess.

I gather up the tests and shove them in a shoebox in my dressing room. They'll be safe there. I take all the trash with me and hide it in the bottom of the large trash bin outside, gagging as I move garbage bags out of my way. Once I'm convinced I've hidden all the evidence, I head to the school. Game face firmly in place.

"Where's Sawyer?" I ask as the boys pile in the SUV, one man down.

"His dad picked him up an hour ago," Cole answers.

"Why?" I ask harsher than I want, but I don't have a good feeling about this.

"Don't know. They called Sawyer to the office and then he was gone," Dane chimes in.

"Call him," I order and pull away from the curb, heading toward the Lancasters' house.

"Tried to. It's goin' straight to voicemail," Jake informs me.

"Call Nick," I instruct.

Jake complies instantly.

"Hey," Jake says into the phone.

"Sawyer's dad picked him up early from school and we can't get a hold of him. Aunt Kay's drivin' to his place now and wanted me to call you."

"Yeah...okay...sure...later."

"He's on his way," Jake says shoving his phone back in his coat pocket.

I pull into the driveway of a large Georgian home with a perfect façade like all the others in this town. I hate *Stepford*!

"I'll be back," I say, swinging my legs out.

"Kat," Jake warns.

"Stay in the car. I'll be right back," I command and he obeys.

I ring the bell and wait with a tap of my foot, my arms across my chest. After longer than I'm comfortable waiting, I ring the bell again...twice. I continue waiting until I'm certain they're not answering the door. I begin to move around the house to look for a point of entry. Something's off. I can feel it in my bones.

I can sense Jake's eyes boring into me as I walk around the house. I wish I wasn't in heeled boots. It would make it easier to get through the half foot of snow on the ground. I have the urge to kick the Christmas lights off the house as I trudge through, but I don't. When I get to the back of the house, no curtains are drawn and I get a clear view into the home.

Sawyer is on the floor and a chubby red-faced man, Harold Lancaster, is kicking him. I run to the French doors at the side of the house I just passed and try to yank them open with no success. I have no weapon on me and no right to break in the house. I'm trespassing as it is. I don't give a shit. Let me get arrested. Jess will get me out of it. She may be pissed at me, but she'll always take care of me.

I pick up a large paving stone, heave it through the glass door and quickly kick away the jagged edge. I'm in the house...somewhere. I can hear Sawyer's whimpers and his dad screaming. I guess they didn't hear me break in. I move stealthily through the large room I'm in, some kind of office or library shrugging my navy heavy down coat. I unzip my boots and pull off my socks. Bare feet are better for a fight.

I pull the door open and move into a long hallway. I head left toward the back of the house. Sawyer's screams are getting louder as is the shouting. I pick up my pace and look around for a weapon as I move. I spy a large silver candlestick and settle on it. It's heavy in my hand with a natural indention for my grip on the ornate spindle. I ready myself for a fight as I move into the room where the assault is occurring.

"Get the fuck away from him," I seethe.

The fat man spins around, shock and rage covering his round face.

"Who the hell are you? Get out of my house!" he bellows.

"Sawyer, can you get up?" I ignore the abuser.

He whimpers in response. I take that as a no. I step to help him and his father cuts off my path.

"I will cave in your fuckin' skull if you don't get outta my way. Now!"

"I'm not worried," he says with a cocky smile and then advances on me.

I tee off, catching him under his double chin causing a good spray of blood. He stumbles back almost falling over Sawyer. The idiot bends down and grabs Sawyer to use as a shield. I crack my neck from side to side.

"Let go of my son," I command in a demonic voice.

If I had my gun I'd put a bullet right between his eyes. Sawyer's quivering in fear and shrieking in agony.

"He's *my* son and you've broken into my house and assaulted me," he rages at me.

"I'm gonna give you one more chance to put him down. If you don't, you will die in this house in about thirty seconds."

"You're fuckin' crazy, bitch. Get out!" he roars.

"Sawyer, sweetheart, it's okay. I'm comin' to get you now," I say softly. His eyes are swelling shut and he shows no evidence he hears me. He's fading from consciousness as his father holds him by the throat, cutting off his air supply.

I decide to make my move. I rush straight at Harold, shocking him. He sweeps Sawyer's now limp body in front of me. I advance again, forcing him where I want him. He's choking the life out of Sawyer. I can't watch him die right in front of me. I fake left and move right, but the fat man keeps Sawyer in front of me. He's not breathing.

I quickly switch the candlestick to my left hand before crushing it into his shoulder that's attached to the arm strangling Sawyer. His grip falters at the connection and Sawyer's limp body falls in a heap to the ground. I strike.

I lift my leg, bend my knee and kick out viciously, landing my foot in his blubbery gut. It knocks the wind out of him and he trips over the ottoman I was leading him toward. He violently kicks and flails to keep me away as move above him. I land a punishing blow with my weapon against his shin causing him to stop and cradle it. I take the opportunity and repeatedly smash his face with the candlestick until I'm splattered with his blood and he stops moving. I don't check his pulse. I don't need to.

I drop to the floor and try to revive Sawyer. He's not breathing and I can't find a pulse, though I don't try very hard. I start compressions while I beg him to wake up and come back to me. I can't lose him. Please I can't lose him. Someone help me! I get to thirty compressions and blow twice in his mouth. Nothing.

"Sawyer! Please!" I scream as I pound away on his chest.

"Kat!" Nick hollers.

"Back of the house!" I bellow.

He comes flying in with all the boys in tow.

"Call 911," I gasp. I'm getting worn out. I can feel Sawyer's ribs cracking beneath my hands as I cave his chest in. Please wake up.

"Let me take over compressions," Nick says calmly, kneeling on the other side of Sawyer's body.

I nod. When it's time for breaths again, I let Nick take over.

I can hear the boys freaking out and Jake on the phone, but I'm solely focused on Sawyer. There's no way the universe is this cruel. Give him back to me! I refuse to be pregnant just to lose a child. My child. Sawyer's as much mine as the child inside me. His black hair is caked with blood, his face swollen to the point of being deformed, his arms and hands bruised and bleeding from trying to defend himself...I'm losing him. I can't lose him. Not after everything else I've lost...please. Please.

"Sawyer, please, baby wake up. I'm so sorry. Please come back to me. Please," I sob in his ear, tears streaming down my face.

I always believed I was only my job. A chameleon moving through life catching and killing bad guys. After the last three weeks with Nick, I thought I'd never be anything but that. Looking at the lifeless body in front of me, my son, I know I'm more than what I believed. I'm a mother. I can't lose my child just as he's shown me my purpose in life. Please, if there's someone out there listening, please don't take him from me. I need him. My son. Please.

I blow two more breaths in Sawyer's mouth and he gurgles deep in his throat. Nick rolls him to his side as Sawyer sputters up blood, coughing and gagging. A loud sob echoes through the room, I'm assuming from me. I throw my body on the floor facing Sawyer without getting in his face too much.

"Mom," he wheezes.

"I'm right here, sweetheart," I say quietly, squeezing his hand.

After a couple minutes, the house is overtaken by paramedics and cops. I stay glued to Sawyer's side as they work on him. He's in and out of consciousness, but he keeps breathing and his pulse is strong. As the paramedics roll him into the ambulance, I climb in behind them. The sirens scream as we fly through town to the county hospital.

I'm stopped by hospital staff as they move Sawyer into the emergency room. I mindlessly take a seat in the waiting room. He's alive. I keep reminding myself that he's alive. We saved him. We saved him.

Chapter 27

Kat

"Missus Johnson," a male voice calls in the distance.

"Yes," I say fully alert as I scan the waiting room. I'm still alone. I must have dozed off for a moment.

"We've moved Sawyer to a room. I'll have to wait for consent from his parents to give you any updates on his medical status," he informs me in a resigned tone.

"His father did that to him," I seethe. "I have no idea where his 'mother' is. Sawyer has been in my home almost every day and night since September. I don't give a shit about HIPAA laws or your hospital's fucking confidentiality rules. Take me to my son!"

"You can sit with him. There are no issues with hospital rules and you visiting him. Only his medical information is privileged. This way," he says, extending a hand for me to go ahead of him, looking a little scared of the crazy lady.

He leads me through the hospital, up several floors in the elevator and then down a long corridor before stopping at a room. I rush in, dragging a chair to the edge of the bed before dropping into it. I scoop Sawyer's battered hand into mine and press a soft kiss to his bloody knuckles.

He looks no different from when he was in the house on the floor, other than some stitches running from his hairline onto his forehead. There's an oxygen mask over his face, monitors connected to wires covering his body, a tube coming from his chest, an IV in his other hand and a few bandages on his arms. He looks horrible. I feel an immense amount of guilt, crushing guilt. I should've taken Jake with me. He could have helped me subdue that monster faster.

"I'm sorry, Sawyer. I'm so sorry," I whimper into his hand.

I lay my head on the bed next to our hands, listening to him breathe and let the exhaustion take over my body.

"Kat," I hear Nick's voice in my ear.

"Hmm?" I answer, squeezing Sawyer's warm hand in mine. He's still here.

"Kat, I need you to wake up and sign this," Nick says softly.

I sit up and find all the boys in the room with Nick and Shane. I offer the boys sad apologetic smiles before looking up at Nick. He looks as bad as I feel. He's holding forms in his hand and a pen in the other. I release Sawyer's hand tentatively, watching for any signs of distress at the loss of my touch. Nothing.

I pull the paper and pen from Nick's grasp. It's a form for immediate temporary custody of Sawyer. I quickly flip through the pages and find where my signature is needed, just below Nick's. Two kids in one day. We're on a roll. I sign and return the form to Nick who passes it to Shane. I'm thankful when Shane exits the room without attempting to speak to me. I'm still furious with him, but he came for me. I see it in his gaze. My friend was here for me when I needed him even though I'm not sure I'll ever speak to him again.

"Aunt Kay," Cole's voice cracks. "Are you okay?"

"I'm fine, sweetheart," I coo offering him a weary smile. I'm so far from fine at this point that I don't even know what I am, but he wants to know if I'm hurt and I'm not physically hurt.

"Mister and Missus Johnson?" a young woman in a lab coat asks as she moves into the room.

"Yes," Nick answers for us both.

"I'm Doctor Willis. I've been given clearance to discuss Sawyer's medical condition with you as his temporary guardians."

That was fast. Well, not really. I'm guessing my signature was just a technicality. Shane may be a bastard, but he's good at this. He probably had guardianship transferred to Nick and me before he got on a plane here.

"Sawyer has a concussion, several fractured facial bones, we stitched up a small laceration on his forehead, his nose was broken and has been reset, he has five broken ribs and four bruised. His lung was punctured from the broken ribs and collapsed. The chest tube will have to stay in place for a few days. All things considered, we believe he'll make a full recovery. At this point he just needs to rest. If you have any questions I'd be happy to answer them."

"How long does he have to stay here?" I ask.

"Once we remove the chest tube and deal with any infections, we'd like him to be tolerating food and fluids on his own before we discharge him. In cases like Sawyer's I expect patients to be here for a week or more. We'll see how he does," she responds kindly.

"Thank you," Nick finishes for us.

Dr. Willis leaves the room and I feel a slight amount of relief. Sawyer's going to be okay.

"Boys, why don't you go down to the cafeteria and get some dinner?" Nick asks, pulling his money clip from his pocket. None of them makes a move to obey.

"Go eat, boys. We're not goin' anywhere," I assure them.

They all study my face until Cole stands up and comes around the bed to me. He pulls me to my feet and crushes me in his arms. I squeeze him back as I feel two more pairs of arms engulf my body. Tears fall from my eyes as their love seeps into my bones. I have Sawyer, now I have to get the three of them.

"I love you boys," I say quietly.

"Love you too," they announce in unison and smash me harder.

I pull out of their arms and kiss each of them on the cheek.

"Now go eat," I order wiping my face with both hands.

I look down at my hands for the first time and realize they're covered in dried blood. I'm still barefoot and my feet are also caked in blood. Shit, I must look scary as hell.

"It's okay, Kat," Jake soothes recognizing my realization. "There's a shower in the bathroom. We'll go eat while you clean up. Nick can stay with Sawyer."

I nod. He squeezes my shoulder before leading the boys away.

"I had the nurse leave you some scrubs in the bathroom. I'll go get you clothes in a little while," Nick says quietly, standing across the room from me near the bathroom door.

"Thank you," I whisper and finally look into his face. His eyes are on Sawyer. His fake dark brown eyes are haunted and tortured in a way I've never seen. My heart breaks for him. Nick may have hurt me, but he loves these boys as much as I do. This is as hard for him as it is for me.

I walk toward the bathroom and stop next to Nick. I pause before placing my hand on his forearm, offering him a firm squeeze of comfort before I move into the bathroom to clean that monster's blood from my body.

Nick

Almost a year ago I sat waiting for my best friend to wake up from a coma after I failed to save her. This is different, and yet no less painful. As I hear the shower flow in the bathroom, I carry the chair Kat was occupying to the other side of Sawyer's bedside before settling in it. I pull his hand into mine and rub my thumb over his scraped knuckles. If Kat hadn't caved that motherfucker's face in I'd be doing worse to him right now.

The scene I ran into is still racing through my head. Jake calls me and tells me that Sawyer's dad took him from school and they couldn't get a hold of him. I wasn't all that worried about it. Sawyer usually goes home once a week for an afternoon to check on his mother and then comes back to our house. It was weird that his dad was picking him up, but I didn't get worried.

When I pulled up in the driveway and saw the look on Jake's face, I knew shit was bad. I sprinted around the house, following Kat's footprints in the snow and came upon a shattered glass door. That's when my stomach dropped and everything started moving in slow motion. I ran through the office spying Kat's coat and boots, bellowing for her. When she responded, I felt relief and terror combined.

I came into the room where Kat was expertly hammering into Sawyer's chest, a piece of me died. I saw the dead body behind Kat and disregarded it as I started working on Sawyer. The pleas and sobs coming from Kat shattered me. She was desperate. A mother's screams to the universe to bring her child back echoed through the room at a deafening level. Sawyer was drowning on his own blood. When we finally got him back...I don't have words. Elation.

I knew I couldn't leave in the ambulance with Kat and Sawyer. I had to clean up the mess. I called Shane and got the machine that is the DCA fixing shit. The State's Attorney's office was first on Shane's list to make sure Kat wasn't charged with murder. An easy fix. Then he set about getting us custody of Sawyer. There's a legal process that should have been followed that I know wasn't. I don't give a shit. He's ours now and as soon as we can, it will no longer be temporary.

"I'm sorry," I whisper staring at his battered face.

Sawyer never mentioned his father being violent. I have no clue what precipitated a beating this vicious, but I'm going to find out. If I discover anyone other than that dead fat fuck had anything to do with it, I'll unleash my monster like I never have.

Sawyer groans a little and moves his hand to his face to pull at his oxygen mask.

"Sawyer, you're all right. Leave that mask on, bud," I soothe, grabbing his hand away from his face.

"Dad," he whispers cracking one swollen eye open.

"Don't talk. I know your dad did this. He's not gonna hurt you anymore," I assure him, squeezing his hand.

"No," he mutters, shaking his head.

He flops his hand up to his face and drags the mask down to his chin. His breath is labored and wheezy.

"Please, leave the mask on. You need it," I urge, standing up to place it back over his face.

He grabs my hand, stopping my progression as I gaze into his tiny slit of an eye.

"You're my dad," he breathes out with conviction.

"Yeah, bud," I say through a smile. "Love you. Keep this mask on."

"Love you too," he says wincing in distress.

"Stop talkin' now. We'll talk when you're better. You're safe now. Get some rest. We're not goin' anywhere."

I put the mask back in place as he barely nods in agreement before immediately falling back to sleep. I press my lips to the least injured part of his forehead as Kat comes in the room. She's in scrubs, her hair up in a towel, feet in fuzzy socks. Her face looks gaunt with deep dark circles under her eyes. She looks like her soul's been tortured and is trying to work its way out of her skin. It's agonizing to witness.

I move around the bed and pull another chair up for Kat to sit in. She regards me cautiously but takes the seat. I go back to the chair on the other side of the bed and hold Sawyer's IV clad hand gently rubbing his knuckles, studying their damage.

"Did he say anything?" Kat asks in a whisper.

"He said I'm his dad and that he loves me," I answer honestly.

I peer up into her hazel eyes. She gives me soft. Fuck that feels good. There's the woman I fell in love with.

"He's ours now."

"Always has been," I state confidently.

"No one can take him," she says with a crack in her voice.

"No one is gonna take him."

"I feel so guilty," she admits sheepishly.

"What? Why?" I ask taken aback. She saved him.

"I should've taken Jake. He could've helped me. I took too long to save Sawyer. He was still conscious when I got in the house. That motherfucker used Sawyer as a shield and choked him to death in the process. I wasn't fast enough."

"Kat, you saved Sawyer. You were unarmed and unprepared. Jake needed to stay in the car with the boys. You didn't know what you were walkin' into. Cut yourself some slack."

She's silent for a few moments, studying Sawyer and me.

"We'll have to work out custody," she says blankly. Her mask is back, cold and devoid.

"Let's just get him back on his feet," I mutter.

She nods and runs into the blackness, leaving me behind with the sweet taste of her still lingering in the air.

240

Chapter 28

Nick

"Get out!" I hear Kat bellow as I make my way to Sawyer's room, causing me to break into a sprint.

I breach the doorway to find Kat making her body as tall and wide as she can in front of Sawyer's bed where she's kept vigil for the last eight days. There's a tall, extremely skinny woman facing Kat with her back to me.

"You can't keep me from my own son," Sawyer's mother, Patricia, growls.

Her blonde hair is stringy from the years of drug use, her frame sickly and drawn.

"Sawyer's not your son anymore. Get the hell out of this room," Kat seethes.

"Mom," Sawyer's voice shakes behind her. I can't see him, but the tone of his panicked voice spurs me forward.

"It's okay, sweetheart," Kat coos at Sawyer.

"He's calling for me," Patricia scoffs at Kat like she's an idiot.

"No he's not!" Kat barks.

I step between Kat and Patricia, looming over the junkie's face.

"Patricia, you need to leave. Sawyer is no longer your concern. Kat and I have custody, you know this. Your parental rights have been removed. Now, I'm asking you to leave without any further scene. Sawyer's been through enough. He doesn't need this stress."

"Who the hell do you people think you are? You move into town and start stealing people's children right from beneath them. I've called the Ashcrofts and the Benningtons, they're coming home from Europe to get

241

their boys away from you people before you ruin their families too. She murdered Harold and stole my child!" Patricia screams.

"Get out," Sawyer growls behind us. Kat and I spin to look at him offering Patricia her first view of his healing body. She doesn't even wince. CUNT!

"You're my son. I'm not leaving and how dare you speak to me like that!" she wails.

"You're dead to me. Kat and Nick are my parents now and they have been for months. I never wanna see you again. You were upstairs while he was beating me to death because I wasn't home to check on you. This is your fault. You almost got me killed. My mother saved me. Not you. Get out!" he roars wincing in discomfort. His ribs are his sorest injury at this point even with pain meds.

"I was sick and you never even came to check on me," she replies in a selfish pout.

"You're a fucking drug addict that ran outta meds."

"Sawyer," she gasps, shocked at his honesty.

"Patricia," he replies blankly, his brown eyes devoid of any love for the woman that gave birth to him.

"I need money," she seethes. "He left everything to you."

Sawyer barks out a laugh and then crumbles in agony. Kat lunges at the bed to help him get comfortable while Patricia looks on without a single concern on her face.

"I won't give you a dime," Sawyer fumes as Kat smoothes his long black waves away from his face. "Dad," he says to me, needing me to step in.

"Time to go, Patricia. If you come back I'll get a restraining order," I say glaring into her hollow dark brown eyes.

"Are you gonna wave a piece of paper at me if I come back?" she asks defiantly.

"No. I'll let my wife go to work on you like she did your piece of shit husband. Get the fuck out or I'll move out of her way and let her get at you now."

Her face pales at my threat before she squares her shoulders.

"I'll be telling my attorney about that threat."

"I'm sure a judge will believe a drug addict over me any day," I snark. "Move!"

She jumps when I roar and makes a hasty retreat.

"You okay, bud?" I ask moving around the bed to take my chair.

"I'm fine," he says through a small smile. "Thanks for that."

"You don't have to thank us for that. We'll always protect you," Kat assures him while she takes her seat across the bed from me. She might as well be an ocean away.

"I know. I'm ready to go home," he huffs.

"Tomorrow," I guarantee him.

"'Kay," he says closing his eyes.

"Sawyer, you said you didn't remember anything before the attack. How do you know Harold was mad because you weren't home to check on Patricia?" I ask before he falls asleep.

With the head trauma he endured, the doctors have told us memory loss around the attack is normal and usually permanent. I'm shocked he seems to have some recollection of the events of that day.

"I remember him screaming 'When's the last time you saw her?' at some point," Sawyer says groggily.

"Do you remember anything else he said?" Kat encourages with a small squeeze of his hand.

"Huh uh," he mutters before giving into the exhaustion and pain meds.

I pick up his hand and stroke the almost healed skin. This situation is horrible, but I'm going to use it for the op. I can approach the Bookers about domestic help now. To be honest, we actually need it...help, not a

243

slave. Kat can only be so many places at once and she's running herself ragged right now. She looks like she's lost a little weight and she didn't have any to lose in the first place. The circles under her eyes are darker, more haunting than the weeks previous to this. She looks tired all the time and that glow she always exudes is almost completely stoked out.

"I need to finish Christmas shopping," Kat says bringing me out of my head.

"'Kay," I respond quietly.

"Thanks for havin' my back earlier."

"Always."

"Not always," she scoffs. I drop my head and shoulders in defeat.

"I'm sorry, Nick. That was a cheap shot."

"It's fine," I say dismissively. "I'll stay here while you shop."

"Are you worried about the Ashcrofts and Benningtons?" she asks softly.

"No. I'll call Shane and have him get us custody. I figured Patricia would pull some shit like this so he's expecting a phone call. I'll get you the papers once I have 'em."

"Really?" she asks disbelieving, her hazel eyes swimming in confusion.

"What?"

"You're gonna do that?"

"Kat, I know you think I'm a piece of shit and you're right, I am. But I love the boys as much as you do. I won't let them be taken from us. Not without a fight. Their parents have abandoned them for months. Even if we went the legal route, no judge would side with them. It's a non-issue," I assure her.

"Mindfuck," she mutters for the first time in a month.

"Back at you, Sunshine," I say through a small smile.

She snorts, but the corners of her mouth tip up.

"Are you guys gettin' divorced?" Sawyer asks sheepishly. FUCK!

"What?" Kat asks horrified, realizing Sawyer just heard our very honest interaction.

"You guys haven't been right for weeks. I'm sorry I was eavesdropping," he whispers.

"We're fine. Just a rough patch, sweetheart. It happens in all relationships. Nick and I will work it out," she lies.

"You're good at that," Sawyer remarks plainly.

"What's that?"

"Lying."

"I..." Kat trails off. Shit.

"It's okay. I'm used to bein' lied to. I know you have your reasons. But if you guys get divorced you won't send me back to her will you?"

"No," I answer immediately, pinning him with a fierce gaze.

"Good," he says relieved.

Kat has tears brimming in her hazel eyes as she stares at Sawyer guiltily. She's good at lying, but her mask hasn't been as expertly crafted as it usually is. She's too worn out with reality. It's my fault. Now I feel shittier than I have for the last month.

"Sawyer, I'm not lying to you. Nick and I are fine. We had a bad fight a few weeks ago and we haven't gotten over it yet, but we will. We're *not* getting divorced. I just need to get you home and get through the holidays. Then I can fix things with Nick."

"You said you needed to work out custody the first day I was in here," Sawyer says with an accusing glare.

"I'm sorry you heard that. I was just upset after your attack. I didn't mean it," she states strongly.

"Promise?" he asks with need in his voice.

"I swear," she says honestly.

My head is swimming right now. What the fuck? She's saying the things I want to hear, but I have no idea where this is coming from. Is this just for his benefit? That would be cruel and horrible to do to him. She would never lie right to his face like that. She doesn't have it in her.

"You fucked up, huh?" Sawyer asks me.

"Yeah, bud."

"You won't leave us, right?" he asks nervously.

"I'm not a quitter. I'm not goin' anywhere."

I hold Kat's eyes with an intense gaze after I answer him. She gives me a small smile. My heart pounds so hard in my chest it hurts my ribs as I maintain eye contact and soak in the soft glow coming from her. What just happened?

"Merry Christmas!" the four boys bellow in unison, bursting into our bedroom.

"Merry Christmas, boys," Kat coos at them from her side of the bed.

Jake, Cole and Dane jump on her while Sawyer watches from the end of the bed with envy in his chocolate eyes. His ribs are too sore to dog-pile his mother. Kat giggles and wiggles to get away from their assault.

I climb out of bed and wrap Sawyer in a hug, carefully.

"Merry Christmas, Dad," he murmurs into my shoulder.

I haven't gotten used to the feeling of him saying that yet. It feels like a shot to the heart every time I hear it and he says it a lot, as if he's reminding himself that he has parents that love him for the first time in his life. It's one of the greatest things I've ever experienced.

"Merry Christmas, bud," I mumble into his messy black mop.

The boys stop attacking Kat and help her out of bed. She secures her robe before wrapping her arms around Sawyer.

"Merry Christmas, sweetheart," she whispers before pressing a long kiss to his cheek. "Let's go see what Santa brought us."

"Yeah." The boys light up like little kids.

Our house looks like the North Pole threw up on and in it. There's garland everywhere with red twinkle lights embedded to look like berries. I've lost track of how many wreathes and Christmas decorations line the walls at this point. It smells like cinnamon and pine throughout every room in the house. It's warm and inviting, offering much needed comfort for my family.

We have three Christmas trees, because why not, I suppose. Outside is a winter wonderland of lights and decorations that you can see from outer space. We descend our embellished staircase and head into the family room where Santa was fucking busy last night. Santa's a bit tired this morning.

The boys run to their stockings and start ripping through them. Kat and I sit on the couch next to each other and watch with huge smiles on our faces as we peruse our stockings. She grabs my hand and interlaces our fingers. I've gotten something small like this from her every day in the last week since we got Sawyer home. I always let her lead and never push for more. Kat only does this in front of the boys, but it's not a mask when she does it. This is real. She's letting me back in.

"Presents now or after breakfast?" Kat asks as the boys finish their stockings.

"Now," they all answer in unison.

Kat went nuts with gifts. Well, we all did really. We got the boys a ton of clothes, Celtics, Bruins and Red Sox tickets. Skateboards, video games, new sports equipment, snowboards and surfboards round out most of their gifts, capped off with a family trip over Spring Break to Tahiti. We over did it and it feels unbelievable.

The boys got me ties, denture cream (ha ha), tee times at the country club for the entire season, a humidor for my cigars and a year of monthly whiskey delivered from the best distilleries around the world. I'm blown over.

The boys got Kat the most expensive tracksuits on the planet. Can someone explain five hundred dollar sweat pants to me? I saw that receipt when the boys got home from shopping and almost passed out. It's worth it though, because Kat looks to be in heaven imagining wearing them. Totally worth it. They also got her a spa weekend, a year of manicures and pedicures and a book of pictures from the months we've been together. That almost made her cry when she opened it, but she held it together. I think the next present will send her over the edge.

"This is from all of us, but it's Shane's gift for you," I explain, handing her the wrapped box.

She furrows her brow at the box and hesitates taking it. I push it toward her. She studies it a moment longer before Sawyer tells her to open it with excitement. She acquiesces and pulls the box from my hand, carefully peeling back the paper. She drags it open slowly and gasps when she sees what's inside.

Permanent guardianship papers for Cole, Sawyer and Dane are the first things she finds.

"Oh my God." She clutches the papers to her chest as tears fall from her eyes.

"Can we call you Mom too?" Cole asks sheepishly.

"Yes," she answers in a teary chuckle.

"One more, Sunshine," I point out.

Kat looks into the box to see a birth certificate inside. Jake Rivers is now Jake Cooper, with me listed as his father and Kat listed as his mother. Kat breaks into hysterical sobbing and I pull her onto my lap. She curls into my chest clutching at my shirt as she bawls. She's more emotional than I thought she would be, but I don't care. I'm feeling her entire body against mine for the first time in almost five weeks. I'll take it however I can get it.

It takes a few minutes for her to calm down before she tips her head back to look up at me. Her eyes are rimmed in red, her lashes wet and clumped together. I look beyond that into her blue-green-grey hazel eyes to see love pouring out. I can't hold back any longer. I lower my head down and gently press my lips to hers. She sighs and kisses me back. Fuck yes!

I work my lips against hers before sweeping my tongue across the seam of her plump pillows. She opens to me and I slant my head to devour her mouth, sweet Kat. My dick twitches under her ass as I massage her tongue with mine, drinking her in. A moan flows into my mouth from hers and I growl, thrusting my tongue in and out. Until I hear an ear piercing whistle along with cheers and hollers from the boys. Oh yeah, we're not alone. We both snicker into each other's mouths as I stop the kiss. I place a soft chaste kiss on her flushed cheek before turning my gaze to the boys. They're beaming.

Kat slides out of my lap and envelopes each boy one by one in her arms, whispering words of love and appreciation to her kids. Our kids. I'm thirty-three years old and I have four teenage sons. It's an indescribable feeling that fills me with warmth and comfort I didn't know existed.

Kat comes back to me with a small box in her hand. She sits on the couch next to me and sets it in my lap. I rip away at the paper more like a kid than an adult, causing everyone to laugh. I shoot Kat a wicked grin before lifting the lid on the plain white box. My breath catches in my throat and tears threaten at the back of my eyes.

Inside is a tiny white baby outfit that has *I Love Daddy* in swirly pale green print across the front. I pull it from the box with shaky hands. I'm in shock. The boys gasp when they see what I'm holding. I guess this is a surprise for everyone.

"Kat," I whisper.

"I'm sorry I could only give you one and you gave me four," she jokes.

We all snicker at her.

"When are you due?" I ask, trying to wrap my head around this, staring at the tiny outfit in my hands.

"I don't know. I haven't been to the doctor yet. It should be in August sometime."

"You're sure you're pregnant though?" I ask, not wanting to get my hopes up.

"I have twelve positive pregnancy tests. I'm sure," she answers with a laugh.

"Twelve?" I ask dazed.

"That's kinda crazy, Mom," Cole pipes in.

"I was feeling a little crazy," she admits.

"How long have you known?" I ask scooping her into my side, pressing my lips to her hair.

"I found out the morning of Sawyer's attack," she whispers.

My entire body goes rigid. If I were doing my math, I would have known she was pregnant when she killed that motherfucker, but her admitting it aloud rocks me.

"You risked the baby to save me?" Sawyer asks stunned and guilty.

"Sawyer, I would've died before I stopped trying to save you," she says pointedly.

"Thank you," he mumbles as one big tear rolls down his cheek.

"No, sweetheart. Thank you. All of you have given me something that I never thought I'd have. You'll never know how much I've wanted you...how much I love you. I'll spend the rest of my life showing you all. I promise you that."

"You're gonna make us all cry," Dane says choking back tears. "This pregnancy's gonna turn us all into a bunch of pussies."

I chuckle along with the room, thinking he's got that wrong. I feel my inner caveman raging to the surface as each second passes.

"What if it's a girl?" Jake asks showing a bit of his own caveman.

"Uh, she'll hate us," Sawyer says in a duh voice.

"What? Why?" Kat questions with concern.

"Because she'll have us for older brothers and we'll beat down anyone that tries to touch her. And she'll probably look like you so we're fucked," Cole huffs.

Kat giggles, but the rest of us remain stoic, thinking Cole's right.

"I'd like a little girl," Kat says quietly, looking up at me.

"You want me to go to prison?" I ask with my brow raised.

"Don't you want a daddy's girl?"

"Only if I can lock her in the house until she's thirty."

"Caveman."

"Damn straight."

She rolls her eyes at all of us.

"How many more kids are you guys gonna have?" Sawyer asks as we finish breakfast.

Kat didn't eat much and looks slightly green. I believe morning sickness is coming.

"As many as she's willing to have," I answer honestly.

"Really? What if she wants twenty?" Cole chimes in with big blue eyes looking at me like I'm crazy.

"Then we'll have to get a bigger house," I respond without hesitation.

"Mom, how many kids do you want?" Dane asks, trying to get a real answer.

"I don't know, honey. I always wanted a big family."

"This'll be five kids for you guys. That's a big family," Jake adds his opinion.

"You think I can't handle more?" She pretends to be offended.

"No. I think you could have twenty and be just fine."

"I think my lady bits might fall out if I try for twenty," she says through a snicker.

"Can we not talk about your lady bits?" Cole gags.

That makes us all laugh.

"To answer your question, I'd like a few more. Maybe three more after this. I like how eight sounds," Kat says, eyeing me with a question in her face. She wants to know if we're really okay. If we're actually doing this together, for the long haul.

"I like that too," I respond to her unasked questions with a loving smile.

"That's good. We can each have one to be responsible for. If they're all girls, that's one we have to protect," Sawyer points out.

"I've got dibs on this one," Jake spouts.

"Hey, no fair. I didn't think to call dibs," Dane huffs.

"Snooze you lose," Jake retorts with a cocky grin.

"I got dibs on the next one," Sawyer jumps in.

"Third!" Coles yells.

"Uh, I guess I got last," Dane looks at me somewhat deflated.

"I'll save the best for last, bud," I assure him.

"Ooh, like twins?" he asks excitedly.

"Triplets," I joke.

"Ha," he gloats. "See last isn't so bad."

"Hey, I want twins," Cole whines.

"You boys have lost your minds. I'm only a few weeks in with number one. You're makin' my lady bits hurt."

They all moan and act disgusted. She chortles and throws a dish towel at them. The four of them start chasing her around the island. Kat squeals and races away, finally breaking free to hide behind me. I protectively hold my hands out, slap boxing with the boys. The house is full of laughter, joy and the bright glow of Kat beaming from every surface. Everything feels right. Perfect.

Chapter 29

Nick

"Shannon Kelly."

"Merry Christmas, Shanny," I say softly.

I'm in the office making my Christmas call while Kat and the boys are napping. I'm ready for a nap too.

"Merry Christmas, Nicky," she says in a relieved voice. She worries too much about me.

"How's Chicago?"

"Crazy as usual. Perfect. It's always good to be home for the holidays." I can hear the smile in her voice.

"I wish I was there with you."

"Me too. Get anything good today?"

"All right, I'm gonna tell you this because I can't keep this shit to myself but you gotta be careful with who you tell."

"Of course," she assures me.

"I've adopted four teenagers and Kat's pregnant."

I hear her spit a drink out followed by moans and laughter from the other people in the room with her.

"Shit! Nicky, hang on," she huffs and I hear her moving away from her rowdy family. "Okay. Say that again and this time put some fuckin' details in that shit."

"This op I'm on is complicated and we ended up with three boys living with us that had been abandoned by their parents. Some strings were pulled by the DCA and we now have permanent guardianship of the three of them. The fourth is a new young recruit that's on the op with us. He comes from some fucked up shit that I don't have any details on other than he's alone in the world

253

and needs some people to have his back. Kat and I have his back now.

"And the biggest shock is Kat's pregnant. I'm reeling from that one. I haven't told you this, but over a month ago I fucked up pretty big with her and have been in the dungeon of the dog house since then. But she's lettin' me back in now. I'm fuckin' elated."

"I'm speechless," she breathes out. "And that's sayin' somethin'."

"I'm happy, Shanny. I never thought I'd have this...deserve this."

"You listen to me and you listen good, Nicky. You deserve everything in this world and more. A year ago you saved my life. You've spent the last year saving my fuckin' life over and over again. You're not the monster you believe you are, goddammit. You're good down to the fiber of your being. You're worthy of love and happiness. You remember that every time you look at your family. You deserve the fulfillment they give you. I'm done listening to you put yourself in a box where you don't belong," she growls.

"I hate that I spent twenty-two years without you, but during that time it was your face and your heart that got me through the shit I had to do. A little girl full of light and love. I love you so much, Shanny. I can't wait for you to meet the people that fill me with so much light everyday that it's blinding. I have this because of you."

"You have what you have because of *you*. I love you, but I'm not the reason you have goodness in your life...you are. Own that, Nicky. You've earned it," she finishes softly. "Now I wanna know when the baby's due. I wanna know everything about the boys. I wanna know if you need anything to make custody ironclad. I wanna know when you're done with this fuckin' op so I can meet these people."

I chuckle at her quick change into attorney/I run shit mode. She's a handful and then some.

"We don't know when the baby's due because Kat hasn't been to the doctor yet, but she thinks in August sometime. I'll email you about the boys because we'd be on the phone for days if I tried to tell you everything. I think we're good on custody, but if something comes up I'll let you know. I'm workin' my ass off on the op because I want my family outta here."

"Can you move to Kansas City so we can live in a weird extended family commune?"

I chuckle deep in my chest thinking that's the best idea I've ever heard.

"I'll ask Kat about that."

There's a long pause and I know I'm about to get it.

"You hurt her?"

"Fucked up pretty bad," I admit sheepishly.

"Got a plan to fix it?"

"Callin' my best friend."

"Good fuckin' plan," she says cockily.

I break every protocol I've ever put in place and tell Shanny everything. I need her wisdom and strength right now. I need this op done. I need Kat back at my side. I need my family free from *Stepford*.

"Holy fuckin' shit," she sighs at the end of my long ass story. "First of all, you're a dick of massive proportions. What is it with men gettin' blood in their dicks and their brains turning to mush?"

"Biological hazard."

"No shit. In the future when you wanna marry a woman and start a family, lead with that. Dummy."

"Noted."

"I'm sorry for what you went through with Sawyer. I can't begin to imagine the torment that caused Kat. I wish I had words of wisdom for your op. I say drop a bomb on that place and call it a day. If I wasn't pregnant and walking with a serious waddle I'd come and blow some people's heads off with you. I'm feeling kinda bloodthirsty after that story. You're right though, domestic help is your in. Work that shit hard and get the hell outta there. Kat and your boys need to be free from that clusterfuck."

"Believe me it's a struggle to spend time with these animals and act like we're friends. If you weren't waddling I'd fly you here in an instant to watch you work. I heard you lent Kieran a hand a while back when he needed some extra firepower."

"Yeah, keep that shit on the down low. If Kel or my family knew about that, I'd be in for it."

"I can't believe you'd go into an organized crime family take over and not tell your man or your family," I say shocked at how ballsy she is. I don't know why I'm shocked. Shannon Kelly is a unique brand of badass.

"*Pfft,*" she blows out. "They would've tied me to a chair if I told them. Kieran's my family and he needed me. He did the same thing for me not long ago."

"That man loves your crazy ass."

"Who doesn't?" she deadpans before falling into raspy laughter. "Hang on."

"'Kay."

"Hey, Kieran just walked out here and says he needs to talk to you now...like important shit now."

"Put him on," I say gruffly.

"He says I need to hear this too," she responds cautiously.

What the fuck? Why the hell does Shanny need to hear anything that Kieran needs to tell me?

"Speaker."

The phone rustles around before she asks, "Can you hear us?"

"Yeah."

"Shannon you're pregnant so you gotta keep your shit together," Kieran orders in his deep whiskey and tar voice.

"Now you're just freakin' me out. Talk," she barks. I agree.

"All right. A few weeks back Nick found a seventeen-year-old girl that had been taken from Chicago about a decade ago. He didn't have a lot of details about her so he asked me to look into it. I've had a hell of a time findin' anything about her, but I've got somethin' now."

"What?" I growl.

"From what I've been able to find out, Cara's father is Vito Mancini and her mother was Deirdre Murphy," Kieran says softly for Shannon's benefit.

This can't be fucking happening. My uncle and Shannon's dead mother...no fucking way.

"You're wrong, Kieran. My mother's been dead for twenty-three years," Shanny states confidently.

"From what I've been told that's not true. Mancini took her and kept her for a few years before he put her out of her misery. I'm gonna go have a chat with Mancini to confirm it, but my sources are good, Shannon."

"Go get Kel," she growls at Kieran and I hear him dutifully obey.

"Nicky, is this even possible? This has to be a mistake," she pleads with me to fix this truly fucked up situation.

"Shanny, I have no clue. I'm just gettin' this information too. You know Kieran though. He wouldn't tell us if he wasn't sure. Fuck," I groan.

"Hey, what's wrong?" I hear Dylan Kellerman tending to his upset fiancée.

"Kieran thinks I have a half-sister that Nicky found a few weeks ago," she explains in a pained voice. No tears, just hurt.

"What?" Kellerman snarls in a low deep timbre.

"My sources are good, man," Kieran reassures Kellerman.

"Shanny, I'm gonna email you an address. I need you to send in a DNA sample and I'll send one in too. We'll know for sure in a few days max." My agent brain has finally kicked back into gear.

"Okay, Nicky," she mumbles, probably into her massive fiancé's chest.

"Hey, Cooper. I didn't know you were on the phone," Kellerman says with a tinge of annoyance in his voice.

He's not my biggest fan. I don't think he likes sharing his woman as much as he has to with her huge family and I just got added to that equation a year ago. I think he also sensed my feelings for Shanny, but I never would have made a move on her and he knew that too. Now that I've got Kat maybe he'll ease up a bit.

"You can be nice to him, caveman. He's got a wife and four kids now. And his wife's pregnant," Shanny chides Kellerman.

"What?" Kellerman and Kieran ask in confused harmony.

I chuckle into the phone at my best friend's amazing ability to just say shit, plain and simple...no bullshit.

"I've been busy," I admit proudly.

"No shit," Kellerman and Kieran continue their unified speech.

Kat comes in the office with a question on her brow when she sees the overwhelmed confusion on mine. I pat my knee and she plops down in my lap.

"Shanny, you wanna say hi to Kat?"

Kat's eyes get huge and then her face breaks in two with a giant toothy smile.

"Hell yes!" Shanny says excitedly as I put the phone on speaker.

Kat snickers at Shanny's excitement.

"Hi, Kat," Shanny says in her soft sweet voice.

"Hi...uh I don't know what to call you. I've heard you have a lot of nicknames," Kat says kindly.

"That's because I'm surrounded by idiots that can't be bothered to say my name," she jokes. "You can call me whatever you want, but my friends call me Shannon."

"It's nice to finally meet you, Shannon. I've heard a lot about you."

"Don't believe a word Nicky says about me. He's a pathological liar. Here, let me introduce you to my fiancé Dylan Kellerman."

"Hi, Dylan."

"Hey, Kat."

"Holy shit what kinda face goes with that voice?" Kat asks animatedly.

The phone fills with laughter as I offer Kat a scowl. She gazes back innocently.

"I love you already," Shanny announces. "My crazy ass cousin is here too. Kieran Delaney meet Kat."

"Hey, Kat," Kieran purrs on purpose.

"Hi, Kieran," Kat says holding back a giggle. "Uh, you got some kinda phone sex side business, Shannon?"

"I know right? I'm surrounded by big sexy men. It's a sacrifice, but I make do," she jokes.

"You two together are gonna be trouble. I feel it," I huff.

"Wait until I get Quinn in on this shit," Shanny fans the flames. "Quinn's Kieran's fiancée. She's tiny firecracker of awesomeness," Shanny explains to Kat.

"Oh my God and all three of us are pregnant!" Shanny spouts excitedly.

"Trouble," Kellerman, Kieran and I grumble in unison.

"Cavemen," Kat and Shanny respond in mirrored harmony.

The five of us fall into fits of united laughter. With what Shanny and I just learned it's a harrowing laugh but much needed.

"Kieran thinks Cara is Shanny's half-sister and my cousin," I explain to Kat as we come back down to earth.

"No fuckin' way. Oh my God that's why she looks like Shannon!" Kat exclaims.

"She looks like me?" Shanny whispers.

"I'm so sorry, Shannon. That was insensitive of me. She does though. Nicky couldn't quit staring at her it freaked him out so much."

"Nicky?" Shanny asks for confirmation.

"It's true. I almost fell over when I saw her face. I felt like I climbed in a time machine when I looked in her bright green eyes."

"This is un-fucking-real," Shanny huffs. "On a side note before I turn into a puddle of hormonal tears, I love that you call him Nicky."

"Me too," Kat says through a sweet smile. I never told her Nicky is the nickname Shanny gave me as a kid. I can see on Kat's face she gets how huge it was for me to suggest that she use it day one. More than that, it means something personal to me beyond words to share it with the woman I love more than life. My sweet Kat.

"Okay. I'm gonna get off here and go bawl my eyes out and then eat a pumpkin pie. Nicky, I'll send in that DNA sample tomorrow. When we're sure Cara's my sister I'm on a fuckin' plane and don't even think about tryin' to keep me away or I'll go commando on your ass," Shanny levels a very real threat.

"Noted."

"It was nice to meet you, Dylan and Kieran," Kat says tenderly.

"You too, Kat," they reply in tandem.

"Shannon...thank you for bein' such a good friend to Nicky. You mean the world to him and that means the world to me. I can't wait to meet you in person so we can get into a shit ton of trouble," Kat finishes with a chuckle.

"I love Nicky. He's the only part of my past that I have and I'm glad he's got you as his future. And we'll definitely be getting into trouble...soon."

We all go about saying a very long complicated five-way goodbye and hang up. My mind is a mess. I can't wrap my head around half the information rolling around my brain so I decide to put it on hold and make out with my wife. She willingly complies.

Chapter 30

Kat

"Hollander," Shane answers gruffly.

"Hello, Shane," I say coolly.

"Kat?" he questions like he's trying to figure out if he's in a dream or not.

"Look, I'm still pissed at you. I just wanted to call and tell you that even though you hurt me and need some serious help weighing your priorities in life...thank you. Thank you for getting us the boys."

"Kat, I'm so fuckin' sorry for hurting you. I'm not gonna try to excuse my actions. I was wrong."

"Yeah, you were," I huff.

"I love you. I really do love you. The last few weeks thinkin' I'd never have you back in my life has been miserable. Bein' in that hospital room with you and not bein' able to talk to you or hold you was worse than any torture I've endured. Please tell me I can fix this. I'll do anything."

"Don't hurt me again, Shane. You and Jess have been the only people in my life since my parents died. I need you. I need you in my life because things are changing for me. My life is growing and I can't imagine what it would look like without you. Don't take what we have for granted again," I say quietly.

"Never," he declares ardently.

"All right, get Jess and put the phone on speaker."

"Uh...okay."

"Hey lady," Jess calls out brightly.

I called and made up with her after Sawyer's attack. She yelled at me for a half hour before she cried and

261

then forgave me. I held this last bit of information from her though. I wanted to tell Nick first.

"Hey you. Merry Christmas."

"Did Santa bring you some happy?" Jess asks noting my brighter tone.

"And then some. I'm pregnant."

I'm met with a long drawn out silence.

"Kat," Shane whispers.

"I'm good you guys. This happened before...well, before."

"You're happy?" Jess asks tentatively.

"I'm over the moon."

"That's freakin' amazing!" I can hear her jumping with excitement.

"You want off the op?" Shane asks professionally.

"No."

"Should I still take you off the op?"

"No," I answer in a snicker. He's thinking about me, finally.

"Should I ask Nick?"

"Shane," Jess warns.

He grumbles something about an assassination in his future but doesn't push anymore.

"Okay, I want details. Hot juicy details, but we're heading to the safe house to spend some time with Cara," Jess says excited for me and the bun in my oven.

"Cara's the other reason I'm calling. I'm gonna pass you off to Nick. I've gotta get back to the boys. I love you both."

"Love you too," Jess coos.

"Congratulations, Kat. Thanks for givin' me a second chance. I won't fuck up again. I swear," Shane spouts confidently.

"I'll sick my husband on you if you do."

"I don't doubt that. Love you, Kat."

"Love you too. Here's Nick," I say handing the phone to Nick who's been watching me intently from the other side of the desk.

He takes the phone and presses a kiss to my palm where he removed the phone from. Fuck, that feels good. I leave the office and head down the staircase to find my boys. I'm relieved in a way I didn't know I could be. I was still so mad at Nick even after Sawyer's attack and finding out I was pregnant that I didn't know how I was going to get through any of it.

Then Nick protected us from that cow Patricia and then immediately assured me he'd get us custody of all the boys. That's when it happened. I realized then that no matter how badly he fucked up telling me he wanted a future with me, it was true. He honestly and truly wants this life with me and the boys. He's not motivated by the op or Shane...he's motivated by his love for us.

I didn't jump back in with both feet at that moment though. I've waited and given myself some time to heal and watch Nick. Even though I've shut him out he's still been taking care of me. He makes me coffee every morning, he deals with the boys before school (which is a task), he walks me to the garage then hovers watching me drive away, he cleans my weapons, he brings home flowers at least once a week, he compliments me often and with sincerity, he takes away my worry at every juncture and above all he shows me that he loves me with every breath he takes.

I wasn't expecting Shane to get us the boys. And as mad as I've been at him, I've missed him. My life has only had two constants since I joined the DCA, Shane and Jess. What Shane did is...beyond agonizing, but I know there was some goodness behind the selfishness. The idiot needs to work on his communication skills. I don't know if our friendship will ever be the same, but I'm not willing to let it go.

Now we've got to get this damn op wrapped so my family can start a real life together. I feel my game coming back full strength and I'm ready to play. I've had enough of *Stepford* and the crazy that encapsulates the space. The Bookers are about to get schooled and I'm going to be their professor of pain.

"Mom!" Cole shouts from the basement where some intense gaming has been going on since this morning.

"Yeah!" I yell back loving the tingle him calling me Mom causes me.

"That bitch that gave birth to me just called!"

Not really a conversation I want to have screaming through the house. I thud down the stairs and enter the land of video games and stinky teenage boys.

"What happened?" I ask as I flop on the huge charcoal sectional couch next to Cole.

"She called me an ungrateful little shit and told me my trust fund is gone," he says in a shrug.

"Merry Christmas," I drone sarcastically.

"No shit. I guess they just got the papers from their attorney about their parental rights bein' removed. She said if I was so lonely I should have spent more time with the staff at the house."

"Jesus Christ," I blow out in frustration.

"My...uh...past dad?" Dane struggles with what to call him. "Anyway, he called too. Told me I'm cut off and to have all my shit removed from their property before they return to the country. I told his dumb ass I moved out in September. He hung up on me. The best thing is I already emptied my bank account before Christmas so I've got enough money to last a while."

"You put that money in your savings account and don't touch it. You're not responsible for providing for yourself. That goes for all of you. That's my and Nick's job."

"You shouldn't have to do that," Sawyer chimes in. "I've got a shitload of money now and once we sell my old house I'll have even more. I can take care of myself."

"I don't care if you can, you don't have to. We're your parents now and that means we provide for you. Your parents have used money as a weapon, whether to buy you boys off or to keep you where they wanted you. That

264

stops now. You boys keep whatever money from your past and use it for your future. But for now, I don't want their money providing for my kids."

"Okay," they grumble in unison.

"Are you worried that we can't give you the lifestyle you're used to?" I ask quietly.

"What?" Cole asks aghast. "No fuckin' way. We just don't wanna be a burden."

"Say that again and I'll ground you," I threaten.

"Okay," he laughs at my idle threat.

"Where's Dad?" Dane asks and I love the sound of it so much I forget to answer.

"Mom?" he prods.

"Sorry. He was talkin' to Shannon and now I think he's wrappin' up some stuff with Shane."

The boys believe Shane is our attorney. It was an easy lie to explain his presence at the hospital with Sawyer.

"Who's Shannon?" Sawyer growls defensively.

"She's his best friend. Really she's the only family he has outside of us. So I guess that makes her like your aunt or something," I explain as truthfully as I can.

"His best friend's a chick?" Sawyer asks like that's the weirdest thing he's ever heard.

"Hey, I'm a chick. What's wrong with havin' a girl as a best friend?"

"I don't know. Doesn't it get weird? Like what if he realizes he wants to be with her instead of you or something?"

"Dude," Jake growls.

"I trust Nicky. He loves me and he loves Shannon, but it's different. Plus Shannon has her own man, a baby and she's pregnant with twins. I'm not worried. They're just friends. When you meet her you'll understand. And you'll love her because she's as crazy as me."

"So Dad has a thing for crazies?" Dane teases.

265

"He has a thing for hot crazy ladies," I deadpan.

"No question," Nick's deep voice echoes through the room.

We all chuckle at his admission as he moves to stand behind us.

"And as for your questions about Shanny, let me clear that shit up. I've known her since I was a kid. In my ten-year-old brain I thought she was the girl I'd spend my life with and then I met your mom and I realized I would spend my life with Shanny...as my best friend. Because Kat is everything I want and need in life. She gives me things that Shanny never could. Shanny found her future with another man and I found mine with your mom. It doesn't change that we love each other. We're just friends though...well that's not true. She's my family just like you are."

"You think she'll like us?" Cole asks sweetly.

"She'll fuckin' love you all. And be warned she's a unique brand of crazy. She'll boss you around and spoil the shit outta you," Nick finishes with a kiss to my hair and a squeeze of my shoulder.

"Sounds good to me," Dane spouts, turning the video game back on.

It feels good to give the boys some honesty about our life. I'm glad that Nick has Shannon to offer the boys. From what I know of her she'll be a good addition to their lives. And the boys deserve as much good as they can get. I hate that they just assume a husband being around another woman means trouble. I want them to see that relationships mean something outside sex and money. I've only got a few years before I lose them to college and I want them going into that time in their lives confident about what their futures can hold.

"My turn," Nick announces jumping over the back of the couch, snatching a controller away from Sawyer.

"Prepare to have your ass handed to you, old man," Dane goads.

A cocky smile splits Nick's face as he enters some game where they go about killing zombies and other

266

creatures. I don't watch the game as much as I watch the boys. Sawyer stays glued to Nick's side and plays vicariously through him, often barking out orders. Dane and Cole chide and tease along with encouraging and defending their father. This is the life we all deserve. I fall asleep with a smile on my lips and a stronger beat to my heart than I've ever experienced. Fulfilled.

Chapter 31

Nick

"I hear you've made some enemies," Phil whispers as we greet each other for our first poker night since Christmas.

"That so?" I ask releasing his hand, preparing for whatever is coming.

"The Benningtons and Ashcrofts are not happy with you and your wife," he says with a pointed look.

I offer a shrug of indifference. I don't give a fuck what they think or how they feel.

"How's the Lancaster kid doin'?" He changes the subject quickly as Tony joins us.

"Sawyer's healing. Broken ribs take time and he's losing patience, but other than that he's doin' good. Thanks for asking."

"And your wife?" Tony asks with a peculiar look on his face.

"It's been rough on her," I lie. "She's seeing a local therapist and it seems to be helping. It's been good to have the holidays at home for her to recover. I don't think she'll ever get over that day though."

This is the lie we've been carefully spinning. Kat had to murder a man to save Sawyer and she's struggling with it. I don't think Kat's actually ever thought about it again. It's how we're trained. If anything, I think she feels good about it. Maybelle needs to believe the opposite. They need to think it was as traumatizing for her as it would be for any normal person. This is also the in for us. Once people know she's pregnant on top of having the boys officially as ours it's easy to start looking for domestic help. Slow and steady it is.

"I can't imagine how you're managing with all that," Phil responds with a little aggression in his voice that I recognize from the real world outside *Stepford*. Either he genuinely feels bad for me or he's uncomfortable with the attention of the murder and rumors. My guess is the latter.

"It's not easy."

"Well, let's play some poker so you can kick all our asses," Phil says with a clap on my back.

I offer him a chin lift and move to the table. Phil and Tony stay where I left them, whispering about something. I wish I had a bug in here now. Kat tried to get one in this house yesterday. She was here for a lunch with some other *Stepford Wives*. When she got back she said she had the distinct feeling it was a test. Like Trish was watching her and sizing her up in a way she hasn't before. With that in mind, she kept the bug. If the Bookers sweep their house for bugs as often as I do, they'd know it was Kat that planted it.

The murder and guardianships have gotten us a lot of attention. It's been mixed at best. The boys will go back to school in a couple weeks and have found most of the kids they go to school with don't really give a shit about anything that's happened with custody. They are very intrigued about the murder. The texting and facebooking and whatever the hell else the boys do to interact with their peers has been in overdrive. Teenagers.

The boys have kept tight lipped about the murder outside of our house. We've told them they can discuss it with people or not, it's up to them. We've got Sawyer in therapy and offered it to the others, but they've declined so far. I'm still not certain the beating was because Sawyer wasn't home to check on Patricia. I know what Sawyer remembers as he took his beating is true, but something doesn't play for me. I've beaten enough people in my life that I know what motivates that behavior. A uninterested parent and absent husband doesn't beat his kid to death for behaving the same way. Jess has been digging into every aspect of the Lancasters' life to

270

try and get a handle on what was actually going on in that house. She'll find it, whatever it is.

The townspeople have been cautious with us. Most of the looks Kat receives are that of pity or curiosity. I've seen plenty looks of disdain too. The boys have gone into protective mode of their mother, Jake being the worst. If they see any looks or hear anything they don't like they're quick to cut that shit off. I've had no effect on this behavior, yet I beam with pride every time I witness it. I have good kids. No, I have great kids.

I've settled into this idea quicker than I anticipated I would. I'm a father. No question, no hesitation, nothing but proud love. I have four sons and I'm going to have a baby this summer. Tomorrow is our first doctor's appointment, and fuck if I'm not nervous and excited. Tomorrow's a big day all around because we're expecting the results of the DNA test for Cara. The more I've thought about it the more convinced I am that Cara is Shanny's sister. Kieran hasn't been able to get answers out of Vito Mancini as of yet. I'm confident he will though. Kieran has ways of persuasion that he'll be employing. I bizarrely feel like Kieran and I are becoming friends. Even though I've known him my whole life we didn't run in the same circles. It's the connection to "the life" that offers us common ground combined with our love for Shanny. Fucking weird and good all at the same time.

Kat and Shanny have been talking on the phone a lot since I introduced them a few days ago. They chat with Quinn too. The three of them are sure to cause massive amounts of trouble once they're in a room together. I'm thankful they're all pregnant and living in different cities at this point because it will lessen the shit they can do, barely. But those three not pregnant for a night out...God help Kieran, Kellerman and me (the world at large).

All of this family building and friendship creating has me craving a normal life more than usual. I want what we have in Maybelle without the rest of the shit swarming around us. I want evenings with basketball practice and family dinners. I want lazy weekends playing video games with the boys. I want nights with Kat wrapped in my arms followed by mornings where she hasn't moved from my grasp. I've had a few days of that back and I feel like a crack addict getting a fix after a dry spell. I haven't had sex with Kat yet. I don't think she's there with letting me back in. I'm dying to get back inside her. I'm jacking off more than the boys combined and that's saying something. The whiskey tonight isn't going to help my resolve to let her work at her own pace.

We're a few hours into the game and I'm a few grand up, not really even trying, when my phone buzzes in my jacket pocket. I swipe the screen to find a text.

Sawyer: Help

I jump up from the table knocking my chair back with a thud. Most of the group startles as I slide my arms into my jacket without an apology.

"Nick, what's wrong?" Phil asks with concern in his voice.

"Something's wrong at the house," I growl, stalking out of the room.

I hear the men grumbling and a few footsteps following me. I burst out of the front door and sprint to my driveway. I can hear slaps of feet pacing me, but I don't check to see who's with me. I wish I had a weapon on me right now. There's a car in my driveway...Patricia's. Fuck!

I go to open the front door and find it locked.

"Do you have keys?" Phil asks out of breath.

"No," I snarl. "I'm goin' around back."

"Let's go."

He takes off running like he's as nervous as I am. I come to the glass wall at the back of the house to find it dark. There's no movement inside, no lights on. Shit. I try the back door, locked.

"You wanna break the glass?" Phil asks, looking around for something to use to shatter a window. The house is outfitted in special glass that won't break on

272

impact. I don't really want him to know this. So instead of answering, I take a step back and scan the house for an open window. It's winter so I'm doubting there will be any open, but it's my only shot. The laundry room on the top floor is cracked open. The boys' dirty clothes stink so bad that Kat airs it out every once in a while.

"Window's open," I say nodding at it.

"And how are you gonna reach it?" Phil looks at me like I'm nuts.

I pull off my jacket and heave myself up the drainpipe running the length of the house. It's wavering under my weight so I move quickly. Climbing a wall in slacks and dress shoes is not something I'm used to so I'm moving slower than I'd like. I slip a few times and feel the pipe pulling away from the house, spurring me to move faster.

I reach the cracked open window and fight to push it up while I support my weight on the windowsill. Silently, I slink in, sliding over the counter. When my feet hit the ground I pull my shoes off. The heels make noise on our hardwood floors and I don't want anyone knowing I'm coming.

The house is pitch-black as I move room to room searching for my family. The silence is bothering more the lack of light. I want to know what I'm looking for. I make my way to the office and ease myself in the room. I scan the monitors for any movement or motion sensors lighting up. I find them in the basement. There's low light in the theater room so I don't have a good view, but the motion alerts are flashing from their movement. I grab two guns out of the safe and head in that direction.

Phil is still standing outside and I make a rush decision to let him in. If Patricia's on drugs, armed or not alone I'd like the extra set of hands. He eyeballs my gun in my hand as I open the door, holding my finger to my lips and then indicate where we need to move.

"Give me your other weapon," he whispers.

I take another risk and hand him the gun out of the back of my pants. He cocks it and holds it at the ready like a pro. Who the fuck is Phil Ganesly? He toes off his shoes and we move. Yeah, he's not Maybelle. I open the basement door and ease my way down the stairs with my back against the wall and my gun aimed in front of me. Phil follows, mimicking my stance.

I can finally hear something when we reach the bottom of the stairs. The door to the theater room is shut so I lean against it, hoping to gain an idea of what we're walking into. I can't make anything out. I can hear voices, but nothing I can discern. I lock eyes with Phil and he nods. We're going in.

I kick the door open and scan the room quickly as I enter. The boys are huddled on the ground shielding Kat. She's unconscious. I see red. I see nothing but crimson Martin Scorsese red. Patricia is standing menacingly over the group with a gun in her hand and a crazy gaze focused on me.

"Jake," I growl. He nods, understanding what I want.

"Boys close your eyes," I order and they immediately comply while covering Kat with their bodies.

"What—" Patricia's cut off as I unload two rounds in her. One in the gut, one in her leg.

She doesn't flinch. She's on drugs, meth probably. Jake jumps into action tackling her as she shoots rounds in my direction. I fly at her as Phil makes his way to the boys. She's fighting Jake like a feral animal. Jake's trying to get the gun out of her grasp as she fires rounds in the room.

I jump into the mêlée and land a knee in her leg wound. Jake is lying across her chest, pinning her gun to the ground as she shrieks and squeezes her trigger. She flicks her wrist and aims the gun at Jake's head before firing her last round. She misses, almost grazing the side of his head. I release her legs and stand up, kicking her wrist and relishing in the sound of bones snapping in her arm as the gun flies across the room. Her fight doesn't lessen.

Patricia is clawing, kicking and hitting Jake as he tries to subdue her. He hasn't hit or harmed her. He's a good person. I'm not. I reach down and pull Jake off of her before landing a vicious blow to her head with my fist. She fights back, not reacting to the impact. I continue pummeling her head before connecting with her jaw with such force I feel it break beneath my knuckles. She's finally unconscious.

I'm heaving and shaking as I stand from her body and fling myself to the boys and my wife. Phil's hovering over Kat with his phone to his ear. I don't see a mark on her as I scan her body.

"Pistol whipped her," Jake growls.

"Ambulance is on the way," Phil murmurs, ending his call.

I want to hold Kat to my chest, but I don't want to risk furthering a head injury by moving her. I bend down to her ear and talk to her instead, crushing her hand in mine.

"Kat, wake up," I order gruffly. "Wake up now. The boys need you to wake up. I need you to wake up. Wake up."

She doesn't. She doesn't wake up while we wait for the ambulance. She doesn't wake up while they load her on a stretcher. She doesn't wake up while we ride to the hospital with Phil driving the boys behind us. She doesn't wake up as they wheel her away from me into the emergency room.

She doesn't wake up.

Chapter 32

Nick

"Nicky," I hear a familiar voice call in the distance.

I flutter my eyes open to find Kat asleep, my hand still cradling hers. I lift my head off the edge of the bed and find my best friend standing across the room with her fiancé behind her pushing a stroller with a sleeping Johnny in it.

"Hey, Shanny," I croak.

Her face is a mask of fierce fury and empathy. A year ago she was in Kat's place and Kellerman was in mine. His features are incensed and pained, behind his support of his fiancée.

Shanny moves to me quickly, considering the size of her belly. She engulfs me in her arms reminding me of the strength her thin body contains. Her lips press a firm kiss to my forehead before she releases me and moves to Kat's face. Shanny rubs the back of her fingers across Kat's cheek before placing a kiss to her skin then whispering in her ear.

Shanny moves to the other side of the bed and sits in the chair Kellerman pulls there for her. She scoops Kat's hand into her own before locking eyes with me. Her bright green eyes are craving vengeance for a woman she barely knows. She may want vengeance for Kat, but the look she's offering me says she give it to me.

"How'd you know?" I ask softly as Kellerman drags a chair next to Shanny after parking the stroller at the end of the bed.

"Some guy named Shane called me," she explains with a waver in her voice.

She thought I was hurt or worse.

"How is she?" Kellerman asks with compassion in his voice.

"Hasn't woken up. The baby's okay and they say Kat'll wake up when her body's ready. I'm sick of fuckin' waiting."

"I know you are," he says pointedly.

He's been here and he blames me for that. I blame me for that too.

"I'm sorry," I pronounce, meaning it more now than any other time I've said it to him.

"You don't have anything to be sorry for, Cooper. It's been a year. I'm done bein' an ass. I got Shannon back and you made sure that happened. We're good."

I hold his strange teal eyes and let that information sink in. I don't know if I'd be that forgiving of me, but I take it. I nod and move my gaze back to Shanny.

"You could've just called. You shouldn't be traveling," I admonish her.

"Fuck you very much, Nicky," she growls. "You need me and I'm here. Careful not to piss me off. I'm packin' and I'm not in the mood."

"Noted."

"Dad, we didn't know what you—" Sawyer stops in his tracks at the sight of Shanny.

Jake, Dane and Cole smash into Sawyer and then each other like a train piling up. I laugh for the first time in twenty-seven hours.

"Holy shit," Sawyer mutters staring at Shanny.

She's wearing a plain white sweater and jeans and she's fucking stunning. Always is. She has this effect on men, boys...even women. The woman is breathtaking, though Kat's the one that steals my breath now. Shanny unleashes her megawatt smile and I see the boys tremble slightly in response. Kellerman looks at me and rolls his eyes. Shanny's a handful.

"Hi, boys," she coos as she stands up and walks toward the group that has unsmashed and spread into a semi-circle. "I'm Shannon."

"Hey," Cole squeaks out in a very unmasculine voice.

"Hi, Cole," she says shocking the shit out of him. I sent Shanny pictures of the boys and she's obviously committed them to memory. She wraps her arms around him and he turns scarlet red looking at me with huge blue eyes. I snicker along with Kellerman.

"Hi, Dane," she continues and grabs him in a tight hold. He closes his eyes and soaks it in. He'll be my trouble maker for sure.

"Sawyer, I'm gonna hug you gently so I don't hurt your ribs, but it doesn't mean I don't wanna squish the hell outta you," she informs him. I love that she didn't want him to feel left out.

"Hey, Jake," she purrs as she pulls him tightly to her. He holds her snugly with a small smile on his lips. Shanny's the closest thing to Kat he's had in more than a day.

"I hear you've got some game on the court," Shanny inquires as she makes her way back to her chair.

"I do all right," Jake lies.

"Liar," she retorts.

"This is my fiancé Dylan Kellerman," she introduces.

Kellerman climbs to his feet and the boys' eyes widen at the sight of the massive man. He's about six foot five and near two hundred and fifty pounds, it's a lot to take in. He shakes all their hands without saying much. Kellerman's a man of few words, super laid back.

"That's your cousin Johnny," Shanny says nodding toward the stroller.

I smile at that introduction. Shanny's family to me, but I haven't been confident where I fit in her life since everything that's happened. I shouldn't have questioned it. She doesn't do half-assed. It's all or nothing with Shannon Kelly.

The boys eye the baby with curiosity. Thinking what it will be like to have one of those soon.

"We didn't know what you wanted so we got you a bottle of water," Sawyer finishes his original sentence.

"Thanks, bud."

The boys take the couch at the end of the room staring at Kat with gloomy eyes.

"She's gonna be fine," Shanny states assertively. "You boys just keep tellin' her how much you love and miss her. She'll come back."

They nod in agreement.

"Now, where's the cunt nugget that did this?" she growls at me. I look at Sawyer to see if my best friend's colorful language bothers him, but his face is blank.

"At the end of the hall," Jake responds for me.

"Armed guards?"

Shit. Shannon Kelly is planning an assassination.

"There's local PD outside the room," I inform her with a knowing gaze.

"Huh."

"Shanny," I warn.

"What?" she feigns innocence.

"Kellerman, help me out."

"Kiddo, you know you've gotta keep your shit together. You're pregnant," he grumbles for me.

"I didn't do anything. I'm just talkin'," she lies.

"Liar," Jakes retorts.

She turns her gaze to him and offers a smile promising mischief at a level none of us are prepared for.

"What's she gonna do?" Cole asks wanting in on the secret.

"Nothing," I groan.

"What's she wanna do?" Dane pipes in.

"Inflict misery and torture at a level that I shouldn't discuss in front of you," Shanny answers honestly.

"What?" Sawyer asks shocked.

"I'm sorry, Sawyer. I shouldn't have said that about your mother in front of you," she says with regret.

"You're holding my mother's hand," he growls.

Shanny's face gets soft while something resembling relief washes across her features.

"Well, for your mother, your father and you boys I'd like to put a few bullets in that bitch and watch her bleed out for hours."

"You'd do that?" Dane asks with some excitement in his features.

"Yes."

Shanny holds the boys' gaze intensely as she lets her words sink in. She'll protect them no matter what. It doesn't matter that she just met them for the first time. They're her family now and she'll do anything for them. I feel immense relief at this realization. Because these boys have lost everything other than us and some old ass crotchety grandparents that none of them have any type of relationships with. Shanny just gave them herself and all the family that comes with her.

"Dad says you're crazy and you'll boss us around and you'll spoil the shit out of us," Dane spouts causing a deep laugh to rattle in Kellerman's chest.

"Nice," she says to me, rolling her eyes before pushing Kellerman in the shoulder for laughing.

"I figured honesty was the best way to go."

"I bet you did," she snarks at me. "When you boys come to Kansas City you'll see how I am. I'm not that crazy and I'm only bossy when necessary. I do spoil the shit out of my family so that you can believe."

"When are we goin' to Kansas City?" Jake asks with furrowed brow.

"Probably this summer when you're outta school," I answer in a shrug.

"You lookin' at basketball camps for the summer?" Kellerman asks Jake.

"Yeah."

"Coach said some college scouts are comin' to the next game," Cole builds on Jake's one word answer.

"You thinkin' about playin' ball in college?"

I know Kellerman knows the details of this op, but he's playing the dumb role well. I appreciate it in this moment. The boys could use the distraction.

"Haven't thought about it. I'm only a sophomore. Feels kinda early," Jake lies.

"Dude, you're better than most high school point guards in the country already. Just wait until you're a senior. Schools will be all over you," Sawyer encourages his friend.

"What about you? You still thinkin' about playin' baseball in college?" Jake turns the tables.

"It depends on them," Sawyer nods at me and Kat.

"What about us?" I ask completely confused.

"It depends on what you guys want me to do."

"We want whatever you want. Whatever makes you happy."

"What if I wanna be a crackhead?"

"Then I'll kick your fuckin' ass," Shanny spouts without looking at him.

The boys snicker along with me.

"What she said," Kat's voice filters into the room.

Chapter 33

Nick

"Mom!" the boys holler in unison.

She winces at the sound and Johnny wakes up with a start. Kellerman hurries to pick him up out of the stroller as I squeeze the shit out of my wife's hand.

"Kat," I murmur into her cheek as I hover over her body. "How do you feel?"

"Like I got my fuckin' head smashed in," she says through a grimace.

"You did, Sunshine."

"The boys okay?"

"Yes."

"The baby?" she asks holding a protective hand over her flat belly.

"Fine."

She slowly peels her eyes open and locks her blue-green-greys on mine searching for a lie. She doesn't find it and relaxes. I rub my thumb across her cheek before smashing my lips to the soft skin.

"I love you," I whisper in her ear.

"I love you too," she whispers back.

My breath hitches, but I steady it quickly for the boys benefit. Kat's never told me she loves me. Those words have just set an unbalanced thrum within my chest. She squeezes my hand and I retake my seat at her side as the boys come over and hug and kiss her. A few tears are shed quietly, but mostly the room is filled with relief.

"Hey, Kat." Shanny leans into her face.

"Thanks for comin'," Kat replies with genuine appreciation.

"Always."

Shanny leans her belly over the side of the bed and wraps her arms around Kat in a tight hug before releasing her.

Kellerman is last to approach my wife as he hands off Johnny to Shanny.

"Hey, gorgeous," he purrs placing a kiss on her cheek.

I growl earning me a chuckle from Kellerman's throat.

"Sucks doesn't it?" he asks shooting me a knowing glance.

"Dick," I mutter through a grin.

"You need anything from us, say the word," Kellerman says as he returns his gaze to Kat.

"I need you guys to take the boys back to Kansas City," Kat replies earnestly.

"Okay," Shanny and Kellerman answer immediately.

"What?" the boys ask in shock.

Kellerman retakes his seat his face a mask of seriousness.

"Jake, shut the door," I order gruffly.

I guess it's time to be honest with the boys. Shit!

Shanny takes her seat at Kat's side and scoops her hand into hers, offering her strength and warmth. I wish Jess and Shane were here right now. Jess has a horrible stomach flu and didn't want to risk getting Kat sick. Shane flew in and back out quickly once we knew Kat was stable.

"I want you boys to listen to me without interrupting," Kat orders.

They nod in unison.

"Nick and I work for a government agency called the Domestic Crime Agency. We're undercover in Maybelle to find a human trafficking ring. After everything that's happened I need you boys safe while we finish our job in Maybelle. You'll be safe with Shannon and Dylan."

"We fuckin' knew it!" Dane spouts.

284

"Huh?" I ask shocked.

"We knew it. After what happened at the Lancasters' we were sure," Cole responds.

"Why didn't you say anything?" Kat asks.

"We figured it wasn't safe or something," Sawyer answers in a shrug. "I saw you that day in my house. I knew you weren't a housewife the way you attacked him. Then you killed him and never said a word about it. A normal housewife would've been fucked up about that shit."

"You're not mad?" Kat's gaze is tentative.

"No," all three answer in harmony with conviction.

"What about you?" Cole asks Jake.

"What about me?"

"Are you one of them?" Dane asks offering him a pointed look.

"Not yet."

"You're not their nephew are you?" Sawyer chimes in.

"No."

"You're not fifteen are you?" Dane continues with twenty questions.

"No."

"Fuckin' crazy," Sawyer breathes out before falling back on the couch.

"Are we really your kids?" Cole whispers.

"Yes," all four adults spout loudly making Johnny jump in Shanny's lap.

"Everything we have on you guys is legal. It wasn't obtained that way, but it doesn't matter. You're ours and no one can take you from us. Our legal names and signatures are on the guardianship court orders. You're our kids," I state emphatically.

"What are your real names?" Sawyer inquires.

"I'm Nick Cooper and Kat's name is Katherine Russell."

"You're not really married?" Dane asks with huge eyes. SHIT!

"No, we're not. We just met in September," Kat answers sheepishly.

"Wow...do we know anything about you guys?" Sawyer asks, becoming offended.

"A lot of the facts are lies boys. It's to keep us safe while we're undercover. But everything we've experienced together is real. We haven't been anything but ourselves when we're with you. And as far as Nick and I go...we may not have been together for ten years, but we're together now and we're not faking that. I love him and I'm having our baby. We'll get married as soon as the op is wrapped. Anything else that you wanna know about us feel free to ask. No more lies," Kat says genuinely.

"What's your name?" Cole asks Jake.

"Jake Cooper."

"How's that?"

"Nick and Kat adopted me before Christmas. That wasn't a lie that day."

"Can we change our last names?" Sawyer asks me.

"If you want to."

"Really?" Cole asks shocked.

"You're my kids. I'd love nothing more than for you to have my last name," I answer honestly.

"I'll get to work on it when we're back in Kansas City," Shanny pipes in, attorney mode in full effect.

"Are you two agents too?" Dane asks disbelievingly.

"No, I'm an attorney and Dylan's in marketing."

"How can they keep us safe then?" Sawyer asks me confused.

"Shanny isn't an agent, but she's got skills like one. She's probably better than me. I trust her with my life. She'll keep you safe."

Kat squeezes my hand and I squeeze back. I don't want to send the boys away, but Kat's right. Shit is getting too dangerous. We were reckless getting involved with them. I don't regret it for a second, but we need

286

them safe to finish the op. After this latest clusterfuck it'll be easy to sell to Maybelle.

"Is Jake comin' with us?" Dane asks sheepishly.

"Yes," Kat answers before Jake can say no. "You're goin' Jake and don't argue with me."

"You need me here," Jake huffs.

"I need you safe."

"And I need you safe."

"I don't wanna go either," Dane chimes in.

"Me neither," Cole and Dane finish.

"Well, it's a good thing I'm your mother now and you don't get a say," she says pointedly. "Jake that goes for you too. I'm your mother and I know you're an adult and I don't give a shit. I can't let you stay here."

"Then I'll go back to headquarters so I'm close if you need me," Jake barters.

"No. You'll go with Shannon and Dylan and finish your senior year of high school as Jake Cooper and then you'll go to college and play basketball like you deserve to."

"You can't make me leave the DCA," Jake growls.

"Jake," I warn him of his tone. Kat ignores it and pushes forward.

"No, I can't. But I want you happy and life in the DCA isn't a happy one. You on the court is where you're happy. Take the opportunity. Allow yourself the happiness you deserve. I resigned from the DCA. This is my last op. I'm done. This is Nick's last op too. We have the chance to build whatever life we want and I want us to have a normal one."

"I don't belong in a normal life," he grumbles.

The room gets silent as Kat and I struggle with what to do with that. We both feel that way too, but our reasons are different than Jake's. We feel that way because of the DCA. Jake feels that way because of life.

"Jake can I tell you a story?" Shanny asks quietly.

"Sure."

"Once there was a little girl that had everything in the world. She had a rich and powerful father that could've given her anything. She was full of love and opportunity. Then one day someone murdered her father and tried to kill her. Her uncle rescued her and spent the next ten years training her to be a machine so she'd never be in danger again. A machine that could kill anyone that got in her way. A machine that could stay calm in any situation that she might face. A machine that didn't belong in the normal world. That girl went off to college trying to find a place where she fit in the normal world. She didn't have a friend or family left other than her uncle that was dying of cancer.

"So on her first day of class at college when three annoying cocky boys invited her to a party she decided to take a chance at normal. It was the best and scariest choice she ever made in her life. That night at the party she was attacked and almost raped. It didn't matter that she was a machine because she was alone in the world and needed someone to have her back. Those three boys found her and saved her from the monster that was attacking her.

"That night she got the family she didn't have. She found her family in an unconventional place, but it gave her normal. It gave her the chance to build her own normal world where a machine could learn to live and breathe. She didn't belong in the normal world either...until she found the place where she could be the normal she needed to be," Shanny finishes her green eyes never leaving Jake's big browns.

Kellerman picks up his fiancée's hand and kisses the palm. He knows that story better than most I'm sure and it still causes him pain. It causes me pain.

"Are you happy?" Jake asks Shanny softly.

"Yes."

"Do you think you could teach me how to live and breathe?"

"Yes."

A small sob breaks from Kat's chest. I squeeze her hand, but I keep my eyes trained on Shanny and my son.

"I have to be able to shoot to breathe," Jake admits sheepishly.

"Me too, sweetheart," Shanny coos.

"Okay, Mom. I'll go to Kansas City," Jake says leaving Shanny's gaze and looking over to Kat.

Kat doesn't say anything, she just nods with tears streaming down her cheeks. We still don't know the details of Jake's life, but knowing that he feels a connection to Shanny's story paints a bad enough picture that it's gut-wrenching to imagine.

Kat and I have been a lot of things in life, but Jake needs someone like Shanny. I'm even more thankful for my friend in this moment. She can help Jake heal in a way that I'm not sure we could. And looking into Kat's eyes right now she knew that. As his mother she knew we didn't have enough in common with him to help him. My wife continues to stun me at every corner.

"Do you have enough room for all of us?" Sawyer breaks the tension in the room.

"Man, we've got plenty," Kellerman answers in a chuckle.

They live in a monster of a house that Kellerman just finished adding an even bigger addition to. I think last Shanny told me it had something insane like fifteen bedrooms and twenty bathrooms. They've got room for my four boys.

"Can we call you Aunt Shanny?" Sawyer whispers.

"I'd love that. And you're gonna make me cry and I don't cry, so knock it off," she finishes in a huff, steeling herself against the tears pricking her eyes.

"I wish I could do that," Kat scoffs wiping her tear stained cheeks.

"No, you don't," Shanny says grimly. That's part of the machine.

Kat squeezes her friend's hand in understanding.

We go about setting up plans to get the boys and their stuff to Kansas City. It won't take much work so it's a short conversation. Which is good, because Kat's doctor comes in and starts poking and prodding my wife as soon as we finish talking. I growl and scowl at the man as he does his job. Kellerman offers me empathetic gazes and a few smiles. I think he may be a new friend for me. I'd like that. I think moving to Kansas City is looking more and more like the best option for my family after the op is wrapped. The look on Kat's face as she watches her boys banter and jack around says we're thinking the same thing. Normal life here we come.

Chapter 34

Nick

"Cooper," I bark into the burner phone.

"Nick, we've got the DNA results for Cara," Shane informs me.

"Yeah?"

"She's Shannon's sister and your cousin."

"I need you to put Cara on a plane here. Shanny's taking the boys back to Kansas City, Jake included. Shanny's here at the hospital. Thanks for callin' her by the way."

I'm speaking in short clipped sentences because my brain is beyond tired and overwhelmed at this point. I don't have much to offer.

"I'm not sure Cara's ready to make a move like that."

"Shane, I need your help here. I don't wanna cause Cara any more trauma, but if you don't send her here, Shanny's comin' to her. You don't know Shannon Kelly, but you don't wanna have to deal with her on your own."

"I did some digging on your friend. You've been keeping some talent hidden."

"Yeah and she'll stay that way. I wouldn't advise you trying to do anything about that. If she doesn't kill you, one of her family members or I, will. In case you're wondering, that's three fathers, two mothers, nine brothers, a crime boss cousin, and a few others that I can't even begin to explain. Stay the fuck away from Shanny," I growl.

"Nick," he huffs, "I wasn't givin' you shit. I was just pointing out the obvious. You're clearly not in the head space for it."

"No, I'm not. I'm gettin' ready to tell my best friend some shit that'll hurt her. I've gotta put my boys on a plane to move half way across the country. I've got a pregnant wife in the hospital. I've got an op to wrap. I'm not in the mood for your shit."

"Right. Sorry. I understand you movin' the boys out. It's a good plan. I'm not sure about Jake goin'. He's an asset to the op."

"He's goin'. Kat's made it clear that he's goin'. You can speak to him on your own, but I want him off the op. Shanny's takin' the boys and she'll take Cara too. Jake can help Cara. They had a connection the night we found her. It works for the good of everybody."

"Good point. All right, I'll speak with the psych team and see what they think. I can't move her if it's gonna be a setback for her. She's fragile, Nick."

"I get that. But living in a safe house isn't what's best for her. She needs support. Shanny will ensure Cara gets whatever she needs and then some. Get her on a plane."

"I'll call you with the details. How's Kat?"

"She's conscious and pissed. I think the finesse of this op is gone. We're gonna have to reassess how we're approaching this."

"I agree. Get her home and then we'll run through our options. Let me get to work on this stuff with Cara. Give Kat our love."

"Will do."

I hang up and move back toward the hospital room. I lock my gaze with Shanny's bright green eyes filled with understanding...she knows. I don't have to say the words or explain anything. She knows.

"Where is she?" Shanny demands, meeting me in the corridor.

"She's in a safe house. I've asked the DCA to send her here," I respond wrapping her in my arms. She nods into my chest clutching at my back.

"How bad is she?" she murmurs.

"Bad."

"Fuck," she huffs pulling away from me.

We move back to the hospital room and Kellerman who's holding Johnny. I reach for the baby so he can tend to Shanny. I'm shocked at the weight of the six month old in my arms. He's definitely his father's son. Johnny grabs a hold of my bottom lip and giggles as I mouth it like I'm eating his fingers.

"You're gonna be a big brother soon," I inform him while I retake my seat as Kellerman holds Shanny in his lap speaking words of love and comfort. They speak quietly, shielding the boys from their conversation since we haven't told them about this clusterfuck.

"You look pretty good holding a baby," Kat compliments from her bed.

"I look good all the time, Sunshine," I respond with a cocky grin.

"True," she whispers as her eyes flutter shut and she falls back to sleep.

"He's a big baby," Jake says from the couch, watching Johnny intently.

"Have you seen his dad?" Cole asks in a duh voice.

"Do you know what the twins are?" Sawyer asks as Shanny shifts in Kellerman's lap to face the group.

"More boys. I have the market cornered," Shanny says with a grin.

"That's good because we already have a system for girls and if you had one or two comin' we'd have to change the rules," Dane explains.

"How's that?" Kellerman asks curiously.

"We all have dibs on the babies comin'. This one's Jake's. Mom and Dad said they're gonna have three more so that gives each of us one to watch out for. If they're girls then we only have one we have to protect all the time from guys like us," Cole explains. "We didn't know we'd have cousins too. Jake you gonna take Johnny as your cousin to watch out for?"

"Yeah."

"I get the first twin," Sawyer jumps in.

"Second," Cole pipes up.

"Uh...I'm not good at this game," Dane says dejectedly.

"You can have the next one," Shanny says sweetly.

"You're gonna have more?" Dane asks stunned.

"I don't know if we'll have another one or adopt, but we'll have more kids," Shanny explains.

"That's cool."

"You've got good kids, Cooper," Kellerman says, offering me respect in his gaze.

"I know."

"They must get it from their mother," he jokes.

"No doubt about that," I confirm with a chuckle.

Johnny has taken to eating my finger with a large amount of drool. It's gross and cute. I may turn into a pussy after all. Kat's been asleep most of the day. She wakes up here and there, but more than anything she's sleeping. She looks exhausted and they can't give her anything other than pain relievers since she's pregnant. So we're all letting her rest as much as we can.

"Cooper, why don't we take the boys home? Let you and Kat have some time alone," Kellerman suggests.

"Thanks, man. Boys, you set them up in the guest room for me. I'll stay here again tonight."

"Okay," they respond begrudgingly. They don't want to leave Kat any more than I do.

"I'd offer to stay at a hotel but that would just be bullshit," Shanny admits with a smile.

"Come on try. I wanna see what fake Shannon Kelly looks like," I goad.

"Want me to kick your ass in front of your kids?"

"Maybe some other time."

"Just let me know when."

"Can she really kick your ass?" Sawyer asks with big brown eyes bugging out at our snarky conversation.

"Yes," Shanny answers plainly.

"Really?"

"She has more training. I have more experience. It'd be a good fight," I offer the boys that are beyond curious about the anomaly that is my best friend.

"No, it wouldn't. You'd be on the ground crying like a little girl," Shanny teases.

"I'll take you up on that."

"Would you let them fight?" Dane asks Kellerman who's packing the baby up.

"Nothing sexier than watchin' her kick someone's ass."

"But he's a guy." Sawyer tries to understand what's going on.

"And?" Shanny asks offended. Only she would get offended by that question.

"He's a lot bigger than you, stronger than you. You can't actually beat him."

"What the fuck are you teaching these kids?" Shanny offers me a glare.

"That boys shouldn't hit girls."

"Well that's true, but I'm not a girl so we're good."

"You look like a girl to me," Cole says with a small smirk on his lips.

"I have lady parts, but that's where most of the girl in me stops. I don't think like a girl or act like one most of the time. I haven't spent any time around women in my life until recently. Being raised by men and then only having male friends made me different. And I definitely don't fight like a girl," she explains honestly. I know Shanny can lie, but she's truthful at all times. It's refreshing to see after what Kat and I have lived the last ten years.

"Can we not talk about lady bits? What's with that lately?" Cole releases a gag just like he did a few days ago.

"Do you prefer to talk about manly parts? I'll talk about that all day long if you're more comfortable."

"Jesus, you're nuts. I don't wanna talk about any parts."

Shanny lets out a loud raspy belly laugh as she swings an arm around his shoulders.

"Sweetheart, you're gonna be very uncomfortable in my house."

"Dad where are you sending me?" Cole asks with a bit of terror dancing in his blue eyes.

"Shanny'll explain this to you, but she lives with a lot of guys and they're pretty disgusting from what I remember. It'll be a learning experience."

"You live with a bunch of guys? What about? What?" Dane fumbles trying to grasp that information.

"I've lived with the same guys from my story earlier since I was seventeen. We'll always live together. It works for us."

"Your fiancée lives with a bunch of dudes?" Dane switches his honey eyes to Kellerman.

"Yup," he pops his *p* in response. "She was a package deal when I met her. I got my future wife and new best friends. It worked out well for all of us."

"I don't think I could deal with that," Dane grumbles.

"You deal with a lot in life for love, bud."

"No shit."

"All right, boys, let's get you home," Shanny directs.

All the boys kiss Kat tenderly, trying not to disturb her sleep. Shanny wraps me in a rib crushing hug before placing a soft kiss on my cheek.

"Love you, Nicky," she murmurs into my skin.

"Love you too."

I press a long kiss to her forehead before releasing her. Kellerman shakes my hand before I pull him in for a manly back patting half hug.

"Thanks for everything. I owe you," I say locking eyes with him.

"You don't owe me shit. You saved my woman's life and defended her when I couldn't. Three fuckin' times. I owe you. I'll keep your kids safe."

His words knock the breath out of me so I just offer him a chin lift as he walks out of the room with everything I love in the world other than my wife. I trust him to keep them safe. It's a relief I can't describe. Now I can focus on Kat and getting her home. Once I have her home I'm turning our basement into a torture chamber and dragging the Bookers down there until they give me what I want. The monster has one last kill before I release him forever. I better make it good.

Chapter 35

Kat

Everything is covered in fluffy white pillows, twinkling with hidden Christmas lights. The ride home is quiet and I take advantage, absorbing the false beauty of Maybelle. There's over a foot of snow on the ground and more snowflakes are pouring from the cloudy grey sky. Nick drives slowly, carefully attending to the road. I just want him to hurry up and throw caution to the wind. I want my boys in my arms as much as I can have them before they leave.

Waking up yesterday with all the boys in the room along with Shannon and her family...I knew. Nick and I can't keep the boys safe and wrap the op. I need to know they're away from here and protected. I've spent days talking to Shannon for a few hours off and on. It's not a lot, but it's enough to know she'll keep my family safe. And after getting eyes on her gigantic drop dead gorgeous fiancé, I felt even better about the decision. Nick trusts Shannon above anyone and I trust Nick. So I'm shipping my newly acquired kids to the Midwest. I hate it.

"How're you doin'?" Nick asks as we turn on our road.

"I'm okay, Nicky."

He's asked me that question about twenty times since I was discharged from the hospital this afternoon. It's driving me nuts and making me happy.

As we approach the house, I notice our driveway is full of cars including a Maybelle Police cruiser. And just like that my head doesn't hurt, my mind is clear and Nick drives at an appropriate pace.

I jump out of the SUV as Nick storms into the house. I follow quickly, skidding to a stop at the sight in front of me. Shannon is about two inches from Officer Burke's face, while Dylan is in a protective stance in front of the boys. The Ashcrofts and Benningtons are standing behind Burke, looking pale.

"Are you aware that kidnapping children is a punishable offense?" Shannon asks in an intimidating growl.

"Ma'am, we have court orders," Burke says in a cocky tone.

"No, what you have are motions for hearings to consider parental rights reinstatement. Can you read?"

"Ma'am, typically in these cases parental rights are reinstated. There's a request for visitation included."

Nick and I slide into the fray, flanking either side of Shannon. I let her continue to work though. She's an attorney after all.

"I can guarantee you parental rights will not be reinstated to those people and they'll never get visitation. I'll work day and night to make certain of that. No judge in this state will give children back to parents that abandoned them for months with little to no contact during that time. While the request indicates the children were left with able bodied staff to care for their needs, there is no evidence to support this claim. The children moved into this home with no concern from the biological parents. They had no idea who was caring for their children for months. That is classic abandonment."

"Ma'am, you can argue your case to the judge."

"You bet your ass I can. Now, I suggest you leave this home before I call the Chief of Police and inform him of your persistent harassment of my clients. Don't come back to this property without a warrant. And you four," she directs her verbal assault to the parents. "I suggest you save your money and your time and drop this case. I'll bleed you dry and tie you up in court until the boys are eighteen. I'll also dig into your lives so far that I'll find every salacious thing you've ever done. If you're willing to fight that hard for the boys, good luck."

"She murdered a man and he shot Patricia Lancaster in front of all the boys," Mrs. Ashcroft complains like a petulant child.

"Both of those events are unfortunate. I'd like to point out that those incidents were in the defense of the child abandoned by the perpetrators. Nevertheless, I can see you must be concerned since you're here for your children. Were you concerned before or after the motion for you to reinstate the boys' trust funds came through?"

I stand stock still not knowing anything about reinstatement of the boys' trust funds. I keep my mask on and stare down the quivering puddles being assaulted by my friend.

"We shouldn't have to pay for them if we're not responsible for them," Mr. Bennington grinds out.

"All right, I'll revoke the motion and you'll leave the boys alone from now on. No contact at all. If you attempt to contact them again, I'll come after every dime you have. I'm aware of some SEC violations that could be very problematic for you Mr. Bennington. And Mr. Ashcroft, I suggest you get your financials in order before you enter a courtroom with me. Hookers and blow can only be hidden so well."

She's met with stark silence. I'm in awe.

"If there's nothing else, I believe you should see yourselves out," Shannon finishes fiercely. "And Officer Burke, heed my advice. If you come near my clients again for any reason without cause, I'll come after your badge."

He flares angry eyes at her until Nick and Dylan take a step toward him. That causes the punk to pale to a shade matching the idiots behind him.

"Time to go," Nick growls.

The five of them turn swiftly and head to the front door, Nick and Dylan following with menacing glares on their faces. When they're out of sight I wrap my arms around Shannon as hard as I can.

"I'm so fuckin' sorry," she murmurs into my hair. "That was my fault. I wanted to draw them outta the woodwork with the financial threat. I should've told you and Nicky about it. I didn't think they'd have the balls to show up here with a dirty cop. I'm sorry, Kat."

"Nothing to be sorry for. You were lookin' out for my boys," I assure her softly.

I release her from my grasp and pull Cole and Dane into my arms.

"You okay?" I mumble into their hair.

"We're good. Aunt Shanny had that shit under control. And Uncle Dylan was about to smash Junior Burke's face in," Cole says with a chuckle.

I chuckle along with him. They're okay.

"My turn," Nick announces at my side.

I release our boys and fold myself into Dylan's arms. He holds my body so snugly I can barely draw a decent breath.

"Get off my wife, Kellerman," Nick growls in a teasing tone.

"Payback's a bitch," Dylan snickers squeezing me harder before letting me go.

"What was that about?" Nick asks Shannon as he pulls her into a brief hug, smirking at Dylan. These men are ridiculous.

"When you told me they pulled financial support I submitted a motion to reinstate the trusts. That money is technically the boys'. It was accruing interest and set in place while they were still in their custody. That money should go to the boys. I figured it would give us the opportunity to push the biological parents off permanently when you told me they were posturing to try to get the boys back. I didn't anticipate them rolling in here with Officer Douche to try and steal the kids. I'm sorry, Nicky. I was tryin' to help."

We got word a few days ago that the Ashcrofts and Benningtons were making moves to try and get custody back. Shane assured us that wouldn't happen, but I told Shannon about it. I guess she decided to fix it on her own. I don't care that those idiots showed up here.

302

Shannon just scared the shit out of them and I'm confident they'll go away for good now. They don't love the boys. This was about money and them trying to get custody was about saving face in *Stepford*.

"You did good, Shanny. Scared the shit out of 'em too. I don't think we'll hear from them or Officer Douche again," Nick compliments.

"Aunt Shanny," Dane says tentatively as we all congregate around the breakfast bar.

"Yeah?"

"You're kinda scary when you're pissed."

"I didn't mean to scare you. I'm sorry. I would never treat you boys that way."

"I wasn't scared of you...it was just scary. Kinda like Mom gets scary."

"I told you we're a lot alike, Dane. Shannon was just keeping you safe," I say softly pulling him into my arms as I sit on a stool. He steps between my legs and folds himself into my chest, breathing me in. I return the sentiment, burying my face is his messy dirty blond locks.

When Johnny starts crying on the baby monitor Jake jumps up from his stool, beating Shannon and Dylan to the punch. I guess Jake has dibs on Johnny.

"Hey, buddy," Jake's grunts filter through the monitor. I'm sure he's lifting the sizeable baby.

Johnny starts giggling and spitting as Jake makes his way down the stairs. When Jake comes back in the room it's the cutest sight I've ever seen. He's holding Johnny up to his face and tickling the baby's belly with his mouth. Johnny squeals and kicks in pure heaven. Jake walks past us all before sitting on his stool and plopping the baby on the bar in front of him. I see the sparks of love between the two and it warms my soul.

Shannon pulls out her phone and starts snapping pictures as the other boys jump in on the action. I move to stand up and get hit with a dizzy spell, flopping back onto my stool but not before Dylan notices. I try to smile it off. It doesn't work.

303

"Cooper, your woman needs a hand," he points out.

Nick looks over at me with a scowl before stalking toward me.

"What's wrong?"

"Just a little dizzy. I need to lie down."

He scoops me to his chest before I finish talking. I don't get the opportunity to talk to anyone as Nick carries me up the stairs to our bed. I sigh in relief as my body hits the cool sheets. I'm so thankful the boys bought me these sweats for Christmas. They'll be my new uniform.

"Thanks," I mumble as Nick pulls the duvet up to my chin.

"I wanna climb in there with you, but I need to make some calls and spend some time with the boys. Text me if you need me. Don't get up on your own," he orders.

"'Kay."

I close my eyes and fall asleep before he leaves the room.

I wake up as warm muscled arms engulf my body from behind. I snuggle my hips against Nick and interlace our fingers over the home of our baby. We both missed the first sonogram. I was unconscious in the emergency room and Nick was in the waiting room while they did the scan. We'll go next week for another one once I'm feeling better. At least we have a due date now, August fourteenth.

"Hey," Nick whispers against my hair.

"Hey."

"Feeling better after your nap?"

"Yeah. My head doesn't hurt anymore."

"I need to get some food in you. Just wanted to hold you for a few minutes," he says breathing deeply.

"Everything okay?"

"Shanny has the house under control. Don't worry."

"I'm so glad she's here. I wish Jess and Shane were here too. It's nice to be able to rest and know you're all taken care of."

"I'm glad she's here too. You wanna talk about sending the boys away. We haven't really had the chance to talk about that."

"Nothing to talk about. They need to go. Jess and Shane work so we can't send them there. Shannon's at home and has a house full of help. It's the best place for them to go. I don't wanna send 'em away. I fuckin' hate this. I feel guilty that we involved them in this op. But I can't imagine not having them now. So we have to do what's right. They have to go."

"I know. You wanna tell me what happened with Patricia?"

"The doorbell rang and Sawyer went to answer it. We were down in the basement. She came in the room with her gun at Sawyer's head. I launched at her, but she was like fighting ten people at once. Next thing I know I'm waking up in the hospital."

"I'm sorry," he murmurs into neck before kissing the sensitive skin.

"Nothing to apologize for, Nicky. You came and got us. That's all that matters."

I roll to face him. His deep brown eyes carry equal amounts of worry and promise of violence. I don't think we'll be able to keep up the front of *Stepford* anymore. It's time to get creative and I have the best partner for just that.

"You're gonna have to quit lookin' at me like that," Nick grumbles.

"Like what?" I feign innocence.

"I'm not having sex with you until the doctor clears you. So quit."

"I don't recall the discharge orders requiring celibacy."

I run my hands up his chiseled torso before looping them around his neck, pulling his face down to me. I press a soft kiss to his warm lips and wait for him to take over. He always takes over. I work my mouth against his as my tongue tickles the seam of his. He growls in his chest, rumbling against my tender breasts before opening his mouth and taking over. We make out like teenagers exploring each other's faces, necks and ears until we're both panting with desire.

I make the move and grab his throbbing dick through his jeans. He snatches my wrist before I can stroke him once.

"Don't," he growls.

I huff and release him. He's got more willpower than I do.

"Now you're pissed," he says with a smirk on his lips.

"No, I love bein' rejected by the man I love after goin' without for a month and a half. It's great," I snark.

"Kat," he breathes out in defeat.

I roll my eyes and remove myself from his arms. I'm going total chick here and I don't care. I want his hands on me, his mouth devouring me and his dick inside me. I'm not above using guilt to get it.

I thud down the stairs to find Shannon in the kitchen cooking up a storm alone.

"Hey lady," she calls over her shoulder until she sees the look on my face. "What?"

"Men," I huff, saddling up beside her.

"Tell me about it," she says with a snicker.

I take over chopping duties for her while Shannon continues at the stove.

"He won't have sex with me," I complain as I assault some potatoes.

"Why?"

"Because of my head."

"Kel went down on me while I was still in the hospital last year. Best fuckin' thing in the world. In a coma one minute, comin' like crazy the next."

"Stop bragging," I groan.

We both chuckle and fall into friendly conversation like we've known each other for years. It feels like we have.

"Hey pussy," Shannon calls out as Nick and Dylan stroll in the room.

"I know she's not talkin' to me," Dylan says through a deep chuff.

"I'm not talkin' to you, Kel. You're not afraid to fuck me."

"Jesus Christ, Kat. Really?" Nick groans in annoyance.

"I'm just talkin' to my friend."

"Your friend has a limited brain to mouth filter."

"No, I don't," Shanny says pointedly. "She's not gonna break. Kel went down—"

"I don't wanna know," Nick says putting his hands up to stop her.

"You *are* a pussy. Who knew the big bad Nick Cooper was really just a little bitch?"

"Are you really tryin' to bully me into havin' sex with Kat?"

"Yup."

"I knew you two would be trouble. Fine. Come on, Kat," he orders holding a hand out to me.

"No, that's okay. Shannon's filled me up vicariously. Dylan, I'm really—"

I'm cut off as Nick hauls me over his shoulder, stalking toward the stairs.

"Caveman carrying should always be a last resort," Shannon yells as Nick runs up the stairs two at a time.

He kicks the door shut and flicks the lock before lying me down on the bed gently. His eyes meet mine and are anything but tender. He's pissed and horny, desire washing over me. This should be interesting.

Chapter 36

Nick

I drink in the sight of Kat's golden locks spread across the pillow. It looks better than I imagined it would the first time I saw her. It's even more intoxicating with her blue-green-grey eyes sparkling with want. I've just been bullied into fucking the woman I love. I'm pissed. I'm tired. I'm so fucking horny I feel like I'm fifteen again. This is not how I wanted to do this.

I strip Kat quickly trying to be careful with her. I'm out of my clothes even faster. I cover her body with mine before pulling her hard nipple into my mouth. She hisses and pulls away from my mouth.

"Sore," she apologizes.

"Sorry."

I leave her tits alone and travel south. I kiss and worship her soon to be not so flat stomach, causing goosebumps to rise on her skin. Moving further down, I'm elated to find her dripping wet and quivering beneath me. I pull her hips to my face and feast, spearing my tongue in her hole, lapping her juices. As her legs constrict around my ears I move to her clit, flicking rapidly. She begins to quake with her orgasm as I release her from my mouth and before she can complain I plunge my dick inside her.

She screams.

She comes with such force she almost pushes me out of her. She rips and tugs at my back devouring my mouth as I thrust forward fast and hard. Another orgasm rips through her throat almost immediately. I growl into her mouth pushing deeper, my hips grinding against hers.

Kat's eyes roll back in her head as she releases my mouth. She silently mouths yes over and over again as she comes again, her pussy clutching my cock. Pregnancy is making her more responsive than she was before.

I nuzzle into her neck biting and kissing away the hurt as I pound into her. Her nails draw blood on my back as I pull her ear lobe into my mouth, nibbling and caressing.

"Nicky," she pleads for release.

I pull her legs around my hips and give her what she desires. My pelvis rocks against her clit while my dick rubs her sweet spot deep inside. My balls are dripping with her come, slapping against her tight ass. I drive forward bottoming out against the womb that holds my child sending her into her final earth shattering orgasm as I fill her with my come.

I stroke myself inside her sliding in and out slowly until she catches her breath. Finally, her legs and arms drop from around my body as exhaustion takes over. That's right. You wanted it and I gave it to you.

I kiss her deeply, reveling in the flavor of her pussy and her mouth mixing in mine. My dick twitches as she flicks her tongue over mine drinking from me.

"You want it again?" I growl against her mouth.

"Yes."

So I give it to her again. I slam into her until she begs me to stop. Until she can't take another orgasm...then I give her another.

I plod into the kitchen, hair still wet from my quick post-coital shower. Kellerman eyes me from the breakfast bar and holds up his fist. I pound it before dropping onto the stool next to him. Shanny slides a bowl of soup in front of me with a shit-eating grin plastered on her face.

"Anyone ever tell you you're a pain in the ass?" I ask before spooning delicious winter squash soup in my mouth.

"Pain in the dick is what I'm usually referred to," she answers with a shrug.

"That too."

"Where's Kat?" Shanny asks hoisting Johnny higher on her chest.

"Passed out."

"Then you did your job well. I'm gonna go lay him down."

Kellerman climbs to his feet to place a gentle kiss on Johnny's head then another on his fiancée's lips. He watches them meander away before joining me at the bar again. Beer in hand, he clinks it against mine before shooting me a wicked smile.

"Never turn down your woman...especially when she's pregnant," he instructs knowingly.

"Noted."

"Your boys are down playin' video games like they're goin' outta style."

"They do that."

"I made a call to a guy I work with. He's friends with a coach at the local high school. Pulled some strings and thinks he can get Jake and Cole on the team after winter break."

"Thanks, man. Wait 'til you see 'em on the court. Magic."

"How long do you think it'll take you guys to finish up here?" he asks curiously, not put out.

"I'm not sure. We were tryin' to finesse our way in, but there's so much heat on us now I don't see that workin'. Once Kat's back on her feet I think we'll have to go at it old school."

"No school like the old school."

We sit in silence a bit longer while I eat my soup.

"How's Shanny holdin' up with the Cara stuff?"

"You know her. She's a steel trap for shit like this. Not bein' able to get Cara here because of the storm is makin' her tense. Other than that she's good. She'll dive into it with Cara like she does everything else."

"How are you holdin' up?"

"We havin' a girl moment?"

"Yeah," I answer in a chuckle as I throw the last of my beer down my throat.

"I'm good, man. Seein' Kat in the hospital was a little too close to home for me, but other than that I'm good."

"Prepare to get your eyes on Cara. It's rough."

"I figured," he huffs draining his beer.

I climb off of my stool and grab us two more beers before returning to my spot with another bowl of soup and half a loaf of homemade bread.

"I'm gonna say this one more time because I wanna get it off my chest. I'm sorry for not keepin' Shanny safe last year. I wanted to more than I can tell you. I didn't read the situation well enough and that's on me. I know what you went through in the hospital waiting for her to wake up from the coma and I hate myself even more now. I never wanted anything bad to happen to her."

"Cooper, I was a dick. You saved her life. You wrapped your hands around her head and saved her life from that bullet. I was jealous and scared and bein' a little bitch. You have a connection to her that I'll never get and I took that shit personally. You have a nickname for her that her fuckin' dad gave her. Every time I'd hear you say it I wanted to bludgeon you. It's irrational caveman shit. I can see that now. She loves you and that's good for her. I know you wanted her. I also respect that you never made that move. You fell in love with a girl and she came back to life right in front of your eyes. I never considered the struggle that would be for you.

"I didn't give a shit at the end of the day. I was too fucked up to think about anyone but her. You've spent a year bein' a good friend for her. Supporting her and gettin' through shit after everything. Don't carry that guilt anymore. It's not yours to carry. You saved her life.

You've done right by her since then. Now that damn nickname makes me fuckin' happy instead of homicidal. We're good, Cooper."

"You're a better man than I am," I mutter.

"Nah, I'm just growin' up. I've got everything I never thought I'd get. Puts shit in perspective. You've got that with Kat now. It'll mellow your shit out and make you a fuckin' idiot. It's a balance at the end of the day."

"What're you two talkin' about?" Shanny's voice rings into the kitchen.

"You," we both answer honestly.

"Boring!" she yells causing us all to laugh loud and hard.

"What's boring?" Kat questions striding in the room glowing. Sweats, no make-up, hair piled on her head and a pair of my socks on her feet...fucking perfection.

"These clowns," Shanny informs her friend.

"Hey, gorgeous," Kellerman purrs pressing a kiss to her cheek.

I don't growl (try not to growl).

"Hey," she responds beaming a smile at him.

I pull her between my legs pressing a long kiss to her pillowy lips.

"Sunshine," I murmur into her mouth.

"Nicky," she says through a grin.

"You want some soup, Kat?" Shanny asks.

"I'd love some, but I doubt I'll keep it down. I believe morning sickness has descended."

"Shitty. You wanna try some crackers and ginger ale?"

"I can get it."

"*Pfft.*" Shanny waves Kat away.

"Dad!" Cole shouts from the basement door.

"Yeah?" I yell back.

"You comin' down?" he asks peering into the room. His soft blues sparkling in the light as his blond hair falls into his eyes.

"You up for some gaming?" I ask Kellerman.

"Yup," he replies, picking up his beer and padding to his woman.

He drops a kiss on her lips as she drives her long fingers into his surfer-styled blond hair. Not to be out done, I capture Kat in a searing kiss of my own and force myself to pull away when a moan trickles from her lips.

"Jesus it's like a porn studio in here," Cole huffs.

"You'll get this someday, bud," Kellerman says through a wicked grin.

"I get that shit now. Just don't like seein' the parentals goin' at it."

Kellerman and I laugh as we make our way to my son and fall into the teenage lair of gaming and potato chips that they've smuggled in the house. It's a perfect man cave.

Chapter 37

Nick

Shane and I lead Cara into my family room where Kat, Shanny, Kellerman and Jake are waiting. We'll introduce the boys in a little while. Explaining the situation to them was a lot for the boys to take in. Cara needs to feel comfortable before we add them into the equation.

We've discovered Cara has more trouble with women than men. I think the night we found her she was so exhausted she just accepted Kat because she was there and being soft with Cara. Apparently, it was a woman and a man that tortured her in the dungeon. Cara wasn't in the same place for the decade she's been gone. She was moved around a few times. We haven't gotten the details on what she's endured at this point. She's been tight lipped with the psych team. She'll talk eventually and when she does she'll have the strongest support system in the world to unload on. Until then, I don't need to know details to know what a horror story her life has been.

Cara pulls up to a halt as we enter the room. Her eyes scan Shanny's face with shock and confusion at the similarities gazing back at her. We showed Cara pictures to prepare her for this, but in the flesh it's even more staggering.

Shanny offers a small kind smile but remains seated, clutching Kellerman's hand. It's taking every ounce of self-control my best friend has to not engage right now. Kellerman is soft and stoic as Cara peruses him. I want to sweep this girl to my side and hold her like the family that she is, but I don't. She's not there yet.

Cara moves her gaze to Kat and a small smile plays at her lips. Kat beams back at her, but stays seated next to Jake, waiting for Cara to make the move. Then it happens. Cara strides away from us right toward Jake. When Jake realizes her trajectory, he jumps off the couch and engulfs her in his arms as she flings herself into his chest.

"Hey, sweetheart," Jake murmurs into her auburn hair.

She's wearing Jake's hoodie, which I've been told she only takes off in order to shower or wash it. Cara's gained some weight, making her look closer to her seventeen than the original fourteen I thought she was. She makes no move to pull out of Jake's arms as he brushes his hands up and down her back.

"You wanna sit down with me?" Jake asks tenderly, pulling back to look into Cara's face.

She nods.

Jake sits on the couch and Cara curls into a tiny ball at his side as he sweeps his arm around most of her slight frame. I finally turn my gaze to Shanny to find her face a collage of emotions running from hurt to pride. Kellerman is still stoic, though there is a caveman bubbling beneath the surface toward the girl. Protective and enraged for the terror Cara's endured. Kat has tears rolling down her cheeks as she witnesses her son being the kind of man you pray your children become. It doesn't matter how Jake came to be hers. She's proud. I know how much pride she has because my heart's soaring with it. I lock my eyes with my son and do everything I can to let him know how in awe of him I am. After a few beats he breaks our eye contact to peer down at Cara with the slightest ghost of a smile playing at the corner of his mouth.

Shane and I take the chairs at the end of the room and wait to see what Cara's going to do. Psych said to let her make the moves. So we wait.

"Sweetheart," Jake encourages.

"I'm sorry," she immediately apologizes, uncurling from his side backing into Kat who pulls her in tight.

Jake schools his features even though that movement has distressed and frustrated him.

"Nothing to be sorry for," Jake whispers.

Cara avoids looking at him and studies her hands instead.

"Cara," Shanny starts causing Cara to jump a little. "I'm really happy to get to meet you."

"Shane said we have the same mother," Cara offers blankly.

"That's right."

"She was evil," Cara grumbles.

"Yes."

"Are you evil like her?"

The question tears at everyone in the room who knows Shanny is nothing like her monster of a mother. Shanny's mother hated her from the time she was born and culminated that hate by giving my Uncle Vito the information he used to execute the hit that killed her father and almost Shanny. Cara doesn't know those details so I don't blame her for asking, but it's still excruciating.

"No, but I don't expect you to believe that just because I say it. Trust takes a long time to earn and I'll do my best to show you that you can trust me. And I promise you right now, Cara, you can trust me. I'll keep you safe and I'll make sure anyone and everyone that's ever hurt you pays," Shanny finishes in a tone promising the things only Shannon Kelly can.

Cara's features soften at the tone and posture that would make most people uncomfortable. Kat rubs Cara's hand in comfort and she flinches. Kat stops and looks at me with remorse in her face. She just wants to help.

"I'm gonna live with you now." The tone in Cara's voice makes it sound like a death sentence.

"Not if you don't want to. It's up to you. I'll let you live wherever you feel the most comfortable. If you're unsure where that is, I'll work with you to help you figure that out. I'm not here to make your life harder. I'm here to make it better in any way that I can."

"What if I don't want anything to do with you?"

"Then I'll leave you alone," Shanny answers plainly.

This is beyond heart-wrenching to witness. I've met fucked up people, but Cara's carrying demons that will take a lifetime to expel.

"What if I wanna kill the people that did this to me?" Cara asks in a voice that mirrors Shanny so much I watch her mouth to be certain it's their origin.

"Then I'll train you to be able to do just that," Shanny replies definitively, her eyes flaring with excitement at the prospect.

"Can you?" Cara asks with fascination on her face.

"Yes."

"You can train me to kill people?" Cara clarifies, searching Shanny for the lie.

"I can train you to be anything you wanna be in life. If you wanna kill the people that did this to you, I'll spend every day training you like I've been trained in order to do that. If you don't think you want that, then I'll kill every single fucking person that had anything to do with this myself."

"I want them to pay."

"Me too," the room clamors in unison, making Cara jump.

"You live with all men? No women right?" Cara asks Shanny, starting to ease up with the tension she's carrying.

"I'm the only woman."

Ding, dong.

Everyone in the room goes rigid as the doorbell sounds. I take a breath before pushing to my feet. We smuggled Cara in the house seamlessly. It doesn't matter though, we're all on edge. I stride to the door and peer through the peephole to find the Bookers standing like a fucking Christmas card. I pull my *Stepford* mask on before opening the gleaming black door. I need these people out of here. They watch the house enough that they know we're home. It'll seem strange and out of character if I don't answer the door. I'm so sick of caring about shit like this. I'm ready to wrap this op.

"Nick, I hope we're not intruding," Trish apologizes loudly. She's trying to get a look at Shanny based on the timbre of her voice. Nosey bitch.

"We're actually busy right now, Trish. I'll have Kat give you a call once she's feeling better," I offer in a placating tone.

"Yes, of course. We just wanted to offer our help if you need anything."

"We've got family friends in town. We're all set. Thanks for stopping by."

"Oh, Kat, you look just awful," Trish cries out dramatically pushing past me into the foyer.

Tony huffs at his wife and follows her in my home. This is not good.

Trish has her arms holding Kat tightly when I turn to ask them to leave. The look on Kat's face is murderous when I meet her gaze. What the hell is going on?

"Shut the door, Nicky," Kat growls in a menacing tone.

Trish drops her arms from Kat and takes two steps back running into Tony when she hears Kat. I do as my wife instructs and lock the door for good measure. I'm putting pieces together quickly as I see Shanny come into view holding two guns. Her favorite Springfield 9mm that she's a ninja with and a small .22 that she always carries in her purse. Shit.

"Get on your knees," Shanny growls.

Trish yelps in fear, throwing herself to the ground dramatically while Tony lowers to his knees with his hands over his head, fear etching his features.

Shane stomps in the area with a roll of duct tape and immediately covers Trish's whimpering mouth. He continues by zip tying Trish's wrists behind her back before moving to Tony, taping his mouth and zip tying his wrists the same as Trish's.

"Weapons," Shane growls once he's done.

Kat launches up the stairs two at a time while I watch Shanny use every fleck of self-control she has to not blow these people to smithereens. Kat thumps back down the stairs looking like G.I. Jane. Four 1911s, two Glocks and an MP5 strapped across her back…maybe the sexiest I've ever seen her.

She passes me my weapons, Shane a 1911 and shoves the other 1911 in the back of her pants before leveling her aim at the Bookers in tandem with Shanny. All right we've got them covered.

"On your feet," Kat commands.

The Bookers stand shakily, as Shanny backs down the hall never leaving Trish's gaze. When we enter the kitchen I find Jake holding Cara around the waist from behind while Kellerman's hulking presence lingers in front of them.

"Stop," Shanny growls. "Let her see."

Kellerman obliges his fiancée and moves out of the way so Cara can look at the Bookers. She studies them long and hard before shaking her head dejectedly.

"I have to hear their voices," she mumbles, grasping Jake's forearms firmly.

A gleam of torture brims in Shanny's eyes as Shane forcefully removes the duct tape from the Bookers' mouths.

"Say hello to Cara," Kat instructs in an ominous tone.

"Hello, Cara," Tony says with a quiver in his voice.

Cara's brow furrows. She doesn't seem to recognize Tony, which is making me question what the hell we're doing.

"Tell me I'm a bad girl," Cara commands.

His face blanches as his throat bobs in disgust. Huh.

"You're a bad girl," Tony barely forces it out.

"That's not him," Cara says gloomily.

"Now you," Shanny barks at Trish who shakes her head silently, not uttering a word.

"Either you talk on your own or I'll do shit to you that'll make you scream the words I wanna hear," Kat seethes in her ear.

Trish's big blue eyes bug out with fear and then I see it. As she locks eyes with Cara, I know Trish Booker did this to her. I see the flames of a monster's fury billowing from her perfect façade.

"You're a bad girl," Trish seethes and Cara's green eyes alight with fear, anguish and finally rage.

Cara flails and screams in Jake's arms as he holds her from launching at Trish.

"Let me go, Jake. THAT'S HER!!" she wails.

Jake holds her tighter as he awaits her fight to wither. Cara kicks her legs and throws her arms, writhing and thrashing. Jake remains immovable, allowing her assault.

"Sweetheart, calm down. She's not goin' anywhere. I don't want you to hurt yourself. Please," Jake soothes in Cara's ear as the fight falls away from her and sobs begin to wrack her body.

"Trish, what in the world is going on?" Tony pleads with his wife looking at her like a stranger.

"Shut up, Tony," she snarls in a tone I've never heard the *Stepford* queen use and neither has Tony based on the expression of horror on his face.

Tony shifts his gaze to me as Cara's sobs quiet.

"Nick," his voice shakes. "I don't know that girl. I've never seen her in my life. Whatever Trish has done, we can work it out. Just let us go. I won't call the authorities."

In this moment I have a tiny amount of respect for the man. He's still trying to protect his family. It won't work, but he's trying to be a man.

I crouch down in front of Trish's face and she bores her lifeless pale blue eyes into mine.

"Do you wanna tell your husband what a filthy cunt you are or should I?" I ask in a taunting tone with a small smirk on my lips. My monster has come out to play.

She hawks back and spits in my face. As soon as she does Kat stomps on Trish's calf causing a feral cry to rip from her mouth. Tony lunges to protect his wife, but Shane buries the barrel of his piece in his temple stopping his movement. I pull my shirt up and wipe away the creature's drool before climbing to my feet.

"She does that," Cara says blankly.

"Spits?" Shanny asks with repulsion in her voice.

"Every time."

Simultaneously, Shanny and Kat unleash a torrent of mucus-filled spit showers on Trish's hair and face. When they're finished Trish is shaking and screaming at them to stop.

"We need to move this elsewhere," Shane instructs.

"Kat," I say pulling her from her blinding rage. "You and Shanny take her to the wine cellar. Shane and I'll take Tony to the office. Kellerman and Jake you stay with Cara. The boys'll be here in twenty. They don't need to know about this so get them to leave the house again."

Kat tosses the extra 1911 to Kellerman before she and Shanny drag Trish down the stairs by her hair as she wails and fights her removal.

"Move," Shane commands Tony, pulling him to his feet by his bound wrists.

Tony obliges, keeping his gaze on his feet not even looking in the direction of where his wife was just dragged. He's figuring some of this out. Once both our captives are moved I turn back to Cara and Jake.

"Cara," I say in the softest tone I can create.

Her green eyes are shimmering with torment and torture, leaking tears silently.

"Sweetheart, she'll never get you again. I need you to stay with Jake while we get information from them. Can you do that for me?"

"Will you kill her?"

"She'll die. I swear it." I pin her with my eyes so she can search for the truth in my words.

"I'll stay with Jake," she says confidently. "I want to see her die though."

I really don't think that's a good idea. This girl's had enough in her life to scar her. She doesn't need a dead body to add to that.

"Cara, I don't think that'll give you what you want," Kellerman says softly.

"How would you know?" she grinds out.

"I know," Jake murmurs into her hair. "Let's talk about it and then you can decide."

His grip hasn't loosened one bit since I've come into the room. He's holding onto Cara for dear life and she's clinging to Jake for every breath of support he's offering her. She relents to his words and his soft touch, nodding.

"Kellerman, if you're not comfortable with Shanny doin' this I'll step in down there," I inform him with a knowing look.

His teal eyes hold mine for a moment while he considers it.

"She's not in any danger and neither are the twins. If I pull her outta this she'll serve me my nuts for dinner. I fuckin' hate it, but I have to let her do this," he groans.

I know the feeling because I don't want Kat doing this either, but I don't get to make that decision. Trish is zip tied and Shanny and Kat are armed to the gills. They're safer than anyone in this house. I offer Kellerman a chin lift and head for the stairs as Jake starts to move Cara back into the family room. Kellerman tags the baby monitor, shoves the 1911 in the back of his pants and follows closely behind them.

I run up the stairs two at a time welcoming the monster that's taking me over with each step. I can taste the death, but I crave blood first.

Chapter 38

Kat

"Get some more tape on her mouth," Shannon complains as Trish wails and screams. I agree.

I rip off a piece of duct tape with my teeth before slamming Trish's head back with force as I cover her obnoxious hole.

We wrestled Trish into a chair and zip tied her ankles to the legs before securing her wrists to the arms. With her mouth taped shut, I can take a moment and think this through.

The wine cellar is at the back of the basement, surrounded in concrete about twelve feet high. The walls hold deep mahogany wine racks that glisten with the jewel tones of wine bottles. There's a small round ornate similar hued wood table in the room with four amber leather wrapped chairs. I flop into a chair next to Shannon and take my moment, staring at what will soon be my playground.

The doorbell rang and we all got tense. Not a surprise really. Then Trish's voice echoed through the house and Cara turned as white as a sheet in my arms and became rigid like stone. I tried to coax out of her what was wrong, but she was stuck. Frozen like a deer in headlights. Jake leapt into action when I couldn't get through.

He pulled Cara into his lap and cupped her cheeks, forcing her haunted eyes to focus on his.

"Sweetheart, do you know that voice?" he asked her in a pointed yet soft voice.

A tiny almost imperceptive nod followed and I jumped into action followed by Shannon and Shane. We all knew it in that moment. No questions to ask. No information required. Trish Booker tortured Cara.

Now two pregnant women are going to torture and kill a *Stepford Wife* and enjoy every second of it.

"I'm gonna go get some tools. Are you good on your own?" I ask Shannon who's studying Trish like a lion stalks its prey.

"Yup," she responds like this is the easiest thing she's ever done. I know she's been trained to stay calm in a crisis, but seeing it in person is pretty impressive. I'm also calm, but she's like a sleeping baby. This is going to be fun.

I sprint up the stairs and find Jake holding Cara to his side while Dylan sits across from them on the other couch in the family room.

"What's wrong?" Dylan asks climbing to his feet, concern marring his perfect features.

"Nothing. Shannon's got it under control. Trish's zip tied to a chair. I need tools," I say a little winded from running around. "Go down and wait with her if you're more comfortable."

He nods and heads that way. I love Dylan Kellerman.

"Cara, honey," I call out, making my way to her. "Everything's gonna be okay."

"I know," she says through a teary voice. "I wanna see her die, but Jake thinks it's a bad idea."

I flop down on the coffee table in front of her. I'm still strapped with weapons so I don't look all that comforting, but I try to soften my features for her.

"Watching someone die is hard. It sticks with you for the rest of your life. Shannon and I have been trained to deal with that and you haven't. You've been through enough, honey. Don't do that to yourself too. Let us carry that burden for you. You don't deserve anymore hurt from that monster."

"I'd rather have her dying in my head than what I have now," she starts strong with her insistence then wavers in the end.

"I understand that. I really do. But you're wrong, Cara. It won't help you to see her die. It'll hurt you. It'll tear away at your soul. Because I promise you, I'm gonna make it horrific. I can't let you see that. Please, honey. Trust me when I tell you this is for your own good," I urge her.

"She told me the next time she came for me she was gonna use a knife on me...down there," Cara says with a fierce growl.

"Did she hurt you like that?" I ask, pushing the gag and fury from my voice.

"No. They did other things to me. I..I don't want you to know," she whispers to Jake.

"If you wanna tell Kat, I'll give you some privacy."

She nods into his chest and he quickly uncurls from her and moves from the room toward the horrid formal dining room before closing the door.

"It was important that I was a virgin. I was gonna be sold to someone that wanted a virgin. I was given *training* about what they wanted from me. They hurt me so badly, Kat," she quivers with memories.

"Okay. I understand."

I don't need any more fucking details to understand what *training* means. Someone buying a sex slave only wants a certain type of slave.

"How long did they have you?" I ask gently.

"Two years or so. Before that I was with people that made me clean for seven years. Before that I lived in a cage until they found somewhere for me. Before that I lived with a bunch of other girls who were sold. I don't remember much before that."

"Do you remember your mother?"

"Only that she hated me. That's what they all told me," she growls.

I know this to be true because Shannon and Cara's mother was a fucking evil bitch.

"Do you remember your father?"

"No. I've never been with anyone that I knew as family. I've always been alone. I think I was in an orphanage or something like that from what I've read in books. When I was at the house I cleaned, one of the older girls taught me to read and write and would give me books all the time when we weren't working."

"And you were in the orphanage until you were seven?"

"Yes."

"But no one came for you or adopted you?"

I'm so confused by this.

"They told me nobody wanted me. That I came from evil people that no one wanted a child from," Cara recalls blankly. "Then one morning I woke up in a room full of other girls that I didn't know. I've never really known where I was since then."

"Why haven't you told the DCA about all this, honey?"

"I don't know," she says with a shrug. "It didn't really matter. I never thought anyone would find the people that did this to me. No one cares about me."

"We care about you, Cara."

"I think I believe you," she whispers staring at her hands.

"I need to get back downstairs now. Are you gonna be okay with Jake and Dylan?"

"I feel safe when I'm with Jake. I don't understand it, but I feel so safe with him," she admits with a shaky voice.

"You're safe with all of us, but you're definitely safe with Jake. I'll go get him and then I'm gonna head back."

She nods and I resist the urge to wrap her in my arms. She feels safe in Jake's arms so that's where I'll put her. I hurry to the formal dining room and push the door open to find Jake already moving toward me. He wraps his arms around me as tightly as he does when I hold him after his nightmares. I squeeze him back just a fiercely.

"I'm so proud of you," I murmur into his hair. "She needs you now."

He nods and releases me, speedily running across the house to get back to Cara. I watch as she dives into his arms, clinging to his body like he clings to mine. I watch for another breath as Jake gathers her body onto his lap and caresses her auburn hair lovingly before I move into the garage and grab Nick's toolbox. This should do.

I make my way back down to the basement hefting the toolbox with me. When I enter the room Trish is unconscious and Shannon is smiling.

"She kept whining," Shannon says through a wicked grin. "I had to knock her out."

I nod and start going through the tools as Dylan kisses Shannon and tells her he loves her and to be safe. I feel his massive arms encapsulate my body from behind.

"Be safe," he orders into my hair.

I nod and pat his hands before he lets me go. He shuts the door with a click as he leaves.

"You've got a good man, Shannon," I compliment as I grab a pair of needle-nose pliers.

"Yes, I do. You do too."

"I know," I say through a smirk. "I talked to Cara and got a bit of background. Trish and whoever she was workin' with were *training* Cara to be sold to a buyer that wanted a virgin. They've had her for two years. Before that she was a domestic for seven. Before that she lived in a cage. Before that she was in a slave cattle call. Before that she lived in some kind of orphanage in Chicago."

"Jesus," she blows out at the barrage of information. "I can't wait to make this bitch bleed. I know you need information from her so I'll keep my shit in check until it's time, but when it's time, I've got this."

"Agreed."

I move to Trish's unconscious body and grasp her thumb before using my pliers to remove the perfectly

329

manicured white tipped nail. Trish wakes up screaming, her eyes panicked. She thrashes around in the chair as I hold the nail in front of her face.

"You're gonna lose all of these then we're gonna talk," I inform her coolly and go about removing the other nine fingernails she's spent a fortune on keeping properly *Stepford*.

The tape muffles her screams as I work while Shannon watches with a grin on her lips. I feel one on mine too. Once I remove the final pinky nail, I sit down next to Shannon and wait for Trish's sobs to stop.

"That felt good," I inform the room.

Shannon claps me on the back before striding to Trish and ripping the tape with a good amount of skin from her face.

"You stupid fucking bitch. You have no idea who you're fucking with. You're a dead woman," Trish threatens me.

"The only dead woman in here is you. Tell me what I wanna know and I'll leave you alone and let Shannon here get to work on you. Don't tell me and I'll stretch this out for days. I've got all the time in the world. Now who's the man that hurt Cara?" I ask clearly.

"Fuck you," she spits.

"Well that was easy," Shannon snarks.

"Toenails it is. Tape her mouth shut again. I have a headache. I don't wanna hear the screaming," I say to Shannon like I'm talking about the weather.

Shannon tapes her mouth again and then backhands Trish for good measure. I go about my business removing some very ugly toenails. Some people aren't fortunate in the feet department. I decide to break a few toes for good measure as I finish up.

"I'm gettin' sweaty," I say to Shannon as I flop in the seat next to her.

"Let's take a break. I should check on the baby."

"Okay."

We stand up and leave an unconscious Trish in the black cavern of the wine cellar and head upstairs to take a break.

Chapter 39

Nick

I'm glad to have the soundproof office and the virtually soundproof wine cellar. I'm also loving having security feeds all over the house so I can monitor everyone with ease.

Shane has Tony zip tied to a wooden chair at the wrists and ankles, his mouth taped shut again. Tony's panicked and breathing hard watching Shane and I move around the room. We have a problem with Tony because I'm not sure he has a hand in this. I have to be certain, but either way, I'm not sure Tony's making it out of this alive. He's seen us and will know what we've done to his wife. The DCA doesn't leave witnesses.

"Tony," I begin coolly, "I'm gonna remove the tape from your mouth. This room is soundproof so you can scream all you want, but I suggest you don't. Screaming has a tendency to make Shane aggressive."

Shane plays the role well, cracking his neck from side to side while rolling his sleeves up. Shane hasn't been in the field for five years, but you never forget how this works. I'm not worried about his abilities. The Ken Doll looks more like a G.I. Joe right now.

I pull off the tape, gently. I'm going to try this differently from what I can see Kat and Shanny doing on the monitor. Fingernails right off the bat for Trish.

"Nick, you've made a mistake. I don't know what you think we've done. Please let us go," he pleads.

"I appreciate you fighting for your wife, but you know she's not what you think she is. Or maybe you know what she is and you're a better actor than her. That's what we're here to find out."

"How does that girl downstairs know Trish?" he asks in a pained voice.

"You tell me."

"I have no clue. I'm not lying to you. I've never seen that girl before in my life. She doesn't have a face you'd forget."

"She knows your wife."

"It would seem so," he whispers dejectedly.

"Do you like to rape little girls?" I goad.

"WHAT? NO! I have a daughter. Are you insane?!" he responds ferociously.

"Your wife likes to hurt little girls. She hurt that girl downstairs for a long time," I offer blankly.

"That's...I can't...This can't be happening." He stumbles and fights the reality soaking in.

"Listen to this," Shane instructs.

He turns the sound up in the wine cellar.

"You stupid fucking bitch. You have no idea who you're fucking with. You're a dead woman." Trish's threatening far from *Stepford* voice shrieks through the speakers.

"The only dead woman in here is you. Tell me what I wanna know and I'll leave you alone and let Shannon here get to work on you. Don't tell me and I'll stretch this out for days. I've got all the time in the world. Now who's the man that hurt Cara?" Kat responds blankly.

"Fuck you," Trish spits and Shane cuts the sound.

"She's not denying anything. She did this. Now I wanna know if you did this too?"

"I've never heard her speak like that in my life. I've known Trish since we were kids. How? How can this be happening? She's the mother of my children. You're telling me she hurt that girl downstairs? Did she hurt my kids? How do you know all this? Who are you people?" Tony's freaking out and looks like he may vomit. Most people in this situation do that or worse.

"I'm not here to answer your questions. I need my own answers. Are you telling me for the last fifteen years you haven't been running a human trafficking ring and Trish has been…right under your nose without your knowledge?" I ask disbelieving.

I've spent the last four months "married" to Kat and I know everything she does in a day. There's no way this man is married to a woman and is that clueless.

"What?" He's not keeping up and I feel my patience waning.

My phone vibrates.

Jake: Texted the guys saying it's not going well with Cara. They're hanging at the Lancaster place until we reach out.

Nick: Good. She doing ok?

Jake: I've got her.

Nick: I'll check in later.

Jake: Ok.

Shane's brow is furrowed in concern at the texting. I offer him a chin lift to let him know everything's good.

"Are you trafficking people?" I growl at Tony, yanking his head back by his perfect hair.

"No."

"You've got a big house, a lot of money and a good life for a computer engineer. Your financials don't look good for you," Shane pipes in.

"Phil and I have a side business," he explains quickly.

"And that is?"

"The church charity," he offers in a grumble, avoiding my eyes.

"We know the charity's bogus and you're profiting what about twenty million a year from that?" Shane confirms.

"More like forty," Tony huffs.

"You people are fuckin' disgusting," Shane grunts.

"And that's not funding your petulance for little girls?" I prod.

"I don't do anything to little girls. I don't do anything to kids. I'm not a pedophile," Tony spouts confidently.

"Well, that's not exactly true. You're married to a woman that does horrific shit to kids and you've been standing by her side through it all. How is that? I know everything Kat does. How could you not see what your own wife is doin'?"

"We live separate lives. I rarely see her. The kids have a nanny that deals with everything. We're like roommates that put on a show for Maybelle. Behind closed doors there's nothing."

"Seriously?"

"She's still the woman I married. She just doesn't love me anymore, but we agreed to never get divorced. Too much to lose financially for both of us."

"That's just sad," Shane says through a chuckle.

"I could help you. I could find out what she's been doing," Tony offers his first bargaining chip.

"And how would you do that? You couldn't see it when it was right in front of you. I don't think you'll be any more successful now."

"I don't know, but I could try. If she's hurting kids I should try," he answers honestly.

"I think we're more likely to get answers from her than you. Are there any men that she spends time with? There was a man torturing Cara along with your wife."

"Hoyt Burke," he answers in a growl.

Fuck. Fuck, fuck, fuck. That's it. That has to be how Cara got away and others haven't. Cara was at the Burke's and broke free once they ran off. How long had they left her in that house alone?

"I need to talk to Kat," I say to Shane.

He nods and moves to stand in front of Tony. I don't want to kill Tony. Maybe we can hand him over to the feds for his charity fraud and he can spend a few decades in white collar prison.

I check the monitors to see the wine cellar is pitch black. They must be taking a break. I thud down the stairs to find Shanny, Kat and Kellerman standing at the breakfast bar with Johnny perched on the edge.

"Hey," Kat calls moving toward me.

I press a firm kiss to her fat lips before releasing her and wrapping my arms around her waist to face our group.

"Jake and Cara?" I inquire not seeing them anywhere.

"Jake's room. She was really tired so he took her up," Kellerman answers with a knowing look my way.

Jake would never put the moves on Cara, but there's something about having the woman you care about in your bed and in your arms that brings a man peace.

"Got some interesting intel from Tony."

"What?" Kat asks eagerly.

"Trish spent her time with Hoyt Burke."

"Fuck!"

"I thought the same thing."

"Hoyt Burke's that assistant principal you ran off after his fuckwad kid sucker punched Jake and got his ass handed to him?" Shanny clarifies.

"That would be him," Kat huffs. "We have any idea where he is?"

"I'm sure Jess does. We'll have Shane call her. End this shit with the Bookers and send another team after Burke. We can't use the house much longer. Need to get the boys home."

"I need some time with Trish to get details about Cara. We can have Burke shipped to a black site for the trafficking intel, but I'm not letting Trish go. Have Shane get a cleaner on stand-by," Kat instructs, sounding more like an agent than she has since I met her.

"Shanny, why don't you let me head down with Kat to work on Trish? You don't need to be involved in this anymore than you already are."

"Nice try, Nicky. Cara's my sister. That bitch tortured her. Threaten to fuck her with a knife the next time she came for Cara. You guys can squeeze every drop of information from her, but her life is mine to end,"

Shanny dictates, pinning me with her emerald eyes. She's getting her way.

"She threatened to do what with a knife?" I ask in a monstrous snarl.

"I talked to Cara earlier. She knows more than she's let on. It makes sense that Trish threatened her that way if Burke wasn't around anymore. Maybe Cara wasn't as important without Burke. They were *training* her to be sold as a virgin slave. Two years they had her. Seven years before that she was a domestic. Before that she lived in a cage. Before that some kind of slave cattle call. Before that she was in an orphanage of sorts in Chicago."

"Let's go," I rumble.

Cara may be Shanny's sister, but she's also my cousin. The only blood family I have left other than an uncle that's about to be murdered in prison as soon as I get word to Kieran.

"I'll go help Shane," Shanny offers.

I flick my chin at her and Kellerman before stalking toward the basement. I've never hurt a woman before, other than Patricia and that doesn't count because she was drugged up enough to fight me like a man. I refused to take jobs that involved women the entire time I worked for my uncle. I don't know if I have it in me, but if there was ever a woman I'd want to hurt it's Trish Booker.

I throw the door open and flip on the lights in the wine cellar, startling a sleeping Trish. Kat shuts the door and stands at my side as I stare down the petrified cowering bitch. She wasn't afraid of Kat and Shanny, but she's scared of me...of the monster.

"You like gettin' fucked with knifes? That a turn on for you?" I purr into her face before ripping off the tape covering her mouth.

"I didn't do it. She's still a virgin," she blabbers quickly.

"You *trained* her for two years. How did you train Cara?" I continue to purr close to her ear in a voice that's promising unbridled torture.

Trish doesn't respond so I step back and study her from afar before moving to my toolbox. I rummage around until I find my weapon of choice, a steel file. I pass it to Kat who pulls a chair up to Trish.

"I think you need a manicure," Kat chirps brightly and begins to file the raw flesh where Trish's fingernails used to be.

The screams and pleas that flow from her lips are music to my ears. I love this. I shouldn't enjoy this, but it fills me with delight to here evil beg for help. No one is coming to help something as depraved as Trish Booker. Never.

"That's better," Kat announces gleefully as she completes one hand. Trish's flesh is filed down to the bone and she's vomited and pissed all over herself. It's not enough. It'll never be enough.

"Would you like Kat to continue or are you ready to answer questions?"

"She was beaten, whipped, choked, face raped, bound, gagged, suspended, shocked and burned," Trish gasps out.

Kat leaps out of the seat in front of Trish, pushes me aside and rummages through the tools. She grabs a hole borer and lunges at Trish, plunging the steel tip into her arms, hands, thighs, shoulders, the places that hurt and don't risk bleeding to death.

Trish screams and cries until no sound travels from her. The agony smothers the reverberations within her. She weeps. She doesn't deserve to weep.

"Where's Hoyt Burke?" I growl leaning into her face as Kat flops into a chair.

"Carrington, New Jersey," she sleepily drawls out.

"Are you the top of the trafficking ring?"

"Yes."

"How long?"

"Since I took over for my father. Seventeen years."

"Who else are you working with?"

"Everyone," she answers through a snort.

"Where are your books?"

"Bunker under the church."

"When's your next shipment of girls?"

"Yesterday."

"Where?"

"They're gone. You won't find 'em. That's why it works. No trail."

"And when you and Burke are gone?"

"Someone else will step in somewhere," she says with a smirk.

Kat leaps to her feet smashing her fist into Trish's nose, shattering it. I relish the sound of the bone crushing married with the wails of suffering. How loud did Cara scream and no one stopped?

"I'm gonna sell your son and daughter in your next shipment. Your daughter is going to the person that wanted Cara. If you weren't so ugly I'd sell you too. Maybe a brothel is South America would take you. You think?" I ask Kat.

"I'm sure we could find one for her in a favela in Brazil," Kat answers thoughtfully.

"You think I give a shit what you do with those kids or me? You don't know me as well as you think," Trish scoffs.

"That's right. You wanted to be fucked with a knife. I don't have a knife in here. Is a box cutter good enough?" I rumble into her ear in a sadistic tone.

"You don't have the balls," Trish dares me.

"Does Hoyt Burke?"

Her face blanches at the suggestion.

"I guess he does. So we'll get him here and let him work on you instead of us workin' on you. Then I don't have to come in contact with your putrid skin."

"Hoyt won't hurt me," she hisses.

340

"That man knows no loyalty. He'll fuck you six ways to Sunday when I tell him to if he believes he'll walk away with his life. The worst part of your undoing is the woman upstairs waiting for you. You hurt her sister and she has abilities and rage that make Kat and I look like pussy cats. She's comin' for you sooner rather than later. She will not relent. She will not stop. She will not turn away when your screaming begins to deafen her. She'll push harder. She'll smile as you plead for your last breath. That's what you've got coming. And come to think of it, I'm ready to be done with you so I can watch the show."

"Let me go and I'll tell you where I got the girl. You wanna know where I got her. It's not in my books. It was a private deal. You'll never be able to find out if you kill me," Trish pleads.

"You wanna know the best thing this job teaches you?" Kat questions. Trish moves her wary gaze to Kat's cool calculated one. "You can spot a liar. You're lying. I can smell it on you even through the piss and puke. I think I smell shit too. Did you shit yourself, Trish? Ah, what would Maybelle think of that? Disgusting cunt of a whore like you lunching with the wealthy, shits herself when she's scared. Pathetic. Tell us where you got Cara now and I'll ask Shannon to cut it short. Say anything other than that and I'm leaving this room and bringing her down here to have her way with you as long as she wants. You know what people call Shannon? A machine. She's a killing machine.

"I feel sorry for you. Something truly fucked up had to have happened to you for you to turn into this monster. Nick won't touch you because he can't bring himself to hurt a woman even though you're nowhere near anything I'd consider a woman. Shannon doesn't have those issues. She doesn't feel sorry for you or care that you're a woman. You hurt her family and have become an object to exact her revenge on. Enjoy your last breaths. Where did you get Cara?"

"Harold Lancaster. Please just shoot me. Don't let that woman down here," her voice quivers with fear.

"How the fuck is Harold Lancaster involved in this shit?" Kat demands.

"We had an order for a girl. Auburn hair, green eyes, tall, American and eighteen. Harold had some contacts that he offered us in exchange for some other services. He found the girl somewhere in the Midwest as a domestic."

"Why did Harold beat Sawyer?" I ask, starting to put pieces of a fucked up puzzle together.

"He thought Sawyer figured it out," Trish offers blankly, sweat pouring down her face from nerves and trauma.

"Why did he think Sawyer had figured it out?" I snarl in her face.

"I told him. I saw Sawyer looking at a picture of Cara on his phone and told Harold."

"You saw Sawyer looking at a picture of the woman that's comin' to take your life you stupid cunt!" Kat rages.

I hawk back and spit in her face before turning to Kat who's shaking with adrenaline. This can't be good for the baby. I don't worry about Shanny coming in here and ending this because her pulse will be below resting rate as she does it. This will soothe Shanny while it's riling Kat.

"We're done. We don't need anything else. Think about the baby and the boys," I speak softly to Kat, trying to calm her.

"Two minutes alone and then send Shannon down," Kat says clinically.

"Two minutes and don't hurt yourself," I instruct holding her hazel eyes.

She nods as Trish begins to beg. I leave the room after brushing my lips across Kat's golden locks. Her body is speckled with Trish's blood and her face is thirsty for more as she moves away from me to avenge our son.

Chapter 40

Kat

Trish killed Sawyer. I watched him die and had to bring him back to life. She's the reason that happened. All because Sawyer used Nick's phone at a basketball game and scrolled past a photo that had Shannon in it. I doubt Sawyer even remembers it. I didn't until this very moment. I promised Shannon this life in front of me and I'm going to be a liar in sixty seconds time.

Trish Booker hurt Shannon's family, but she killed my son. Her death is mine.

I stand in front of Trish, grab her by the shoulders and repeatedly ram my knee into her ribs until they begin to crack from the force. I don't hear her screams. I hear Sawyer's whimpers calling out for me to help him.

I pummel her face with my elbows and forearms, saving my knuckles from any damage. She's coughing and choking on the blood filling her mouth from the teeth I've knocked loose. I grab a hammer and crush her hands and knees when she starts to lose consciousness, bringing her back around. I'm panting heaving breaths from the workout.

"This is what my son felt because of you," I seethe into her swollen deformed face.

I wrap my hands around her neck and constrict with every bit of strength I have in me. The wine cellar opens and Shannon comes to my side but doesn't intercede. She watches as Trish strains and wiggles beneath my grasp trying to fight for her last breath. I clamp down harder seeing my son's face as Harold choked the life from him. I squeeze so hard my fingers burn with a fire that warms my soul.

A soft hand settles on my shoulder bringing me back to the room. It's silent, shimmering with reflections of glass and wine. Peaceful.

"She's gone," Shannon whispers, running her hand down my arm to help me release my cramped fingers.

"I'm sorry," I say genuinely, peering into Shannon's face.

"She tried to kill your son," Shannon says pulling me into her arms, her pregnant belly smashing into mine. "You did good."

I release a giant breath I didn't realize I was holding as we stand embracing each other for a long while.

"Cleaner's here," Nick announces from the doorway.

Shannon and I separate offering each other comforting squeezes as we do. She moves to Trish's unrecognizable body before spitting on her corpse. That pretty much sums it up. So we leave the wine cellar together climbing the stairs feeling lighter, freer.

"I need a shower," I declare when we hit the kitchen.

A slight man with grey hair and wire rimmed glasses nods at Nick before descending the stairs with a large black bag over his shoulder. He'll wash Trish down the drain in the basement bathtub. It's better than she deserves.

"Shanny, I need your clothes for the cleaner," Nick says kindly.

He needs mine too. I should have changed out of my new favorite track suit the boys bought me. I'm irritated that I didn't think about that. Luckily, they bought me five.

Nick follows Shannon and me up the stairs, leaving me at our room with a soft kiss before following Shannon up to the guest room to wait for her clothes. I quickly strip and bag my clothes for Nick before climbing into a excruciatingly searing hot shower. I scour every inch of my body twice, removing any trace of Trish or her death from my body and my mind. I'll never think of her again after I get out of this shower.

She's gone from the world and gone from my mind. Never to be considered again. I feel no guilt. No remorse. No regret. I feel avenged and peaceful as the last of the suds funnel down the drain. My soul is clean for the first time since I began this job. I feel whole and right in the world. Serene.

I cut off the water and dress in a heather grey track suit. I'm no longer *Stepford*. That's a relief I don't have words for. I can't wait to get out of this house. The boys are mostly packed already. I want out tomorrow. I'm done. I'm done with this life. I'm done with the DCA. I'm ready for normal.

Hair piled on my head in a messy lump and make-up free I run into Shannon on the stairs. She looks much the same in a long sleeved pale yellow T-shirt and yoga pants. We're a sexy pair. The doorbell rings and Shannon and I hurry down the stairs to find Phil Ganesly walking in shaking Nick's hand as he does.

"Kat, meet Federal Agent Phil Ganesly," Nick introduces as I hit the bottom stair.

I nod but make no move to greet him.

"Phil, this is my best friend Shannon Kelly."

"Pleasure," Phil says shaking Shannon's hand professionally.

"It's nice to meet you, Agent Ganesly," Shannon returns.

"Phil has been undercover working to get Tony Booker on charity fraud," Nick explains.

"I knew you were workin' an angle here. Just wasn't sure what it was. When your prints on your business card didn't pull up any hits in our system, I figured you were lookin' for an in on the charity fraud. When you hooked up with the rest of the poker group I was almost certain. With the surveillance you were able to collect on them, they'll be goin' away for a long time," he says to Nick and then turns his attention to me. "I'm sorry for how rude I was to you, Agent Russell. I had no idea who you were. I'm glad you're recovering well."

"No offense taken. I know how the job works. Thank you for your help with Patricia Lancaster. I'm feeling much better," I reply professionally. He's a good agent because he had me convinced he was the classic Maybelle asshole.

Phil smiles kindly at me, not a hint of that jerk I met before in sight.

"If you wanna follow me, your mark's up here," Nick says to Phil, leading him up to the office.

I guess Tony didn't have anything to do with this and gets to go to white collar prison. At least he'll have his poker buddies with him. I just want him out of this house so I can get the boys here and packed to move. Shannon and I plod into the kitchen and then the family room where Dylan is laying on the couch watching ESPN with Johnny asleep on his chest. Those two are so laid back. Shannon climbs over her son and settles on her side draped over her man and baby.

"You want in on this?" Shannon asks sincerely.

"I'm good," I respond through a smile, collapsing on the other couch. Exhaustion hits me quickly and I'm asleep in moments as basketball drones in the background.

"Mom," Sawyer's voice tickles my ear.

"Hmm."

"We're home," Cole announces softly.

I peel my eyes open to see the three boys perched on the coffee table watching me.

"Hey," I say through a large stretch.

"You were sawin' logs," Dane informs me with a teasing smirk on his lips.

"I was worn out. That's when I do my best lumberjack impersonation."

They all snicker at my joke as I stretch my aching body.

"We met Cara," Sawyer says sympathetically.

346

I sit up and face my kids. They look happy and normal. None of this has touched them other than Sawyer and he'll never know that. I'll shelter him from this until the day I die.

"How'd that go?"

"Fine I guess. She's stuck to Jake like glue, but she laughed at Dane so I think it went well," Cole says with an easy grin.

"You guys hungry?"

"Nah, we ate." I love it when they answer in unison like that.

"You have much more to pack?" I ask as I sit up to face them.

"You're really makin' us go," Sawyer complains dejectedly.

"I'm really makin' you go. And I'm comin' with you."

"What?"

"Really?"

"How?"

The three of them fire off in harmony.

"We wrapped the op this afternoon. I can't tell you much more than that, but we're done. I think we could all use a change of scenery. Kansas City seems like the best option for us at this point. Nick and I don't have any family. The only people I have are Shane and Jess. I love them, but I don't wanna raise you boys in the shadow of the DCA in Virginia. I'd like us to be in the Midwest where I'm from. With Shannon and her family in Kansas City I think we'll be happy there. What do you boys think?"

"Sounds good to me," Dane says with his typical laid back shrug.

"Me too," Cole agrees.

"What about Jake?" Sawyer whispers.

"What about him?"

"You think he'll go with us now? He doesn't need to look out for us anymore. Maybe he'll decide to stay in the DCA."

"He's going with us," I state emphatically.

"Okay," Sawyer says with a glint in his ebony eyes.

"Where's everyone else?" I ask as I stand to go search.

"Aunt Shanny went up to nurse Johnny. Shane's in the office. Dad and Uncle Dylan are down in the gym and Jake and Cara are in the game room," Dane answers as we walk into the kitchen.

"All right, you three go up and finish packing. I'll be up in a while to see where you're at."

I kiss them each on the cheek before padding down the stairs to the basement. I can hear the slap and crunch of the heavy bag being brutalized before I enter the gym. I stand in the doorway and watch Nick pummeling away as Dylan braces the bag. These two with their shirts off should be illegal.

"Hey," I call out stopping Nick mid-swing.

"Hey," they respond in unison.

Both men start unwrapping their hands as I stare at their god-like physiques. I think a little drool is pooling in the corner of my mouth.

"Should be fuckin' illegal," Shannon whispers in my ear.

I look over my shoulder catching her mischievous green eyes and we burst into laughter.

"What's wrong with you two?" Dylan asks, striding his massive frame toward us. Two, four, six, eight...that's an eight pack and a man V Batman would be jealous of.

"Pick your jaw up, Kat," Nick admonishes me.

"You too," Dylan chides Shannon who's staring at Nick.

Her and I exchange looks again and fall into fits of laughter so deep that my sides hurt and tears are running down our cheeks.

"You two are trouble," Dylan grumbles, sweeping Shannon into his arms.

"You like me bein' trouble," Shannon says through a sexy smile.

"Can we talk a second?" I ask Nick as he yanks me roughly to his front, rolling his eyes at Dylan.

"Yeah," he says gruffly, still annoyed at me.

"I'm gonna hit the shower," Dylan purrs into Shannon's hair.

"You wanna hit this in the shower?" she replies with what would be a suggestive wiggle if her belly wasn't the only thing moving.

His deep timbre chuckle reverberates in the hall as he drags her away.

"Good workout?" I ask, wrapping my arms around Nick's sweaty neck.

"I've got other ways I'd like to work out," he mumbles into my ear before nibbling the lobe.

Something about him being sweaty and warm mixed with his spicy musky scent has my hormones in overdrive. I drag my nails across his scalp as he moves his lips and teeth along my jaw before taking my mouth in an aggressive passionate kiss that steals my breath instantly. Our tongues mingle and massage as our bodies crush into each other.

I move my hands down his sculpted back, rubbing beads of sweat into his olive skin. His hands find my ass and he roughly grabs my cheeks causing a startled and turned-on squeak to break from my throat. Nick grins against my mouth before releasing me.

"Not fair," I mutter, disappointed at his self-control.

"Sunshine, we've got a house full of teenage boys, a teenage girl, Shane and the Kellerman clan...not really the time to fuck you in the middle of a room with a glass wall."

"Right," I huff, untangling myself from his arms before flopping on the weight bench. "I'm gonna go to Kansas City with the boys."

349

"What's that?" Nick asks, sitting on the floor in front of me stretching.

"The op's wrapped on our end. I don't wanna stay here and I don't wanna go back to Virginia with the boys. I have Shane and Jess there, but I wanna be away from the DCA. I'm ready for normal Midwestern life. I don't expect you to go with us. I know you've got a job waiting for you in Virginia and we need to talk about what that means for all of us. So this is me talkin' to you."

"How do you want this to work?" he asks with a furrowed brow.

"However it's best for everyone."

"Why do I get the feeling this is an attempt at a break up?"

"Are you feeling okay?" I ask, looking at him like he's nuts. "Did you just kiss me or were you havin' an out of body experience? I'm pregnant, Nicky...with your baby. Why the fuck would I be breaking up with you? Did you let Dylan hit you with those giant mitts of his?"

"Uh."

"Yeah," I scoff. "You've got mushy dick brain. We'll talk about this later when you can form actual coherent sentences. I'm gonna go help the boys pack."

I move to stand up only to be pushed back down as Nick springs to his feet in front of me.

"Let's do something about my mushy dick brain," he purrs in my neck as he climbs on top of me, running his hand up my shirt. Sounds like a plan to me.

"Sorry to interrupt," Jake says through a chuckle.

Nick groans and collapses in defeat. I pat his back in consolation before pushing him off. I sit up to find Jake grinning at us like the teenager he is. I'm surprised to find him alone. I don't think he's been away from Cara for more than a few seconds since he came out of the formal dining room earlier. Just as I complete the thought, she strolls up to his side where he immediately sweeps his arm around her shoulders.

There's some tension in Jake's face that I can't quite place. Looking out for Cara all day is surely starting to weigh on him a bit. This day has been full of emotion and exhaustion and I don't really know what's gone on with Jake and Cara throughout the situation. She's so comfortable at his side and he seems content to have her there. I knew their connection could be difficult for both of them. I hope we're not hitting a rough patch already.

Chapter 41

Nick

"What's up, bud?" I ask as I watch Jake holding Cara with a level of comfort that looks like she's been at his side his entire life. Yet, there's a little concern etched in his features. It's been a rough fucking day so I'm just feeling him out before I become worried.

"I need to talk to you about where I go from here," he says sheepishly.

And now's the time to worry.

"Go pack your stuff. We're still going to Kansas City," Kat chimes in.

"Who's we?"

"Me and you boys."

"What're you doin'?" Jake asks me.

"I've still gotta talk to your mom."

"I'm gonna head back to the training farm," Jake says blankly.

What?

"What?" Kat whispers.

"It's where I should be now that the op's wrapped. I need to get back to training."

"Jake we talked about this already. I don't want that for you. I want you to have more than this. Jake, what's goin' on with you?" Kat asks with confusion in her voice.

Cara peals herself away from Jake, starting to understand our conversation.

"You're not comin' with me?" she asks, staring at the floor.

353

"You've got your family now, Cara. I need to get back to my job. The Kellermans, the boys, Nick and Kat will all make sure you're all right."

Something cold and dark is hanging over Jake's head. If I didn't know any better I'd say he was angry, but I don't think that's what I see in him. Cara lifts her head and looks into Jake's face with a mask of...I don't know how to describe it. She looks hollow, like a shell of a human being.

"I understand," Cara says in a robotic voice before turning on her heel and walking up the stairs.

Jake watches her until he can't see her anymore before turning his gaze back to us. He's in pain. That wounded him and I have no clue why he did it.

"Jake," Kat says with a plea for him to explain.

"I can't be what she needs. I'm not what she needs. This is better in the long run. I wish I could go with you to Kansas City and play ball, but I've gotta be realistic. I'm not meant for that. I'm meant for this life. I love you guys. Thank you for adopting me and treating me like your flesh and blood. I'll visit you as much as I can, but I've gotta go."

I can hear soft sobs from Kat, but I keep my eyes on my son. Something happened that's got him scared shitless. If he thinks I'll just let him run away from us into the blackness that we've been working to pull him from, he's got another thing coming.

"Kat, give us a minute."

She nods and moves to Jake. Kat pulls him into her arms snugly and he returns the hug with defeat on his face. She whispers in his ear before pressing a soft kiss to his cheek then releases him. Her shoulders heave in silent sobs as she walks up the stairs.

"Tell me what's really wrong," I instruct, nodding for him to sit down on the bench I was just humping Kat on.

"I'm freaking the fuck out," he huffs as he flops down.

"I'm gettin' that. Why? Did something happen with Cara?"

354

I take a seat on the bench next to him holding his brown eyes with mine.

"Nothing's really happened. She doesn't talk much, but she hasn't left my side. She feels so fuckin' good there. I don't have words to describe it. It's wrong though. She's seventeen and comin' out of an extremely fucked situation. She needs help. I can't help her. If I go to Kansas City and she's there, I won't be able to stay away from her. I've gotta go back to the farm."

"I lost Shanny for twenty-two years," I begin quietly and his eyes focus intensely. "When I found her she was moments away from bein' raped. The girl that I fell in love with was alive and about to be raped right in front of my eyes. I can't tell you what that was like, but I'm guessing you can imagine how horrific it was.

"So here I was an enforcer in a crime family, ten years running. What the hell could I offer Shanny? I was a monster and she'd been taken by my family. The worst part was I couldn't even keep her safe. I slit that motherfucker's throat, but she still got shot four times and died in my arms. The week I waited for her to come out of her coma was excruciating. Then when she woke up it was almost worse. I felt like she was wary of me and unsure where or if I'd fit in her life. At that point it didn't matter. She was safe and alive...that was enough.

"That woman is somethin' else. She refused to see me as the monster I saw myself as. Shanny let me be who I needed to be and never pushed for anything else. I got to be her best friend and stand by her side when she needed me. Little by little I started to believe that I was more than a murderer and torturer. Then I met you and Kat...I got something that I never thought I deserved. Then the boys came and I got everything I'd ever dreamed was possible in this life. Then Kat got pregnant and my life became real, no longer a dream. It was real for the first time in thirty-three years with you boys, a wife and a baby on the way. I finally got what Shanny was tryin' to get me to see this last year. I'm not the monster, he lives within me, but I'm more than that. I'm a husband and a father...a protector.

"Don't let the blackness of your past dictate your future, son. Let it shape you, carry the lessons, but don't let it become everything you believe you are. You're an amazing man, Jake. I'm proud of you. I'm proud to call you my son. If you need help, let me help you. Let Shanny help you like she offered in the hospital. Please don't run into the blackness," I urge him reaching out a hand, squeezing the side of his neck.

"I was bein' honest in the hospital. I can't breathe unless I shoot. This op has been excruciating for me without a rifle in my hand. How do I leave that behind? How do I just turn everything off that I know and walk into a normal life like it's always been that way? I'm too fucked up to give Cara what she needs and that fuckin' kills me. I wanna give her everything she needs. But what the hell can a man that still has to climb in bed with his mom after a nightmare offer anyone?"

The torment filling his deep brown eyes makes my chest hurt. I feel it like it's actually happening to me.

"Don't you dare fuckin' do that," I scold. "You'll never heal if you beat yourself up for needing comfort and support. That's why we don't want you to go back to the farm. How can we give you the love and support you need if you're halfway across the country from us? Leave Cara outta this for a minute. Jake, what do you need?"

"I need to shoot," he whispers his eyes shimmering with unshed tears.

"Does that have to be for the DCA?"

"I think the government will have an issue if I just randomly start murdering people," he snarks.

We both chuckle, releasing some of the tension.

"What if you just worked as a contractor for the agency? Instead of bein' a full-time field agent, you could just take a few contracts a year," I suggest with a tinge of hope in my voice.

"Does that job even exist in the agency?"

"We'll talk to Shane about it. He's got the ability to pull strings. I'll call in every favor I've got comin' to me in the agency to make this work if that's what you need."

356

"You'd do that for me?" Jake asks with disbelief in his voice, furrowing his brow.

"I'd do anything for you. I love you, Jake. You're my son no matter how that came to be. You're mine."

The tears that were threatening his big brown eyes finally spill down his cheeks as he launches into my arms. I stand up and gather him tightly to my chest as sobs wrack his smaller frame. I hold him until he calms down before setting him back to arm's length, forcing his gaze to mine with my fingers under his chin.

"I love you too, Dad," he says strongly.

That's the first time he's called me Dad. The other boys jumped on it quickly, but Jake's held back. Now my eyes are fighting the tears as I rip him back to my chest roughly.

"I still have a year of sniper training to complete," he murmurs into my shoulder.

"I know. I can't let you go for a year. I just got you, bud. Can't do it."

He snickers before stepping out of my arms, a small smile playing at his lips.

"I promise to call," he says in a snarky teenager voice.

I tag him around the neck, leading him out of the gym to go find Shane and more importantly to form a plan for our future.

"You better fuckin' call," I say with a chuff.

Jake and I walk through an empty kitchen and up the stairs where I can hear the boys and Kat laughing and jacking around as tape screeches and rips, sealing up our lives. We enter the office to find Shane on the phone in professional mode, barking at people. He's good at his job. He'll help me figure out how to heal my son. I trust him with that job like he trusts me with Kat's heart.

357

Chapter 42

Nick

"A year to eighteen months?!" Kat shrieks at me from her dressing room as we're getting ready for bed.

"He needs the training...you know this," I respond with a small smirk. She's hot when she's flustered.

"Oh no you don't. Don't you dare try to placate me with sex. Pervert!" she shouts, heaving her bra at me. Not really a good incentive to not want to have sex with her.

"Showin' me your tits isn't the best way to turn off my hormones," I chide, moving into the room.

"Well, tellin' me you're okay with sending my son away from me for a year and a half isn't the road map to my pussy," she sneers.

"I don't need a road map, Sunshine. I have the route memorized," I purr into her ear as I reach down and palm her naked ass cheeks. The red thong she's wearing doesn't really count as underwear...not that I'm complaining.

We haven't mentioned the Bookers once in the house today. When it was done, it was truly done for us. Shane sent a team after Hoyt Burke and I'm sure he'll be in custody before dawn. My only other loose end to clean up is my uncle. First I need to feel Kat's warm body beneath me.

"Prove it," she dares me.

I shoot her a cocky smile before lifting her onto her marble topped dressing island.

"Are you attached to these?" I question, tracing the top of her thong with my index finger.

"Not parti—" I cut her off, ripping the fabric away from her body. "—cularly."

"Good," I whisper as I push her down onto her back before pulling her hips off the edge and up to my face, draping her long slender legs over my shoulders.

I devour her pussy, thrusting my tongue in her fiercely. I move up to her clit when her thighs begin to clamp down on my head with a slight tremble. Arching her back so that only her shoulders remain on the cool white stone, she rocks against my face climbing toward her orgasm. I suck her clit deep before releasing it to press long soft licks across it.

"Yes, yes...fuck yes," Kat moans as her come covers my chin.

I lower her hips and pick her up under her arms, dragging her naked sweaty body to mine. I drop my boxer briefs before commanding, "Wrap your legs around me." Kat's sex-hazed eyes sparkle with anticipation as she quickly complies. I spin her around and slam her against the wall before sinking her onto my straining cock. I set a punishing pace, thrusting long and hard. I feel her nails ripping the skin on my back as I pummel her mouth with my tongue in tandem with my dick in her tight pussy.

I grip her ass firmly, squeezing her soft cheeks as I drop my head to her neck nibbling and kissing her sensitive sweet skin. She nips my ear, causing a growl to thunder from my chest and my thrusts to increase making the wall shake. "Nicky," she gasps as a violent quake travels through her entire body as she comes. I hammer away until I feel the tingle build at the base of my spine. Slamming home, Kat screams her way through another orgasm as I groan and grunt through mine.

Panting like we just completed a marathon, we hold each other close.

"I think you took a detour," Kat heaves out, making us both to chuckle.

"I fuckin' love you," I stutter out through my laughter.

"Love you, Nicky," she replies sweetly with love pouring from her hazel eyes.

I move us from the dressing room, Kat still wrapped around me. I lay her on the bed and devour her again, slow and sweet. We make love until we're so exhausted that we fall asleep still attached, sweaty and tangled. Heaven.

He's screaming. My legs are up and moving before the thought registers. I barely pull my underwear over my hips before I sprint up the stairs as Kat yanks my T-shirt over her head, following closely in my wake. We burst into the room to find Shanny holding her gun at the ready, Kellerman trying to assure her everything's okay, the boys huddled around Jake and Cara standing in the corner watching with horrified eyes.

Kat throws herself on the ground and Jake curls into her like every other time. The boys turn helpless eyes at me and I offer them a sad smile. It hurts all of us. Kat rocks and shushes Jake as I crouch down to them.

"Come on, bud," I say quietly, scooping his lanky frame into my arms.

I lock my eyes with Shanny's bright greens as I walk past her. She's schooling her features, but I see the recognition in her eyes. She can't hide that turmoil from me. Shanny approaches us and I pause for a moment.

"You're loved now, Jakey," she murmurs into his blond mop before pressing a long kiss into it. The tension melts away from his body as I move us out of the room. I hear the boys rush into their rooms and back out before thudding down the stairs. As I lay Jake in the bed, the boys make up pallets on the floor and snuggle in as Kat runs into her dressing room to get on more appropriate sleeping attire. She launches herself into bed moments later and Jake clutches at her, painfully based on the wince on Kat's face.

"Easy, son," I whisper, reaching around Kat's body and grasping his shoulder.

He nods into Kat's chest and loosens his grip on her. I hold the two of them all night, wishing I could heal Jake through my touch, my love, my fury at whoever hurt him...something. It's a restless night as I constantly reassure Jake while holding Kat. As the sun peeks through the curtains, wisps of gold dancing around the room, I squeeze Jake's shoulder once more before rolling out of bed.

I pad down the stairs to find Kellerman in the kitchen staring at the coffee machine, willing it to work faster.

"Morning," I grunt.

"Morning," he grunts back.

Caveman conversation before coffee doesn't move much beyond that.

"So you see when I find out who hurt your cousin, I'm gonna leave a trail of bloody destruction in my path. Yes, I am," Shanny's voice coos in her sugar coated momma voice at Johnny through the baby monitor. "Nobody messes with Momma's family and gets away with it."

"How does she make murder sound so sweet?" I ask Kellerman as I put the last of my coffee to my lips.

"It's a talent," he says through a smile at the rim of his mug. "That shit fucked with her last night. She had bad nightmares after she was attacked when she was seventeen. I guess she had a few after she got home last year too. She couldn't sleep without Kavanagh wrapped around her like a security blanket."

Aaron Kavanagh is one of Shanny's best friends/brother/roommate/savior. He's one of the guys from Shanny's story she told Jake in the hospital. Kavanagh slept in the same bed with Shanny for four years after that fateful night he saved her from being raped, holding her closely to protect her from her demons. Kellerman is a strong man to allow his woman to seek comfort in another man's arms, but that's why he's perfect for Shanny. He understands the relationships she has with her guys. Kellerman was ripped away from Shanny last year at Christmas by his crazy ex girlfriend and couldn't be there for Shanny after

362

she was released from the hospital. He had to entrust her to her guys.

The other two guys from her story, Brian O'Sullivan and Ryan Callaghan, each offer Shanny comfort and peace in their own way. O'Sullivan is her entertainer, constantly joking with her and making her laugh. Callaghan is the sweetest dude you'll ever meet. He's Shanny's comforter, always at her side when she needs someone soft. They're good men that saved Shanny when blackness took her over. I feel indebted to them. I also feel sorry for them because meeting Cara is going to bring up some difficult memories. I have no doubt they can help Cara the same way they helped Shanny.

"So what's the plan?" Kellerman asks refilling our mugs. "Shane blazed outta here in a rush yesterday after you and Jake talked to him."

"His fiancée is really sick so he needed to get back, plus he needs to be at headquarters to get our next moves ironed out."

"What are the next moves?"

He flops onto the stool next to me, turning his sparkly teal eyes to mine. He looks like something out of a fairy tale expect for scarier and bigger...so not really at all other than the eyes.

"Jake's goin' back to the farm for twelve maybe eighteen months of sniper training. Kat already retired, so this is her last op. This is my last op too, but I was supposed to take Shane's job. That's not happening now. Kat wants to move to Kansas City."

I let that hang in the air to see what kind of reaction it garners. He and I have bonded lately, but he hasn't been my biggest fan so I'm not sure we're welcome in his neck of the woods. Kellerman studies my face for a few breaths and then cracks a wide grin, crinkling the edges of his damn fairy tale eyes.

"Domesticating?" he asks with a quirked brow.

"I spent over a decade living as a rogue criminal. I'm not sure I can be domesticated...or that I wanna be. Kat's amazing at the job, one of the best, but she's done, man. She can't do the job and be the kinda mom she wants to be. She wants the kids back in the Midwest. I can't argue with that. So I'm not takin' Shane's job. If you're good with us movin' your way, then I'll just take contract work from now on. Only a few overnights a month. I can be around for Kat and the boys...and Cara."

"There's a house for sale on our street," he states matter-of-factly without looking at me.

"So we're gonna go from you hating me to bein' neighbors?"

"I didn't hate you."

I offer him a look that calls bullshit on that statement.

"Okay. I hated you in the beginning. You woulda hated me too if our positions were switched. I don't hate you now. I haven't for a while. You're Shannon's friend. Not just that, but you're her only connection to her father. That means something to her and that meaning something to her means something to me. She'll love havin' you close. She'll stop worrying about you all the time. Her family and Kieran bein' in Chicago is about as much distance as she can stand. I'm good with you comin' back to Kansas City with us. You're welcome in my home any time. Stay with us until you find a place."

He claps me a couple times on the back as the boys pad into the kitchen looking like zombies.

"Morning," they grumble in unison.

"Morning," Kellerman and I reply as the boys flop into their stools.

"Morning," Shanny calls out in a grumpy tone as she makes her way over to Kellerman with Johnny. She's not a morning person.

Kellerman sweeps the baby to his chest and pats Shanny's ass once, never uttering a word to her. She wouldn't respond if he did. Her sweet cooing voice first thing in the morning is reserved only for the baby. She heads to the stove and starts making oatmeal.

"Are we leavin' this afternoon?" Cole asks, his blue eyes barely visible under his messy blond hair.

"That's the plan."

"And Jake's really not goin' with us?" Dane asks in a tortured voice, studying his hands resting on the bar.

"No, he's not."

Sawyer drops his shoulders while Cole and Dane steel themselves against the disappointment.

"Who's gonna take care of him?" Sawyer whispers.

"Jake can take care of himself, bud," I reassure him.

"He can't when the nightmares come," he says softly, turning his deep brown eyes to meet mine. He's worried about his brother. They're always reminding me what amazing kids I've got.

"Shane's getting him some help for the nightmares. Jake wants to go back to training. As much as I hate that, I also understand it. He'll be fine, boys. You're not losing your brother. Just think of this as him goin' away for college."

"Will we get to see him at all while he's away?" Dane asks in a shitty tone.

"No."

"It's not like fuckin' college then."

"Dane," Kat scolds from the entryway to the kitchen. "Watch your tone."

"Sorry," he says to both of us sheepishly.

I didn't take offense. He's struggling and he's fifteen. Shitty tones are to be expected, though I haven't heard any of the boys use one since they've been with us.

Kat strides up to Dane and wraps her arms around his shoulders from behind.

"It's okay to be sad. I'm sad too. But don't take that out on your dad. It's not his fault. It's nobody's fault."

Dane spins his stool around and buries his head in Kat's neck, squeezing her around the middle. Kat strokes his dirty blond locks lovingly, locking tormented eyes with me. Okay, so we're all really fucking sad about

Jake leaving us. I hate it and I'm also proud of Jake. He's doing what he wants. I can't fight him on that.

"Cole and Sawyer get over here," Shanny barks from the stove.

They quickly comply and Shanny pulls them tightly to her, hugging them snugly.

"Jake needs to take care of himself for a while. That doesn't mean he doesn't love you. It doesn't mean this is easy for him. But sometimes people like Jake and me need to do things a little differently in life. He'll come back to you guys," Shanny murmurs into Sawyer's raven hair.

"Is he leavin' because of me?" Cara whispers as she pads into the room wearing Jake's hoodie and a pair of black yoga pants.

"No," all the adults respond in harmony.

I want to comfort her so badly as she stands at the end of the bar unsure what to do with herself. I can't take it. I slide off my stool and approach her cautiously. I stop a foot from her and wait for Cara to make the move to me. And she does. She collapses against my chest, wrapping her tiny arms around my ribs. I hold her head with my hands, stroking her auburn hair.

"Does he hate me? I did this to him. I can see it on his face. Something about me makes him uncomfortable," she mumbles dejectedly into my chest.

I tip her face up to mine with a finger under her chin.

"This isn't about you, sweetheart. Jake has some things to work through on his own. He'll come back to us when he's ready. Don't blame yourself for this. He's not uncomfortable with you. He's just struggling with everything that's happened."

Her bright green eyes search my face. She's looking for a lie. It's not a lie. Jake may think he can't give Cara what she needs, but the truth is he can't give himself what he needs right now. He has to be confident on his own before he can offer anyone a piece of himself. This isn't about Cara. It's about Jake.

"Okay," she whispers.

366

Sawyer and Cole move back to the bar as Shanny starts passing out bowls of cinnamon apple oatmeal. Sawyer stops next to us. He grabs Cara's hand off my back and pulls her under his arm.

"Let's eat," he says with a reassuring smile.

She grins at him as he leads her to a stool. I think Cara's found three protectors in my boys. Jake's going to have to relinquish that job now that he's leaving. Cara's like a new version of Shanny and more than in just the looks department. Shanny had her three protectors from the time she was seventeen too. I can see in my boys' faces that they recognize Cara's beauty, but they're more concerned with helping her heal. They'll watch over Cara like Shanny's guys watch over her. That puts a grin on my face as I meet Shanny's gaze. She's watching the boys and Cara with the same thoughts as me based on the contented smirk on her lips.

Kat pushes her oatmeal away and closes her eyes.

"Ginger ale?" Shanny asks, pulling the bowl completely away from her.

Kat nods.

"I'm glad that part is over," Shanny says, sliding a glass in front of Kat.

"As long as I don't try to eat, I feel fine," Kat snorts sipping a small bit of her drink.

"You've gotta eat, Sunshine," I chide her as I wrap her in my arms from behind.

"Well, you run shit so tell your baby that," she huffs.

Kellerman chuckles next to us causing Johnny to laugh right along with him. I press my lips to her hair before releasing her from my grasp. I scoop up a bowl of oatmeal and lean against the counter watching everyone smile and giggle at the baby. Maybe I can be domesticated because I could get used to this. The smile beaming from Kat's face is the only motivation I need.

Chapter 43

Kat

As I drive away from the home I've built a family in I feel tears prick my eyes. Yes, the house was a torture chamber and a place that brought me a good deal of heartache and anguish, but as I look back I see the boys bantering and bonding. I see Nick peeling away at the thick layers that encased his heart in order to let me in. I see myself learning to take off the mask to stay in the present. I thought I was born when the DCA recruited me. I was wrong. I was born in Maybelle when I became a wife and a mother and chose to no longer run into the blackness.

I glance over at Jake in the passenger seat...his face is blank. He's been blank since we packed the rest of our stuff this morning. The DCA's moving company showed up as we were climbing in our vehicles. They'll store our belongings until we set down roots somewhere.

I reach over and interlace my fingers with Jake's and he returns with a squeeze. The boys are riding with Nick so I can have a little alone time with Jake. This is hard for all of us, but I'm struggling more than anyone. My pregnancy hormones aren't helping.

"Jake," I say quietly.

"Yeah?"

"You're scaring me."

"What?" he asks in a shocked tone, finally leaving the blank behind.

"You're not yourself. You're all closed off and blank. If you're havin' second thoughts about this, you can tell me. We'll change plans."

"I'm not havin' second thoughts. I've never had anyone to say goodbye to. It's harder than I thought it would be."

"It's okay to be sad," I whisper, choking on my emotions.

"Yeah," he says in a huff. "Cara won't even look at me. The guys look so hurt I don't know what to say to them to make it better. You're forcing yourself not to cry. I feel like I'm hurting everyone I care about."

"You're not hurting us. We're just hurting. There's a difference."

As the snowy peaks pass us by, I try to muster the strength I need to watch him walk away in a few minutes. He'll be different when he gets done with his training. That's the point of training, to make you different. I'm terrified he won't want us when he's done.

"I'm not leaving you," he states strongly. What is he a damn mind reader? "I need to do this. I talked with Aunt Shanny about it. She thinks it'll be good for me. The training she got helped her a lot. If I thought she could train me I'd go with you guys. But she's got Johnny and the twins are comin'. She can't take me on, especially with her having Cara now. Even though she told me she could and kinda cussed me out for underestimating her," he finishes in a chuckle.

"Well, I'd caution you in ever underestimating Shannon Kelly. That woman's like a super hero. I'm thinking of buying her a cape," I say through a snicker.

"You're my super hero, Mom," he says quietly turning his big brown eyes to me.

"I love you, Jake."

"Love you too."

"I know you won't be able to call much, but you better call me. I'll fly to the farm and kick your ass if you don't," I threaten weakly.

"I promise, I'll call when I can," he reassures me with a squeeze of my hand.

"And you'll come home when you're done," I state plainly.

"I'll be a little old to be livin' at home," he says through a snort.

"What about basketball?"

"I figure I'll go to college once I'm done. Try to walk-on a team," he says with a shrug.

"I like that plan," I respond with a grin.

Jake and I continue to hold hands as the abandoned air strip comes into view. Two jets are waiting for us, one to take my family to our new home and one to take my son to heal. I stroke the back of Jake's hand with my thumb as I come to a stop behind Nick's car, Dylan parking their rental car behind mine. Several DCA agents pile out of one of the jets to clean and dispose of our vehicles. There will be no trace of the Johnsons by the end of the day.

Goodbyes are going to be quick because it's below freezing and a storm is blowing in. All of us huddle near the jet stairway that will take Jake back to the farm. Dylan claps Jake on the back in a manly embrace before passing Johnny off to Jake. Jake nuzzles into the baby's neck whispering sweet words as he does. Before tears begin to flow, Jake passes Johnny back to Dylan and they climb into Shannon's jet.

All three boys converge on Jake, squeezing him with all their might. They each make him promise to call. Cole and Dane peel away and rush onto the jet, each wiping tears from their cheeks as they go. Sawyer tugs Jake into a rough hug as his shoulders shake with sobs. My heart feels like it's palpating from the force I'm using to maintain any semblance of calm.

"Swear to me you'll come back," Sawyer demands, locking their brown eyes in a pointed gaze.

"Sawyer, I don't wanna promise something I'm not sure of," Jake says quietly.

"Don't fuckin' do that. You don't get to run away! You're my brother damn it. Jake, you can't just take off. We're a family now. Family sticks together. Promise me you'll come back!" Sawyer finishes his plea with a crack in his voice.

Jake studies his brother for a few breaths before closing his eyes and whispers, "I'll come back when I'm better."

"Swear," Sawyer demands.

"I swear," Jake responds strongly.

"I'll take dibs on this baby. You can have the next one," Sawyer assures Jake.

Jake's face pales and my resolve fades into tears streaming down my cheeks. Nick pulls me roughly into his side, pressing his lips to my wooly cap. Jake won't be here when I have the baby. He probably won't even meet the baby until it's almost a year old.

"It's okay, Sunshine," Nick murmurs into my neck.

Jake doesn't respond to Sawyer other than to offer him a sad smile and a clap on the back. With that, Sawyer starts to climb the jet stairs before stopping and looking down at Jake.

"I love you," Sawyer calls out.

"Love you too," Jake says back with a giant smirk on his lips.

Sawyer finishes his ascent with a big wave.

Cara takes a small step toward Jake before halting her progression. Her green eyes are full of hurt and agony as she pulls her winter white beanie a little tighter over her auburn hair. She stares him down for a few moments before speaking.

"Thank you for bein' kind to me. I hope you find whatever you're lookin' for," she says coolly before running up the stairs of the jet, removing any chance of Jake responding.

I see Dane pull her into his arms when she gets on the plane, crumbling into tears. Jake watches her for a while before facing us again. Shannon approaches Jake, grabbing his face in her sable grey colored mitten covered hands.

"You take all of your pain, all of your hurt and all of your fury and you channel that shit into your skills. You use that to motivate you to be the best sniper you can be. When you breathe through your shots let the things that haunt you bring you calm. Let the memories that torture you steel you against any future harm. Release the demons through every bullet, every target. When you think you can't go on, remember you're a survivor and nothing can beat you. If you're alive, you've won. You're the center of your strength. Always trust your gut, Jakey. Your instincts will never lead you astray," Shannon finishes with a small hitch in her voice.

I know she was speaking those words, but I swear it was through someone else. It's like she was channeling another person. Jake roughly rips Shannon into him as his body trembles with emotion. She grips him fiercely, smashing the twins between their bodies.

"Why do you call me Jakey?" Jake asks in a shaky voice as he pulls back, still remaining in her arms.

"My dad called me Shanny. It's how I show love to change names the same way. You're a piece of me and every time I call you Jakey you'll know it means I love you. You go do your eighteen months with the DCA and then you come and give me six months to fix whatever they fuck up," she commands, switching from sweet to serious. Nick and I chuckle quietly as Jake beams a smile at Shannon.

"You'll be busy, Aunt Shanny. I think the DCA's got it under control."

"You wanna go to training after gettin' your ass kicked by a fat pregnant lady?" she questions sternly.

"No thanks."

"Do your eighteen months and come to me. It's not a question, Jakey."

"Okay."

"Okay."

She hugs him once more before kissing his cheek and releasing him from her grip. She climbs the stairs with the calm that only that woman possesses.

"Fuck, she scares me," Jake says through a ragged breath.

"Me too, bud," Nick agrees, tagging Jake behind the head and crushing it to his shoulder.

"I'll miss you, Dad," Jake whispers.

"I'll miss you too. You need anything, you call me. I don't care if it's something small and inconsequential, you call me. If you're struggling with anything I wanna know. If you're kickin' ass and takin' names, which is what I think you'll do, I wanna know. Once a month, you call," Nick demands.

"All right."

"I love you, Jake. I'm proud of you."

"Love you too."

Jake squeezes Nick one last time before Nick lets him go with tears shimmering in both their eyes. Nick places a soft kiss on my cheek before climbing on the plane with one last wave to his son.

I lock my hazel eyes with his big browns and release a small sob. Jake moves to me, almost knocking me off my feet with his force. He curls down into my chest as we both cry, quaking with emotion.

"I love you so much," he stutters out.

"I love you too," I whimper. "I don't want you to go. I understand why you need to, but I need you to know that I want you with me. I wanna see your face every day and hold you in my arms whenever I want. I want you Jake. Do you understand me? You're wanted in this life. Never question that."

"Thank you...for everything. I wanna be with you, with all of you. But I've gotta do this. I need to be better. I'm not leaving you, Mom. I promise you, I'll come back."

Jake squats down and holds my hips before he talks to my parka covered stomach.

"Be a good, baby. Go easy on Mom, she deserves that. Sawyer'll watch out for you until I get back. Love you, baby."

I'm crying so hard now I feel like I'm going to puke. How am I going to live without him with me? I don't know how parents do this. I feel like someone's ripping a piece of my soul from my body.

Jake swipes his thumbs across my cheeks when he climbs back to his feet.

"I've never had someone love me as much as you do. I'll carry that with me while I'm away. I'll use your love to get better. You'll help me escape the blackness," he murmurs against my face before pressing a long kiss to my wet cheek.

I can't say anything so I nod and hug him one last time.

"I love you, Mom."

"I love you too, Jake."

He lets me go and climbs the stairs to the DCA jet, waving one last time before the flight crew pulls up the stairs and closes the door. I try to regain my composure as I climb onto our jet, but I lose the battle as Nick pulls me into his arms. He places me in a seat and buckles me in as sobs wrack my body. As our plane taxis, I fight the urge to vomit and curl into Nick's side as closely as I can get.

"I'm so sorry, Sunshine. Love you," Nick mutters into my hair as he cradles me as best he can.

"Love you, too," I whisper back allowing the emotional exhaustion to pull me into a deep sleep.

I dream of Jake's smiling face, free from torment. It's a good dream even though it hurts. This anguish won't go away until he's back with me. I'm sad.

Chapter 44

Nick

"Wake up, Sunshine," I whisper into Kat's golden hair as the flight crew lowers the stairs. The kid—he can't be older than twelve—that flew our plane has turned an unusual shade of red as Shanny smiles at him.

"Kiddo," Kellerman growls at her flirtatiousness.

"Oh, stop it," Shanny says, rolling her eyes with a delighted smirk playing at her lips.

It should be noted now that we're in Shannon's world everyone that talks to her will call her Kid. She got that nickname when she was seventeen and it's stuck.

Kat stretches and flutters her bright red-rimmed hazel eyes open.

"Sorry," she croaks.

"You needed the rest. Let's get back to Shanny's and you can get some more sleep."

"'Kay."

I help her to her feet and follow the boys out onto the snow-dusted tarmac where two black SUVs are waiting for us. One, with Shanny's bodyguard, Thomas—a mountain of a man who's not to be fucked with or questioned—behind the wheel. I was pretty surprised he wasn't with Shanny in Connecticut until she told me Thomas isn't a fan of flying.

"Quick trip?" Thomas grumbles, walking up to Shanny with a furrowed brow.

"I called. We got held up, Thomas. Don't get your panties in a wad," Shanny admonishes.

Thomas lets out a *humph* before a small smile cracks his usually rigid face.

The other SUV is just idling with no one behind the wheel. I offer Thomas a chin lift and lead Kat and the boys to the empty SUV. Thomas helps load in the Kellerman clan and we take off toward the fortress that houses a unique brand of crazy.

"Holy shit!" Dane exclaims as we pull in Shanny's gated driveway. Yeah, it's a lot of house.

"I second that," Kat says through a smirk.

"Prepare yourselves for the world of Shannon Kelly, boys. This should be…educational," I inform them as we come to a halt in the driveway. We all pile out and follow everyone through the garage and into a kitchen twice the size of the one we just left in *Stepford*. It's part of a great room meant to hold an NFL team. This house was big to start, but it's a monster now that Kellerman has more than doubled its size.

We move past the gleaming white marble topped counters and stop as the men in Shanny's life descend upon us. Kavanagh is the first to make his way to Shanny.

"You're lucky you're fuckin' pregnant, Kid," he growls, wrapping her in his giant python arms. He's built like a linebacker, about six foot one and as wide as a refrigerator, capped off with a cocky attitude…I like Kav.

"Kavy, don't be such a little girl," Shanny admonishes him squeezing him back.

Brian O'Sullivan rips Shanny away from Kav grumbling in her ear, "Where you go, we go."

"I'm fine, Sully," she reassures him. Only Shanny gets to call him Sully. To the rest of the world he's O'Sullivan and nothing else. He was a fighter all through college and still carries the swagger associated with it. He's Kieran's cousin and they grew up fighting together until Kieran went with the criminal life and O'Sullivan made his way into criminal law. They're still close even though they live on two separate sides of the criminal coin.

His chocolate eyes shimmer with mischief as he runs his hand through his dark brown hair.

"Pain in the dick," he huffs, passing Shanny off to Ryan Callaghan.

The man is a gentle giant, six and a half feet of sweetness. Callaghan has dreamy (yes, I said dreamy) bright blue eyes, shiny blond hair and dimples that look like they hurt. He's a man of few words, but always in the action with this crowd.

"No more of that shit," Callaghan reprimands Shanny, scooping her off the ground in a tight hug.

"Cally, I was with Kel. You worry about me too much."

"Uh huh," he grunts, setting her back on her feet.

"Cara, come over here and meet the guys," Shanny calls out kindly.

Cara's hiding behind me huddled into her own posse of boys. I'm in some sort of space time continuum looking at Shanny and her guys mirrored by Cara and my boys....it's weird. Cara holds her position, not complying with Shanny's request.

"You want us to go with you, sweetheart?" Sawyer whispers behind me.

I turn to see her nuzzled into his side, holding hands with Dane while Cole hovers at her back. She's found her safe place. A small smile plays at the corner of my mouth as I lock eyes with Kat, who's grinning right along with me.

"Yes," Cara murmurs. Slowly, Sawyer and the boys lead Cara past me into the view of the guys who let out audible gasps at the sight of her. Her body goes rigid at their reaction, causing Sawyer to clamp down on her harder and Dane to squeeze her fingers.

The guys' faces are pale and wearing varied levels of astonishment as the kids stops in front of them. The two groups stand and stare at each other, two ends of a fifteen-year continuum assessing the other.

Kav snaps out of it first, approaching slowly. He stops a foot in front of Cara and inspects her from head to toe with love and hurt shimmering in his blue-grey eyes.

"I'm Aaron Kavanagh," he says in his deep bass voice, extending a large mitt toward her.

In order to shake his hand she'll have to let go of Dane, that's not happening.

"I'm Cara," she says softly.

Kav pulls his hand back and rubs his buzzed brown hair vigorously.

"I've been searching for the last fourteen years to find anyone that could hold a candle to Kid. You've just ended my search, Baby Girl," he says with that cocky Kav grin on his lips.

Cara's face turns bright red and a giggle bursts from her lips, causing the room to release a ton of the tension that was sinking down on us. Kat and Shanny beam knowing smiles at each other.

"No way you're gettin' dibs on this one," O'Sullivan chides Kav, nudging him out of the way. "I'm Brian O'Sullivan. I'm funnier than any of these idiots and you're simply breathtaking."

The blush that Kav created has bloomed even more, causing Cara to hide her face in Sawyer's shoulder.

Callaghan strides toward her without uttering a word. He simply stands in front of her and holds her eyes for a long while in silence. She stares at him with the strangest contented look on her face. I look to Shanny who's now holding tears at bay. Her and Callaghan have this connection where they don't need words to communicate and I think Cara has just created the same thing with him.

Cara peels away from her boys and steps right into Callaghan's space before reaching her slender arms up, barely circling his neck. Effortlessly, he scoops her off the ground, allowing her feet to dangle a half foot off the ground as she buries her face in his neck.

"I've got you," he murmurs into her hair.

She nods in return, squeezing him harder.

"Okay, Cal's got us fuckin' beat," Kav grumbles, not meaning a word of it.

"Whatever. I'm not a quitter," O'Sullivan huffs.

Callaghan sets Cara back on her feet and offers her a dazzling dimpled smile and she beams right back at him. It's a short lived moment as she scurries back to her boys and Cole wraps his arms around her from behind while the other two interlace their fingers with her.

Time to introduce my family.

"Guys," I say with a chin lift, pulling Kat toward the group. "This is Kat Russell."

"Hey, Kat," Kav purrs.

"It's nice to meet you," Kat says through a sweet smile.

"Cooper where'd you find this one? She's...hot," Kav compliments.

"No shit! Gorgeous," O'Sullivan says, placing a kiss on her knuckles.

These guys are obnoxious.

"She's the kinda girl you marry," Callaghan says with a broad smile.

"Huh?" Kat asks.

"Two types of girls in the world. The kind you...uh...well...sleep with and the kind you marry," Kav stutters, trying to avoid his usual foul language.

"I'd like to think I'm both," Kat says with a quirked brow.

"Love her," Shanny beams through her announcement.

Cara whispers something to Sawyer before turning her green eyes up to him with a questioning look.

"Marry, sweetheart," he says gently.

Her face lights up as she snuggles further into Cole's arms.

"No question," O'Sullivan says, offering Cara a wide Cheshire grin.

"These are our boys," I introduce. "Sawyer, Cole and Dane."

"It's like goin' back in fuckin' time," Kav says with a chuff in his voice.

"Dude, if we're lookin' at our future I get to be you," Dane says with a huge smile on his face.

"Good choice," Kav responds through a chuckle.

"Then I'm O'Sullivan," Sawyer pipes in.

"Better choice," O'Sullivan goads Kav.

"You're idiots. I'm Callaghan, gettin' the hugs from hotties," Cole finishes with a toothy grin.

"Best choice!" Callaghan shouts.

Kat pulls my ear down to her mouth and whispers, "And Jake will be you. He gets the top spot."

My heart pounds in my chest at the sweetness of her words as I smash my lips to hers.

"Too much mushy shit for me to stomach," Kav says with a gag as I pull away from a snickering Kat. "Come on boys, I'll show you where you're stayin'."

The boys and Cara follow Kav and Callaghan to the giant staircase at the end of the great room. As they walk away, all I can imagine is what the next fifteen years hold for Cara and my boys.

"So that was fuckin' weird," Shanny points out the obvious, passing Johnny off to O'Sullivan who immediately starts eating the baby's cheeks to his giggly delight.

"That it was," I agree.

"Kid, she's like a damn carbon copy of you. That shit felt like freshman year all over again. My dick didn't get hard this time though," O'Sullivan admits through a snort.

"That was pervy back then. Now it would be illegal and buy you the business end of my gun," Shanny replies with a pointed look.

"Last I checked you liked the perv that I was."

"Is that so?"

"Oh you can try to lie about it now, but you thought I was a sexy piece of meat and you were ready for dinner."

"You were like beef jerky that I wanted to feed a dog, Sully," Shanny says through a chuckle before sweeping Kat away from my side.

"Your boys are ten times better than my guys were back then. Don't worry about Cara bein' with 'em," Shanny reassures her, leading us to the world's largest horseshoe sectional known to man.

"I'm standing right here, Kid," O'Sullivan complains.

"I see you," she deadpans.

Kat and Shanny flop down and Kellerman and I wrap an arm around each of our women while O'Sullivan drops to the floor to roll around with Johnny.

"Should I go up and check on Cara?" Shanny asks the group.

"She's good with the boys," Kellerman reassures his fiancée.

"Realtor tomorrow?" Kat asks me.

"Yeah."

"There's no rush. You can stay here as long as you need to. Aidan's at a conference this week. Aidan is the baby Callaghan brother," Shanny clarifies for Kat. "He lives here too. Finn, the oldest Callaghan, lives a couple miles away, but he's here all the time."

"So you're just surrounded by men all the time?" Kat asks with a little mischief in her voice.

"That I am," Shanny responds with a smirk on her lips.

"It's a nice view."

"No question."

"You two are trouble. Maybe we should look at houses in Alaska," I grumble.

"Isn't the male to female ratio in Alaska like two and a half to one?" Shanny asks in her I know you're full of shit voice.

"Not the place to scope for pussy," O'Sullivan chuckles, flying the baby above his head while he lies on his back.

"You don't scope for pussy anymore," Shanny says pointedly.

"Uh, scoped, sampled and savored last night, Kid."

"Is that so?"

"Yup," he responds popping his *p*.

Shanny furrows her brow but doesn't respond as Kellerman nudges her to shut up.

"Your sons are rolling a lot today," Shanny grumbles, trying to find a comfortable position.

"They're happy to be home," Kellerman beams, placing a large hand on her swollen belly.

I can't wait for Kat to get that far in her pregnancy. I'm ready for the hand on the belly move. Even though she's sick all the time right now, she's still got that pregnant glow about her. It keeps my dick at a semi most of the day.

"When are you due?" O'Sullivan asks Kat, quirking an eyebrow at me.

"August fourteenth," Kat says with a shine in her voice and a rub of her flat stomach.

"So we're workin' a baby every two months at this point huh? Kid in April. Kieran and Quinn in June and you two in August. Who's pickin' up October?" he jokes.

"You," Kellerman and Shanny say through a laugh.

"I like my baby gravy smothering buns not uteruses. Plus, I like pussy too much to settle on one flavor," he scoffs.

"You just haven't found your favorite yet," I inform him with a cocky smirk.

"Kieran said the same thing. What the hell? Who would've thought you and him would ever be givin' out that kinda advice?"

"Shit changes," I answer with a shrug.

If you told me six months ago I'd be where I am right now I would have laughed in your face and advised you to get your head checked. I found my flavor though and I can't imagine wanting a different one in this lifetime. And apparently I've turned into a pussy, so there's that.

384

"I'd like to head up to Chicago to check in with Kieran after we finish up house shopping," I say to Kat.

"All right," she responds tentatively.

She knows what I'm going to do in Chicago. She'd rather be at my side than here in Kansas City, but I've got to do this on my own. It's time to remove the demons. I'm ready to rid this world of the evil that has caused the people that I love torture and anguish. I'm going to kill my uncle once and for all.

Chapter 45

Nick

"I'm worried about my swimmers," Kieran grumbles as we sit and wait for my uncle to be brought into the visitation room at the federal penitentiary he's currently serving a life sentence in.

"How's that?" I ask, thinking that's the weirdest thing he could say to me right about now.

"You knock up Kat after one maybe two tries. Kellerman knocks up Shannon in one shot...with twins. It took me a few months with Quinn. There's gotta be somethin' wrong with me."

"You're fuckin' insane," I say through a chuckle.

"No Mancini Family left in the city. I took the last two out last night," Kieran informs me bringing us back to business. "We take care of your uncle today and you're good to go, man."

"I owe you."

"Nah, this motherfucker's had it comin' since he went after Shannon. He fucked with my family, so I killed his," he states nonchalantly.

The door opens and my uncle staggers as his eyes land on my sapphire blues. No more contacts after today. I'm coming back to the life I fought to earn.

The guards sit the stunned old man down and handcuff him to the table before leaving the room with knowing nods at Kieran. I'm not here as Agent Nick Cooper. I legally changed my name when I joined the DCA, but today, I'm in this room for the last time as Nick Scarso, nephew and enforcer for Vito Mancini. Today Nick Scarso dies right along with his uncle.

"Nick," my uncle says in a haunted voice.

"Vito," I return coolly.

"So the feds got to you?" he asks in a resigned tone.

"I am the fed. I've been the fed since I walked into your office almost eleven years ago," I admit confidently.

His classically Italian features harden at my admission. I see him plotting who he can get to carry out a hit on me. Nice try old man. Not happening. He'll be dead before he can get to a phone or a contact in here.

"You fuckin' ratted on your own family?" he growls in disgust.

"I did my job and helped bring down the biggest piece of shit to ever grace the streets of Chicago and I did it with fuckin' pride."

"And now you've aligned with this fuckin' mick?" he spits.

"This fuckin' mick has eliminated every last person in your family," Kieran snarls.

"You're a sad excuse for a boss, Delaney. Your day'll come sooner than later," Vito threatens.

"I'm not a stupid old man that kidnaps women and sells his own children. I'll take my chances, Mancini."

"Sells my own children?" Vito questions.

"I found Cara," I state simply. "I'm here to find out what the fuck you did with her."

"How?" he grunts.

"How did I find her or how am I gonna find out what you did?"

"How'd you find her?"

"Naked in my backyard runnin' from a sex slave dungeon," I growl, feeling my fury begin to boil at the memory.

"Deidre Murphy was a fine piece of ass," he says through a grin.

"I guess you have a thing for sex slaves," Kieran grumbles.

"She'd been on my cock for two years before I offed her pussy husband."

"So you lied about how you killed her?" I ask trying to get answers to questions for everyone involved in this crazy shit. When Vito was finally brought down last year he pled guilty to the murder of Shannon's mother. Only he fucking lied and said he killed her a few months after he murdered Shannon's father and tried to kill Shannon.

"I didn't kill her. She died a few months after she gave birth to Cara from complications from the birth or some shit."

"Why the fuck did you say you killed her then?" Kieran demands.

"Didn't want anyone pokin' around for Cara," he answers blankly.

"What'd you do with Cara?"

"Gave it to a black market baby selling ring. I couldn't keep a baby with me when Deidre died. I didn't want the kid anyway. I only let her keep it because she didn't want an abortion. Horny as hell when she was pregnant. She didn't want that fuckin' baby. She never paid it any attention. More work than it was worth in the long run. Killed Deirdre in the end."

"You're a sicker motherfucker than I gave you credit for," I huff.

"I'm not a pussy like you."

"You know what, if bein' a pussy means I'm nothin' like you I'll wear the title proudly."

"I'm disgusted I gave you anything in this life. I shoulda let the O'Boyle Brothers take you out when they wanted to," he growls.

"Well, I blew those motherfuckers' brains out so you can ask me to take out Nick if you need some help," Kieran taunts.

"Fuck you, Delaney," Vito snarls.

"The only one gettin' fucked in this room is you," Kieran retorts pointedly.

I see the realization seep into his features as he figures out he's a dead man. A smile breaks across my face as fear etches itself in his.

"You're nothing to me. You've never been anything more than a mark to me. These are your last breaths in life. I hope you can enjoy them."

I climb to my feet and pull on the crime scene coveralls stored in my messenger bag. The cameras have been turned off in here so there will be no evidence of what I'm about to do. Kieran's paid off the guards and the warden to make this mess I'm about to create go away with no question. The only reason I'm covering my clothes is so that I won't be covered in Vito's blood when I walk out of here. I remove my knife from my messenger bag and approach my uncle slowly.

I meet eyes with Kieran and his murky blues are sparkling in anticipation. If he could kill Vito he would and he'd do it in style. This is my life to take. This man has hurt every person I love either personally or in some weird six degrees of separation. My monster is ready to retire with Vito Mancini's blood.

"You may be a nark now, but you'll always be the monster I created. You can try to have a normal life, but I'll always haunt you," Vito threatens as I stare him down.

"After today anything you've ever been to me will be gone," I purr sadistically.

I set about carving his body up like a turkey. His screams go unanswered as they should. As my blade drags through his flesh like a knife through warm butter I shudder in relief. As his blood pools on the floor the gleam brings a smile to my face. As he gasps and gurgles on his own blood I relish the sound of death capturing the evil life he's lived.

When there's nothing but silence in the room I peel out of the suit and retake my seat across from Vito Mancini's corpse. His skin is flayed from his body exposing bones, tendons and organs. That body didn't have a soul to release, but if it did, it ran like a scared little bitch when I worked him over.

"Fuckin' poetic," Kieran beams, clapping me on the back. "You ever wanna put those skills to work, just give me a call."

"I'll keep that in mind," I say through a chuckle at the bizarre relationship Kieran and I have with death, murder and torture.

"Let's head out," he says climbing to his feet, grinning at the corpse one last time.

I look once more as well, feeling peaceful for the first time in my life. Nothing from my past can touch me now. I can be Nick Cooper without shame from this day forward, a father, a husband and a protector. The blackness is gone as I stride from the room into the light.

"It's done," I murmur into Shanny's hair as I hold her close.

She nods into my chest in relief. The last monster to harm her and her family is gone. She can live in peace.

"Thank you," she whispers, pressing a soft kiss to my cheek.

"Nothin' to thank me for."

"You took care of me. I'll always be thankful for that."

I kiss her forehead before crossing the room to Kat beaming a full smile at me.

"Hey, Sunshine," I mutter against her lips before capturing her them in a passionate kiss that steals her breath.

I tangle our tongues and palm her ass until a throat clears behind us. I break from the kiss and look over my shoulder to find my sons furrowing their brows at me in disgust.

"Dad, you've gotta stop doin' that," Cole admonishes me.

"Never."

They all smile and approach me for hugs as I release Kat from my hold.

"So the blue eyes are fuckin' weird," Sawyer says, staring at me.

"I love 'em," Kat and Shanny say in unison.

"You'll get used to it, bud," I assure him.

The boys amble off to find Cara based on the conversation I hear as they climb the stairs.

"Got some good news while you were gone," Kellerman says, walking in the room with Kav.

"Yeah?"

"They accepted your offer on the house. Willing to close next week," he informs me before offering his fist for a bump.

"Welcome to the neighborhood," Kav says with a clap on my back.

"Thanks, man."

I turn to see Kat and Shanny talking excitedly about the new house, both of them glowing with pregnancy. They're so bright I feel the need to squint.

"So, you ever fuck up with her," Kav says nodding toward Kat, "I'm goin' in for the kill."

"Not happenin'," I respond with a chuckle.

"Just sayin'. She's fuckin' hot, funny as hell and cool as shit. I bet she's awesome in bed too."

"Jesus you're an asshole," I scoff. "Stay away from my wife."

"Uh...you put a ring on it when I wasn't lookin'?"

"She's my wife and don't forget it," I warn with a pointed look.

He offers me a cocky smile and then beams a panty-dropping grin at Kat before leaving the room. Such a dick. He'd never go after Kat. He's just making sure I know what I've got. I'm aware of what I have without his shit, but I appreciate him looking out for Kat. He's got a soft spot for her already. That's saying something for him because soft spots for women are not what he's known for.

"He's got a point," Kellerman says, offering me a beer.

"Which one?" I ask, bringing the bottle to my lips.

"She's not your wife."

"She's my wife. I just haven't married her yet."

"That's some fucked up math," he responds with a deep chuff.

"Do you think of Shanny as your fiancée?" I ask through a quirked brow.

"Not really," he says in a shrug. "She's just mine."

"There you go. I'm no different than you. I just use the word wife because Kat would cut off my nuts if I referred to her as mine all the time."

"I don't think chicks work like that, man," Kellerman replies, gazing at Shanny with love and pride as her and Kat pass Johnny between the two of them.

"Work like what?" I ask, watching the Kat with the same amount of love and pride as Kellerman.

"Kat called you her partner to the real estate agent earlier. You're lucky Kav was there because that real estate agent was comin' in for the kill until Kav swept his guns around her shoulder and offered a glare I was proud of. I had the same issue with Kid. That rock on her finger gives men at least a warning there's something out there that'll kick their ass if they don't stay away. It's not much, but it's something."

"She called me her partner?" I ask incredulously, shocked that's the word she'd use to describe me.

"What else should she call you?"

"Her husband or boyfriend or something more than that fuckin' business term," I huff, draining my beer.

"There's no ring on her finger. She seemed lost at what to call you. I get you're in a weird situation, but you need to make that shit solid sooner rather than later," he says with a pointed look.

"I just bought her a fuckin' six million dollar house. We have four kids together and she's pregnant with my

393

baby. I don't feel like there's a lot of question in my level of commitment," I scoff.

"Five point eight," he says with a cocky grin at his win in negotiating our house price. "Women are different from us. I should already have Kid at an altar. I swear her Pop coulda killed me when he found out I knocked her up with the twins and we still weren't even engaged. Kid's in no rush to get married. She never wanted to get married so she doesn't have a dream wedding she's already got planned. I want it more than she does, but I've been goin' at her pace. She'll be my wife a few months after the twins are born if I have to drag her to the courthouse."

"Which Pop was gonna kill you," I ask curious what it's like to have in-laws to worry about.

"All three," he retorts in a chuckle.

I don't doubt that. Her having three fathers has to be a lot to contend with. Not to mention the nine brothers. Kellerman's a brave man to take all that on, but I swear it's one of the things that made him love her.

"You doin' anything tomorrow?" I ask quietly.

"Saturdays are family dinners around here. Otherwise it's just sports and fuckin' around."

"Wanna go shoppin' with me?" I question with a small grin on my face.

Kellerman's become a friend...a really good friend. I like the idea of him with me for this.

"Do I have to carry your purse while you try on clothes?"

"I'd rather you came in the dressing room with me."

We both fall into quiet chuckles, trying not to catch the attention of Kat and Shanny.

"We'll head out in the morning," he says with a sly grin.

He knows where we're going and what I'm doing. Yeah, Kellerman's my friend. I apparently need to thank Kav for running off the real estate agent too. Kansas City is going to be good for us in more than one way. We'll be happy here.

Chapter 26

Kat

"Hey," I say into the phone, relieved she's calling me.

"Hey," Jess groans.

"God are you still sick?"

"I'm not sick," she huffs.

"Jess, what's wrong? You're scarin' me. It's been almost two weeks now."

"We found out what's wrong with me yesterday."

"Jess," I say with a quiver to my voice, terrified there's something really wrong with my best friend.

"That motherfucker, Shane Hollander, got me pregnant," she grumbles. "I've got hyperemesis gravidarum. Which is apparently the Kim Kardashian of morning sickness."

"Kim Kardashian?" I ask in a chuckle, feeling relieved at her news.

"Yeah, nauseating, annoying, makes you vomit uncontrollably, can't make it go away and you're never happier than when it ends...Kim Kardashian," she deadpans.

I double over in laughter at my friend's ability to make something that's really hard for her hilarious.

"Okay. Are you healthy other than the HG? When's the baby due?" I ask, bringing myself back to good friend mode.

"I'm fine. I'm annoyed more than anything. How the hell do you get pregnant on the pill? I'll never fit in my wedding dress now. Shane's tryin' to convince me to just scrap the wedding and head to Vegas. Can you believe that shit?" she screeches.

"Jess, it's gonna be fine. Women get married pregnant all the time. We'll get you a new dress or something. It's not the end of the world, honey. Do you not want the baby?" I whisper.

"Of course I want the baby!" she yells in a more normal Jess voice. "I just wanted it after we were married. I've worked my ass off on this damn wedding and now it's all fucked up."

"It's not fucked up. You'll be just a perfect as before, with a gorgeous pregnant glow. You're hormonal and scared. Everything with the wedding is gonna be just fine," I assure her.

"I don't want it anymore," she says quietly, switching her stance. "It doesn't seem important anymore. Watching you and Nick move off to the Midwest for the normal life with the boys and your baby coming...it made the wedding and all the other shit seem unnecessary. I had all this planned for what our future was gonna be and now it's all changed. I'll go to Vegas and marry Shane tomorrow if that's really what he wants. I'm more mad at myself than anything. Shane and I have been so focused on work that I feel like we've wasted more than a decade that we could've been building a life together."

"Jess, you guys are right where you're supposed to be. Trust that. You've had an amazing thirteen years together and now you get to build on that foundation. Nick and I are the ones doin' everything backward. If you want your big wedding with ugly bridesmaid dresses, have it. If you wanna jump on a plane and head to Vegas, do it. I'll wear the hideous dress or stand at your side in front of Elvis with pride. Find joy in what you have."

"Such a good friend," she says in a teary voice.

"So are you. Now, when are you due?"

"August fourteenth," she says in a giddy voice.

"Shut the front door!"

"I shoulda shut the front door a few months ago cause that thing's about to be stretched into the Lincoln Tunnel."

That gets us both rolling in happy tear-inducing laughter.

"Love you. And tell Shane congratulations," I say as we wrap up our conversation after going through all the fun stuff in our shared due dates and mutual pregnancies.

"Love you too. Kiss all your boys and those hot as fuck temporary roommates you've got."

We hang up and I feel lighter and brighter knowing Jess is okay. There's a bit of sadness knowing we could have been in the same city pregnant together, but it's fleeting. I'm so happy here in Kansas City I can't imagine being back in Virginia. I feel like I've come home for the first time since my parents died. Nick's bought us a house that'll be the home we'll live in until we die. The people in Shannon's life are amazing and quickly becoming good friends. I like normal life.

"What're you so smiley for?" Kav's deep rough voice powers through the great room.

"It's just a good day, Kav," I beam brightly.

He flops down on the giant chocolate colored sectional next to me with such force my body bounces. Kav offers me a cocky grin as I snicker at his goofiness. He's got a reputation and then some for being an asshole and a slut, but I think he's sweet...and a slut. He runs women through this house like a Union Station turnstile. I'm impressed with his abilities, frankly. Where most guys seem to run through girls like they're trying to prove something, Kav's just being himself. There's nothing to prove...it's just him.

"So when are you leavin' that douche Cooper and givin' a real man like me a try?"

"What a sweet offer. I'm not sure I've had enough vaccinations to give you a try though."

His booming laugh warms me to the core.

"Fair enough. Like we said the first day, you're the marrying kind and I'm not on that program," he assures me with a smirk, his blue-grey eyes dancing with mischief.

"Think that'll ever change?" I question honestly.

"Not really. I know it seems like I'm just fuckin' around all the time, but the truth is my career demands a lot. I've got Kid and her babies when I'm home. I can't imagine anything beyond that even tempting me to cut down on my life. I don't hate marriage or have anything against it. It's just not for me. I've met enough women that think I just need to meet the right one and I'll change my whole way of life. Funny, they all think they're that woman. Why don't women get that if you're with a guy, you don't want him to change to be with you? If you're changing a man then you're not really with the person you met," Kav finishes pointedly.

"Makes sense. I don't want Nick to be anyone other than the man I met back at DCA headquarters. I know what he's done in life and what he'll continue to do. I'd be a pretty selfish person to meet him as one thing and demand he become something else," I agree with an easy smile.

"See, now you, I could marry," he lies with a wry grin.

"Yes, you could. If I met you and your slut-o-licious ways and decided I was willing to be one car on your booty train, we could totally get married."

A load chortle reverberates from his chest as I snicker along with him.

"I'm tellin' you now. Cooper fucks up you're marryin' me," he orders with a suggestive eyebrow wiggle.

"I consider myself warned."

"I've spent a lot of time tryin' to find someone like Kid. That wasn't just a line I fed Cara the other day. The way that girl looks...hits me in the gut every single time. It hurts and feels amazing all at once. Then you and Quinn come along and I swear Kieran and Cooper are into voodoo. You two aren't exactly like Kid, but you're enough like her and then what each of those dudes need that's just slightly different. Those motherfuckers must've made you two in some witch's brew," Kav scoffs, rubbing his buzzed chestnut head flexing his massive biceps.

"I thought you weren't lookin' for anyone?" I ask with a quirked brow.

"I met a girl when I was eighteen and a freshman in college. Everyone thinks one of us guys shoulda ended up with her. She's gorgeous, funny, sweet, fuckin' mean as hell, loyal like no one you'll ever meet. She loves like a person who's been through her life shouldn't be able to and gives us each something that we need from her that's just for us. The thing is...it's not like that with Kid. I can't explain it, only that she's more than a girlfriend or a wife to me. She's a piece of my soul. I love her. That love will never die or change, but it's not romantic love. If I ever tried to take it there, it'd ruin everything we have and that's nothing I'm willing to risk. So I've been lookin' for the next best thing for fourteen years," he responds with a shrug.

"So if you found Shannon's clone you'd settle down, get married, have some kids, keep your dick in one place for the rest of your life?"

"Uh...that sounds awful," he admits honestly.

"I don't think you're really lookin' for someone like Shannon. I think you use that as an excuse to not look for anyone without pressure. Don't be ashamed to be happy with where you are. If you're happy in this life, own that. You've earned it I'm sure."

"If I thought I could kill Cooper and get away with it, I'd marry you. You might be the first person other than Kid that gets me," he grumbles.

"Not every person needs the traditional happy ending to be happy in the end."

I wrap my arms around the big man's neck and he squeezes me around the middle with his python arms.

"Dude, Cooper comes in here and finds you puttin' the moves on Kat we got problems," O'Sullivan says in an alert voice, coming down the stairs.

401

"Just a hug between friends," I assure the sexy fighter who gifts me a Cheshire grin before flopping on the couch next to us.

"Can I get some of that friend action?" he asks with too much sex in his voice.

"Back off, O'Sullivan," Kav growls protectively. He sounds like my older brother...if I had one.

"She's like Kid two point oh," Callaghan says quietly, sitting across from us with a dimple-puckering smirk.

"No shit," O'Sullivan huffs.

"I think Cara's more like Kid two point oh and Kat's like double oh seven because of her spy shit. Why do we meet women that rock and then all we want to do is protect 'em?" Kav questions seriously.

"You boys are a trip. I appreciate you bein' protective of me, but I'm all right on my own. As far as Cara goes, she needs everything you can offer her. My boys seem to have become her safety blanket and that couldn't make me happier...or more proud. Cara's got a chance in life now and she'll need all of us to make that happen."

"Nothin' will happen to Cara ever again. That you can rest assured of," Kav states in a primal growl. "I wasn't the man I am today when we met Kid. Cara'll have benefit of the fourteen years I've had to grow up and get fuckin' meaner."

"I think her boys might give you a run for your money," O'Sullivan says with a knowing smile. "They're all sleepin' with her at this point."

I gasp in horror and move to fly up the stairs and rip my kids new assholes, when O'Sullivan snags me back to the couch by my waist.

"I said sleepin' with, not fuckin'," he says in a smooth calm voice for my benefit.

I search his chocolate eyes for a lie, trying to cover for my boys, but I don't find it.

"I've heard 'em goin' in her room at night. I peaked in this morning and all four of 'em were cuddled together in her bed. We were the same way with Kid after her attack. Shit we're the same way now. Somethin' about touchin' Kid lets us know she's good. Your boys are doin' the same thing. You've got great kids, Kat," he assures me with a sweetness that the constant entertainer is usually missing.

"She misses Jake," I whisper sadly.

"He's comin' back though, right?" Callaghan asks with concern on his face.

"I don't know," I answer sincerely. "He's got a lot of shit to work out before he'll come back. I'm afraid it might be a lifetime of shit."

"Kid says he's a lot like her," Kav pushes gently.

"They definitely have a connection."

"Then he'll come back to his family," O'Sullivan spouts confidently.

"You guys are pretty sweet," I say with a teasing smile.

"Don't spread that shit around. We've got reputations to maintain," Kav replies horrified at my admission.

"I'll be sure to spread the asshole rumor to all my new friends. Oh wait, you're my new friends. Thankfully, I've got Shannon now and her and I can gossip about you all we want."

"You two are gonna be nothin' but trouble," Callaghan huffs with a glint of approval in his eyes.

"You all keep sayin' that. What exactly do you think we're gonna do?"

"One night out and we'll all end up in prison, I'm sure of it," Kav grumbles.

"Why's that?"

"Look at you two. Men'll be sniffin' around and causin' fuckin' problems. You're too hot to be allowed outta the house often. I'll have to talk to Cooper and see what his plans are for you," Kav says humorlessly.

"Uh, I don't think Nicky's gonna have a lot of say in what I do, guys. I'm not one to be told what to do or how to do it. Nicky runs shit and I'm good with that to a point, but I'm not plannin' on bein' barefoot, pregnant

403

and chained in the kitchen," I scoff. "When Shannon and I aren't pregnant anymore I'm thinkin' we'll go out on our own without the caveman convention residing here in Kansas City."

"Bull-fuckin'-shit you are," O'Sullivan growls.

"Is there somethin' in the water around here that lowers IQs or somethin'? I've got the same skills as Shannon. I think her and I can take care of ourselves," I say irritated, getting a bit annoyed at the constant protectiveness. I get it from Nick and my boys enough already. Taking on Shannon's group is becoming suffocating.

"Kat, there's no question you can take care of yourself. The thing is, when we care about someone we take on that responsibility. It's not to demean you or to put you beneath us. It's to take away that burden. Cooper's got your back and that's a good thing. We're here to fill in the holes for him. He's done that for us with Kid for the last year. We owe him the same thing with you," O'Sullivan explains, back to his sweet voice.

"All right," I say softly.

The pregnancy hormones have me all over the place, but that was sweet and comforting in a way I wasn't expecting. I see now why Shannon keeps these men in her life and in her home. They're more than friends...they're family.

O'Sullivan sweeps an arm around my shoulders pulling me into his side when the alarm chirps, alerting us that Dylan and Nick are back from whatever they've been out doing. I move to push away from O'Sullivan's grasp, but he clamps down on me with a shit-eating grin on his face. Here comes trouble.

Chapter 47

Kat

"You're gonna lose that fuckin' arm, O'Sullivan," Nick growls from behind us.

"Just keepin' her warm for you," he purrs back suggestively, causing me to roll my eyes dramatically. "Dangerous thing leavin' a pretty single woman like this around."

"She's not single, dick. Get off," Nick grumbles with a little amusement in his voice, knowing O'Sullivan is fucking with him.

"I could get off for hours, Cooper."

That spurs me into action. I run my hand up O'Sullivan's torso, causing him to go rigid. I look up at him with the best bedroom eyes I can muster and see panic racing through his. I stop on his pec before shooting him a seductive smile. The panic is turning into plain fear at this point. Teasingly, I trace across his pec toward his nipple with my index finger.

"How many hours?" I rumble hotly.

"Kat," Nick says in a tone warning everything O'Sullivan fears in this moment.

"Uh," O'Sullivan mumbles, darting his eyes around for an escape.

I reach his nipple and pinch the hell out of it as he screams, trying to get out of my grasp as the men in the room howl in harmonious laughter.

"You don't like it rough?" I ask innocently.

"No! Fuck, let go! Ow, ow, ow," he whimpers.

I release him and smack his chest a few times before crawling to my feet in front of him.

"Jesus you're just like Kid," he grumbles, rubbing his bruised man boob. "Sorry," he mumbles the apology I was hoping for.

I wink at him before rounding the couch to Nick's awaiting arms. He's not laughing like the rest of them are. His features are a mask of frustration and his sapphire eyes are possessive in a way I've not seen before.

"Kat," he growls, pulling me roughly into his chest, forcing my arms to fly to his chest to brace myself.

"Nicky," I say sweetly, tipping my head up to him.

"No."

Jesus, am I a dog? I feel like a scolded child, as I bury my face in his chest. I wasn't doing that to make him jealous. I was doing it to make a point to the guys. One, I can take care of myself, and two, I'm not up for grabs. I know none of them would make a real move on me. All of their shit is for Nick's benefit. Like they're reminding him what he has in me, which is sweet is some backward fucked up way.

"That's the funniest thing I've seen a chick do since Kid about ripped my fingers off the first day we met," Kav stutters out, gasping for air through his laughter. "Lighten up, Cooper."

Nick grunts in response, but the tension in his body remains. I fear this brings back memories of the first night Nick and I were together when he found Jason Ross with me. Now I feel like a jerk.

"Let's go," Nick instructs, releasing me from his grip.

His hand settles on my back, pushing me down the hall toward our room. I meet eyes with Dylan as I move past and he offers me a weak and knowing smile. The guys are still laughing and giving O'Sullivan shit for screaming like a girl as we get out of earshot.

We pass multiple doors and take two turns before we end up at our room at the back of the house. Our boys and Cara have been holed up in the basement theater room most of the day. It's nice to see them being typical teenagers. Shannon's been asleep upstairs for an hour

406

or so. I can only imagine how exhausted she is being pregnant with twins and an infant to take care of.

Nick shuts the door behind him and flicks the lock. We're completely isolated at the back of the house. If we get in a big fight no one will hear us screaming at each other, so that's a bonus of the world's largest house.

I flop down on the end of the king size bed with luscious champagne colored linens and an upholstered cream headboard. It's like staying in a hotel for all intents and purposes with the attached marble encased bathroom. I feel like I've been on vacation for the last week and a half we've been here. We're moving into our new house next week so I've been shopping like crazy with Shannon and her awesome assistant/best friend Karl. Thomas the bodyguard is always with us, silently shadowing our movements. I'm making a home for the first time in my adult life and it feels like nothing I've ever experienced.

Nick's expression is still not a happy one as he crosses the room to stand right in front of me, forcing my gaze up to meet his. His sapphire eyes are stormy seas of emotion, not settling on any one too long. I'd prefer the fake brown ones right about now.

"You made your point," he growls.

"I'd hope so," I scoff.

"If you can't behave around these guys we need to reassess shit and quick."

"I'm sorry?" I ask, completely offended and no longer feeling bad.

"If you're gonna be climbing all over the guys, this won't work. Either you and I won't work or we'll need to move where you can control yourself better."

I'm up and on my feet before he finishes his truly off base statement.

"First of all," I say poking his chest with my index finger as I go. "Fuck you. I'm in complete control of myself at all times, Nicky. How dare you accuse me of doin' anything other than bein' completely faithful to you! I see those guys as nothing more than friends.

O'Sullivan was tryin' to get a rise outta you and it fuckin' worked. I was makin' a point to the guys that not only can I take care of myself, but I'm also not up for their shit. You wanna go and get all insecure that's your issue, not mine. And if this is gonna be a constant problem for you, then you're right, this won't work with us."

I've poked him all the way back to the door during my rant.

"You looked at another man the same way you look at me," he grumbles.

"No, when I look at you I mean it. What he got was Agent Russell. You've got me."

He drops his head in defeat as I spin away from him, my anger currently boiling over. I stomp over to the closet and begin rifling through for some different clothes. I've been in jeans and a sweater every day since we got here. It's been heaven on earth. I need something different on right now.

"What are you doin'?" Nick asks in a resigned voice.

"Goin' out. If I'm gonna be accused of bein' a whore I might as well act like one, right?" I sneer, snatching a little black dress from the back of the closet.

Prick!

"Kat," Nick says with warning in his tone as I brush past him.

I slam the bathroom door and lock it for good measure before pealing out of my clothes and jumping in the shower. Making quick work, I hop back out before the room has a chance to steam up. I dress quickly and then spend some time on my hair and make-up. My resolve to leave has hardened with each minute that's past. Slathering lip gloss on my lips, I inspect my final look.

A simple black scoop neck form fitting black dress with my hair up and a smoky eye. I look good if I do say so myself. I take a breath to calm my anger before exiting the bathroom expecting to see Nick on the other side of the door, scowl in place.

408

I'm shocked to find Shannon sitting on my bed.

"That's what I thought," she huffs. "Where are we headed?"

"Out," I grunt.

I notice she's got on black slacks with a tuxedo stripe down the side and a cap-sleeved silk violet maternity shirt that sets her green eyes alight more than usual.

"Let's go," she encourages.

I slip on some sky high black strappy heels and we head out. When we enter the great room all the men are on the couch including my boys. Cara is sandwiched between Cole and Dane, while Sawyer sits in front of her on the floor. She's cocooned by love.

"Mom?" Sawyer questions from the floor, the first to notice my appearance.

"I'll be back later," I reassure him as he pushes to his feet.

"Shit," I hear Kav grumble.

All eyes in the room are on Shannon and me now and the gazes are weighing me down like a bolder on my shoulders.

"Have a good evening, gentleman," Shannon says brightly, tugging me along toward the kitchen and garage. "Don't wait up."

"Kiddo," Dylan warns, gifting him a dagger-filled stare from Shannon.

"I've got my gun," she says pointedly.

"Me too," I chime in to ease the tension.

Nick's sapphire eyes are churning with fury as I quirk an eyebrow at him.

"You two have made your point," Callaghan relents.

"No point bein' made. We're goin' out!" Shannon says with a slight shimmy. "Love you!" She offers the room a big blown kiss before winking at me.

"Love you boys," I say sweetly to my kids that are staring at me like I'm an alien invasion of their mother.

"Love you too," they respond in unison.

Cara has a smirk on her lips. She gets it. I don't know how she gets it, but she does. I send her a grin before turning my back on the room and following Shannon to her SUV. We climb in and speed off before anyone has the chance to follow us based on the acceleration Shannon uses.

"Turn off your phone," she orders. "You know he'll try to track you. I've already got mine off."

"What about the baby? Don't you need to be available?" I feel bad I've dragged this heavily pregnant woman out of the house on a Saturday night in January.

"Kel knows how to find me," she assures me with an ornery grin. "Time to teach Nicky a much needed lesson."

Yes, it is.

Chapter 48

Nick

"What did you do?" Cole demands as Shanny and Kat exit the garage.

"Pissed her off," I answer honestly.

"Did you just see her?" Sawyer asks. Shocked that I'm still sitting here after his mother just left the house looking like a model headed for a runway.

"I did."

"And you're just gonna sit here while her and Aunt Shanny go out lookin' like they do?" Dane asks exasperated at me.

"I don't feel like gettin' shot," I respond in a grumble.

"You know dudes are gonna be all over her. Uncle Dylan, I know Aunt Shanny's pregnant, but she looked awesome too. You're really just lettin' 'em go?" Cole sounds distressed, his soft blue eyes brimming with distrust for the men in the room.

"What would you do if you were us?" Kellerman asks respectfully.

"I'd be in a fuckin' car followin'. I sure as shit wouldn't be sittin' here like bumps on a log. It takes nothin' to lose people. Women like that are treasures and any man that sees them tonight's gonna know that. Act like you give a shit!" Sawyer screams at me.

"Sawyer," I try to soothe him.

"Dad," he responds harshly, puffing his chest at me.

"Jake's rubbed off on you," I compliment him.

"Yeah and if he was here he'd kick your fuckin' ass."

"True."

411

"Fine. If you two aren't goin', we are. Cara, we'll be back once we find Mom and Aunt Shanny," Cole growls, standing up off the couch.

"Guys you're not gonna be able to find 'em," Kav steps in. "They just need a few hours to cool off."

"I thought you were her protector?" Dane sneers, bucking up to Kav.

"I am," Kav responds plainly.

"You fuckin' suck at it," Dane scoffs in return, yanking his phone out of his pocket.

Kav scrubs his hand over his head as my son orders a taxi like a man while the men in the house sit around like frightened teenagers.

I have beyond fucked up with Kat and I'm at a loss with what to do. When she looked up at O'Sullivan with those sexy hazel eyes, my gut flip and my heart stopped. I never want to see that again as long as I live. I know she was playing and it wasn't serious. I knew it in the moment, but it fucked with me nonetheless. Then, like a supreme asshole, I basically called her an out of control slut. I'm such a winner. Now I've sent her out into the night with Shanny to get into God knows what kind of trouble. SHIT!

"Love your kids, man," Kav says in a chuckle at their protective ways.

"Cab'll be here in thirty," Dane announces to his brothers who all start to move to get ready to leave.

"Thanks for callin' us a cab, boys. We've got it from here," Kellerman assures them, offering me a pointed look that says get my ass in gear.

"'Bout fuckin' time," Sawyer grumbles, flopping on the couch next to Cara.

She curls into his side with the same grin on her lips that's been there since she laid eyes on the girls.

"Where are we headed?" I ask, looking down at my appearance in sweats thinking I'm not dressed for the evening we're about to tackle.

412

"Not to the gym," Callaghan scoffs, eyeing my clothes too.

I offer him a wry grin. We're all wearing the same fucking clothes.

"Guess we've got twenty minutes to get our asses in gear," Kav says happily.

He's enjoying this too much.

"You all okay on your own?" I ask my kids that are still good and pissed at me.

"Yeah," they huff in unison. "Go get Mom and we'll be better," Dane finishes for the group with a meaningful glare.

"Right."

"Johnny's asleep and should stay that way for the rest of the night. Can you four keep the baby monitor with you and check in on him a few times while we're gone," Kellerman asks the group.

"I'll take care of my nephew," Cara says, showing the maturity she possesses.

"I know you will, Baby Girl," Kellerman responds with a wink.

Cara smiles in return. I love that she's changing so much already. She's relaxing and accepting everyone fawning all over her like a champ. Her and the boys can hold down the fort so the adults can attempt to behave like adults for once.

I race down the hall and take a five-minute shower before pulling on dark jeans, a tight navy T-shirt and a dark grey blazer. I slip on brown leather boots and run back down the hall to meet the other guys all wearing similar outfits only differing in the color of shirt and jacket. We look like some kind of boy band for sure.

The cab pulls up and the five of us lumber out to the yellow minivan shouting goodbyes to the teenagers as we go.

"Where to?" the driver asks as we smash ourselves in.

"Bar," all the guys and Kellerman answer in unison.

"Any particular bar?" I ask as we pull away.

413

"Bar is the name of the club, man," O'Sullivan explains with a sly grin on his lips.

"Right."

We ride in tense silence to Kansas City's Power and Light District, which is hopping with people pouring out of restaurants, bars and clubs. When we pull up in front of the seemingly old warehouse the line around the block to get in is not a welcome sight.

We pile out of the cab and follow O'Sullivan to the doorman at the head of the line. They talk for a few seconds before shaking hands. The doorman lifts the velvet rope and we stride through to the discontent of the people waiting in line. I feel bad for about two seconds before I'm enveloped by the bass of the dance music and the wide-open space in front of me with a sea of people moving in harmonious waves of undulation.

It's going to take time to find the girls in here. From the looks of the club the main floor is the dance area with bars and some tables at the edges, while the second story balcony looks like a VIP area. We head to the left up to the VIP area. It'll give me a good vantage point to spot my woman if she's on the dance floor.

Past another velvet rope, and we're in a quieter area with soft couches and chairs in creams and greys. There are glass barriers muffling the music from the main part of the club below us. We're led to a table and immediately brought bottles of vodka and tequila. I barely notice as I lean over an open part of the balcony with Kellerman next to me, searching for our women. It's dark, other than lights and lasers making my scan more difficult.

It takes us maybe ten minutes to finally locate them. By this time, all five of us are searching. I spot Kat near the middle of the floor dancing like crazy with Shanny. There's a large group of men surrounding them, watching like panting dogs. Before I do something stupid, I take a moment to stand and watch them. Kat and Shanny seem oblivious to their revelers as they swing and spin each other, their heads tipped back with huge smiles.

414

I can feel the tension flowing away from all of us as we watch the women we love glow brighter than any of the women in here. A club full of well over five hundred people, and two pregnant women have stolen the show. I feel a ghost of a smile sweep across my face.

It's short lived because a guy comes up behind Kat and Shanny each, grinding and humping at their asses. I'm moving before I register it, Kellerman and the guys right on my heels. The crowd parts for us easily. I'm sure we look scary as hell prowling toward our women. When we get to the girls they're alone again dancing with each other. Shanny's facing me and gives me a pointed look. Yeah, I'm aware I fucked up.

I wrap my arms around Kat's waist snugly, pulling her warm slightly sweaty back to my front. She slouches in defeat before pushing my arms off her.

"I'll tell you what I told every other man in here," she yells without looking at me. "I'm married!"

"Is that so?" I whisper in her ear. Her entire body goes stiff before she slowly turns to look at me. She's only a few inches shorter than me in the skyscraper heels she's got on.

Kat levels me with an icy glare placing her hands on her hips dramatically.

"Yeah!" she yells over the music.

Kellerman scoops his arms around Shanny and they start dancing together both observing us intently. The guys are surely here dancing with other women, but I'm focused solely on mine.

"My husband's a real dick sometimes though," she continues yelling at me.

"Any guy that's a dick to you is a fuckin' fool," I yell back.

"I'm thinkin' about gettin' a divorce."

"I'm thinkin' about gettin' married."

We stand and stare at each other in the middle of the dance floor. The bodies around us fade into the background and the music dims along with them. I'm the luckiest motherfucker on Earth to have this woman. There's no way I'll lose her because I've turned into an idiot. The ring in my pocket feels like my only lifeline at this point. I wanted to do romance. I wanted to do sweet and soft, just for her. A sweaty club will have to do.

I drop to my knee in front of her and her hazel eyes go from pissed to stunned in the blink of an eye.

"I love you. I want my life to begin and end with every breath of yours. I'm at peace for the first time in my life and that's because I share every day with you. I'm not a changed man because of you...I'm the best version of me. I'll spend the rest of our lives proving to you that I deserve everything you offer me. I'll be the best father to our eight kids. I'll be the best partner at your side, offering you support and love at every turn. I'll love you more each day because I fall in love with you a little more every morning. Marry me, Sunshine," I finish quieter than I started because the house lights have come on and the music has stopped. All eyes in the club are on us.

I pull the ring out of my pocket. An eight-carat pear shaped diamond with a smaller pear shaped diamonds on either side. I hold it out to her, waiting with baited breath for the only answer I'm prepared for.

Kat hasn't looked at the ring. She's staring at me with tears in her eyes and a hand over her mouth. I really hope she doesn't vomit. That would make this proposal even worse than it already is.

Finally, she nods only a tiny movement.

"Yes?" I clarify that she's not had some kind of tremor.

Her hand drops from her mouth as she squares her shoulders and beams the biggest smile I've ever seen cross her breathtaking face.

"Yes!" she screams at the top of her lungs to the glee of the club that breaks out in cheers and hoots of support.

I climb to my feet and slide the ring on her finger. She never looks at it. As soon as I'm done, she throws her arms around my neck and smashes her lips to mine. The club lights come back on as "When a Man Loves a Woman" filters through the space. I kiss Kat and rock her body with mine as people clap me on the back and shout congratulations.

Our tongues dance along with our bodies as happiness envelopes our embrace. I keep her crushed against me as firmly as I can, wishing we were alone and naked. Kat finally breaks our kiss, panting and wiping tears from her cheeks, her new ring blinding me.

"I love you," she says with adoration and love framing her features.

"I love you too."

"All right," Shanny says at our side. "My turn."

She wraps Kat in a strong hug as Kellerman pulls me in for a back slapping man hug. We switch quickly. Shanny squeezes my neck so tightly I have to gasp for breath.

"I love you even more right now, Nicky," she murmurs into my neck.

"Thank you," I mumble back, meaning that for more than the compliment she just paid me.

She pulls back and looks kindly into my face and I have a memory of an eight-year-old girl and a ten-year-old boy in a backyard saying goodbye to each other. My heart hurt that day like I've never felt since then. My heart hurts now too, but it's with a love so deep it's working its way into crevices that aren't used to feeling. Shanny opened my heart and Kat took it over. I have everything I could ever want in life. In this moment, I'm content and complete.

Shanny shoot me her megawatt smile before sliding back to Kellerman as the guys pass Kat around. Each of them scooping her off the floor and spinning her around like she's their little sister. They may be assholes, but they care about the woman I love. The glow bouncing off Kat's face is proof that having them care about her is important. I won't ruin that for her by being a dick about it. I'll just enforce some strict boundaries with those guys. A five-second rule for touching or something.

O'Sullivan passes Kat to me with a pointed look promising me bodily harm if I fuck up with her. I shoot him a cocky grin as I scoop Kat into my front, kissing her forehead.

"Take me home," she whispers, laying her head on my shoulder.

She doesn't have to tell me twice. I offer our group a chin lift and lead my soon to be legal wife out of the club. It takes forever with all the congratulations, but we make our way out eventually. We jump in the back of a cab and go back to Shanny's house.

We make out in the backseat like teenagers all the way there. When the cab stops my dick's so hard it hurts and Kat's hazy sex-filled eyes are not helping the situation.

The boys throw the front door open and our happy mood ends as soon as we see them. They're still pissed at me and worried about Kat.

Kat hurries toward them and I fall in step behind her.

"Are you okay?" Cole asks, wrapping her in a tight hug in the foyer as I close the door.

"I'm great, sweetheart," Kat assures him.

Sawyer pulls her in next, followed by Dane.

"Boys, I'm fine. I needed to get out for a bit and cool off. You have to trust that your dad and I can work through our problems. I mean actually work them out. We're not gonna do the things you're used to in relationships. We'll fight, argue, disagree and all of that's okay because in the end we'll always come back to each other. We love each other enough to fight for each other more than against each other."

The relief that passes over their faces is an amazing sight to witness.

"What the hell is that?" Sawyer shouts loudly, pointing at Kat's left hand.

"I proposed," I answer in a smirk.

"Nice," he says through his own smirk.

Cole and Dane join along in the smirking, letting me off the hook simultaneously.

Kat finally looks down at her hand and her breath hitches.

"Nicky," she whispers, staring at the gigantic ring.

"Do you like it?"

"It's a lot," she says through a snort.

"You deserve even more."

"Yeah she does," Cole agrees, his blue eyes dancing with happiness.

"I have everything I deserve and more with you all. This is just a bonus."

The boys all smile and converge on their mother almost knocking her off her heels. They let her go and attack me just the same. I hold them in my arms as tightly as I can, relieved they're not holding earlier tonight against me.

"Let's go the rest of the way in the house, guys," I say, releasing them from my grip. Cole and Dane sweep their arms around Kat's waist as I keep Sawyer under my arm. "Where's Cara?"

"Takin' a shower," Sawyer replies as we enter the great room. He tags the baby monitor off the coffee table before announcing, "We should go wait for her."

"You guys sure are sticking to her like glue," I point out the obvious.

"She needs us," Cole retorts with a shrug before peeling away from Kat.

"We're goin' up. We'll probably just sleep in her room again," Dane says.

"What's that?" I ask baffled at his last statement.

"We've been sleepin' in her bed every night since we got here, Dad. You're already losin' your spy skills," he teases.

"By sleepin' you mean?" I ask, hoping like hell they mean drooling and snoring.

"Dad," Sawyer huffs at my question. "Sleeping."

"Noted."

The three of them kiss Kat on the cheek and give me hugs before running up the stairs to their girl. I'm filled with pride at the men they're becoming. If Jake could see them he'd be proud of his brothers too. They're keeping his girl safe until he can come back for her. That'll be a good story.

"Take me to bed, Nicky," Kat purrs in my ear.

"Fuck yes," I groan, sweeping her off her feet and basically running down the hall as she cackles with laughter at my behavior.

The sound of her joy mixed with the beam of sunshine that's just her, sends a warm rush right through my heart. She's mine. I have this for the rest of my life and I'll appreciate it every moment. I know what the blackness looks like and I'm happy to turn my back on it and walk straight into the light.

Chapter 49

Nick

I kick the door shut on our new master bedroom at the end of a long moving weekend carrying Kat bride-style, which has been done a lot lately. We've been engaged a week now and life has been fan-fuckin'-tastic. Hoyt Burke was finally terminated after being held at a black site for the last few weeks. He gave the DCA all the intel he had and then he was disposed of. Thousands of girls have been traced all over the country. We succeeded in our op and we've excelled at life.

Kat and I had our first sonogram and doctor's appointment this week. She's progressing perfectly in the pregnancy and the morning sickness is getting slightly better. Seeing my baby that looked oddly like a blob was a life changing moment for me. I fought with everything I had not to cry as I watched the tiny flicker of its heart while I cradled Kat's hand and she cried. We created that little being together in the blackness that had surrounded us for years and years. I now believe in miracles.

The boys started school this week, which was difficult because that meant they had to leave Cara for the first time. Cara's in an accelerated home school program with multiple tutors to catch her up to where she needs to be. She'll still be a bit behind age wise, but all the experts around us believe she'll be able to go into her junior year of high school with the boys next year.

That girl has the same fight in her as Shanny. I have no doubt she'll battle her way through therapy and school to get where she needs to be. In the few weeks we've been here, I can see her beginning to heal. While it'll be a long and slow road, I'll be proud to stand by her side and support her for the duration.

We haven't heard from Jake since he went back to the farm. I knew we wouldn't, but it's difficult. Kat's struggling with it more than anyone, mostly due to her pregnancy hormones. He'll call. He'll come home. He'll heal. I keep reminded her, the boys, Cara and myself of this as the days pass with no word. I trust my son to follow through.

I lay Kat down in our California King dark mahogany four-poster bed gently. Kat chose all the furniture and linens and pillows and art and whatever else is in this house. My life savings has taken a hit buying the house, cars, her engagement ring and home furnishings. I don't give a shit. Everyone I love is happy and healthy. The DCA pays me well and I made a shit load of money while I worked for Vito Mancini. We're good.

I slowly peel Kat out of her silk pale blue robe that she put on after her shower this evening. I'm delighted to find her completely naked and ready for me as I slide the liquid material from her body.

I don't take the same care yanking off my sweats, but I'm not really that concerned with myself right now. Once I'm naked, I cover Kat with my body diving in to devour her fat lips. She arches into me with a moan that causes my dick to twitch. She notices and runs her hand between us, pumping me with her fist as our tongues lick and lap each other.

I move away from her mouth and trail my teeth down her neck straight to her overly sensitive nipple. My dick is no longer in her grasp as my tongue softly flicks her. When her nails drag painfully over my scalp, I know she's close. I pick up my tongue's pace and pressure while my thumb and forefinger pull and tug in rhythm.

One more firm tweak and she's crying out, "Nicky," quaking from head to toe.

"Fuck that's hot," I murmur against her stomach as I make my way down.

"It's only for you," she whispers.

That little piece of information causes me to growl before kissing the womb nourishing my child. Kat hikes her legs back like I want them without a word or movement from me as I attack her pussy with my mouth. I spear my tongue in her hole as it clenches around me, quivering and begging for more.

I move to her clit and slide my middle finger in her. Her delight reverberates around the room in mewls and groans that rev me to get the job done faster. Hardening my tongue and adding a finger, I pound into her curving my fingers to hit that spot that undoes her every time.

"Nicky! Fuck!" she yells slamming her pussy against my face as she comes.

I hop up on my knees before she catches her breath, palming my dick and slowly feeding it into her. As she clutches me with her pussy, always needing a moment to accommodate my size, I reach under her arms and pull her into my lap.

Kat wraps her slender arms and legs around me before peppering my face and neck with kisses as she begins to rock against me. I help her motion, gripping her ass, moving her up and down, back and forth. I lean my forehead against hers and watch the passion that fills her blue-green-grey eyes while another orgasm builds.

If love were tangible, this would be the moment I'd be holding it. Kat in my arms, peaceful and vulnerable, giving me every piece of her.

"I love you, Nicky," she whispers, her voice full of emotion and sex.

I tip her back down onto the mattress and power into her with long paced strokes.

"I love you, Sunshine," I murmur into her neck.

Kat constricts her arms and legs around me, her nails scoring my back. I surge forward. Filling the room with slaps and groans of pleasure. As my spine tingles with my own orgasm threatening, Kat shudders with her own.

I capture her screams of ecstasy with my mouth, tasting and savoring the woman I love as I fill her with come. I pump and pump into her, releasing the biggest load I've ever had. Goosebumps cover my skin as my last shaky thrust buries me deep inside her.

"Holy shit," I breathe out collapsing on top of Kat.

"I second that," she gasps in exhaustion.

As our breathing evens out I feel sleep taking us over, so I roll Kat on top of me, my dick still inside her. I cover our bodies with our new duvet and kiss her hair as sleep pulls her under. I follow not a minute later.

The alarm chirps letting me know a door or window has opened. I sit up to find Kat already climbing out of bed. She wraps her silk robe around her body as I tug on my sweats. I run down the hall to be stopped at the vision of Dane carrying Cara up the stairs.

"She can't sleep, Dad," he whispers.

I nod and follow him into his room where he lays her down in his bed. Kat comes into the room with a groggy looking Sawyer and Cole. That is until they spot Cara. They both clap me on the back before climbing in bed.

Dane crawls behind Cara pulling her back to his front. Sawyer lies in front of her as she snuggles her head into his chest. Cole situates himself at the end of the bed before wrapping around her legs. She's cocooned by love. Her breathing evens out almost immediately followed by the snores of my boys as Kat rests her head against my bare chest.

"You wake the boys up?" I whisper.

"She needs 'em," she says quietly.

I nod in agreement before leading us out of the room. As we plod back to ours, I feel a grin on my lips. I have my wife in my arms, my baby safe within her and my boys caring for my cousin all under my roof. I'm at peace...almost. I need Jake home and safe for everything to be right in the world. Until that day comes, I'll hold this moment dearly as a second best for us as a family. We didn't get here the conventional way, but we got here all the same. Together we found unconditional love.

424

Jake

"Cooper?" Jase Mitchell, my future spotter, whispers from the bunk next to me.

"Yeah," I whisper back.

"Were they really talkin' about your parents out there today?"

"I guess so," I reply with a shrug.

Some of the instructors were talking about past recruits today in the mess hall at the table behind us. Apparently, Nick Cooper and Katherine Russell have left some big shoes to fill. I'm happy to have the goal and proud that everyone here knows they're my parents.

"You think your brothers'll come into the DCA?"

"Nah," I say nonchalantly, knowing I'd fight them tooth and nail if they ever tried. "Sawyer's got baseball. Cole and Dane are really smart. They'll do the college thing for sure."

"Your parents good with that?"

"Yeah. They just want us to be happy."

"You happy here, Coop?"

"Happy as I'm gonna get, Mitch. Get some shuteye. They'll be comin' for us soon," I order.

He's two years older than me, but I'm definitely the leader of our team. I like being the leader of our team.

"Night, Coop," he says, trying to get comfortable.

"Night."

The bunks here suck. My back's killing me and I feel like I haven't slept in days. Probably because I haven't slept in days. Sniper training is kicking my ass and I'm loving it. I need this to feel human at the end of the day. Coming her was the best decision for me. No matter the sorrow it caused.

Every night at the same time I feel like a warm beam is splitting through my center. I know it's her, Cara. I know she needs me and I can feel that need burning in my soul. That's some crazy shit to think, much less experience, but I know that's what's happening. I've never felt it before she came into my life. I've never felt anything like I did before she came into my life.

When the time is right, I'll make sure she gets all of me like she deserves.

She deserves everything I can give her and the stuff I'm learning to give her while I'm here. It's been almost three months and I feel different. Part of it is the physical training I'm going through. Part of it is the emotional turmoil the training has taken on me.

I haven't had a nightmare since I got here. When the instructors have allowed it, I've had peaceful, quiet sleep in a way I didn't know I could. My mom gave me that. Her love holds my head above water at every turn. My dad offers me the strength to push when everyone around me is crumbling and I want to lay down in defeat right along with them. I have strength and love because two people decided to have my back when no one ever has.

I miss my brothers like crazy. Those guys showed me what happy feels like. Always accepting and forgiving, they showed me that a smile can mean something. I hurt them when I left and that kills me every day I'm away. I never wanted to hurt anyone. I only wanted to heal. They get that. I promised to come home when I'm done here, but I'm not sure what done means for me. I don't think it'll mean training completed. I think I'll have to spend some time in the field in order to feel ready to join the normal world with my family. If I do what's best for me they'll understand.

I keep trying to imagine what a normal life looks like. I can't picture it yet. My past has clouded that vision. Now that I have the support of my family, my sight is becoming clearer. With the training the DCA is giving me, I have an outlet for the torment that makes my everyday hazy. If I can just find a way to let the past go, I can join the people I love with confidence. We'll see what happens tomorrow when I get a glimpse of their normal. When I see my family. When I share in one of the best moments of their lives. When I escape the blackness for just a little while and step into the light.

Epilogue

Kat

I'm so calm. I thought I'd be a ball of nerves, but I'm completely calm. There's no tremor in my hand. No racing heart. No need to vomit or run for the hills. I'm ready for this. I'm excited for this.

Tahiti for spring break had to be held off with Shannon's due date looming in a few weeks. We wanted her here with us for this. I've bonded with her over the last few months so closely I feel like she's my sister. Her family has taken Nick, the boys and me on like long lost cousins. I feel full to the brim with love and affection enough that my parents not being here today only stings instead of being a fatal wound to the day.

All of Shannon's family is here with us today. Nine brothers, three fathers, two mothers, her crazy cousin and his family, her uncle Butch, Karl and even Thomas. Jess and Shane are here with us. Now that Jess is feeling better, she's been here to help with the fast planning. Her and Shane went through with their wedding, but made it more intimate with only a small ceremony and reception. I didn't have to wear an ugly dress either.

The wedding planner cracks the door open telling me five minutes. I turn and take a last look at myself in the full-length mirror. I asked my girls to give me these last few moments alone. I started this whole thing alone only six months ago and I wanted to have one last memory that my life is no longer empty.

My ivory silk dress clings to my body in all the right places. I have the slightest baby bump and I swear it makes the dress flow even better across my hips. The neckline plunges only hinting at my cleavage while the straps connect to a lace racer back. The lace is soft and delicate running down my spine where it connects to the dress at the base. I decided to go without a veil and have my hair swept away from my face with an antique hair clip that Shannon's mother, Mary, lent me. It's covered in diamonds and pearls, shining brightly in my honey curls.

My bouquet is a mix of calla lilies, orchids and irises. My bridesmaids are wearing violet dresses that match each of their body types and pregnancy bumps in the case of a few.

I'm ready to do this. I smile at myself in the mirror as the door behind me opens and the tears I've been promising myself I won't shed immediately skirt my lashes at the sight of him.

"Can I take you on a short walk?" Jake asks my reflection, offering me a spectacular smile.

I drop my bouquet on the table and rush at him. I heave myself into his waiting arms and let the tears flow. That's what waterproof mascara was made for.

Jake's shoulders are wider and he's taller. He looks like a man more than a teenager. I gaze up into his big brown eyes and run my fingers over his military buzzed hair. My son.

"Hi," I whisper with a beaming smile.

"Hey," he says through a grin.

"What are you doin' here?" I ask the stupid question.

"I came to walk my mother down the aisle," he says tenderly.

I nod, for fear the tears I've stopped will ruin his suit and my face.

"You're the most beautiful bride I've ever seen," he murmurs into my cheek before kissing it softly.

"Thank you," I say in a whimper, fighting my emotions.

He swipes my cheeks clean with his thumbs as he studies my face.

"Normal looks better on you than any mask you've ever worn, Mom. I'm so happy for you."

"Jake, you've gotta stop. I'll never be able to fix my make-up," I scold him weakly.

"Right. Let's get you out there so I can have a mother son dance with you."

"Not helping the tears," I say through a sob.

"I love you," he says as he squeezes me tightly.

"And I love you."

We hold each other until there's another knock from the wedding planner.

"Showtime," he says through a broad grin.

I tentatively release him to collect my bouquet and glance at myself in the mirror. This is the best I've looked after crying, no contest. It's a wedding miracle.

Jake pushes the door open and leads me down the hallway. We're getting married at the Loose Mansion in Kansas City. It feels like getting married at home. I love the cozy atmosphere mixed with the grand architecture.

As Puccini echoes through the space while my bridesmaids make their way into the Grand Salon, I feel my parents smiling down on me. I'm not one to believe in those things, but I feel lighter in this moment holding Jake's arm about to meet my husband.

"Trumpet Voluntary" begins and Jake leads me toward the aisle. Kieran and Quinn's daughter, Ashling, is our flower girl and Johnny is our ring bearer. Ashling just turned one so there aren't a lot of flowers on the cream runner, but there are some as I step onto it. I make my way around the corner and keep my gaze on Nick's. His gaze begins with my eyes and his breath falters when he takes in the rest of me. I do the same at the sight of him. He's in a black suit with a black tie and I've never seen him look better than he looks right now. His sapphire eyes shimmering with love and adoration, making my knees knock.

Then he catches sight of Jake and the tears he's been holding spill, one large drop falling from each eye. I look to my boys standing next to their father, all of them his best men, as they also release a few tears at their brother's surprise. I look to Jess, Shannon, Quinn and Cara next. Jess and Quinn are crying while Shannon steels herself like only she can. Well not only her, because Cara is doing the same thing. Her green eyes are locked on Jake, but she's calm and collected as she watches us approach.

When we come to a stop in front of the wedding officiant, Nick grabs Jake away from me and wraps him in a hug so tight I'm afraid he's hurting my son. We're all here. Every loved one is here to share in this moment with us. I take a breath and absorb the light and vow to myself never to run into the blackness again. I'll bask in the glow of the light for the rest of my life.

Nick

I hold Jake so tightly I'm sure I'm crushing his ribs and I can't bring myself to let up.

"Dad," he mumbles against my shoulder. "You've got somethin' else to do right now."

I chortle before clapping him on the back and releasing him with a squeeze to the side of his neck.

"Love you, son."

"Love you too."

He moves next to me and hugs his brothers quickly while I take Kat's hand in mine and get this wedding in gear.

She's the most beautiful bride the world has ever seen. The glow coming off her skin is blinding in the best way. Her dress fits her like a glove and shows the tiny baby bump she now has. I run my hand along her back and find it naked other than a scrap of lace running down her spine. I stop listening to the wedding guy and take a step backward to look at her back.

I let out an audible hiss that earns me hoots and hollers from the men in the room. I think I hear something about a spank bank being filled, but I don't pay attention.

Shanny sends me a warm smile before a suggestive eyebrow wiggle making me smile so big it hurts as I take my place at Kat's side.

"Surprise," she says through a shy smile.

"That is was. Sorry," I apologize to the guy marrying us.

"It's not a problem," he assures me and continues with the ceremony.

"You may now kiss your bride," he announces what feels like seconds later and I obey.

I capture Kat's mouth in a searing kiss, dipping her back as she laughs against my mouth.

"I present to you Mister and Missus Nicholas Cooper," he says and the place erupts in more raucous applause.

I race down the aisle, stopping at the front door of the mansion where the rest of the wedding party meets us and begins the never ending congratulating. I skip most of it for my son.

He's bulkier and taller already. He looks like a man now and I'm filled with pride at the sight. I keep him at my side while I introduce him around. Kat fulfills my social duties until it's time for pictures.

After a thousand photographs, it's finally time for our reception. We start off with our first dance to "When a Man Loves a Woman" just like it was played when we got engaged. I hold Kat close and kiss her often as we sway to the music.

"I love you, Missus Cooper," I purr into her ear as our dance ends.

"I love you, Mister Cooper. Thank you for giving me all of this. I was just existing before I met you. You've allowed me to thrive in a way I didn't know was possible. I can't wait to see what the future holds for us, Nicky," Kat whispers lovingly against my cheek.

"Sunshine, with you at my side, our lives will be perfection."

I move my lips against hers, pouring all of my love into my wife. She's mine. I have a treasure in my arms that I'll never relinquish. I did this. I fought for the love of my life and while the battle was brutal, it was worth every wound.

When I pull back from our passionate kiss, my heart stops at the smile breaking across Kat's face. There she is. Every piece of her. Just for me.

"Let's wrap this thing up a so I can peel you out of this dress," I murmur into her neck.

"Okay," she mumbles against my cheek and slides away from me to get the show on the road.

Instead of a father daughter dance Kat elected to do a mother son dance. Each of the boys takes their turn with her, causing her to unravel into a pool of tears as they whisper words of love. When Jake gets her in his arms, his words wreck more than the others'. Of course it could just be his presence along with the pregnancy, but I'm sure my son is saying words that are filling her with those tears of joy.

Not having a mother to dance with, I decided to dance with Shanny and Cara. I start with Cara and she hangs onto me snugly as I lead her around the dance floor. She remains silent in my arms, but squeezes me with love before I let her go.

Shanny comes into me as closely as she can with her gigantic belly that's about to burst.

"I'm proud of you," she murmurs into my ear as we sway slowly. "You earned all of this love. You let yourself find the light and then you held onto it even when you thought it might burn you. I love you, Nicky."

"Love you too, Shanny," I whisper before pressing a long kiss into her cheek.

When the song finishes I go to my bride and take our seats at our table at the head of the ballroom. A room filled with the weirdest mix of people I've ever seen. Criminals and saviors mix together without barriers or

434

concern for the other. An unconventional family built on love and loyalty.

I interlace fingers with Kat, rubbing my thumb across her wedding band. She gifts me that beaming Sunshine smile and I see it. That light I was afraid to live in, I now crave. There's no blackness defining me anymore, only light that I've found and built on. I deserve the glow and I'll let it warm my heart every day for the rest of my life. The monster within me is dormant, content to live in the peace that remains.

The End

Coming Soon

Blackness Within
Brian O'Sullivan's Story
September 2014

Escaping the Blackness
Jake Cooper's Story
Winter 2014

The Blackness Series

Blackness Takes Over

Blackness Awaits

Shrouded in Blackness

Stay tuned...

Follow me at one of the links below to keep up to date with my newest projects. Sneak peeks are always available to those on my mailing list. You can sign up at my website below. Thank you again for your support. Please leave reviews if *Into the Blackness* made an impression on you. I take the good with the bad, appreciating honesty above all.

www.normajeannekarlsson.com

www.twitter.com/NormaJKarlsson

www.facebook.com/AuthorNormaJeanneKarlsson

www.goodreads.com/normajeannekarlsson

About the Author

Originally from Kansas City, Missouri, Norma Jeanne recently found herself relocating to the United Kingdom. Now living in Belfast, she took hold of the opportunity to kick the 9-5 job for a chance to become an author. The best part: working from her home office, she gets to spend more time with her cast of crazy characters (written and real).

In her free time Norma Jeanne is a voracious reader and consumes books as readily as meals. She is a people watcher by nature and uses her experiences in life, observed or otherwise, to build the worlds and characters that thrive in her books. A believer in the strength of the human spirit, Norma Jeanne writes the stories of people that persevere when all appears to be lost.

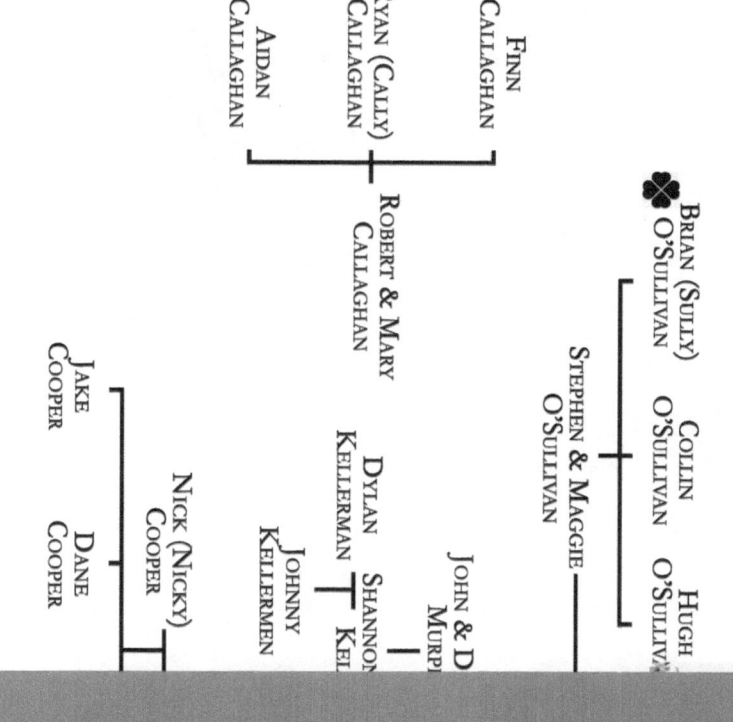

The Blackness Se...

Finn Callaghan

Aidan Callaghan

Ryan (Cally) Callaghan

Robert & Mary Callaghan

Brian (Sully) O'Sullivan

Collin O'Sullivan

Hugh O'Sulliv...

Stephen & Maggie O'Sullivan

Jake Cooper

Dane Cooper

Nick (Nicky) Cooper

Dylan Kellerman

Johnny Kellermen

John & D... Murph...

Shannon Kel...

Denotes Shani...

www.ingramcontent.com/pod-product-compliance
Lightning Source LLC
Chambersburg PA
CBHW032139270626
47172CB00009B/400